Eternity

Eternity
A Trilogy

TOM KNIGHT

ETERNITY
A TRILOGY

iUniverse books may be ordered through booksellers or by contacting:

iUniverse
1663 Liberty Drive
Bloomington, IN 47403
www.iuniverse.com
1-800-Authors (1-800-288-4677)

Because of the dynamic nature of the Internet, any web addresses or links contained in this book may have changed since publication and may no longer be valid. The views expressed in this work are solely those of the author and do not necessarily reflect the views of the publisher, and the publisher hereby disclaims any responsibility for them.

Any people depicted in stock imagery provided by Getty Images are models, and such images are being used for illustrative purposes only. Certain stock imagery © Getty Images.

ISBN: 978-1-5320-6627-6 (sc)
ISBN: 978-1-5320-6628-3 (e)

Library of Congress Control Number: 2019900390

Print information available on the last page.

iUniverse rev. date: 01/23/2019

~

THIS BOOK IS DEDICATED TO:
MY MOM
AND MY DAD
and ROSALIE,
my precious wife, today, tomorrow, for all eternity...

AND...

TO ALL THE BRAVE AND UNSUNG HEROES
BOTH THE DECEASED AND THE SURVIVORS.

ALL THOSE WHO HAVE HAD
TO FACE TRAGEDY
AND CALAMITY IN THEIR LIVES...
THIS STORY IS SINCERELY
AND HONORABLY DEDICATED.

Special Thanks to God for this Divine
Epiphany, along with the
perseverance and tenacity to see this
project to its completion.

The Mysteries of the Ages that will be revealed are:

Why were you Born?

What is your Divine Purpose?

What is your Ultimate Quest?

What is your Divine Mission?

... and **Where is your Divine Destiny**?

And many more questions will be answered within these revealing pages!

May God bless all the readers of this book!

Note: All quotes from the Holy Bible are
from the Authorized King James Version.

CONTENTS

PREFACE

There is a vast unknown land that lies just beyond our reality. A strange world, a paradox of mysteries and wonders that we, as human beings, cannot begin to understand. Extrinsic and incredible enigmas that baffle the mind lie in wait for us, from the natural world to the vast unfathomable cosmos.

Eccentric and bizarre phenomena, inexplicable riddles, anomalies and conundrums that we are only beginning to comprehend pique our intellect forward. Like an iceberg floating in the ocean hiding four fifths of itself under water, there exists many unusual events beyond our paltry three-dimensional existence.

Logic and our limited reasoning may not let us probe into phenomena outside the boundary of our known reality. All the laws of science fall short when dealing with the values that make us human—the concepts of love, truth and justice. Why is our morality of knowing right from wrong and that good conquers evil imbued into our subconscious minds?

Unsolvable puzzling phenomena that cannot be

explained with our five senses, such as prayers, miracles and angels, may exist just beyond our perception. How does an infinite all-knowing, all-loving God fit into our cosmos? Where does the concept of life after death originate?

Many scientists are frustrated by God and the Bible. They experiment in a three-dimensional universe with laws of chemistry and physics. They are perturbed because they cannot dissect the soul or place love in a flask. Nor can they find Heaven through a telescope or Hell through a mine shaft.

Science cannot probe the mystery of prayer. Nor can it place angels, demons or divine miracles under the microscope. They comprehend a complex universe where 96% of it is still unknown. Nor can they go back in time and see the creation of the cosmos, nor the creation of humanity.

Scientists can only formulate their theories of how things work when they do not have all the facts. Nor can they solve the problems of evolution. Their theories are forever changing and are constantly altered. Science cannot answer the great cosmic question of our existence: *Do we have a purpose beyond this life?* We need the answers to these profound questions since we are only human and are living a finite existence.

We are trying to understand an infinite, divine God, a God who is omnipresence, omniscient and omnipotent. Divine knowledge goes beyond the normal into the paranormal, beyond psychology into the parapsychology, beyond the physical into the metaphysical.

Even Christ stated that he was "not of this world." We have learned that we cannot find God through materialistic, naturalistic, or humanistic means. Science nor any mundane philosophy can open a spiritual doorway to our supreme God. Some ministers even present a watered down biblical theology denying a Heaven and a Hell, the virgin birth, and Christ's miracles.

Have our hearts been hardened—have our ears become deaf? How much longer can we survive the apathy in our society? Is there any hope for our world?

So, the final ultimate questions are: *How do we find God? How much do we want God's power in our lives? Do we really want God's peace, tranquility and love? Do we want God to be our Supreme Guide, giving us the best advice, bestowing upon us His mighty blessings and divine favor?*

> "Fear them not, therefore, for there is nothing
> covered that shall not be revealed;
> and hidden, that shall not be known."
> —Mt. 10:26

How can we unravel the ultimate answers the human race is so desperately seeking? How will God reveal his Divine Secrets, his Divine Glory, and his Divine Power to us?

So, let us break free of our physical time-bound world in which we live and enter *terra incognita*—the Land Unknown.

Let us proceed beyond what science can offer. Let us enter into the mysteries of an unexplored universe beyond the realm of death into a vast intellectual and spiritual dimension.

As the telescope has revealed the vast cosmos, and the microscope a clandestine world of the invisible, we may wonder just how many other foreign and strange worlds still lay in wait before some visionary reveals them to us.

—The Author

"Call unto me, and I will answer thee,
and show thee great and mighty things,
which thou knowest not."
—Jer. 33:3

"I will open my mouth in parables;
I will utter things which have been kept secret
from the foundation of the world."
—Mt. 13:35

Has God been silent before you?
Now let Him speak directly to your heart
about His Divine Mission
and His Special Purpose for your life.
Let God reveal His Divine Mysteries—
and your Divine Destiny.
Travel beyond your wildest imagination...
into a surreal world of hyper-reality—
and enter into the very presence of Almighty God!
—The Author

"Someday you will hear that I have died.
Don't you believe it!
I will be more alive then than I am now."
—Billy Graham, Evangelist (1918-2018)

The Ultimate Quest

I realized that the world is rampant with evil,
that suffering, disease and sorrow is universal.
What caused this hopelessness of the human condition,
its vanity and despair?
So I was inspired to write a book to ameliorate society—
making it my Magnificent Obsession
to help those wanting
and desiring a more meaningful and fulfilling life.
I wanted to explore the world's most intriguing mysteries,
to discover the source of success and happiness.
I dreamed of a more enlightened world,
and started the Ultimate Quest,
to be the grand legacy to all people for all time.
I now release it on its Divine Mission
to heal and bless all those that are seeking
the clandestine answers to life and death—
and that your life ... those around you,
and the whole earth will be changed
for the good of all humanity.
—The Author

"That the God of our Lord Jesus
Christ, the Father of glory,
may give unto you the spirit of wisdom and
revelation in the knowledge of him,
the eyes of your understanding being enlightened;
that ye may know what is the hope of his calling,

and what the riches of the glory of
his inheritance in the saints,
and what is the exceeding greatness of his power
toward us who believe, according to the
working of his mighty power, …"
—Eph. 1:17-19

"Great ideas often receive violent opposition
from mediocre minds."
—Albert Einstein

A Dim Lamp

"We live from birth to death...
as a person on the edge of infinity...
trying to comprehend the world and our existence.
Yet we, through all our knowledge only light a dim lamp,
groping through a dark night full of ignorance and terror,
superstition and trepidation ... learning
a little here and a little there,
but leaving eternity and most of the vast cosmos unknown
and as mysterious as the day we were born."
—The Author

"The cosmic religious experience is the strongest and noblest driving force behind scientific research."
—Albert Einstein

Alfred Nobel, inventor of dynamite, mistakenly one day,
read his own obituary in the newspaper.
He then realized he did not just want to leave a legacy
as the person that gave the world
the power to blow itself up.
So, instead he established the Nobel Prizes
to those esteemed in literature, science, peace and culture.
Therefore, I also realized that few things in this world
are truly lasting, so I resolved to write a book
illuminating the divine mysteries of the Great Beyond—
as our inspiration, talents, and
imagination manifest themselves
into a magnificent journey that will
continue… for all eternity.
--The Author

INTRODUCTION

*T*he Lord revealed that I, through the written word, could reach a needy and starved humanity promulgating the miracles of our LORD and his great and marvelous Creation. I believe God has given me the divine insight to reveal only a tiny portion of the wonders of the next world to come, that glorious Kingdom of God!

"For I neither received it of man, neither was I taught it, but by the revelation of Jesus Christ."
—Gal. 1:12

Thus, through divine prophecy this book was born. Each and every one of us must travel that road of destiny and face the dark mystery of death. Is death the horrible specter that many believe or just another phase or journey we must all partake in? Why should we have great trepidation upon this universal and vital enigma facing each and every one of us sooner or later.

"To fear death, gentlemen, is nothing other than to think oneself wise when one is not;

for it is to think one knows what one does not know.
No man knows whether death may not even
turn out to be the greatest of blessings
for a human being; and yet people fear it as if
they knew for certain that it is the greatest of evils."
—Socrates

May this revelation be a wonderful comfort for all of humanity, and be a solace for those who have just recently lost a loved one.

We go on with our lives knowing full well that death lies in wait for us all. We are the only species that realizes that we shall someday die. Yet we are complacent and continue ignoring the fact that we are but mere mortal beings.

We are aware of death everyday. We see it on the TV, on the radio, in the movies and in the obituaries and in thousands of other ways. Yet we never seem aware that it will someday happen to us.

Engraved on an actual tombstone:
Born 1914
Gave up smoking 1959
Gave up booze 1973
Gave up red meat 1983
Died anyway 1989

What an unsettling thought! To cease to exist is incomprehensible! Life cannot fathom this pit from which none have escaped. With the exception of Enoch and Elijah experiencing death, all others, including Jesus himself, has gone through its shadow.

Yet, will our reality of the world in which we live stop at our death? Or will it be enhanced?

"Out, out brief candle!
Life's but a walking shadow, a poor player that struts
and frets his hour upon the stage
and then is heard no more.
It is a tale told by an idiot, full of sound and fury,
signifying nothing."
—Macbeth (Shakespeare)

Yet most of us believe the soul survives death. Why is this? It is as if God himself has placed in our vast minds that intangible thing called faith with an inborn intuition that we will survive death and attain immortal life. Why is this?

Can we comprehend that our life will someday cease? Have we lost that security of living each day to its fullest and without trepidation, knowing full well that we are but mere mortals, having only a limited number of days upon this earth?

"As sand through the hourglass,
so are the days of our lives."
—Unknown

No wonder we are neurotic and have anxiety over this phenomenon called *death*! We have all been cursed by the fall of Adam and Eve and have reaped its dire consequences eating from the tree of the knowledge of good and evil, thus gaining the forbidden fruit of "sorrow and death."

What happens after we die? That is the *ultimate question*, for without the answer, we as human beings, are swimming in an unfathomable dark and senseless ocean treading the water of fear and terror, wondering forever why we were born, where we are going and what we are doing in this vast deep abyss. We will be forever searching for life's ultimate meaning, rendering this circumscribed existence as a senseless insanity, never to be repeated and never to be remembered in the vast ocean of sidereal space. Our world and all life upon it is only one tiny speck of cosmic dust evaporating with the demise of our sun into cosmic oblivion, totally forgotten in the eons upon eons of endless nothingness.

Or is there something more?

O death, where is thy sting?
O grave, where is thy victory?"
—1 Cor. 15:55

This theophany presents a *fresh look* at the Holy Bible and its message for *everyone*. Prayerfully and after many years of research, I have finally discovered the very mysteries of life and death ... and our purpose in the universe.

Now enjoy this epiphany before you and may this *Word of Knowledge* bring all the tranquility, peace and hope the author has intended ... for all eternity.

"If I have told you of earthly things
and you do not believe,
How can you believe if I tell you of heavenly things?"
—Jn. 3:12

"But it is written, Eye hath not seen,
nor ear heard, neither have entered into the heart of man,
the things which God hath prepared
for them that love him.
But God hath revealed them unto us by his Spirit;
for the Spirit searcheth all things, yea,
the deep things of God. ...
But the natural man receiveth not the
things of the Spirit of God;
for they are foolishness unto him,
neither can he know them,
because they are spiritually discerned."
—1 Cor. 2:9-10, 14

"We are confident, I say,
and willing rather to be absent from the body,
and to be present with the Lord."
—2 Cor. 5:8

"For to me to live is Christ, and to die is gain."
—Phil. 1:21

"I seem to have been only like a boy
playing on the seashore,
and diverting myself in now and then
finding a smoother pebble

or a prettier shell than ordinary, whilst
the great ocean of truth
lay all undiscovered before me."
--Sir Isaac Newton (1642-1727)

Eternity

Book One

I Believe in Angels

CHAPTER ONE

Beautiful dreams seem to carry me along on a journey. Strange places, vaguely reminding me of my own home and city, but somehow incorporeal and intangible. I watched Faith, my precious wife, in an old oak swing, holding our daughter, Elizabeth, laughing and smiling with the thrills of life in our backyard. God created such a sweet little miracle, a perfect little human being—one of his grandest masterpieces—a small wonderful innocent child.

Such is the mystery of the phenomenon we call life. Beth, our daughter, dead at the tender age of one year of Sudden Infant Death Syndrome (SIDS). Never to learn the joys of learning to ride a bicycle, or playing in the water sprinkler on a hot summer afternoon.

She will never learn to climb a tree or build a tree-house. Nor will she ever learn to water ski or learn to dance, or play the piano. She will never win a science fair ribbon or become a Girl Scout. Never will she rejoice in having birthday parties, nor rejoice in the blessings of Christmas.

This young child of mine will never really know her

mother or her father, how they loved her, how their hearts ached for her—to hold her, to wipe away her tears.

A thousand other things come to mind as I dream. She will never see her first prom dress, her first wonder of love, or that first sweet kiss, or that first date. She will never grow up, fall in love and get married. She will never know the joy of marriage, and the joy of having children of her own.

Now that tiny casket—her funeral. Time to say good-bye. The rose which I placed gingerly across her grave. Heartache. A buzzer sounds—

My alarm clock. I must get ready for work. I look at the time, turn over and feel the warmth of the bed. I nudge my wife to get up, as I drift once again into dreamland. The buzzer again wakes me a few minutes later and I think about my little precious daughter that died. Sweet Beth. I can't think about her now. Block it out. Must get ready for work.

A twinge of pain and stiffness in my right leg which took a bullet at the '93 government siege at Waco. That bullet put me in the hospital for over a week. The Branch Davidians were held at bay for fifty-one days on illegal weapons charges, while negotiations deteriorated and the Bureau of Alcohol, Tobacco, and Firearms (BATF) and the Federal Bureau of Investigation (FBI) forced their way into their compound at Waco, Texas. The raid was to seize the illegal weapons and to release the children thought to be in jeopardy there.

I dressed, unlocked the safe-box and took out my SIG Sauer 9mm semiautomatic pistol.

You just can't be too safe with small children running around the house these days, I thought to myself.

Donning my shoulder holster, I checked the weapon,

cocked it back proving the chamber was empty, clicking off the slide, and snapped in the loaded clip. Placing it on safety, I inserted it into my holster, covering it with my coat. There was hardly any bulge of it showing. My wife, Faith, had coffee made by now and the kids dressed. Breakfast was fixed and the twins, Hope and Charity, both three years of age, gathered at the table to eat.

Now I kissed my wife good-bye and fetched the kid's lunch sacks that contained sandwiches and some of their colored Easter eggs left over from Easter Sunday, the weekend before. Then the twins and I left the house and traveled the twenty miles to work from Bethany to Oklahoma City. They loved Sunday School and we sang some church hymns on the way to work, namely, *He Lives*, and *What a Friend We Have in Jesus*.

A quote entered my mind as I was driving down the highway—

"Our Creator would never have made such lovely days
and have given us the deep hearts to enjoy them
unless we were meant to be immortal."
—Nathaniel Hawthorne

I wondered if I should continue teaching my senior high Sunday School class. I had taught Bible to 4th and 6th graders, middle school, and high school classes in the past. Though time consuming, I found it fulfilling for it made me study the Word of God. Preparing my next lesson on the Holy Spirit, I wondered about the nature of the Holy Spirit—how it touches the believer and how it changes the heart of the sinner before and after salvation. Is salvation dependent on being baptized by the Holy Spirit and receiving gifts of the Spirit such as healing, prophecy, and the working of miracles?

Okay, I told myself, *what is it you are really searching for? Are you going to sit in your comfortable air conditioned church and patted pew, and listen to a cute little story? Are you going to see a sermon—or be a sermon? Is the Word of God going to translate before your eyes into that realm of power and glory? Will the mystery of the actual truth of God's Word permeate into the very depths of your heart, where the life of Jesus and the miracles of God become a reality? Could these results then be manifested into great wisdom and in blessings beyond your wildest dreams?*

While driving I realized that this is Wednesday, "hump" day as we at the office call it, being in the middle of the week. Let's see—Wednesday, April 19, 1995.

Cool morning. The sun is shinning brightly. Wonder what God has in store for us today. I remembered what Hope, after church Easter Sunday, asked me about when Jesus died on the cross, where did he go? I remembered stating that I thought she was too young to be asking such questions—that she had a lot of living left to do. When she grows older, then I will then explain it to her. I wondered what happened myself, and where I could find the answer.

While driving along the freeway, a thousand other things came to mind that I must do. Being a Special Agent of the Foreign Counterintelligence Division of the FBI, I am trying to discover the whereabouts of Eyad Ismoil, who masterminded the plot in 1993 to drive a bomb-laden van into the World Trade Center.

The twins and I arrived at the Alfred P. Murrah Federal

Building, turning into the lower parking deck and found those reserved for the FBI. After parking I grabbed Hope and Charity by the hand and entered the elevator and traveled up to the second floor to the America's Kids day-care center. Kissing and hugging them good-bye, I proceeded to my office on the ninth floor. Mary Ann, my secretary, hadn't arrive as yet, it being 7:50 A.M. Allen Erikson, one of my coworkers waved to me out in the hallway, handing me a book.

"What's this?" I inquired.

"*The Turner Diaries.* A book written by Andrew MacDonald.

"Is it any good?"

"Oh, Iben, some rebels make a bomb from heating oil and fertilizer, place it in a stolen delivery truck and blow up a FBI building as it opens for the day. Far-fetched, maybe, but never-the-less intriguing!"

Mary Ann, my secretary, hadn't arrived as yet, it being 8:00 A.M. Allen and I decided to spring for coffee. Daniel Norris was already in the break room pouring his.

"Iben, good morning to you and Allen. Hope we have an easy-going day. I didn't sleep very good last night, and I'm still a little tired this morning."

Daniel had already checked the mail before I arrived. He handed me a sealed envelope which had just arrived from Washington D.C. The cover of the envelope read:

TO: Agent Iben Thayer
CONFIDENTIAL
CAUTION: To be opened by Iben Thayer only

I ripped it open and found the following document:

SPECIAL BULLETIN
FROM: KAREN SPENCER: ATTORNEY GENERAL
FEDERAL BUREAU OF INVESTIGATION,
WASHINGTON D.C.

TO: SPECIAL AGENT: IBEN THAYER
FOR YOUR EYES ONLY / HIGHLY CONFIDENTIAL

Iben, your next assignment is to proceed to Elohim City on the Arkansas border, north of Muldrow, Oklahoma. You will do surveillance on the leader of the Aryan Nations, a white supremacist organization.

On April 19, 1985, state and federal officers invaded a remote compound at Bull Shoals Lake, Arkansas. Here the FBI discovered plots to destroy state and federal property with stolen munitions from a nearby army arsenal.

Make note that they all have a mission—to overthrow the U. S. Government.

Be cautious, Iben, for they also have FBI clothing with facsimile insignia and fake I.D. cards so as to impersonate federal agents. Also, a number of them are underwater demolition experts having experience in plastic and C-4 explosives.

Other extremists, all who live in Elohim City, carry automatic weapons and preach the white-separatist ideology. One such person is acting as Richard Wayne Snell's spiritual adviser, who is awaiting execution on death row.

Arkansas will execute convicted cop killer Richard Wayne Snell for the murder of a Texarkana pawnbroker. Snell will die of lethal injection on April 19, 1995, around

10 P.M. at the Cummins Unit maximum security facility, Grady, Arkansas. At Snell's death his body will be driven back to Elohim City to be buried there.

Therefore, Iben, please be careful while in Elohim City. These white-supremacist of the Aryan Republic Army are considered armed and dangerous. They are very serious about the overthrow of the American Government by any and all means they can muster.

You remember Randy Weaver, when Weaver's wife and son were shot to death along with a federal marshal in the 1992 confrontation on Weaver's land near Sandpoint, Idaho. Many of those in Uniontown and Elohim City are all close friends.

You, Iben, will be traveling to this little community next Wednesday, April 26, 1995, driving your personal vehicle so as not to arouse suspicion. You will be staying in an undisclosed motel. I will contact you with more technical details as the week proceeds.

—End of Document

At my desk, I now typed in my security code searching through numerous access files for pertinent documents that needed by immediate attention.

U.S. DEPARTMENT OF DEFENSE
OFFICIAL REPORT:

TOP SECRET
FOR YOUR EYES ONLY
(File in a secured cabinet)

Federal Bureau of Investigation
Washington, D.C.

The United States had thwarted a terrorist attack involving deadly nerve gas at Disneyland, CA during the crowded Easter weekend, April 16, 1995.

Japanese terrorists were planning to release nerve gas at the California tourist attraction over this last Easter weekend.

Federal authorities caught two Japanese men at Los Angeles International Airport just before the Easter holiday. Found on these men were the instructions on the manufacturing of Sarin, the highly toxic nerve gas used in the terrorist attack in the Tokyo subway.

The Aum Shimrikyo doomsday cult executed a poison gas attack in March, 1995, in the Tokyo subway. Exposure to the nerve gas sarin killed 12 people and injured over 5,000. This cult has actually contacted the Russian nuclear agency searching for nuclear warheads at Russia's Kurchatov Nuclear Weapons Institute and also scanned the Internet for bomb-making experts.

Iben, please review the following United States Department of Defense Official Reports #21, #71, and #116.

Sincerely,
Karen Spencer, Attorney General
Washington, D. C.
April 18, 1995
—End of Document

U. S. DEPARTMENT OF DEFENSE
OFFICIAL REFORT #21:

TOP SECRET   TOP SECRET

U.S. DEPARTMENT OF DEFENSE
OFFICIAL REPORT

FOR YOUR EYES ONLY

WEB OF TERRORISTS: THE BOJINKA PLOT
National Security Agency
Ft. George / Meade, MD

The Bojinka Plot was a planned attack upon the American airlines to be the worst terrorist attack in U.S. history!

Project Bojinka was a plan to blow up 11 U.S. airliners in retaliation against the United States. Muslim terrorists were to plant virtually undetectable bombs aboard 11 big passenger planes.

The U.S. government accused Ramzi Ahmed Yousef, the Pakistani terrorist, of engineering the New York World Trade Center bombing, Feb. 26, 1993, killing 6, setting 200 cars ablaze, injuring over 1,000 and causing $300 million in damages. As you remember, a rented Ryder van containing an 1,800-pound bomb exploded in their underground parking garage destroying 5 underground floors. Six Islamic militants were caught and convicted to life in this attack. The terrorist, Ramzi Ahmed Yousef, allegedly masterminded this bombing, including the Bojinka plot.

There were also plans to assassinate Pope John Paul II

while he visited the Philippines. That plan is now believed to have been designed to deflect attention from their plan to destroy the planes.

Intelligence experts said that the investigation into the Bojinka plot has brought to light a worldwide network of terrorists financed by Osama bin Laden, a Saudi millionaire. Many terrorists have received weapons training and brainwashing indoctrination from such terrorists in certain countries like Afghanistan and Iraq, who are determined to attack the "Satanic" United States for its support with Israel.

—End of Document

CHAPTER TWO

I was working steadily and realized that my coffee was cold, so I decided to take a break and strolled over to the window to stretch a bit. That was when I saw a yellow Ryder van nine stories below parked at the curb in front of the building. A thought went through my head and I remembered renting an almost identical van when I moved to Oklahoma City a few years ago from Stillwater, after graduating from the University of Oklahoma.

The phone rang...

"FBI—Iben speaking."

"Hey, Iben? This is Mary Ann. My children are sick and I decided to take the day off. There's not anything pending that you really need me for today is there?"

"Not really," I replied. "I'm just going over some files and it should be a relatively easy-going day. Stay home and take care of those kids and I'll see you tomorrow."

"Thanks Iben—bye."

So her kids are sick. I noted today, April 19, as a sick day on her desk calendar.

Then I saw a strange effluvium for an instance surrounding me as an aura, filling my heart with a harbinger of trepidation. I shivered and adjusted my chair looked at the wall clock which had 8:45 A.M., then I pulled up the next document —

U.S. DEPARTMENT OF DEFENSE
OFFICIAL REPORT #71
Bureau of Alcohol, Tobacco, and Firearms

This file is in reference to the killing of Idaho white separatist Randy Weaver's wife and son. Randy Weaver retired to rural Idaho with his wife and four children and a family friend.

On August 22, 1992, six marshals, one equipped with an assault rifle, shot Weavers' dog. Weaver's son, Samuel, outraged at this, charged the marshals shooting his weapon as he ran toward them, killing U.S. Marshal, James Logan.

(I knew Logan and remembered when this happened. He was a fine friend, and a cool head under fire. We had training seminars together and went out for lunch when he came down to attend them. I miss him).

Samuel Weaver's son, was shot in the back as he retreated. This reinforced Weaver and Harris to refuse surrendering to the authorities.

National Guard and FBI Hostage Rescue Teams were now called in and shot Weaver in the arm as he went to check on Samuel. Vicki Weaver was killed by a sharp shooter as she held her baby in her arms. Harris was wounded by a smoke grenade.

—End of Document

U. S. DEPARTMENT OF DEFENSE
OFFICIAL REPORT # 116
BRIEF HISTORY OF TERRORISM
National Security Agency

There has also been a recent discussion by the Deputy Secretary of Defense on a plan by foreign nationals to develop a "dirty bomb" using cesium-137. These radioactive bombs could be detonated over any large city to produce radiological contamination. These dangerous bombs are not nuclear nor do they need to cause a huge explosion. A pipe bomb sealed in a radiological contaminated suitcase can be classified as a "dirty bomb." It does not need enriched uranium or plutonium—only languished radioactive materials such as stolen from a hospital lab. It would mostly become a "panic" weapon ... not to destroy, but to cause mayhem in a populated city.

Chechen separatists marked their first anniversary of their conflict with Russia by planting a "dirty bomb" in a popular Moscow park. Also, a device containing cesium-137, the same isotope that triggered the 1987 contamination panic in South America—was recovered in Brazil—before detonation.

—End of Document

I now glanced up at the clock and saw it was 8:50 A.M. Allen wanted me to look over the fax that had just arrived from the FBI in Little Rock, Arkansas. I told him to wait for a few minutes, until I had finished reading my documents. He placed it in my file basket.

Agent John Kidron just arrived, he was always in and out on assignments, and I didn't see much of him anymore. He stated that he was springing for some coffee and that he would see me next Friday.

I glanced at the wall clock ... time 8:57 A.M.

I reached in the file basket and picked up the newly arrived FAX which Agent Erikson had placed there.

TO: SPECIAL AGENT IBEN THAYER/FBI
Alfred P. Murrah Federal Building
Oklahoma City, OK

FROM: CHRIS HALL
The Federal Building/FBI Headquarters, Little Rock, AR
FAX TIME: 8:36
APRIL 19, 1995
Iben, I was requested by Washington, D.C.
to forward the following information
that might be pertinent for your next assignment.
Thank you, C. H.

Be aware of extremists such as ZOG, short for Zionist Occupation Government. They are against gun control, the Brady Bill and the 1994 federal ban on assault weapons. They were sympathizers with the Branch Davidians at Waco, Texas on April 19, 1993. Waco is the militia movement's Alamo, where 86 men, women, and children died in the siege which began to seize the Davidians' illegal weapons and to check on the improper treatment and incest of their children.

April 19, 1995: Today, is the date scheduled for the execution of Richard Wayne Snell, a white supremacist, who is convicted of killing a pawnshop owner in Arkansas. He will be executed by lethal injection at 10 P.M. tonight CDT.
—End of Document

I glanced at the clock ... 9:02 A.M.

CHAPTER THREE

I felt a vibration under my feet—a swaying ... the clock was knocked from the wall. Pictures crashed down—a shock wave rumbled and shuttered throughout the building. Files toppled over, my computer and the lights blinked out—a clap of thunder blasted into my ears. A red-orange fireball lit up our office shattering the windows and blowing my desk against the wall, pinning me against it. Shards of glass blasted from the windows—excruciating pain. I thought I might have a broken rib or two, then the concrete floor split, heaved upward, then there was a falling sensation...

Earthquake, I thought.

Smoke and detritus—shards of glass and plaster—blood all over me. I looked up and saw the carnage of the building bellowing black smoke into the blue sunlit sky. Glass cascaded down like rain. Parking meters blown from solid concrete. Roofs on nearby buildings destroyed. Eviscerated bodies scattered everywhere—

Masses of concrete, steel and rebar twisted in grotesque shapes. Computers dangling from wires hanging from the ragged edges of the floors. Dust and plaster permeated the air—a still, unnerving quiet replaced the cacophony of noise. An eerie silence permeated throughout the chaos of crushed steel and sheet rock.

I glanced upward through the smoking building. I noticed checkbooks scattered everywhere and that I was resting on vast amounts of money. The safe of the Credit Union that once resided on the third floor was shocked open by the blast. All sorts of currency lay scattered before me. In another world I could have greedily plucked some of it up—but now I gazed upon it as some foreign substance—having no use.

I had drifted from my prostrated body. I was now strangely outside the office building. I realized just what a ghastly specter it was. A gaping hole from the collapsed floors crumbled into a massive heap of concrete, steel and rubble, still smoking and burning. Cinereous bodies scattered the street in front of the building and many cars were still burning. I could hear sirens of the police and firetrucks, along with the ambulances and even those of the police dispatchers and the 911 calls!

What on earth had happened, I wondered. *A natural gas leak?*

I could easily see the huge crater where possibly the gas line had been.

Then, a trepidation came over me as I realized this was the very exact spot where the Ryder truck had parked a few moments before.

How many of my friends had also perished in this calamitous disaster?

I felt as though I was in a phantasmal dream world. I could feel a certain necrosis creeping through me.

Take that last deep, heavy breath Iben, and exhale very slowly. This will be your last one ... forever ... as my body was engulfed by a vast unknown—

Now I groped for some other thing. Is there something else here at the very last moment of life? What?

Something more miraculous, more amazing, more extraordinary, more divine, more loving than the mind or imagination can conceive. Blackness—nothingness ... then an unconscious, floating void ... the darkness of infinity.

My mangled body revealed only a shattered chrysalis. I turned away from its ghastly sight—

Something ethereal and shadowy left my body — brushed across by pulverized face and in an instant vaporized into thin air.

What was that? I shivered.

Nothing but silence—deadly silence.

Other mangled truncated bodies lay beside mine, but I couldn't recognize any of them for the detritus and thick smoke surrounding me. I began to dream—

Am I now on the earth ... or on a journey ... Is there a north or a south? An east or west ... I now realize how utterly silent it is ... I can even hear the beating of my heart...

But my breathing ... has ceased ... and yet I feel no distress ... my thinking seems to vibrate my whole self.

Only now as pulsating waves of blackness engulf and permeate ... can I even comprehend how God felt before the creation of the universe.

I realized I was now hovering above ground and still viewing the carnage of the federal building. Fifth Street, in front, where the explosion occurred cars were demolished, still afire and smoking. The YMCA day-care center was destroyed at the corner of Fifth Street and Robinson Avenue. In the Oklahoma Water Resources Building the windows were shattered. Behind our building I could see the Federal Courthouse, where there were some workers injured by falling glass. Their roofs were peppered with tiny shreds of some blue plastic material.

Strange.

Now an Oklahoma City police sergeant passed a little limp, blood-splattered baby into the arms of a firefighter. I remembered this fireman from the time I took my children to visit their station last year. I saw at a glance that this little tattered child was that little baby girl who had a birthday party with my children at the day-care center the day before, where she just turned three-years-old.

Across the street was the Journal Records Building— which sustained heavy damage. Strangely, I could hear people actually praying in the building—intense prayers of those like me facing death, and those badly hurt waiting for rescue workers to find them.

I must relate at this moment to those which had lost love-ones here that I could see other wondrous beings, supernal supernatural entities. They were ministering to and comforting those dying and those severely hurt. I could see the effluvium of those which perished rising up from their bodies, though I could not recognize any of them as my friends or co-workers for their intense brightness.

The Red Cross arrived and hearing the conversations of other newcomers, I realized that Tinker Air Force Base even sent their personnel to help. Nurses and doctors also arrived from St. Anthony Hospital nearby.

I watched all through the night while rescuers pawed through the rubble with cranes, backhoes and acoustic equipment, listening for signs of life. Dogs trained to sniff human scents prowled the carnage; so did cave-rescue specialists and crews equipped with fiber-optic cameras.

A triage medical team was forming at the corner of Fifth Street and Harvey Avenue to help those in immediate need. My eyes had such a distant stare and I could tell that I was badly crushed under tons of concrete with blood trickling down in little rivulets. Then complete silence—my heartbeat had faded away. The stillness of such I have never known.

Having left this carnage, I now realized that I did not belong anymore to the mundane world of which I was born. I embraced the incorporeal world, the world of the spiritual. The mundane world I once knew—was but a memory. I must now bid it farewell—for all eternity.

"Death, a riddle wrapped in a mystery inside an enigma."
— The Author

"The nature of God is a circle
of which the center is everywhere
and the circumference is nowhere."
—Empedocles

CHAPTER FOUR

A light … a light! It was a sparkling diamond of fire in the black velvet of unfathomable infinity. I realized that I was moving toward it as it grew in intensity.

A Voice spoke out, "Go toward the Light, Iben."

"Iben Thayer, go toward the Light."

The light grew brighter and increased in its brilliancy.

"Iben, follow me," the Light quivered.

I turned away from the ruins of the federal building and slowly reached toward the bright dazzling luminosity. I was caught within a vertiginous swirling convolution, a psychedelic beacon in the dark void of nothingness. It was a strange kaleidoscopic gateway into another world.

Its center, an oculus, opened as an iris, and I plunged through. It was a radiant beautiful tunnel, a swirling nebula of luminescence. I could sense a Presence—that of Holiness, and I found myself surrounded by a beautiful aureole of some angelic being.

I had encountered a new empyrean dimension of love, tranquility and euphonious music, light and airy, faint as tinkling fairy wings. The melodious rhythm became more and more intense—

Now appeared thousands of "Hallelujah" Angels in great exultation all praising God. I then realized that I was under the blood of Jesus, a "child of God" being born unto a new life, unto a new dimension, unto a new existence.

Before me were magnificent Luminaria, great emissaries of God coruscating peace, love, holiness and supreme tranquility.

The darkness suddenly ceased as I moved toward these supernatural scintillating beings. Bible verses came softly to me—memorized as a child.

"Yea, though I walk through the
valley of the shadow of death,
I will fear no evil: for thou art with me;
thy rod and thy staff they comfort me…"
—Ps. 23:4

"God so loved the world,
that he gave his only begotten Son,
that whosoever believeth in him
should not perish, but have everlasting life."
—Jn. 3:16

Then the Light spoke:

"I am come as a light into the world
that whosoever believeth in me
should not abide in darkness … follow me."

I then panicked—

I am dead ... I can't be. I have so much to live for. My wife, Faith. My two children—

My twins! They were on the second floor! I must try to find them.

I heard myself scream their names ... Hope ... Charity...

Oh God ... this can't be happening...

Then a peace so wonderful permeated within me. I followed the strange wondrous brilliant luminescence of an angel, the being of immortality and resurrection—

Beautiful and peaceful.

I encountered a strange sensation, a dream, or reality I knew not. Beautiful shades of divine radiances warmed my soul. It was a living undulating prism of twinkling jewels, a wonderful dancing aura—sparkling all the colors of the spectrum.

I was as in a radiant drop of pure sunshine, photons of iridescence, coiling, twisting and dancing. I was within a starry nebula—the nimbus of a Holy Being.

The Light spoke, "I am the Archangel, Anastasia."

I was beginning to focus on the Light without being blinded by it. I watched as an ethereal apparition coalesced into human-like form. This supernal divine being radiated the energy of the divine, perfect, holy and pure.

"Again, I am Anastasia, thy radiant guide —"

All fear left me. So peaceful, tranquil and euphoric.

Synesthesia and ESP

"You, Iben, are now a transformed being, a Child of Light—born unto a new life of immortality having a glorified spiritual body. Welcome to Eternity—that strange parallel dimension between the mundane world and the incorporeal world—the greatest part that life has to offer—the realm of the hyper-consciousness.

"You now have powers beyond the normal senses. The mortal mind can not comprehend what it cannot experience. This is a totally new experience for you—the human soul has no color, race, or nationality, having one language, a godly language of communicating, one universal language, created by God, for perfect communication, which you will learn very soon.

"Iben, you now possess the grand potentially of the human psyche! You have the mental capacity to tap into the infinite mind of the Eternal.

"Differential calculus was difficult for you while upon the earth. Now you can solve one of mathematics most intriguing problems—that of proving Fermat's last theorem!

"Soon you will become a member of the Cognoscente having total omnivorous thought and knowledge and you will see this universe of ours as one great scientific laboratory, beckoning you into strange dimensions of time and space."

I realized that I had an enhanced mind, and therefore had an enhanced world. Perception is relative to the mind that comprehends it. Surely the future is worth all my past! And yet, my past determined the path of my Divine Destiny!

"I notice, Iben, you are pondering what happened to the Murrah Federal Building. The answer is that a terrorist placed a mixture of ammonium nitrate and fuel oil in the yellow Ryder van you saw a moment ago. He then detonated it, blowing up the building along with its day care center and credit union, killing 168 people—including yourself. Over two hundred and seventy structures were severely damaged. The blue plastic shredded material you saw on the roof tops were the containers vaporized from this explosion."

"So this is what happened! The shock of it all! There was so much to do. How can I contact my wife and tell her?"

"No need, Iben, for God and his guardian angels will be with her in her hour of need. The Lord gives us no more than that which we can bear. The churches and ministers will give your surviving family all their support and they will be comforted."

I wondered about the strange sensation I had at the federal building once again. I remembered seeing a mist or aberration just before the bomb went off.

"Dear Iben, you sensed Thanatopia, the Angel of Death. He prepares the way for Christians to find God in great times of distress. He protects God's flock and acts as their guardian angel, directing them towards the Light."

Secular Mysteries

"You are going to love it here," Anastasia continued. "Is it divine wisdom and divine knowledge you are after? You will once again experience the pure joy of learning! You now have an eidetic or photographic memory and the ability to comprehend algebra, differential and integral calculus, and numeric systems unheard of and yet to be invented back on earth. You are not limited to one or two languages, but now know hundreds! The "Anti-Babel Blessing" we call it. Remember in Genesis chapter 11—

"Are you an adventurer? There are jungles we will discover that are many times greater than those of Africa or

South America—greater than those combined, and grand surrealistic worlds just waiting for us to explore."

"Then there are some things that are still unknown?"

"Of course, Iben! One of the greatest wonders of being human (which you still are, of course), is that of the mysterious. God would not take this away from immortal humankind. We will explore the oceans of the world. You will learn the age old secret of chlorophyll, along with the secrets of life, the *elixir vitae,* and that of protoplasm of which all life is composed."

"Then I realized that I was to learn the following:

If Lee Harvey Oswald acted alone to kill President Kennedy.

What happened to Amelia Earhart?

What is Spontaneous Human Combustion?

"What happened at Roswell, New Mexico Army Air Field. Were there little space aliens found alive from a crashed flying saucer?

What about those enigmatic crystal skulls susposely discovered in the Mayan ruins of Central and South America?

What were the 'curses' when Howard Carter, in 1922, opened King Tut's tomb causing many of his colleagues to die?

What happened when Lord Carnarvon opened the tomb of King Casimir in Poland on April 13, 1973—a few days later only two of the original twelve that excavated the tomb were still living. Were these 'curses' caused by the mold *Penicillium rubrum* or *Aspergillus flavus*—or something else?

What caused the Salem witch trials in 1652? Were rye kernels infected with the fungus *Fusarium* or *Claviceps* the real reason why so many town's people hallucinated and burned their children, friends and relatives at the stake?

What happened at Groom Lake, located in the Emigrant Valley? It is an extension of the Nevada A-bomb Test Site, situated 120 miles Northwest of Las Vegas. Also known as—as AREA 51. And what is in the secret complex called S-4 at Papoose Lake, near Groom Lake? Does it contain a crashed UFO and real aliens from another world?

What happened at AREA 52, located in a remote part of Utah? Does it contain the secrets of the Egyptian pyramids along with other strange mysteries...

Have space visitors, or extraterrestrials ever contacted the Earth in the past? Are Erich von Daniken's theories correct? He asserts that technically advanced intelligent aliens came from outer space, teaching humankind how to design and erect advanced civilizations of stone buildings and temples. Von Daniken really thinks this happened ... and has authored numerous books on the subject, namely the best sellers *Chariots of the Gods? Gods from Outer Space* and *Miracles of the Gods.* Iben, what you are about to learn will go *way beyond* what he ever thought or imagined!

Did an alien spiritual visitor arrive from space which landed in Fatima, Portugal on Oct. 13, 1917? This was actually more spectacular than the encounter that happened in Roswell, New Mexico. Seventy thousand people were visited by a strange shiny disc or sphere. Many thought they actually saw a celestial being or the Virgin Mary come down from the heavens to make contact with three little children. Journalists and photographers were present to record the event. You will learn if this story is true, and what or who they actually encountered.

How did a strange earthenware jar, found in Iraq, turn out to be an ancient battery? It contained an iron rod set inside a copper cylinder, resembling a modern dry-cell battery. This discovery could mean that the Iraq had generated electricity 1,600 years *before* the 1800s—the date of the first manufactured modern battery!

How Francis Gary Powers was shot down in his U-2 spy plane over Russia in 1962? Or if a timed bomb was placed aboard the plane by a spy? Russia claimed that one of their missiles shot it down!

The enigma of the woolly mammoths will be solved. How thousands of them were found in Siberia in the late 1800s, frozen to death while eating wild flowers and grasses. Many were discovered with buttercups still in their mouths, grazing on a mild spring-like day. What instantaneous climatic change occurred here thousands of years ago when all of a sudden a fierce frigid wind blew upon them freezing them instantly in their tracks, killing them so fast that they didn't even have time to fall over dead! They were so well preserved that the explorers in the 1800s who discovered them actually cooked and ate their flesh.

What caused the downfall of the woolly mammoth? Was it a magnetic reversal, volcanic activity or maybe a tilt in the Earth's axis that caused this calamity of violent weather? We will soon even solve this mystery of the ages!

How dangerous is the top secret nuclear weapons complex is located near Rocky Flats National Wildlife Refuge, northwest of Denver, CO? Here during the cold war, plutonium triggers were manufactured for the hydrogen bomb program. If inhaled, plutonium can enter the lungs where it can cause cancer.

Biblical Mysteries

And the BIBLICAL MYSTERIES will be solved:

Which prophet wrote Revelation? Was it John the Baptist, John of Patmos, or John the Elder? or another John, lost to antiquity?

"With what weapon did God destroy the twin cities of Sodom and Gomorrah?

How did Joseph interpret his strange dreams?

Where are the actual Ten Commandments?

How did the priests blowing the trumpets destroy the walls of Jericho?

How did God stop the Earth when Joshua demanded that the sun and moon to stand still during the battle between the kings who attacked Gibeon in the book of Joshua?

"What kind of 'great fish' swallowed Jonah? What actually were those sea monsters in the Bible? The Hebrew word, *tannim*, in Genesis 1:21, Job 7:12; Eze. 32:2; has been translated as "sea monster." In the Greek New Testament, the word, *ketos*, as whale, is used in Mt. 12:40. Were they really *whales* as many translators imply ... or could they have been giant prehistoric creatures known as the ichthyosaurs? In the past, there existed prehistoric creatures known as the *Zeuglodon* (80 ft. long). Also, the ancient *Eleasmosaurus*, a member of the plesiosaur family roamed the ancient oceans. There were the archaic giant sharped-beaked armored creatures such as the *Dinichthys* (30 ft. long), a member of the placoderms (prehistoric fish), or the giant alligator-like *Tylosaurus* (56 ft. long), a member of the mosasaur family, all of which were very capable of swallowing Jonah.

What was Ezekiel's Vision of the valley of dry bones?

What ever happened to the Twelve Lost Tribes of Israel?

What actually became of all the twelve disciples of Christ?

What happened during the 'lost childhood years' of Jesus Christ, from his birth till he started his ministry?

Who wrote the Gospel of Thomas, unearthed in a cache of jars which was buried in the fourth century A.D.? It is one of the most important manuscript discoveries of modern times! It is similar to the Gospels of Matthew, Mark and Luke and is as old as these MS. themselves.

What is the 'Angel Scroll'? How was this lost 2000-year-old manuscript, written by the Essenes, discovered? It was found alongside the Dead Sea Scrolls which describes a man identified as Yeshua ben Padiah who in a vision was taken to Paradise by the angel Panameia to visit God's Heavenly Palace.

Is the 'Shroud of Turin' really the actual burial cloth which covered Christ at his death? supernatural powers?

Is the limestone ossuary excavated by looters and placed upon the antiquities market is really the burial box of James, the brother and disciple of Jesus Christ? Etched upon this stone box found around Jerusalem were the exact words written in Aramaic, *Ya'akow bar Yosef akhui diYeshua* which translated states 'James, son of Joseph, brother of Jesus,' written around A.D. 63. If this is authentic, this ossuary is the very first epigraphic mention of Jesus of Nazareth outside the Bible.

Will the 2,500-year old ancient cuneiform tablets, one of the world's earliest scripts, excavated from southern Iraq, be proven to be authentic? Found were 110 cracker-sized clay tablets that provide the earliest written evidence of the biblical exile of the Judeans to Babylon in 586 B.C. These tablets fill in a 130-year gap in their history when they were exiled to Babylon. Then the Babylonians destroyed Jerusalem in the sixth century B.C., and these tablets recently discovered depict dates inscribed on them from about 15 years after the destruction of the First Jewish Temple in Jerusalem proving that the Judeans soon became an important part of the Babylonian empire.

What are the mysteries of Stonehenge, England??

Who build the statues on Easter Island in the Pacific? Any why?

We will learn the secrets of the ancient mysterious pyramids of Egypt and the Great Wall of China.

We will travel to Teotihuacan where the Aztecs produced their glorious pyramids.

We will visit the grand temple of Angkor Wat, the architectural wonder of the Khmer civilization.

We will solve the mysteries of the Piri Reis maps and the enigma of the Bermuda Triangle.

And, I realized that there were a thousand more mysteries just waiting to be solve, strange enigmas waiting to be explored.

CHAPTER FIVE

*A*nastasia continued, "Again, Iben, welcome to glory, the Everlasting Sanctum within the Kingdom of God."

"Therefore, if any man be in Christ, he is a new creature: old things are passed away; behold, all things are become new."
—1 Cor. 15:49, 53; 2 Cor. 5:17

"You now have Divine Mind that has been cleansed of all evil thoughts. You remember that shadowy apparition which left you when your worldly body was uncreated? Well that was all the evil demons you had in your mind that left when you were purged from mortal life.

The Supernatural Mind

"You now have a supraliminal mind of pure reasoning and cognizance which takes the place of complacency in learning. Your sensory acuity has expanded tremendously.

You can hear beyond normal hearing, from the high frequencies of the supersonics or ultrasonics, deep into the low frequencies of the infrasonics. Your visual perception has increased its range beyond visible light, into a type of X-ray vision known as thermalvision (the *Kirlian*, or the *Schlierenvision Phenomenon*). You now possess biotelemetry and can even observe the blood coursing through the heart and brain—seeing broken bones healing and deadly cancer cells in patients.

"Iben, your sense of smell has been greatly increased. So has your taste, among other abilities, all have been greatly enhanced. You, Iben, can now actually taste, smell, and metabolize the pure nectar of Divine Kinetic Energy!"

So, I did hear the police bands of the dispatchers, short wave radios, and all those 911 calls!

"You can receive signals through the air like a radio or TV. These natural abilities have been enhanced, along with the supernatural ability to see and sense things beyond the normal perception."

With this last statement Anastasia, evaporated before my eyes as white wispy clouds in a blue morning sky.

The scene changed and I found myself encountering another luminosity. It came closer and closer, taking on the nimbus of human form, the image of a female. I then realized it was my precious mother, Sophia! She looked young and radiant!

"My son, Iben, it has been many precious years since we have departed. Many members of your family have been waiting for you. We could hardly wait until you were reunited with us!"

Something must be said about these supernal, immortal and paranormal beings, I termed "SUPERNALITES."

Every one of them emanated a radiant effluvium about their countenance and body, a glorious nimbus or *visica piscis* of pure divine energy of the Holy Spirit.

"Iben" Sophia continued, "we are now all living in an anti-senescent existence. We seem not to be over twenty years of age, young and vivacious — the paragon of perfection. We are all frozen in the peak of opulence, never to grow old, never to have senility nor any effete symptoms. We possess a glowing radiance of pure joy and happiness with divine energy imbued with omniscient love."

All these dazzling Beings were the faces of exculpated souls, assuaged and comforted, living without fear or animosity in total peace and tranquility.

How wonderful to be in our prime once again! I knew that they saw me in the same luminosity as I saw them, being full of enlightenment and the metaphysical, full of mirth and ecstatic joy!

Two fast moving Luminaria whizzed past and I recognized them as Hope and Charity, my twins! As they sped past, they turned toward me, but spoke not a word, their eyes enlightening their total bliss, then passed directly into the midst of hundreds of other supernal immortal beings and disappeared into the depths of Eternity, surrounded by a nebula of magnificent angels, the Seraphim, Cherubim and Thrones. The twin's countenances shone as the sun as they were reborn into immortality. What a wonderful visit, though they were gone in a flash, I knew that I would see them again very soon. All these Supernalites I met were in the best of hands, the omnipotent hands of Almighty God.

I realized that pure eternal divine kinetic energy from God now empowers our immortal system. No more need for common foodstuffs, for we were now of God, in a hypostatic union of pure bioplasmic energy, just as Jesus Christ, the human, was connected with God, the Divine.

I then realized that I was composed of sempiternal substances, free of blemishes and impurities as God had meant it us to be before the fall of Adam and Eve.

Strange that if our five senses increase, our perception also increases. Therefore, our knowledge will multiply—our universe will expand from a three-dimension world to a multi-dimensional reality. As our world changes, our minds will dilate, becoming limitless … infinite … and eternal.

Christ's saints (all believers in Christ) now have a mind of supraliminal abilities, not finite, but infinite, vast and mysterious. As the divine substance of God was incorporated into Christ, so we are transformed into glory. We were now embued with the phenomenon of translocation, (*Corporalis/ Spiritus Interstice*), miraculously traveling instantaneously from one place to another.

More Luminaria appeared. They were my young childhood friends, their lives cut short by accidents, maladies and diseases. Appearing before me in all their radiance were those I played with as a child, all of whom died before I did. What a great reunion we had. Such *esprit de corps*!

I did not realize how much I loved and missed them!

Mom stated that she had to leave. There were other pertinent agenda that needed her undivided attention.

With this, she instantly disappeared right before me.

Then in an instant they were all gone—leaving me with a touch of divine love never before experienced.

I was left wondering about these miracles and pondered them in my heart.

The Concept of Time

"God created time so everything
wouldn't happen all at once."
—Erin Biba, a San Francisco writer

Another prodigious divine angel now appeared.

"I am the Archangel of Time Travel—Timaeus is my name. It is I who separate time into the Past, Present and Future.

"This phenomenon of time is technically known as *Translinear Chronometry*, or in layman's terms, the 'Transchronos Barrier.' You will learn how time undulates and fluctuates, and why clocks run slower in a strong gravitational field than they do in empty space. You will learn the exotic concept of time symmetry—that the *past* does not exist anymore—only in your memory; the *future* does not exist (as yet), and the *present*—is an indefinable 'point of reality.' It is neither *past* nor *future*. Strangely, in less than a nanosecond, *the present* is future and then it is past—the *now* exists only in a fraction of time so infinitely minuscule it cannot be measured—not by any atomic clock yet devised, nor by any chronograph ever invented! Time and matter are both exotic concepts of warped and curved space, both major principles of Einstein's special relativity.

"Conceive time in the analogy of a fulcrum," Timaeus

explained. "The past is on the left end while the future is on the right. The present is balanced in the center. If the future is tilted up, it slides into the past—we experience *the present*, the future sliding into the past—time as we now know it, the *illusion* of the present going into the future. But what happens ... if the past tilts up and slides down into the future ... could we travel back in time?

Childhood Relived

"Iben, would you enjoy reliving your childhood once again?"

"Was this possible?"

"Not only possible, but since you have an eidetic memory you can remember it all. It would seem only as the blink of the eye since we were living in eternity time now."

Shards of polychromatic light swirled me through a vast strange vortex—

I remembered everything about my childhood. I lived my whole life over again. It took less than a second in Eternity. Timaeus revealed all my foibles, what decisions I should have made, and the parallel life of what destiny awaited if I had married each of the girls I had dated before I met my wife. Wow!

I now realized that my Dad, Hugo Thayer had much more wisdom than I had remembered. And my Mom, Sophia! What a precious joy to see her in her younger days and how beautiful she was back when I was a mere child. What love she had for me! Both parents gave all their love, courage, wisdom and knowledge to teach me about the world—right from wrong and guiding me to the right decisions to direct my life. What wonderful parents God had given me! Too bad it took death to teach me this!

What a joy to remember all that happened while I was a young boy. I remembered each birthday, each Christmas, and all our vacations, mingled with amity and blessings of family, friends and parents. All the rapport which effervesced from our family in love and sharing.

I then realized that each day is as a precious sparkling diamond to be utilized and cherished to the fullest—for they will each be only once, and then soon vanished as an extinguished candle in the night.

I again relived my long lost school days and listened to all my teachers of whom I had regretfully forgotten through the years. I fully realized the wisdom that many had tried to imbue into me making me wise and strong and of sound judgment.

My childhood school mates now appeared. I learned where they went on graduating from high school, how many children they had, how many times they were married, where they lived, what they accomplished.

All my family stated they would again see me—that I was still a work in progress. With this—the rest of my family all instantly disappeared.

All of a sudden a cortège of Luminaria approached. It took me by surprise and I almost swooned. I was seeing all those Supernalites that were once the people of earth, those that had died in combat fighting the wars of the earth. They appeared as stars falling from the sky—of wars unknown and lost to history—now paraded forward. All those civilians killed in battle marched before me—those innocent victims of war crimes.

Then the heavens alighted with those protectors of our society—the police that had died in the line of duty.

Such commiseration I felt that all this mass of humanity had died violent deaths of hate and crime. That our society has actually prevailed and progressed in the midst of stupidity, greed, envy and hate!

Then I saw the dazzling fireball of an exploding comet that was all those inhabitants of earth that had died from disease. What melancholy spread its sad face before me. What a vast waste of humanity! Think of all the tears and heartache caused by this. I was overwhelmed. I stared at this, tears unashamedly staining my face.

Then a bright nebula of those who had taken their own lives expanded across the dark sky. I wept unashamedly for these, whose lives were cut short by their own hand. God, I learned, will be merciful upon them, for many were mentally sick with the pathos and misery of life, numb from its futility and senselessness.

"Iben," Timaeus continued, "don't feel contrition for these Supernalites, for they are as you. They did not taste the agony of old age having their putrescent bodies crumble as they lived. Death was merciful to most of them. Now they are doing God's work, and they are with great mirth and ecstasy. They know life at its best. Do not pity them. They are as you, you are as them."

Then others passed before my eyes. They were those all over the world that had just died. Tens of thousands transected the portal and started their eternal day just as I have.

There were more streaks of lightning. These are those mortals who are murdered every day. Many were just tiny innocent babies, while others were the very aged which have died today in the nursing homes. Still others came—those all over the world that had died of starvation the night before.

Then those thousands of sweet little boys and girls who were kidnapped from their homes, raped and killed now appeared.

Incredible. I now realized that the true meaning of life was not to be found in mundane things, but spiritual things, not in our worldly possessions, but in our empathy and rapport for our fellow beings.

"But, Iben, do not have contrition for them. They are all better off in this new existence than in the old order of life without their Lord to guide and protect them. Some of these children would have grown up rejecting God, and others would have acquired a drug habit and overdosed. So God picked them early to save them and their parents more heartache. The Lord knows in advance those that will reject him long before they do it. So he chooses them first."

"Timaeus, what about car accidents where people are killed?" I inquired.

"Why would God let one person be killed and yet spare another? How about the bombing of the Federal building in Oklahoma City? Why does God take 168 lives here and spare others? Is it God's will that those 168 people are doomed that day of April 19, 1995? What about Mary Ann, whose children were sick—dodged my fate? Or those people late to work that infamous day, grumbling and cursing that slow traffic, and their lives were spared? In other words, why should some people live while others die?"

"Again, Iben, God is all-wise and all-knowing. He allows things to happen that are beyond our comprehension.

"Why do some men die in war while others survive?" I continued.

"Is there a reason for these deaths, or are they only a random meaningless insanity?"

"My dear Iben, while upon the earth, you have the power to choose good from evil. God gives you the choice of right from wrong and the power and support to meet *all* your needs.

"But, Satan has been loosed upon this earth. As in war *all* hate originates from Satan, *for he is a liar and the father of it*, and *all* sin and evil is this result of not keeping one's mind and heart on God. The good suffer along with the evil. It is the nature of sin and the curse of the earth since the fall of Adam and Eve.

"In the book by Thornton Wilder, *The Bridge of San Luis Rey*, the most famous bridge in Peru collapses in 1714, hurling five travelers to their death plunging them into the deep gorge below. In this novel Wilder tries to explain why God would send these people of different backgrounds to their deaths—and how this affected the other members of their families and friends.

"Iben, in the book, *Alive*, by Piers Paul Read, an amateur rugby team, had their plane crash in the Andes' Mountains, South America (1973). Of the 45 crew and passengers, why did 29 have to die and only 16 live? Why did God spare some, while others perished?

"Another example is found in the New Testament book of Luke, where the tower of Siloam falls killing 18 people and witnesses wondered why the capriciousness of God took innocent lives."

Timaeus looked far into the future and revealed other examples:

"Iben, a bridge will collapse along the Arkansas River on I-40 near Webbers Falls, Oklahoma, killing 14 people.

"And at the Texas A&M Campus at College Station, a 40-foot tower of heavy logs will collapse while building the college's pregame bonfire, killing 12 students.

"Why will God let all this happen, you may ask?"

True, I contemplated, *but what about the babies and very young children—*

Timaeus continued, "Remember your precious Beth, your daughter? And now Hope and Charity, your twins? God is a God of love and His ways are wiser than ours. To live and then have it all taken away—why be born? Also, if death were the end, you could not have faith of a life *beyond* death, knowing that someday you will meet your loved ones again. Is life more than a meaningless pause between two eternities?

"Also, Iben, remember that Jesus Christ, the Son of God, suffered during his, was born in poverty and died in disgrace. *Yet he conquered death.* Jesus Christ has broken the power of Satan and has overcome evil!

"Can a person cope with all this hate, murder, greed and selfishness in the world? Fulfillment, happiness and peace in the material world lies in seeking the kingdom of God and following his will. Life is full of tragedy and only through Christ can we find God's love.

"Praying and knowing God's Word will heal in the time of grief. For you, Iben, can see into the Great Beyond, and known that there is a better place. Blessed more are those that have the faith and yet believe! You now know that God is infinitely wise, and that he will bestow upon you all the desires of your heart. When life's great tragedies commence, the faith of divine wisdom will guide you through them.

"We know that the vicious act against the government in the bombing of the federal building killed many also. Humans know not what calamities lie in their future and the lesson that we need to be ready when death comes, for it comes to us all—*no exceptions.*

"All these souls, you see, have most rewarding lives that would have eluded them upon the earth. We must love our children because we will not have them forever. That also goes for your husbands and wives, your parents, your relatives ... and your friends."

With this ... Timaeus stated that he must be leaving—

The Theurgist (or Watcher)

(Dan. 4:13, 17)

At this moment other prodigious Luminaria materialized. They coalesced into the countenance of my dear wise dad (Hugo) and my dear mother (Sophia).

Dad spoke, "Dear son, I want to reveal something that has baffled mortals for eons—what the deceased do while here in glory. You see, Iben, I am known as a 'Theurgist.' That is a beneficial spirit, or *Watcher* giving divine esoteric knowledge to the enlightened of God, supernatural beings who have transcended death and who work divine miracles. I pass esoteric wisdom from God's Kingdom to the born-again believer. I open secret passage ways of God's divine thoughts into those desiring wisdom on the earth, imbuing them with divine knowledge solving the very mysteries of life itself. I have given thousands of people inspiration to live a fuller and more meaningful existence.

"Ever wonder why people write books, or compose a song? Or how Einstein thought up the Theory of Relativity? Or how James Watt invented the steam engine? Or how Eli Whitney invented the cotton gin? Or how Benjamin Franklin, or F. B. Morse, or Alexander Graham Bell, or Thomas Edison, or Nikola Telsa, *ad infinitum*, thought of their wonderful inventions? Or how Leeuwenhoek invented the first microscope, or how Edward Jenner discovered the vaccination of smallpox. Or how Louis Pasteur invented the pasteurization of milk and developed the vaccine against rabies. Or how Alexander Fleming 'accidentally' discovered penicillin or how Goodyear 'accidentally' discovered the vulcanization of rubber.

"If a mortal really wants an idea bad enough and concentrates upon it hard enough, we intervene with God's permission, to help that person discover an answer or solution to their problem. As a Watcher, we help those people who earnestly pray and profoundly mediate upon their problems with a *divine mind-link*. Through this we can reveal strange deep secrets and profound revelation of age-old mysteries. I believe it is the most rewarding work one could do while in glory.

"Iben, remember F. A. Kekule von Stradonitz, who in 1865 was struggling on the structure of benzene. Then he decided to sleep on it. While asleep, a Watcher came into him in a dream revealing a snake biting its tail and he realized that benzene had the configuration of a ring!

"Ever wonder how an artist is inspired to paint? Or how the author Samuel Taylor Coleridge 'dreamed' the master poem, *Kubla Kahn*?

"Or how the writer Morgan Robertson in 1898 wrote a novel, *Futility,* about a huge fictional ship which struck an iceberg and sank 12 years *before* the *Titanic* did?

"Or how Hector Bywater of the London Observer wrote *The Man Who Invented the Pacific War* claimed the Japanese would attack Pearl Harbor in 1924—*17 years before it actually happened*!

"Scientists believe they are 'gifted' or that 'intuition' did it. It is really Theurgists or Watchers like us that help them, connecting their mind with the pure divine kinetic energy of God's omniscience!"

Dad further explained that they influence their patrons to think acutely avoiding car crashes, or find a lost memo, or a lost article, that misplaced business file, or profile murderers and even prevent suicides.

"Almighty God reveals this pure divine energy unto his angels. They in turn, enlighten their Supernalites, of whom I am a member, and you, Iben, are now also!"

I learned from dad that I will also become as he is, a Watcher. We will go forth to enlighten those mortals that are willing to go that extra mile to read and study and mediate upon the Word, the Holy Scripture, and learn God's ways, trusting and obeying them will receive His *divine gifts*. Remember, "the works that I do shall he do also; and greater works than these shall he do, because I go unto my Father."

"Have the Supernalites influenced any other person with their enlightenment?" I inquired.

"I would like to mention how the Supernalites influenced one other soul—which changed the history of American music! A little boy went into a pawn shop wanting to buy a .22-caliber rifle for his birthday, but his mother wanted him to get something less dangerous. So he decided upon—a used guitar! We helped him through influencing his mother, to change the pattern not only of his own life, but that of the whole world!

"Do you know who I am talking about, Iben?"

"Was it—Elvis Presley?"

"And the Watchers influenced them all!"

"If any of you lack wisdom,
let him ask of God, who giveth to all men liberally,
and upbraideth not, and it shall be given him."
—James 1:5

"Life only makes sense in the contest of an afterlife."
—The Author

CHAPTER SIX

*D*ad and Mom stated that we will now travel to see the FINALE involving my life—or rather, my DEATH.

Again mom and dad spun me through the Transchronos Barrier as prismatic colors swirled—

Back to the Oklahoma Holocaust

Then I once again encountered the noisome stench of death—that of coagulated blood and the burning of bodily flesh brought me back to the Oklahoma federal building.

Mom spoke, "Iben, observe those shimmering Luminaria before us. They are the new arrivals of the Supernalites, those that have just died in the federal building as you did."

Some of them recognized me as I did them. We spoke not a word—all was said in our eyes and countenance, for we were all one in the Lord.

I observed my torn, crushed, lifeless body lying in the rubble. The carnage was terrible. Cars still smoldering, the dead and dying, and my body still and silent. An ambulance passed screaming its siren then screeched to a halt. Wounded people with blood streaming down their faces and clothes were weeping and walking about in a daze. Paramedics arrive along with fire trucks and other emergency vehicles. Destruction was everywhere, the chaos, the police and other rescue units arrive, their sirens blasting in my ears.

My body was one of the first found and was taken to the triage area, and covered with a sheet. Later, it was carried to St. Anthony's Medical Center. Strangely, I watched my own necropsy with rapport fascination. Many of my organs were saved to be used in organ transplants.

Mom continued, "Iben, you see, even in such somber circumstances, good still alleviates the evil. Some die, but because of your magnanimous graciousness others shall live."

I remembered that I had signed a donor card only two weeks before this tragedy to donate my organs at the time of my death. I also had some DNA saved and stored by cryogenics, in case I wanted to have another child someday and couldn't.

Mom spoke, "Iben, you loved enough while on earth to do that great deed of donating your organs. Five people will actually live and one will even have their sight restored because of you! That one selfless act will help other people to live better lives, and you will be blessed greatly in the future."

My body was then embalmed and sent to the morgue. Later it was delivered to the funeral home.

During the vigil I saw my wife, Faith, there paying her last respects, along with many of my close family members.

Then I saw another familiar face. That fateful day, Mary Ann, who called in to work when her children were sick—what strange fate has spared her this tragedy! I noticed her weeping and so entered her mind to solace her. I could actually read her mind telepathically, along with all the other family members and friends in the room. I penetrated their minds to comfort them, for I could sense their nostalgia. Each of them realized they would also taste death someday themselves. All of them thought this. There was not one exception. I could hear what they were thinking—about what kind of person I was, about themselves, what they accomplished in their own lives, and that life, in general, was short.

Mom located a Friday's newspaper containing my obituary. I stared upon it for quite a while and read it through many times without looking up.

My obituary from the daily Oklahoma newspaper:

OBITUARY OF IBEN THAYER

Friday, April 21, 1995

Iben Thayer (32) of Bethany, Oklahoma, a Special Agent, died Wednesday, April 19, 1995 in the Alfred P. Murrah Federal Building holocaust. He was an active member of the Sword of the Spirit Ministries. Survivors are his wife, Faith, and a brother, Nathaniel. He was reunited in death with his children, Beth, who died at only one-year old, and Hope and Charity (his twin little girls) who were both 3 years old when they were also killed in the Federal Building. Mr. Thayer served in the United States Army, and was a graduate of Oklahoma State University and employed with the FBI. Funeral arrangements will be held at 10 A.M. Saturday, April 22 at Sword of the Spirit Ministries, Oklahoma City by

Pastor Goodspeed. Burial will be in New Horizons Memorial Park shortly after the funeral service at 11:30 A.M.

Strange. No matter what you do in life, this fate awaits us all. The grave stands ready to admit us one by one no matter what our status in life, or our reasons for living. Nothing can keep us from the grave.

Strange. We work all our lives for a small piece of literature in the newspaper! It doesn't seem right somehow. But then, this is the fate of all living souls upon the earth. NO EXCEPTIONS! The rich, the poor, the mean and cruel, the saintly and the godly … EVERYONE! Why is this so hard to comprehend? WE ALL KNOW SOMEDAY WE WILL DIE.

I now wished that I had witnessed more about Jesus Christ. To explain the fate of all is death and our only hope is Jesus Christ, the Son of the living God. Thank goodness that someone witnessed to me and that I believed. I had been a Christian for only two years! Attended church for only two years! Why didn't I learn more about this Jesus and God? Eternity lays before us all and our lives are only one second compared to it! A human being knows there is a time to be born, but why doesn't he think that there is also a time to die? Humans are a strange lot!

Now I was to attend my own funeral…

SPECIAL MEMORIAL SERVICE

Eulogy of Iben Thayer
by
Rev. John Goodspeed; Sword of the Spirit Ministries
10 A.M. Saturday Morning Church Service

Upon his pulpit overlooking his reverent and quiet congregation, Rev. Goodspeed, now spoke.

"What kind of person was Iben Thayer? Can I describe his love for his wife and his daughters Beth, and the twins, Hope, and Charity, who also died in the federal building holocaust? Iben's brother, Nathaniel, and all his surviving family and close friends have all been affected in numerous ways. There is now a big gap that will never again be filled by this special agent and father of three.

"Iben was a person who really loved people and freely shared his good qualities and charisma. His humanity and good personality radiated out to all who knew him.

"We are more blessed here because he once walked among us. Iben had short-comings like everyone but whoever came in contact with him became a better person. He possessed an uncommon and unique talent of selfless love toward humanity. I sincerely believe he has given an excellent account of his life here upon this earth while he lived and will be greatly blessed in the life to come. Yet, we must find a way to move on.

"Yes, Iben was many things to us. Besides being a federal agent, he was also a hero, a friend, a helper, a mentor, a deacon, a Sunday-School teacher, a Boy-Scout leader, a daddy, a brother, and a son.

"What lessons have Iben given us? That life is priceless, it can end at any moment, and all our days are more valuable than precious jewels! And to love your family while you have them, for we know not what tomorrow shall bring.

"We know that God has allotted each of us a certain number of days to accomplish our mission here upon the earth. Our lives can be compared to that of the ephemeral

Mayfly. It lives for only one brief glorious day, then perishes forever, as a wind blowing out a candle flame.

"God bless you, Iben Thayer. We have all become richer and wiser because you once walked among us. You will be remembered in our hearts and in our minds—for all eternity."

I observed that the sanctuary was filled to capacity with hundreds of people, family members and friends, and the news media that were also present carrying this memorial and celebration of Iben Thayer's life to the eyes and ears of millions throughout the world.

All present shared common emotions ... grief, loss, sadness and the questionings that always accompany such tragedies ... *why this person ... why this family?* Each person present has found a way to express their comfort and their love to this heartbroken community by being here and paying their respects and honoring his family.

The heart of the service was the reading of the Holy Scripture, from both the Old and New Testaments.

As those ancient, time-honored words of Scripture were read aloud without commentary, one could not help but feel a quiet strength from ages past. How many generations have been comforted by these same God-breathed words of Divinity?

The passages, their beauty, power and mystery brought a solace no one could readily explain or fully comprehend.

Now a prayer was offered, both acknowledging our collective grief and bewilderment and that great hope of eternal life offered by the Gospel. The common bond of prayer brought inner strength and peace that comes only when friends suffer and unite together.

Then the chorale and organ music commenced. The colorful fragrant flowers, the rituals, and the silent message brought by the profession of faith seen throughout the sanctuary gave comfort to those mourning and grieving.

Gathered as one with the Lord, we could gaze into the faces of family, friends and strangers—the whole solidarity of those bereaved. In this setting we could experience the Holy Spirit, and the gentle angels of God giving comfort and strength and empathy to our faithful believers.

"Death is but an open door,
We move from room to room,
There is one life, no more,
No dying, and no tomb."
— *here is No Death* by Joseph Sweeney

After reading the above quote ... the memorial service was now brought to its end.

The clock ticked, the world changed—
and time marches on...

CHAPTER SEVEN

The Graveside Memorial

IBEN THAYER'S HONORARIUM

By
Rev. Goodspeed, Head Pastor, presiding:
Sword of the Spirit Ministries
Oklahoma City

New Horizons Memorial Park
Saturday, 11:30 A.M., April 22, 1995

*P*eople sauntered across the dew-strewed graves and trampled down the tiny white and lavender wild flowers scattered across the sacred meadow. Little tombstones, worn and chipped, covered with lichen were sentinels guarding the sacredness of the graves through which the people paraded. Freshly dug graves with their red gravel mounds were reminders that this is not just a place forgotten, but that recently people have passed this way in the last few weeks. Some monuments were as new, their tombstones, bare of lichen, clean-cut polished marble and granite with no wear upon their surfaces, with pristine flowers, red roses and yellow mums placed reverently upon their crowns.

Then the rows of gray metal chairs were stationed around a grassy hummock, with a dais in the center, covered on one side by the green canopy gently rustling in the cool morning breeze, advertising the name of the funeral home on its frieze.

The pearlescence hearse carrying the polished mahogany coffin arrived at the cemetery with the funeral director. As the pall bearers were carrying the casket, I noticed who each one was—my brother, my uncle, and four of my best friends upon this earth, namely, Grant, Anthony, John, and Colton. It was nice to know such worthy gentlemen presided at my side in this time of lamentation.

My brother, Nathaniel, God bless him! All the wonderful years of being raised together, of growing up together sharing our toys and dreams. All the fun we had! Our closeness while growing up.

My uncle. What good times we had when mother and daddy were away, he would baby sit for them. We would go to a fast food restaurant, then to a newsstand to purchase a comic book.

My friends … now carrying my body on its final journey.

There is Grant … fun times at college, the girls we dated and the adventures we shared.

Anthony, my childhood friend, our birthday parties

together and exploring the neighborhood and nearby woods. Such happy days.

John, my 'ol army buddy. The places we were stationed in Japan and Turkey. The adventures we had in those countries.

Colton, who I knew from the first job I had out of college. We used to pal around together and flirt some with the girls until one caught him and turned his interests. My good friends—my eyes swelled up into tears. I wept unashamedly.

The crowd of mourners, silent and reverent, of both family and friends, along with the news media, were gathered around the casket, which lay at rest on the catafalque.

Few words were spoken as the honored family found their reserved row of oak wood chairs at the proximity of the casket, resting upon its bier, draped with the American flag, Old Glory, with sprays of flowers on each side, reflecting sunlight on this cool April morning.

The Rev. Goodspeed stepped forward to the rostrum. With obvious emotion, he gazed down at the front row of the family seated before him, while many others were sitting and standing reverently beyond.

The TV cameras hummed as he addressed his audience of forty million viewers and listeners:

"Dearly beloved, we are gathered here today to pay our deepest honor and sacred memory and sincere respects to our departed brother in Jesus Christ, the late Iben Thayer, and to his twin children, Hope and Charity, who are still missing in the federal building on that fateful Wednesday, when our world was changed forever.

Iben taught us how to live life. When he was even wounded from gunfire, he stayed positive. He always tried, by his Christian example, to choose gratitude instead of self-pity, kindness instead of indifference, hope instead of despair, and love instead of hate.

"He also taught us that we must make the most of life, for calamities as the Oklahoma City bombing show us just how precious life is. So why do we take our existence so for granted?

"The most proven fact in the world is the death and resurrection of Jesus Christ as seen by hundreds of eye-witnesses.

"Jesus' resurrection proves three things. First, it reveals that there is life after death, second, that the Holy Bible is the word of God, and thirdly that Eternity is a reality! *Jesus Christ is the key that opens this gate to eternal life.* Through the new birth the Christian has a living hope into an inheritance that can never perish—that of immortality.

"The book of Job deals with a profound question: *Why do good people suffer?*

"Job was a man of great wealth and was righteous in the eyes of God. Then God let Satan test him. He lost everything—his wealth, his family and even his health. In the midst of his pain and grief he kept his faith.

> "Man that is born of a woman is of
> few days, and full of trouble.
> He cometh forth like a flower, and is cut down;
> he fleeth also as a shadow, and continueth not."
> —Job 14:1-2

"Job's friends stated that he was responsible for his own suffering. God reveals to Job that true happiness is not found in worldly riches or mundane wisdom as taught in secular college. We do not know our reasons for suffering, but we know that God does chastise those he loves. But God is love and he will guide us through all difficulties. We must continue to trust in Jesus. We must realize that his wisdom and power is beyond our mortal knowledge. We must realize that his love is far beyond our comprehensibility.

"You are a totally *unique individual* in the eyes of God, our Creator! And how precious is this gift of life? That human life is actually created by God for a definite purpose. Ever wonder how and why the Earth, solar system, and stars were formed from nothing?

"We have been created for a *Special Purpose* in God's mysterious Divine Plan. The pain of birth and the tragedy of death prepares us for the great adventure beyond life. God has ordained for us, the Christian, a world *beyond* this world, a new and glorious existence for those that truly do walk in God's Spirit."

The Reverend continued…

"Let not your heart be troubled; ye
believe in God, believe also in me.
In my Father's house are many mansions; if it were not so,
I would have told you. I go to prepare a place for you.
And if I go and prepare a place for you, I will come again,
and receive you unto myself, that where
I am, there ye may be also."
—Jn. 14:1-4

Now let every eye be closed and every head bowed:

"Our Father who art in heaven, Hallowed be thy name.
Thy kingdom come. Thy will be done
in earth, as it is in heaven.
Give us this day our daily bread.
And forgive us our debts, as we forgive our debtors.
And lead us not into temptation, but deliver us from evil.
For thine is the kingdom, and the power,
and the glory, for ever. Amen"
—Mt. 6:9-13

Rev. Goodspeed concluded, "Iben Thayer now has gone from this world of vanity and sorrow … into the Land of Endless Joy, into that glorious *Land Unknown,* to that Promised Land of those who love the Lord."

"The LORD bless thee, and keep thee;
The LORD make His face shine upon
thee, and be gracious unto thee;
The LORD lift up His countenance
upon thee, and give thee peace."
—Num. 6:24-26

"Now may the LORD keep you in the palm of his hand ... for all eternity. Amen."

Now the funeral service was officially over. The crowd began to disperse. The news media began to saunter back to their vans and cars, packing up their equipment. The immediate family stayed on a little longer, hugs and kisses felt, tears shed, and once again humans embraced the abyss between the living and the dead.

How short, I mused ... *Just like a lifetime. Short.*

Mom spoke, "Iben, life eternal is yours. Happiness is yours. Peace is yours. It will be just what you always wanted. Didn't you want to learn the secrets of life and matter? Did you not want to explore the wonders of the earth and the mystery of time and space? The wonders of the universe beckon before thee, Iben. Mighty things God has yet to reveal—phenomena you could not understand while mortal—but will understand very soon!"

All of a sudden—my mom and dad departed. I felt a sudden aloneness then remembered that God and his angels were always nearby. There was so much to see and think about that placed me into a profound pensive state of mind.

CHAPTER EIGHT

*S*uddenly another sparkling Luminarium appeared—bright as a lightning strike.

"Fear me not, Iben, for I will enlighten you to the ways of the Lord. I am an Angelic Divine Counselor, the angel of Abraham, Lot and Jacob. You can call me Mahanaim, for here I was seen by Jacob. Now let us leave this saturnine place, your graveside, to discover new and fantastic wonders of your miraculous existence."

The Criminal Caught

We found ourselves traveling along Interstate 35, sixty miles north of Oklahoma City just outside of Perry, and entered the mind of a state trooper stopped along the highway.

A yellow 1977 Mercury Marquis whizzed by, speeding without a license plate. When pulled over the trooper discovered the driver was concealing a Glock 9-mm semiautomatic pistol, loaded with Black Talon, "cop killer" bullets. The driver was wearing black pants with combat boots. The trooper arrested him for carrying a concealed weapon, driving without tags and having no insurance. Oh yes, the name of the man driving the car: Timothy McVeigh.

I recognized the pungent smell of ammonium nitrate and fuel oil upon his body. The state trooper arrested him on the spot and he was later identified as the person responsible for the Oklahoma City bombing.

Reckless Driving

We then materialized upon the side of I-40, the Interstate from Oklahoma City threading its way into Arkansas—

"Iben. listen to the cars pass. Do you hear anything unusual?"

Even through the glass and metal I heard their conversations as they zipped along the freeway. Oddly enough Mahanaim and I could travel right along with the vehicles!

I noticed a Dodge Caravan packed with an over capacity of 21 people, 15 adults and 6 children.

"Nice morning," the mother stated. "Hope the kids are awake when we arrive in Ft. Smith, AR a couple of hours from now."

"They should be," commented the father, "by the time we arrive it should be around 9:30 A.M."

Strange, I knew at that instant where the auto occupants were from, where they were going and much of their past history by scanning their minds.

Then I noticed an apparition appearing at the top of the auto. It was Thanatopia—

At this instant the Dodge Caravan accelerates around a long line of cars hitting the cab of an 18 wheeler. Tires exploded sending rubber into the air, the stench of brakes abraded the asphalt knocking the van airborne. As the semi-truck jack-knifed and overturned, the van skittered on its side, then flipped over and over, its doors springing open, throwing bodies all over the asphalt before stopping. It now exploded in a vermilion fireball.

The tractor-trailer was carrying Oxalic acid, a highly poisonous substance. The truck stopped about one-hundred feet from the van, still smoking. The driver of the semi opens the door, jumps to safety realizing that his coworker is pinned under it. He tries to lift the cab but to no avail. His traveling partner is trapped helplessly under it crushing him to death. Mahanaim now jolted into action, uses his mind to help the driver raise it, leaving the driver thinking he had the strength to lift it himself! Then the driver drags his friend to safety.

Are angels powerful enough to raise a 3,000-pound cab—?

"Angels are much stronger than this," Mahanaim answered, reading my mind. "Iben remember the Red Sea when Moses cross it? That miracle took only *one* omnipotent angel!"

"Do such powers exist in the universe?"

"Iben, I assure you—such powers exist."

The Dodge Caravan was a conflagration of burning gasoline and debris. Of the twenty-one passengers in the van, none survived—only charred crisp bodies, their flesh still smoldering.

The caravan was in the wrong. All twenty-one occupants dead. The van was vastly overloaded, originally designed to carry only eight. Also, they were speeding and no seat belts were worn. Nor were they using such a simple device as a blinker nor their side rear-view mirror before changing lanes.

Other cars are beginning to pull over and slow down. I watched in horror. Mahanaim stated that humankind, instead of being called *Homo sapiens*, instead should be called, *Homo stupidens,* because this driver at fault was driving too fast, causing this fatal accident!

Too bad his wife and children had to die with him. She should have told him to slow down, therefore she shared some of the guilt.

"Yes, Iben," Mahanaim stated. "How true—the innocent many times pay the ultimate sacrifice because of someone else's mistake."

As I watched, twenty-one wispy effluvium rose up from those who were killed...

"Those emanations rising up from the bodies, Iben, are the incorporeal souls of the deceased. Mortal man, of course, cannot see this phenomenon."

I now witnessed an intense bright light hovering far above us beckoning these souls upward toward the heavens.

How many people have died because they didn't wear their seat belts or were speeding or because they didn't turn on their lights at dusk, or on a rainy or foggy morning? I thought

Mahanaim spoke, "Many people in the United States each year perish from car crashes due to their own negligence, stupidity and egocentric ways. Not wearing seat belts, reckless driving, driving drunk, using drugs, running red lights, falling asleep at the wheel and texting (using cellular phones) are major problems. The death toll is rising daily and may in the near future exceed 40,000, if the trend continues.

"Another thing, Iben. Cars look innocuous enough! But they kill more people than guns each year in the United States! It also should be known that sleep-deprived drivers are as dangerous as those who drive drunk!"

I also learned that in a normal brain there is a gene which regulates a protein called brain-derived neurotrophic factor or BDNF. One in three drivers do *not* have this gene and so have a slower cognitive motor-skill development. In normal drivers this BDNF protein is released, but in many people there is a lack of this protein which makes drivers more aggressive and dangerous on the roads, breaking the speed limits, not wearing their seat belts and weaving in and out of traffic.

"Notably, most cars in the future will be equipped with robotics that will be able to drive *100% better* than *everyone*. These self-driving cars will never get tired and constantly watch the roads. They will *always* obey the speed limits and stop at red lights, never tail-gate, will know how a four-way stop works, always see on-coming traffic, adjust to rainy, icy and snowy conditions. They will also stop when a school bus stops driver slower in school zones, and be aware of all emergency vehicles coming and going. Robotic cars will *always* use their blinkers and *never* text and drive. The reaction time for a human to break is 1/5 second. Your robotic car will be able to sense danger and break before you even see the problem thousands of feet ahead in infrared vision! It will apply the breaks to your car 10,000 times faster than you can react to the situation. Also, your robot car will never drink alcohol, smoke pot, eat while driving ... put on makeup, or have road rage."

Mahanaim stated that he must leave and go forth to the people that were killed in the van accident. He was to welcome them into their new existence as I was welcomed.

CHAPTER NINE

Iben-the-Wise

As Mahanaim left, yet another blinding ethereal Luminarium appeared.

"Fear not, Iben, for I am Peniel, an Angelic Divine Counselor."

I learned that Peniel means "like the face of God." He was also carrying a scepter of ultimate power.

Peniel continued, "Jacob wrestled with me until daybreak. He realized I was a heavenly messenger, when I made him crippled. Then blessing him, I changed his name from Jacob to Israel. When Jacob asked me to proclaim myself, I stayed silent, but blessed him. Jacob called this place where we met, *I have seen God face to face, and my life is preserved.*

"My dear saint. God has sent me on a special mission to bless you. *God has ordained for your name to be changed.* In the Old Testament, Jacob's was changed to Israel, and Abram was changed to Abraham. In the New Testament, Saul, the apostle, was changed to Paul with his conversion to Christianity. Therefore, shall you be known from henceforth, not as Iben Thayer, but as 'Iben Jair.' *Jair* being Hebrew for 'whom God has enlightened' and you will be known henceforth as *Iben-the-Wise*."

I realized that I now had been bestowed with the greatest of blessings and was among the chosen and blessed ranks of Jacob and Paul and honored as a child of God.

Traveling at the Speed of Light

(EMFs)

The angel Peniel and I were inexorably pulled by an unseen electromagnetic force toward a high tension power line. As we came closer and closer to one of these steel colossal towers, like a Herculean giant holding up the power of a mighty city, we began to glow and became visible to mortal humankind as a type of illuminated aberration.

"Iben, we have encountered low-frequency electromagnetic fields (EMFs), a flux from the current of high voltage. We will be seen by mortal man, but they won't recognize us. They will only see a phenomenon known as St. Elmo's fire, or ball lightning flashing across the power lines!"

The electromagnetic field somehow attracted us and Peniel and I shot through this line as fast as the speed of light! This power line led directly into the homes of the upper middle class neighborhood.

"Iben, some scientists think these EMFs cause cancer in humans."

"Yes, I had heard of this before, but nothing was ever proved."

"Iben, these EMFs can mutate specific proteins in the human body forming abnormal tumor cells. They cause cancer by interfering with calcium inside each cell which activates muscle contractions and cell division. EMFs also prohibit growth hormones and enzymes. They can even change the cell's membrane leading to breast and prostate cancer. The hormone epinephrine is also affected by these EMFs."

"Peniel, how does a person receive such EMFs?"

"Many ways, Iben, but normally through computers, TVs, radios, microwave ovens, Christmas trees and even electric blankets!"

Yet sewing machines, I learned, produced the worst emissions! These waves are even powerful enough to penetrate lead shielding! Small children and unborn babies are more vulnerable to EMFs than adults are.

The things I am learning in this enhanced state of glory!

By now we had traveled many miles along this superhighway of electricity entering many businesses and neighborhoods. We soon arrived at one particular home in less than one billionth of a second, one nanosecond, as it is called.

Dangerous Foods

This power line led directly into the home of one typical household. Peniel and I entered the living room through their TV set. It was the home of my coworker, Mary Ann, her husband, Gregory and their two children—Eva, three years old and Jason, six.

In their kitchen we spied the family of four eating supper. On their wall I spied a clock realizing it was the one I had given Mary Ann for Christmas the year before. It was shocked dead at 9:02 A.M. She will soon notice it — but will she make the connection that some imponderable mystery from "The Great Beyond" had actually stopped the clock at the precise time of the Federal Building explosion, April 19, 1995?

If humans are not aware that such things can happen are they less likely to perceive or notice them as being divine contacts from the other side or from another dimension? Could such phenomenon as this be a link to or a proof of things beyond our normal reality?

Mary Ann spoke, "Kids, turn off the TV. We have seen enough tragedy about the federal building. Since you both are feeling better from being sick Wednesday, we are having comfort food tonight—chili dogs and hamburgers, and your dad is finishing up that leftover fried squirrel."

Then they helped themselves to the hot dogs. Their mother had cooked them in the microwave which destroys Vitamin K, needed for blood clotting. The deficiency of this vitamin is a major cause of heart attacks.

We inspected the red wiener she had just cooked in her microwave, still sizzling on the paper towel. It contained harmful chemicals to retard rancidity along with a dye derived from insect scales to give the meat that red color. It also contained nitrates, cancer causing agents, to prevent spoilage from salmonella. I learned that if children eat over twelve hot dogs a month, they have a nine-times greater chance of developing leukemia!

"And I thought hot dogs were healthy!" I proclaimed.

"Don't gulp down your food, Jason!" his mother shouted. "Experts have discovered that even T. Rex chews his food!"

Peniel spoke, "Yes, Iben, Jason will choke to death next week on a hot dog!"

"What?"

"Well, because Mary Ann hasn't heard about the Heimlich hug the child will die."

"Can't this be prevented?"

"Since she has never heard of this hug, a type of squeeze used in first aid on a choking victim, she will not be able to unclog his airway. You see, the hot dog is exactly one half inch in diameter, the same as the boy's windpipe. Jason will get a piece lodged in it and the rest will be history."

"This is very sad. Is there any way we can stop this?"

"Could this be God's will?" I questioned.

"In twelve years from now in his alternate life, this young boy would have dived off a cliff while swimming and would have been paralyzed and wheelchair bound. He would become bitter placing a great strain upon his family which is not well off financially. Then when he reached forty years of age, he would acquire a gun, place it to his temple, and you know the rest of the story."

I thought upon this for a long while and stated, "But he will be saved by Jesus, right?"

"Yes, Jason has attended Sunday School and learned about Jesus, that he is the Son of God, and about the power of his death and resurrection and how to be saved."

"So, Peniel, hamburger meat is safer than hot dogs?"

"My dear Iben, eating hamburgers can produce some diseases in mankind. They sometimes contain the *E. coli* bacterium which secretes *shiga*, a toxin almost as deadly as botulism."

I further learned that many hot dogs contain trichinosis (roundworms) that can enter the intestines and muscles of humans. They can even find their way to the brain. Also, some hot dogs contain *listeria,* a bacterial disease found in many meat processing plants. Luckily the microwave oven also killed this organism!

Then Gregory finished up the fried squirrel, eating the cooked tongue and brain.

Peniel continued, "Iben, Gregory doesn't realize that eating squirrel brains could be harmful. You see, some people have come down with Creutzfeldt-Jakob Disease. This disease is similar to Mad Cow Disease and Chronic Wasting Disease—all dangerous organisms to humans.

"Maybe someday a word of caution will get out to the American public who have this tradition of cooking and eating squirrel—not to eat their brains."

So, I thought, *her family will eat healthier tomorrow at supper time.*

"Not so," Peniel related, reading my mind.

I noticed that Mary Ann was drinking water with her meal.

"I guess that is safe enough?"

"Well, Iben, 53 million Americans drink water daily that violates EPA safety standards. Contaminated water kills a thousand people each year and causes 400,000 illnesses.

Bottled water isn't any better. Some bottles have been discovered that contained arsenic!

"Look close at Mary Ann's water. You see those photons of light? That is uranium in it! It is slightly radioactive! Uranium-tainted water at Pandora Fuels Corp. on the Cimarron River, 40 miles north of Oklahoma City, contains 35,000 times the amount of uranium allowed by federal standards! The uranium leaked many years ago from a solvent extraction building. The material passed through the floor entering into the ground water. It finally ended up in the wells of Oklahoma City where the population thinks it is safe to drink!"

I noticed something else in her water. It was a tiny creature, the protozoan, *cryptosporidium* and *fecal coliform*, kin to the bacterium, E. coli. It can cause diarrhea and stomach cramps, but can be deadly in older people with weakened immune systems.

Peniel explained that this old house in which they were living contained lead pipes which contaminated the water with lead. Mercury was also discovered along with dioxin from their paper mills.

"Anything else in the water, Iben?"

Through my enhanced senses I became aware of something strange—

"Fluoride, Iben. You are smelling fluoride. Since the 1940s it has been put into America's drinking water to prevent cavities. But fluoride toothpaste will do the job of prevention tooth problems just as well (if people would use it)! Sodium fluoride might influence hyperactivity and senile dementia. But too much of it in the water system can cause dental *fluorosis*, mottling or darkening of the teeth and increases the brittleness of bone."

"Wow, that sounds pretty scary!"

"But those without fluoridation have *twice* the cavities as those people not using it. It also should be noted that *bottled water contains no fluoride—thus having no useful benefits against cavities.*"

"Peniel, I bet that honey is healthy!"

"Iben, although honey is an excellent source of the sugar dextrose, it should not be given to children under 3 years old ... because it might also contain traces of botulism."

We found some week-old oysters Gregory brought home from a restaurant. Here we found dangerous bacteria which could make him sick.

I spotted some cans labeled "Health foods."

"Well, these must be healthier than regular foods? Right?"

Peniel and I found *more* pesticide residues in them than any other foods! Many of these nuts, beans, seeds, legumes and dried fruit contained pesticides used to prevent rotting. The lowest level of pesticide residue was found in fresh produce from grocery stores. These showed *half* as much pesticides as the health foods did!

Next we checked their freezer.

"Now Peniel, I believe that the freezer should be a safe place for food items."

"Well, let's see, Iben."

We analyzed the ice cream discovering *salmonella enteritis*, a bacterium responsible for an outbreak in a major chain of ice cream manufacturing plants across the United States.

The frozen strawberries even contained Hepatitis A virus which can cause liver damage. Their frozen raspberries imported from Chile, contained the parasite *cyclospora*.

The frozen catfish contained many strange toxic and cancer-causing substances. Without her knowledge, Mary Ann had purchased catfish imported from China, which has little restrictions on placing toxic chemicals in their food. Imported Chinese and Vietnamese catfish are, many times, raised in unsanitary conditions.

Even the frozen chicken contained dangerous bacteria.

Nutritious Foods

"Is there *any* food items *good* to eat?" I asked Peniel. "This has really opened my eyes."

"Yes, Iben, see that little flat oval can? That little can, packed with vitamins and minerals, is low in calories and high in protein. Read the label."

"Sardines?" I questioned.

"Yes, Iben, sardines! They contain unsaturated fats called omega-3 fatty acids (also found in breast milk) which lowers heart disease and helps the production of serotonin in the brain. They also can prevent migraine headaches, rheumatoid arthritis, manic depression and schizophrenia. Sardines actually prevent fatty plaque and cholesterol which may lead to antherosclerosis. Fish oils lower this cholesterol, alter the blood lipoproteins and lowers triglycerides, thus making the platelets less sticky. Also, the human brain is almost entirely made up of fats, 60% of which is DHA (*Docosahexaenoic acid*). This acid is essential for the neuron rejuvenation and brain growth and can be found in sardines!

"Also, fresh fruits, known as *frugivores,* have great benefits and are healthier that meat eaters. Remember, fruits and herbs constituted the original *God-given diet.* Check out Gen. 1:29 and Daniel 1:12..."

"Even the Dandelion, Iben, brought over from England by the Pilgrims has twice the vitamin B than spinach, six times the vitamin B of iceberg lettuce, 40% more vitamin C than tomatoes, 20% more beta-carotene than carrots and more calcium than milk! It also contains mentionable amounts of phosphorus, manganese and iron.

"Coffee also contains nicotinic acid which can prevent pellagra. It should be noted that Nicotinic acid is useful to people that have high triglycerides in their blood."

Next Peniel and I checked the air conditioning system. Here we found an organism known as air conditioner lung, known also as Farmer's lung. It is caused by exposure to spores in moldy hay. It can cause acute fever, chills and coughing.

"Let's check the gas oven while we're here, Iben."

The gas stove?

Here were traces of nitrogen dioxide.

Is that harmful?

"Iben," Peniel, reading my mind, continued, "Nitrogen dioxide can cause asthma and damage the lungs. This can cause chest tightness, wheezing and shortness of breath leading to chronic coughing."

Well, Peniel, that should cover all the hazards in this house!

"Iben, we haven't even begun to find them! There is a malady known as the 'sick building syndrome.' Many houses contain dust mites along with dangerous fungi such as the green mold, *Aspergillus*, asbestos and even lead paint on their walls."

I could smell a faint strange odor in this house.

"What is that odor?"

"Iben Jair, the normal person can't smell that gas, but in your new enhanced existence you can. You are smelling *radon*—an air pollutant, caused by the decay of radioactive radium. Radon is responsible for over 20,000 lung cancer deaths annually and may be present in over 8 million homes in the U.S. Radon comes from radioactive rock and naturally emanates up through the floor.

"Preventive measures, Iben, are as easy as opening a window and ventilating the home. Also, placing plants in the house can absorb pollutants such as formaldehyde, carbon monoxide and nitrogen dioxide It should be noted that a brick house usually contains more radon than a wood-framed house."

There was a cellphone laying on the table. Peniel noticed that I saw it and stated that a brain tumor called "glioma" can develop from using a cellphone more than an hour a day over the period of a few years. They can also cause face and neck tumors to develop over years of continual use.

I stood in awe at what the angel Peniel was teaching me! I never knew that the world was so unhealthy. *I now realized for the first time that humanity could never solve its problems no matter how smart mortal man became. Scientists will never be able to solve all of society's dilemmas.* I then realized that the human race is nearing its last generation to enjoy tasty gastronomical delights. Overeating foods rich in animal fats and sugar in combination with a sedentary life style causes heart disease, arteriosclerosis and even cancer.

The Insidious Séance

After they ate, Mary Ann and Gregory had some neighbors over. They then lit candles and turned off the lights and called upon the spirits from the dead.

"A seance!" I uttered, as I realized I could see into an alternate world of strange horror.

"Yes, Iben," Peniel continued, "see all these chimera, chupacabras, imps, and demons conjured up from the darkness of the nether world. Your new glorified body has quickened your eyes to see such strange phenomena!"

Now he waved his awesome scepter, which contained the power and might of the Lord. These strange apparitions were vaporized in a millisecond back into the dark void from whence they came.

Seances, I learned, along with mediums, necromancers and spiritualists are all *condemned* by God. The living mortals, those still alive upon the earth, *never* are to converse with the dead (those transitioned beings as we now are). Prayer opens this esoteric pathway between God and his angels directly, but *not* through mediums, etc. The Watcher, through God's Divine Power and *only by His decree and His will*, can give out God's divine wisdom or work miracles. Under *no* circumstances does the Watcher relate his own personal thoughts to the mortals, but only that *Special Knowledge through prayer that the angels or divine beings reveal can they influence them.*

He was to stay with Mary Ann's family and try to convict her husband not to have hot dogs that next Saturday night, because poor little Jason will choke to death.

"So Peniel, you can change the future?"

"Not so, Iben Jair. Our fates are not sealed at conception. We are not slaves to a predetermined destination. The prayers of Jason's parents will be heard by God. I will try to influence Mary Ann and Greg not to let little Jason eat hot dogs that fateful night. I, you might acknowledge, am Jason's guardian angel, to watch over him and his family. So I must leave you. Soon another angel will greet you."

We then left the house and penetrated through the wall on our way outside. I could hear strange rasping noises of something strange within this wall and realized I was actually hearing the termites chewing the wood in their home!

Chapter Ten

Visit to the Hospitals

*O*utside Mary Ann's house, still at the speed of light, I encountered another divine angel, Academia, bright as a luminous comet, full of he essence of life, and the mystery of death. He carried an awesome ignescent pastoral staff.

In less than a nanosecond we toured all the area hospitals in Oklahoma City and found some children critically injured. We unveiled our *visica piscis*, our divine light and soothed their pain. One little boy was badly burned. His little scared eyes were staring out as we unveiled our halation, comforting him and lessening his pain! Another little girl was surrounded by stuffed animals and colorful balloons. Here we unveiled ourselves exposing our aurora and communed to her. As I touched her face she was immediately comforted with peace and grace of the Divine! We also saw a little five-year-old boy recovering from brain surgery. We exposed our bright beacon of divine light before him and he raised his little hand and touched my face and his little eyes and countenance were soothed with the glory of God's Kingdom! He was immediately imbued with divine peace and stopped crying! Yet, in another room down the hallway a young lady was also critically injured. We touched her with the divine miracle of healing, solace and comfort!

What did *all* these above patients have in common? Academia stated they were all victims of the Oklahoma City bombing!

Prayer: It's Definition and Power

One more patient Academia and I visited was to leave the hospital the next day because he was actually *cured* of cancer. This person had a cancerous tumor in his liver the size of a grapefruit. There was nothing the surgeon could do as the cancer was malignant and had spread through other organs in his body.

He was a firm believer in Christ. So the deacons from his church, trained as spiritual Intuitives, anointed him with oil, placing their hands upon him praying for the miracle of healing. This "laying on of hands" (Point of Transference) is known as the *Superheterodyne Principle* (much as touching a laptop computer screen or your smartphone screen, or in the old days, as touching the "rabbit ears" of an old indoor antennae enhanced the reception of the TV's signal). Finally, after only a few months using these intuitive healers, this patient before us that had terminal liver cancer—had been totally cured by the power of God!

"How can these spiritual healers do this?"

"They are communicating directly into the Kingdom of God using the unadulterated anointing power of the

Holy Spirit. As we have seen, sincere praying communicates radiesthetic waves of divine kinetic energy (God's divine healing power) into the mind and physical body of the believer in Christ. You see, Iben, prayer can be defined as a telepathic communication of manifesting divine knowledge into the mind via a psychotronic process of supernatural omniscient Cosmic Intelligence (God) which transcends beyond the range of our normal mental realm.

"Another concise definition of prayer can be defined as *extraterrestrial communication.* This esoteric information and divine knowledge of the invincible miraculous power of the Holy Spirit is being conveyed from a supernatural multidimensional source (the Kingdom of God) into that three dimensional world of reality in which we normally live.

"This is also known, Iben, as intercessory prayer. God's omnipotent power produces divine healing. You communicate to God and God communicates to you. Many people have been totally healed because of these techniques."

Anointing with Oil

"I have always heard about some religions anointing their believers with holy oil?" I asked. "Could you explain this?"

Academia answered, "Iben, this phenomenon is known as the *Katalysia Divinia Energia* or placing the anointing oil upon those who are sick that need healing miracles with the power of the Holy Spirit. This virgin olive oil acts as a catalyst manifesting these divine wonders—the catalyst of Divine Energy — the unction from God. Supernatural Knowledge and Supernatural Power of Healing and Revelation is thus created through the Divine Afflatus to those afflicted in the physical, spiritual, and mental realms of being.

"There are things that are working *beyond our knowledge*. Being *born again* is like this. Salvation comes to us though no physical change is seen ... *only a Spiritual manifestation of God is revealed on faith.* It is an encounter with the Holy Spirit. There is a *mental and physical change* throughout that person—a transforming and renewing of your mind in benevolent and beneficial ways.

"The oil acts as a catalyst as in a chemical reaction which quickens the Holy Spirit inflaming those anointed with Divine Power and Healing."

The Octogenarian

"Another person I want you to visit, Iben."

Academia now led me into the geriatrics ward, then down to a room, cool and dimly lit, quiet, with a very old man resting in bed.

"Iben Jair, this octogenarian has been here for many years. See these tubes in his mouth — they are feeding tubes. See this strange machine, it is helping him to breathe. He has rested here in this coma for many years and his immediate family has trepidation about taking him off life support and letting him die a peaceful death."

His his limp body was already twisted back into the fetal position.

What do people think or dream while in this long duration of a coma?

I realized he was already communicating with the angels

which were watching and protecting him and in his own little dream world, living a peaceful life *beyond* our physical world. No mortal could see the fact that God has sent many comforting angels to watch over this child of God, and I could see that he was just waiting for the moment his family will release him from his mortal bondage of his weak and aged body to be reunited with his divine family in the celestial realm of the Eternal. These angels have been patiently waiting for his precious soul for over twelve years!

Other patients and maladies were studied by Academia and I but could not be written down fast enough. Time to say good-bye to Oklahoma City. Other great wonders and miracles beckon us forward.

CHAPTER ELEVEN

I must regress here a minute. What is it like to travel near the speed of light? Close to 186,000 miles per *second*! Traveling this fast we encountered a strange phenomenon known as *time dilation*. Time seemed to stand still. Cars on the freeway ... people everywhere seemed to be stopped in time, cattle in the pastures, birds in the sky, a child jumping rope frozen in mid-jump, a baseball in mid-flight, a basketball game stilled, with one player four feet in the air making a slam dunk through the hoop! We knew that Einstein was right! The faster you travel—the *slower* time becomes.

He and I now crossed the Great Smokey Mountains, soon arriving at Hartford, Tennessee. Here we discovered a paper mill polluting the area with dioxin, its poison draining into the Pigeon River. It used chlorine in its paper manufacturing which, in turn, produced dioxin.

Indigenous Species

We crossed the Mississippi River and stopped at the White River, observing something very unusual. It was a strange fish with razor sharp teeth known to bring terror to those in South America. Could we now have them in the White River in Arkansas? I caught myself staring into the eyes of a Piranha!

"Iben Jair, these mutants have learned to adapt to the milder temperature of the southern streams—and even breed! Will it be only a matter of time until havoc strikes? In the near future, a person swimming in these rivers may soon stumble upon a school these heinous creatures and actually be eaten alive."

The greenhouse effect might be worse than I had thought.

Next we entered one of the many prisons scattered across the United States, and decided to watch an execution in Cummins Unit maximum security facility, Grady, Arkansas. Here we saw Richard Wayne Snell strapped onto the gurney with an IV in his arm and realized he was to be executed at 10:00 P.M. I glanced at the wall clock and the mixture was already in progress with the lethal serum dripping into his veins ... drop by deadly drop—all frozen in time, for we were still at the speed of light.

Ft. Detrick, Maryland

Academia spoke, "We are now traveling to another bizarre place."

Here before me was a modern complex, not unlike that of a hospital. Yet something was vastly different I could feel.

"Iben, these numerous buildings compose the U.S. Army Medical Research Institute of Infectious Diseases located in Fort Detrick, Maryland."

We entered a modern building, their "Army Biodefense Laboratory." We stealthy passed an armed military guard carrying an M-16 rifle at its entrance. We scurried by him unnoticed and weaved our way down the hall through their cafeteria.

On our left was a locked door titled, "In Vitro Lab/ Authorized Personnel Only." Then I saw the strangest thing ... a room containing a refrigerator unit with hundreds of petri dishes. These sealed dishes, I realized, contained experimental human eggs, human multi-celled fertilized embryos that were stacked upon each other in stainless steel tanks frozen at minus 196 degrees Celsius. They came to Ft. Detrick from a medical facility near Washington D.C. that had acquired them in an experimental program which became too costly for medical research to continue. So they were sent here for temporary storage.

"These embryos, Iben, can live for decades or even centuries. Physicians were experimenting with in-vitro fertilization, then abandoned them. If these fertilized eggs were destroyed, would it be the same as murder?"

Adjacent to this, there was a new state-of-the-art stem-cell research facility originally designed to study amyotrophic lateral sclerosis (Lou Gehrig's disease). Then geneticists started transplanting transgenic DNA stem cells into live human embryos to study their effects upon autism, Parkinson's, Alzheimer's and autoimmune conditions such as multiple sclerosis and rheumatoid arthritis. This program was then expanded to include the genetic transformation and pathology of toxic organisms mainly to enhance organ transplants. This research led indirectly to creating GMOs (genetically modified organisms). But, some of these chimeras (organisms created by these means) it was discovered, could actually be mixed with human brain cells developing strange intelligent life such as the world has never seen. Soon, precocious "teratomas" (strange living tumors) will be kept alive from this vanguard research. Might there soon be designed and created rational and percipient mutant cancerous "blobs" or parasites that could live independent lives *outside* their host?

Behind these refrigerator units Academia revealed yet another double doorway which led into a new strange secured medical laboratory, protected by yet another code. Here we entered through a sealed massive vault emblazoned with the biohazard symbol and this warning:

Top Secret Research Facility
BL-4 Bio-Defense Laboratory
Authorized Personnel Only
Biohazard Area
Protective Suits Required

Slipping stealthy through these doors we encountered numerous quarantine rooms and sterile surgical rooms, made a right turn pass the autopsy rooms for both animal and human patients. This lab had a phone outside their double doors for authorized personnel only. Staff members, including nurses and doctors, must punch a code on the wall for excess to this facility. It is then buzzed open and they can enter.

"This is where the deadly Ebola outbreak was studied." Academia continued.

"Ebola?"

"Yes, Iben, the Ebola virus. A type of Hemorrhagic Fever. This is the deadly Zairean strain. This exotic virus kills 70% of those infected. Ebola has spread across West Africa and has even traveled to the United States. It could be the world's next new plague. To date it has killed over 11,000 people. It could easily become pandemic as passenger jets can easily carry the deadly virus from infected people to many other countries. It could also easily become a terrorist weapon of the future."

We saw epidemiologists donned in their protective virus-resistant blue Chemturion suits, resembling "space suits," roaming this dangerous laboratory of microbes, chemicals and petri dishes. We spotted grounding strips designed to prevent static electricity, thus preventing an accidental explosion. Here resided dozens of hot-box incubators designed to breed different strains of deadly bacteria and viruses that the doctors were experimenting upon to make antibodies and vaccines. Fastened to the walls of this lab were pressurized metallic bottles of chlorine dioxide. In case of an outbreak or leak from this laboratory these bottles would be used to kill almost all known deadly viruses and bacteria known to man. Above our heads were ultraviolet lights used to kill any or all absconded particles which might leak from any of these containment vessels or flasks. Also the air pressure in all these labs is less than the outside, making a slight vacuum making the air flow inward when any outside door is opened making all infected air to stay inside the sealed doors in case of a breach of containment.

We entered the "cryogenics" laboratory. Here we discovered numerous rows containing dozens of chicken eggs and growth medium used to incubate these germs.

"Iben, this is known as a BL-4 laboratory—one of the world's biosafety 'Level 4' facilities known as the 'Hot Zone.' These labs handle the deadliest viruses known. These contagions before you are test specimens in small easy to handle quantities to only be used to create antidotes, antibodies and vaccines."

I noticed that te larger stainless-steel canisters and cylinders containing these dangerous organisms were buried in clandestine refrigerated bunkers in a secured top secret area on the military base to be handled by authorized professional officers trained in biohazard materials."

At this moment, we discovered that these labs are studying:

1) **H5N1 flu virus:** Deadly Bird Influenza: Here were very dangerous viruses *genetically altered* by man into one of the world's most-deadly bird-flu mutants. In the near future this transgenic virus could be produced by a terrorist organization and dispersed into any major city. It can easily be transmitted across any continent via airlines (becoming pandemic), killing millions of people worldwide. This particular weaponized virus was actually created in a Dutch lab and sent to Ft. Detrick. More details on this organism is "Critical

Top Secret" and will *not* be released to the public or news media, nor any details of it will be transmitted via the Internet. (H1N1, H3N2, and others, will continually plague humankind).

2) **Carbapenem-resistant Enterobacteriaceae (CRE):** A bacterium, known as "The Super-Bug." It can cause infections of the bladder or lungs. This bacterium usually springs up in hospitals, nursing homes and health care facilities. The only preventive measure at the present time is complete sterilization of hospital surgical instruments. In the near future it will kill two people in the Ronald Reagan UCLA Medical Center and another 200 will be exposed to this deadly bacterium. It will be spread from ineffective sterilization procedures resulting from their use of the duodenoscope—a thin, flexible fiber-optic tube that is inserted down the throat to search for an intestinal blockage. Study of this dangerous bacterium is ongoing ... to discover how to destroy it, or to develop a vaccine against it.

3) **Legionnaire's Disease:** Akin to *chlamydia*, known as parrot fever and *ornithosis*. (This weaponized recombinant strain of *Legionella* has been imported from the Obolensk laboratories in Russia). Victims quickly suffer from brain damage, shock and paralysis and usually die within hours of infection. Produces symptoms like those of multiple sclerosis, a disease of the central nervous system. A genocide weapon. Mortality rate: almost 100% fatal.

4) **MRSA:** (Methicillin-Resistant Staphylococcus Aureus): This penicillin-resistant bacterium, or

"Superbug," may be the next "modern plague." This particular MRSA strain was responsible for 94,000 infections and has killed over 19,000 worldwide. Two million people have been infected to date, killing between 60,000 to 80,000 people *each year* in the U.S. There is the antibiotic staph **HA-MRSA,** Hospital Associated MRSA, associated with surgeries and IVs, and the **CA-MRSA**, Community-Associated MRSA, painful skin boils that spread through the contact sports like wrestling and also can spread through child-care workers. The flasks lined up before us contained *both* these resistant bacterial strains.

5) **Marburg:** (A type of Hemorrhagic Fever) Akin to Ebola, this exotic virus has *DNA is very different like no other viral organism upon the earth. Some scientists believe it might have come from outer space.* First discovered in Marburg, Germany. Many were infected in West Germany and Yugoslavia by Ugandan green monkeys. One in three infected—die.

6) **Clostridium Difficile: (C. DIFF)** Another dangerous drug-resistant staph infection that troubles physicians. Another super-bug that could be controlled just by washing your hands with hot water and soap before eating and after a bathroom visit. This could prevent millions of infections and thousands of deaths each year in hospitals and nursing homes.

Academia explained that soon another plague such as

this one will ravage the earth. This will be a mutant flu virus composed of avian (bird), swine (pig) and human viruses combined through a process known as *reassortment*. It will start from a swine farm in Mexico and travel to the United States. It will kill thousands of people in these two countries. It will soon become a world-wide pandemic, another dangerous neo-plague of the future.

We now encountered a small sealed flask containing the *Pseudomonas cepacie* bacteria, setting on their lab desk. I learned that it could someday become the new superbug that is so tough it can actually survive in isopropyl alcohol and is a nightmare in many hospitals throughout the world! (Some tenacious species of viruses can even survive in sulfuric acid).

He revealed other items of interest. Here resided an assortment of vials, flasks, syringes, and canisters in neat little rows lining hundreds of sealed sterile glass compartments. Each shelve was emblazoned with the scarlet curved arrows of the sinister warning "BIOHAZARD" which contained the following deadly contagions:

HEPATITIS C VIRUS: This virus has largely been ignored by the public. It has infected over 4 million Americans—4 times as that of HIV! Causes massive liver damage, with 10,000 dying in the U.S. *each yea*r. There is no known cure or vaccine. It is transmitted via contaminated blood transfusions. College students are contacting it by sharing their toothbrushes or through drug use by infected hypodermic needles.

AIDS: (Acquired Immune Deficiency Syndrome): a retrovirus. It has now infected over 45 million people worldwide. In the U.S. around 50,000 Americans have been identified as having AIDS, almost 30,000 of them have already died. Another 1,500,000 are carriers. Around 70% of cases have occurred in homosexuals and bisexual men, and about 25% in male and female intravenous drug users. Worldwide, over 30 million people have died!

"How can a person catch AIDS?" I asked.

"Through sexual intercourse. Drug addicts catch it by using a hypodermic needle infected with HIV. It is transmitted by blood transfusions but the virus is NOT spread by what you eat, by utensils, drinking glasses, sneezes, nor social kissing. Mosquitoes, thank goodness, are *not* vectors (carriers) of this diseases."

Yellow fever, Lassa fever, Dengue fever, Malaria, and African Sleeping Sickness were all here in various strains also.

KURU VIRUS: Indigenous of Papua New Guinea; spongiform disease; causative agent is either a slow-acting virus—*or some new unknown form of microbe.* Derived from an infectious particle of protein, now known to virologist as a "prion." Natives of New Guinea get infected by eating the brains of their dead in burial rituals, thinking this gives them strength and wisdom. Kuru is kin to mad-cow disease, scrapie, Creutzfeldt-Jakob disease and chronic wasting disease (found in deer and elk). In all these cases the brain becomes "spongy," or full of holes, causing mental and physical deterioration. This brain disease may be caused by a primitive kind of virus called a "virino," which is found in "mad cow disease," known also as "bovine spongiform encephalopathy" (also known to infect humans that cook and eat fried squirrel brains). The hot grease is not hot enough to kill these organisms! About 200 people are infected and die from CJD each year in the United States.

I learned that all it would take is a flask from the saliva of an infected pig or cow from a foreign country sent to any city in the United States—and in three days the deadly outbreak of foot-and-mouth (mad cow) disease in America would become epidemic.

A few of the diseases Russia has experimented with included foot-and-mouth disease, and Newcastle disease in exotic game chickens, the latter being an avian virus that spreads much like foot-and-mouth disease. If escaped from this lab could cause the mass slaughter of millions of infected chickens to prevent its spreading.

THE ZIKA VIRUS: Originated from Latin America and the Caribbean. Break-outs have occurred in South America, Central America, Mexico, and will soon be in the United States. Infections cause permanent paralysis in arms and legs. Can be transmitted by sexual contact and through bodily fluids, such as tears, discharge from eyes, salvia, vomiting, urine and stool (diarrhea). Also, possible transmission through blood transfusions. Zika has also been linked to microcephaly in new born babies, producing small heads and abnormal brain development. Also, it can lead to Guillain-Barre, causing temporary paralysis. Vector: Travelers throughout the world that have been infected by the mosquitoes: *Aedes aegypti* and *Aedes albopictus.*

KARNAL BUNT: A variety of small flasks containing a fine cream-colored powdery fungus that is harmless to humans, but sours the taste and smell of flour made from infected kernels of wheat. As a terrorist weapon it could be crippling to America's wheat crop in a matter of months. Also pathogens such as soybean rust disease can also cause much economic damage as animal diseases do.

I now learned that Russia has advanced technology in agroterrorism. Before her fall, Russia employed 60,000 people at more than 100 facilities developing two dozen crop and animal diseases for use against the United States. Russia has released many of these deadly secrets to Communist China and North Korea, and the terrorist nations of Iran and Iraq.

Top Secret Research Facility
BL-5 Bio-Defense Laboratory
Authorized Personnel Only
Biohazard Area
Top Secret
Sensentive Information/Classified

We passed through a vestibule which separated this lab from yet another one. This confined area was lined with triple-sealed bullet resistant glass windows. Two military police were observing all the activities with government issue .45-caliber pistols. On a shelf near the wall adjacent to them, protected under transparent glass with coded access, stood fully-automatic M-16s, loaded and ready. On the opposite wall those officers were surrounded by video surveillance cameras clandestinely viewing the whole complex, inside and outside the building, including their courtyards and parking lot. Also these officers had telephone "hot-lines" in case of emergency tying them not only to the base commander, but also to the experts at the Centers for Disease Control (CDC) in Atlanta, GA and to the Mayo Clinic, Rochester, MN and to the Dept. of Epidemiology, University of Minnesota at Minneapolis.

All virologists that worked within this lab had to pass by these guards, showing their I.D. military badges of authorization. What lay before us was yet another critical top secret ultra-modern BL-5 Complex "Hot Zone" that had been built within the last few years to continue research with their bio-warfare program. Since the government had learned that rogue nations such as North Korea, Russia, Iran, Iraq, and China have continued their biological weapons experimentation, our nation's top officials decided clandestinely to continue vital research in this area to protect our nation from a deadly biological warfare attack. These scientists are genetically engineering these pathogens creating new deadly bioweapons from known viruses, and producing vaccines against them in case we are hit by one (as we already have been with weaponized anthrax).

Numerous medical researchers were poring over wafer-thin lap top computers with 3-D pictures set into the walls analyzing viral genes and cataloging their nucleoproteins. This is an extension of the Bio-4 lab, where the medical teams used rubber gloves built into the walls where germ incubators bred live viruses that were studied behind thick hermetically sealed glass windows using electronic robot arms. Also sectioned off behind this protective glass resided animals (Rhesus monkeys, white lab mice, guinea pigs and rabbits) for pathological studies. This BL-5 lab was separated from the Bio-4 facility but shared double-air lock windows where deadly pathogens in sealed containers could be transferred from one lab to the next. Here I noticed some oblong canisters known as "biogenerators," used to breed genetically modified organisms (GMOs) for further research.

Some personnel were focused over numerous double-ocular light microscopes wired to computer monitors. Lined in neat organized rows were hundreds of vials of infected blood and various rows of slide boxes, petri dishes, lab flasks, test tubes, pipettes and centrifuges. In the center were numerous exotic microscopes, a dark field microscope, a phase contrast microscope and various fluorescence microscopes. Also available nearby were the awesome Scanning Electron Microscope (SEM), an ultramicroscope, and nuclear magnetic resonance imaging microscope (NMR) all uniquely designed to analyze perilous microbes and deadly viruses.

Academia stated that the National Germ Warfare Defense Facility located at Plum Island, NY has now closed. Plum Island was an 840-acre island shared by the Dept. of Agriculture and the Dept. of the Army. Here resided numerous facilities where sensitive biological research on exotic animal diseases were studied, along with viral genetic engineering. It is also where the development of our top secret germ warfare program occurred during the cold war.

The following is a list of the pathogens and deadly chemicals that were relocated to Ft. Detrick for further study until another clandestine biological laboratory can be built (including secured underground refrigerated storage) northeast of Topeka, KS.

Other bio-terrorism contagions and potions of death were shipped to Ft. Detrick from dozens of refrigerated underground storage bunkers once located in Aberdeen Proving Ground in Maryland. Most of these shipments are now relocated at Ft. Detrick to their maximum security installations. A few of them made to to the "Pandora Sector" as it was infamously called.

Academia and I now entered through yet another rather large refrigerated hermetically sealed vault, secured by a thick steel gray door also emblazoned with a white skull and cross bones including a rather large red biohazard symbol.

Section BL-501
Top Secret
Restricted Area
Authorized Personnel Only
Retinal Scan Required

This explosive-proof door could only be opened by a digital combination that activated a bar-coded lock programmed within specified badges. Only then will the newly installed retinal scan for authorized personnel open the door. Unknown by the staff or even to the guards, forced or unauthorized entry would release deadly hydrogen cyanide gas.

In sealed refrigerated bullet-resistant compartments contained the following:

Pandora: Unit I
BIOLIGICAL AGENTS:
Top Secret/Critical
Genetically Engineered Pathogens:
(Bio-Warfare Weapons)

BOTULISM: (*Clostridium botulinum*) A couple of round

fat 500 ml flasks sealed with an innocuous looking dirty-brown substance. These held the weaponized, genetically-altered botulism bacteria, with enough lethal toxin to kill the total population of the world! Many of these toxins from botulism can be 10,000 times more lethal than nerve gas. Could be easily placed in a small drone and sprayed over a target city. Extremely deadly. *C. botulinum* was used as a terrorist agent in Tokyo and against the U.S. military installations in Japan on three different occasions between 1990 and 1995 by the Japanese cult Aum Shinrikyo.

SMALLPOX: (*Variola virus*): Hemorrhagic. Various weaponized strains of variola were frozen in a liquid-nitrogen freezer. This freezer contained a stainless-steel cylinder with a circular lid displaying its temperature keeping these deadly viruses at minus 321 degrees Fahrenheit. It was secured to the wall with two heavy chains.

Notably, the Spaniards in the sixteenth century introduced smallpox into Mexico, killing 3.5 million people. Then it found its way to the American Indians where one half of them died from the disease *before* the arrival of the Pilgrims on the *Mayflower*.

Other tiny sealed flasks were all lined up in little white boxes containing: Weaponized Type *Aralsk strain* (from the Soviet Bioweapons development program) released upon Vozrazhdenie Island, Russia in 1971. Has a 100% mortality rate.

Another virus we discovered, sealed and freeze-dried in small vials, was the war-head grade ***India-1 strain,*** smuggled from the microbiology facility of Obolensk, Moscow. No effective vaccine. Even if people are vaccinated, the normal smallpox vaccine is only good for around 5 years.

BLACK PLAGUE: (Bubonic, septicemic, and pneumonic). Spread by rats infected by fleas carrying the bacterium *Yersinia pestis*. About 15 cases *every year* are still discovered in the United States, but the last epidemic killer plague occurred in 1924. In A.D. 542, the Black Death entered Asia Minor. Then in A.D. 1347—51 it attacked again, killing 25,000,000 people in Europe and possibly brought on the great famine of 1337 in China, killing another 4 million from disease and starvation. In 1900 the plague was discovered in San Francisco, where over a million rats were killed. Eventually the squirrels even became carriers of the disease. (Interestingly, the children's song, "Ring Around the Rosie" came from these plagues. "Rosie" meant the red buboe or pus lumps that appeared, "Pocket full of posies" referred to flowers or herbs to be placed on the victim's graves, and "We all fall down" references the death to all those infected).

Before us in sealed petri dishes were aerosolized spores of plague microbes; GMOs to be an effective weapon of choice. Perfected by Russian and British laboratories during the cold war. If escaped, this *weaponized* form of Black Death could kill maybe half the population of the world.

ANTHRAX: (*Bacillus anthracis*): Three sealed 118 ml flasks. One labeled RMR-1029. Weaponized spores of anthrax laced with silicon to make them more airborne and ready for dispersion. It is a highly infectious, contagious and deadly disease contacted from cattle to humans. Before us was a sample of the Daschle anthrax (Amerithrax) which spread from the postal system, Sept. 11, 2001, when five people died. Another vial contained one liter of the genetically altered freeze-dried powder of Vollum 1B—enough germs to kill the total population of any major U.S. city. This was a sample sold to Iraq some years ago intercepted by American troops. Yet other spores were deadly weaponized bioengineered IL-4 mousepox wrapped in silica nanopowder for wide ariel dispersion which jumped the species barrier. No known vaccine. The next one contained strain 11966, a genetically engineered bacterium developed by Ft. Detrick during their cold war experimentation.

In Fort Detrick, MD, Horn Island, Pascagoula, MS, and Pine Bluff Arsenal, AR have researched and tested many of these deadly bioweapon agents. Most research— still classified.

Q-FEVER: (Query fever) Twenty sealed 10 ml flasks of *Coxiella burnetti* (Australian variety; victor: ticks; rickettsial infection; found on the hides of sheep and cattle). This freeze-dried weaponized microbe can replicate very quickly. This new GMO is fatal in 90% of its victims.

TULAREMIA: *(Francisella tularensis):* An acute plague-like infectious diseased, carried by a tick, first discovered in California. New recombinant version rendered a new deadly disease engineered for biological-warfare production. Imported from Stepnogorsk complex, Kazakhstan.

WEST NILE VIRUS: Exotic deadly gene-spliced virus. Carried by either mosquito, bird, rabbit, squirrel, bat or horse. Genetically modified by the Russians. Death-rate unknown.

CLOSTRIDIUM PERFRINGEN (BW-T): A bacterium that normally causes gangrene in the human body. This mutated strain can be used for assassination of high-ranking officials in foreign countries. Engineered into a new transgenic organism to carry black-widow venom, a neuro-toxin, 15 times more deadly than the rattlesnake.

Pandora: Unit II
Nerve Gas and Chemical Agents
Top Secret/Critical

Row One: Here were a few dozen 283g flasks each containing enriched modified LSD, which produces hallucinations or chemical insanity. Here was enough chemical to incapacitate the total populations of New York City and San Francisco combined, deployed by aerosol or via their water system!

Row Two: Contained 141g canisters with the nerve agent GB and VX ... very deadly. Other little canisters contained pressurized potions of the chemical nerve agent *chlorethylmercaptan*, Soviet war gas, perfected during the cold war.

Terrorist have developed the poisonous sarin gas. They have also weaponized typhoid and are working on the deadly Ebola virus. Many rogue nations have stockpiled cannisters of VX and *chlorpicrin* (both deadly nerve gases).

Row Three: Numerous small 10 ml flasks full of an untraceable clear liquid known as Chaos. It was a modified chemical formula derived from a series of the psychoactive drugs *psilocybin*, *dimethyltryptamine* (DMT), mixed with a *piperidybenzilate ester*. Introduced into a small community's water supply it could incapacitate everyone who drank it, not killing them but rendering them helpless and insane for days.

Row Four: Numerous vials containing dangerous

warfare chemicals were the following noxious agents: tabun (GA), sarin (GB), and soman (GD), along with other volatile organophosphates, such as the nerve agent thionylchloride which reacts against acetylcholinesterase in the human body necessary for nerve function. These chemicals react against this enzyme leading to convulsions and almost instant death.

Row Five: A series of small metallic spray 118 ml canisters containing a deadly biopesticide used originally as a fumigation treatment for insect pests on grain. The Nazi party had it perfected as a death potion during World War II. It was then utilized in the many extermination camps such as Auschwitz, killing millions of Jew and those opposed to the German Reichstag. It is an odorless, colorless gas ... its infamous name: Zyklon-B.

Row Six: Still other rows were lined with noisome vials of the Substance A-232, A-23 and Compound 33, all nerve gas poisons produced from deadly fluorine acetic acid derivatives. Smuggled from Russian labs these substances cause fatal liver damage. These chemicals are so illusive that no trace of them will ever show up even in autopsies.

Row Seven: Contained small ampules of the poison ricin. It is 6,000 times more deadly than cyanide. It is used today as a terrorist weapon of which there is no known antidote or treatment. It is derived from the castor bean plant. The poison is relatively easy to produce and has been linked to the al-Qaida network and linked to other third world countries such as Iraq.

Row Eight: Dozens of bright red metallic 170g canisters emblazoned with a white skull and cross bones of death at the top, and a white hammer and sickle, symbol of Russia, toward the bottom, sealed with the deadliest substance known to humanity. They were smuggled out of Russia and arrived at Ft. Detrick during the cold war. They were clandestinely termed *Novichok* ... being *ten times* more deadly than VX gas, previously the deadliest nerve gas in existence!

The Pentagon has just revealed that the Soviets, North Korea, along with other countries, have new intercontinental missiles, along with various cruise missiles, which have been *redesigned* to carry not only nuclear but *biological* warheads. Could they already be armed and ready ... and aimed at the United States?

Looks like the world has just gotten a little more dangerous.

> "We can return to the Stone Age on
> the gleaming wings of science,
> just as quickly as we can glide into
> the twenty-first century."
> —Winston Churchill

> "Eternal vigilance is the price of liberty."
> —American Proverb

CHAPTER TWELVE

raveling at the speed of light, Academia and I intersect the St. Louis Arch. We flew through its massive loop and noticed in its portals, human beings as tiny ants looking out at the city's skyline—stilled, motionless in time from our hyper-speed. We saw them but they were oblivious to us. I wondered if any of them thought they saw an apparition or even a UFO as we neared it!

We flashed between St. Louis' many skyscrapers as on an invisible roller coaster! Onward we crossed the Shenandoah Valley and the Blue Ridge Mountains.

What a beautiful sight as the twin towers of the World Trade Center came into view. We zipped between them a thousand feet in the air. These towers, representing the commerce of over 80 countries throughout the world, became blinding bright as the sun. But this was *not* ordinary sunlight showering them with her golden countenance, but rather the radiance of uncountable angels crowning both 110 stories of these massive buildings kneeling in holy prayer. I had a sense of forthcoming doom, I knew not why.

Academia spoke, "Iben, remember this day well, for

the world will soon change, and grand icons thought to withstand the perils of time, great symbols of America, will soon perish as dust in the wind. America will be greatly stunned—with skylines altered forever."

We sped on through the Rockefeller Center Plaza, then spiraled up the facade of the Empire State Building and streaked to the top of the United Nation's building. All was strangely stilled in this great city with all those busy city folks frozen in mid-stride, all their vehicles and ships in their harbors—stilled in time.

Then we balanced ourselves upon the rays of the tiara crowning the Statue of Liberty!

Pollution

On through New York State we flew. We observe the contaminated Love Canal area with hundreds of homes abandoned and derelict — a ghost town.

"Love Canal?" I inquired.

"Yes, Iben," Academia continued, "where Hooker Chemicals and Plastics Corp. dumped 21,000 tons of toxic wastes causing cancer, miscarriages and birth defects. Many even had damaged chromosomes in their bodies. In 1978 Love Canal was declared a health hazard, over 200 families were evacuated and the neighborhood turned into a ghost town."

Crossing the United States, we noticed many locomotives we coined, "Death Trains." Freight trains every day travel all over the United States carrying dangerous toxic chemicals. These tank cars, each capable of carrying over 30,000 gallons of liquid, are filled with toxic substances such as vinylidine chloride, phenol, butadiene, chlorine, naphtha, propane, diethylbenzene, sodium picramate, phosphorus, gasoline, dichloropropene, methyl isocyanate, etc. Each one of these trains—could wipe out complete neighborhoods or even take out a small city, killing and injuring hundreds of people. And there are around 2,500 accidents *each year* all across America involving trains!

We arrived in Charleston, West Virginia, discovering a chemical spill from a coal mining facility. Here a storage tank erupted containing 4-methylcyclohexanemethanol or MCHM having a green tint and a smell of licorice. It will soon pollute the Elk River decomposing into formaldehyde, a known carcinogen. We discovered its long-term effects on all the animals, human life … and the developing human embryo.

I learned that coal processing plants have poisoned ground water aquifers causing gross deformities in many animal species. Coal plants are responsible for over half of all toxic pollutants that enter the nation's water supply. Coal ash waste contains poisonous arsenic, mercury and radioactive selenium. Here we discovered—mutated two-headed fish.

Hundreds of other accidents were discussed by Academia. It was revealed just how polluted our old world actually is!

Drugs in America

All across the United States Academia and I located thousands young people using "sherm," the street name for a mixture of PCP and marijuana. These drugs can lead to heart attacks and death. Also, I discovered K-2, fake "pot" or "synthetic marijuana." Even stranger drugs such as "bath salts," are synthetic cannoabinoids, all which can become deadly. Then we discovered yet another dangerous illegal drug young people were using known as "carfentanil," an elephant tranquillizer, 10,000 times more powerful than hydrocodone. It is, even in tiny amounts, very deadly.

We also discovered that Americans are overusing *prescription* opioids (pain-reducing) medicines. Even preschool children have been known to overdose on them which are usually found in their parent's medicine cabinets! Along with the painkillers heroin and fentanyl, opioids are the most common cause of our fifty to sixty thousand overdose *deaths* in the United States each year.

On this journey I also discovered crystal methamphetamine laboratories throughout our grand country. Simply amazing, with all we have in America, our citizens are still not happy with our freedoms and liberties and are still trying to make a fast, illegal buck, not caring that they are destroying the very fabric of our society. But instead, these drugs kill and destroy marriages, families and friendships.

"Yes, Iben, and there are other illegal drugs that are destroying the fabric of our society, such as heroin and Molly."

"Molly?" I asked.

"Yes, a form of Ecstasy, a synthetic illegal drug also known as MDMA. It can cause liver damage, kidney and cardiovascular failure. College students usually use it at rave music shows in their universities and on their college campuses.

"It is a disgrace to our society that with all the mass

media, i.e. TVs, radios and the Internet, the poignant message has been compromised that illegal drugs are still destroying our citizens."

Frog Mutations and Bat Fungus

Still at the speed of light we toured many polluted ponds and rivers. Here we found numerous anomalies of life forms, strange inexplicable phenomena that scientists cannot answer. We even found deformed frogs! We also discovered that many bats were dying by the thousands. I learned that frog eggs and tadpoles are very sensitive to changes in their environment and will show up as mutations quite suddenly.

The bats found in New York and Vermont caves were dying mysteriously from a disease known as "White-nose Syndrome." This fungus could someday actually wipe out the bat population in our country. The cause of these mysterious deaths is still unknown.

Deformed frogs and dead bats, Academia explained, means only one thing—a portent of worse things to come.

CHAPTER THIRTEEN

Niagara and the Great Lakes

*W*e now arrive at Niagara strangely stilled in time from our hyper-speed. Usually 100,000 cubic feet of water each *second* plunge over it. Under the falls we observe the great turbines that generate electricity. They would normally revolve thousands of times a minute generating many kilowatts of electricity.

I fell and bounced across the water above the falls but its surface tension kept me somehow afloat. It was like bouncing upon a trampoline, falling and undulating and bobbing up and down upon its surface. Then I momentarily passed over the cataract composed of billions of tiny prismatic marbles suspended in space—and plunged into the strangely still water below. Hitting the bottom of the falls I bounced to and fro as upon a bowl of jelly. What a ride! And all in 1,000,000,000th of a second!

Now I perceived the world beyond my five senses into even more foreign concepts of wonder. What a strange sensation. Now I had no fear of asphyxiation. This, along with swallowing, I realized, were both worldly traits and forfeited at death. Then I realized that I wasn't even wet! Even the pressure of the water didn't bother me, nor did the blackness of its depths. A bolt of fear struck me, but then I realized that breathing was not needed in my new enhanced spiritual body. I was in the state of *Interdimensional Transposition*, that strange spiritual parallel universe where we can travel through matter without affecting it, or a spiritual universe within the third dimensional universe, yet separate from it. As two cars meet traveling through an intersection at the same time and instead of colliding, they pass right *through* each other—unharmed. I now realized that my enhanced glorified body was dependent only on God's Divine Kinetic Bioplasmic Energy. All mundane foodstuffs and air our old mortal bodies needed wasn't now necessary for our survival. As mothers milk is the perfect food for the nursing infant, so *Divine Kinetic Bioplasmic Energy* is the perfect food for the immortal glorified bodies of Eternity.

Then we spotted the eel-like parasite, the sea lamprey, attached to many fish—sucking out their bodily fluids.

The Algae Pfiesteria

In only a moment we arrived at Chesapeake Bay and discovered another nightmare, known as *Pfiesteria*, a one celled algae releasing a poison that kills fish. Humans swimming in these waters can also experience short-term memory loss. This problem is caused when pesticides run into the rivers from fertilized crops. This algae kills millions of fish in North Carolina and has also infected the waters of Virginia. We also found similar algae stinking up the coasts of Florida.

In many polluted rivers we noticed the dangerous pesticides DDT and PCBs causing fish to have both male and female characteristics. These mutant fish are all precursors of a dying world.

We now found ourselves close to one thousand feet high above Port Arthur on Lake Superior. Here we spotted a depression filled with water.

"Chubb crater, Iben!" proclaimed Academia. "We are at the southern end of Quebec, Canada and what you see is the result of a meteor striking the earth at 37 miles per second thousands of years ago. You probably remember the meteor crater in Winslow, Arizona was almost a mile across and 600 feet deep. Well, Chubb Crater which we see before us … is a hundred times larger than this!"

At the speed of light, we crossed over the province of Quebec, Manitoba, Saskatchewan, Alberta—onward to explore the Canadian Rocky Mountains.

What a pristine sight! Serrated snowy ice capped mountains intersecting an azure sky! Between the provinces of Alberta and British Columbia, the Canadian Rockies extend over a thousand miles with not a city or person in sight! From Elk Island National Park, Academia and I crossed the Rockies and flew high above Jasper National Park on to Mt. Edith Cavell. Then I saw the most majestic peak so far and we soared to its top—Mt. Robson, the highest point of the Canadian Rockies. Here we stood upon its peak and pondered upon God's grand creation.

Now we crossed Yoho National Park and the Rocky

Mt. Trench, heading for the Canadian Yukon. We observed nimble mountain goats climbing along the steep edges of narrow cliffs. Here grizzly bears were frolicking and foraging for food.

Academia and I have now explored the whole span of Canada and the Yukon. Now we journeyed onward to Alaska!

A moment later we spotted the majestic sun-lit peak of Mt. McKinley rising above us into the frigid air, the apex of the Rocky Mountain chain.

We joined a team of British climbers and saw three specks on a cliff dangling from a rope. We proceeded closer and by scanning their minds we learned that their leader was Lucas Johnson.

He revealed that our Divine Mission from God is to rescue this British team of nine members from the perils of this mountain. These three men were struggling to get out of the *Orient Express* a 3,000-foot precipice at the 14,000-foot level—tired, hungry and injured. They had fallen from their companions, six others standing helplessly by unable to help them. Lucas and the other two were determined to climb upward to the ledge of the Orient Express when he realized his legs were broken in the fall and his companions also were hurt. They were numb from the cold, it being with a wind chill of over 80 degrees below zero! Getting dangerously frostbitten Lucas along with his companions were praying for a miracle and desperately needed rescuing from the mountain's precipice. Academia and I comforted them giving them peace and hope.

This is another point upon our Divine Mission—to help

the high-altitude helicopter find these three climbers in peril and safely whisk them from the cloud covered mountain.

With this Academia miraculously opened up a hole in the clouds so the rescue team could find these three climbers. We communicated with the helicopter pilot, gently guiding him through the darkness and poor weather to fulfill their rescue mission.

Lucas had his eyes closed praying for a miracle. Then, as we neared, he finally opened them again seeing us ministering to him! A moment later they all heard the helicopter and then saw its searchlights. We guided these searchlights to these desperate three. Then we left Lucas and his companions to their thoughts and then gently guided the other six British climbers back down the mountainside to safety.

Looking back, I still saw Lucas stilled from our hyper-speed, but noticed that his eyes were filled with hope and happiness of that instant bright flash of glory when he saw us!

Caribou, the grizzly bear and the timber wolf, along with the golden eagle were seen suspended in this time-gap of stilled movement. Then we flew over the Bering Sea where we met some beluga whales suspended in mid-jump high above the water.

Subsonic Speed

We were to once again slow down to subsonic speed for our mission was over to save the mountain climbers! We had traveled over 5,000 miles in less than a nanosecond, traveling all the way from Oklahoma City to Mt. McKinley via St. Louis, New York City, the Great Lakes, Canada and Alaska!

A reverse shock wave as an anti-sonic boom splintering the space-time fabric sent ripples of kaleidoscopic shards of color twisting about us as we egressed from the speed of light. Then the fabric of time oscillated and vibrated—rivers ran downhill, animals once again ran across the tundra. Ships moved upon the rivers, lakes and oceans and the fish moved beneath them. The leaves rustled in the trees and the clouds moved in the sky. The birds and the insects moved once again with the wind. Cars sped along the highways, planes crossed the sky and people moved upon the streets. What a strange world we left as time quivered and then became normal once again.

Business-as-usual.

Then I remembered the mountain climbers. I somehow knew Lucas and his two other companions were rescued from Mt. McKinley and taken to Elmendorf Air Force Base hospital, Anchorage. Here the climbers told of the angelic beings who saved them. The helicopter pilot told of a flash of light that guided him safely to those climbers in peril!

The poison dripped into the plastic tube at Cummins Unit, and that condemned criminal Richard Wayne Snell finally succumbed to Eternity. And those rail cars suspended in mid-air at Duluth, MN finished their fall into a river.

And the beluga whales once again plunged into the depths of the Bering Sea. And the mobile universe I once knew appeared again peaceably before me.

Black bears are spotted crossing the tundra hunting for food. Then this Sunday morning in a small village a modest country church is seen still in session. I could even see the effluvium of their sincere prayers crossing the vastness and infinity of space seeking answers to a fathomless existence.

We transverse miles of coastline spotting dozens of pilot whales and seals beached along the coast and wondered why they would commit suicide this way. Academia was silent upon an answer.

Chapter Fourteen

Russia and Her Pollution

*A*cademia and I transported across the Bering Strait to southeastern Siberia. We encountered a beautiful lake, deep and rich with fish and animal life.

What mysteries will this strange lake reveal to us?

"Iben, this is Lake Baikal, Russia's Sacred Sea. It is the deepest lake on earth, over one mile in depth, 395 miles long and 50 miles wide. It holds one-fifth of the planet's fresh water or 5,520 cubic *miles* of it. Yes, more than all the Great Lakes combined!"

I learned that it also was becoming polluted.

"Lake Biakal truly is the Pearl of Siberia, the earth's deepest land depression, composed totally of fresh water."

I could smell something gross in the air. Many cellulose plants were billowing their pale-yellow smoke of pollution. I learned that much of Lake Baikal was hopelessly contaminated by them!

Thousands of gas flares lighted up Russian oil fields

sending dense black clouds of sulfur dioxide across Siberia. We toured chemical companies where plutonium, developed for nuclear weapons, has been dumped in rivers—and entire nuclear reactors have been buried at sea. This nuclear waste, to our enhanced eyes, was coruscating deadly gamma-rays causing both leukemia and cancer.

We also learned that over twelve atmospheric nuclear test bombs were detonated across the Siberian wilderness, contaminating it with deadly radiation.

Moscow was next. It is a city of nine million where hundreds of waste sites had dangerously high radiation levels.

Now Academia and I toured *Krasnoyarsk-26*, a man-made cavern in Siberia three times as large as the Great Pyramid of Cheops. One hundred thousand convicts carved it out 600 feet below the earth. Here three atomic reactors convert plutonium for the production of hydrogen bombs for Russia's war machine. The left over radioactive waste is dumped into the Yenisey River.

The Mayak complex was explored next. Here September 29, 1957 a huge explosion destroyed the complex. Radioactivity from this explosion forced 10,000 people to evacuate the area.

We toured places where nuclear bombs were tested in 1954, exposing thousands of Russian soldiers to deadly radiation. Many have since died from leukemia. I learned that a similar scenario had taken place in the United States with America's above-ground tests in the Nevada Testing Range, south of Las Vegas.

(Alarmingly, we discovered that many of Russia's *underground* atomic tests leaked high levels of radiation as some of those detonated in the United States, China and North Korea have also been known to do).

Chernobyl

Belarus, in the Ukraine, was contaminated when Chernobyl nuclear reactor exploded and melted its nuclear core in 1986 similar to the Three-Mile-Island complex in Pennsylvania.

Academia and I crossed the Baltic Sea and discovered grotesque fish with malignant tumors. Many lakes were contaminated with deadly radiation from Russian nuclear weapons manufacturing.

In the northern Ukraine we came upon an abandoned city, where hundreds of dilapidated houses and apartment buildings were now strangely silent being without any people. Here resided the infamous atomic power plant, Chernobyl.

Then we cautiously passed by abandoned cranes, trucks and machinery and neared the stone coffin of reactor No. 4 still containing its 180 tons of melted nuclear fuel entombed in concrete.

"Chernobyl," Academia explained, "on April 26, 1986 was NOT the place to be. It was the worse nuclear disaster in recent history. Thirty-one people died when the Number 4 reactor was destroyed by an explosion. Some 500,000 people were contaminated and of these, 300,000 are undergoing treatment. Cancer rates have risen immensely and 92,000 people have been removed from an 18 mile 'hot zone' around the plant. Thousands of children had been removed from Kiev and surrounding areas. Now a new city had been built to replace all these people miles away from this contaminated area. Farmers close by were ordered off their land and told to come back until it was safe — in about 600 years! About 10,000 people have already died so far from radiation poisoning in Russia from this disaster.

"It is the worse nuclear disaster to ever plague humankind. Its deadly plume reached as far as Germany and Scotland where thousands of cattle were contaminated with radiation poisoning. Even in Egypt this radioactivity caused blindness, spinal degeneration, paralysis and death in young children, indirectly exposed. You see, they were drinking milk that was shipped from Germany whose cattle had been exposed to radioactivity from Chernobyl. Some of this contaminated milk was even traced to Brazil! Eventually all of Europe would be contaminated from the Chernobyl disaster. In Sweden pregnant women and small children were contaminated by radioactive iodine. In West Germany milk and lettuce were banned from grocery stores. Italy was cautioned to use only powered milk because regular milk was contaminated. Even areas in Poland had radiation levels one thousand times above normal!"

Next we toured over a dozen cities hopelessly polluted by chemical and radioactive wastes such as dangerous cesium 137.

"Thousands of Russians are dying from this environmental chaos. Many rivers full of noxious poisons have contaminated her air and food.

"Also, Iben, not just Russia is contaminated… the United States still have their nuclear problems. In Washington state, the Hanford Nuclear Reservation has numerous storage tanks still leaking deadly radiation. At Oak Ridge

National Laboratory, TN, they are injecting radioactive waste materials into shale beds deep underground. And at the Yankee Atomic Electric Co. in Bolton, MA, there is thousands of pounds of spent fuel needing relocation because of dangerous radiation contamination. In the past, also, there was a deadly explosion at the Experimental Breeder Reactor No. 1 (EBR-1) near Idaho Falls, ID, and a radioactive core meltdown at Three Mile Island, Harrisburg, PA."

Academia and I now leave the Ukraine and continue—

Pollution of China and India

I learned that over 9,000,000 people each year die from environmental pollution worldwide! Air and water pollution *each year* are killing more people than have died from smoking, hunger, AIDS, tuberculosis and malaria *combined*.

We learned that China has many environmental problems from her nuclear weapons program, her nuclear energy, and from mining coal and rare metals. Also, since her economy has risen in the last few decades, so has her pollution.

India also has major air pollution problems. New Delhi, is now the world's most polluted city.

"What is causing all this pollution in India?"

"Burning cow dung for cooking is their main pollutant problem," Academia continued. "Next comes industrial plants, poor fuel standards, and extensive garbage burning and their use of fossil fuels. They are still developing coal-fired electrical plants that will *double* their sulfur dioxide and nitrogen oxide pollution which produce dangerous lung-clogging particulate matter.

"Iben Jair, we are now going to the sea's surface and beyond. See what wonders await you here!"

Academia stated that he must now be leaving because he must monitor China, who has developed nuclear-armed stealth submarines equipped with long range nuclear ballistic missiles. These Jin class subs *each* carry 12 of these missiles with a range of 5,000 miles. Noteworthy, they also have the land-based mobile solid-fueled missile with a range of about 7,000 miles. Also, he was concerned about Pakistan exploding a nuclear bomb and the development of its nuclear tipped Tarmuk, a short-range missile which could launch a nuclear warhead about 250 miles into India.

Then he revealed that Iran's ballistic missiles soon will have nuclear warheads. North Korea is also testing their nuclear tipped ballistic missiles and submarine launched long-range missiles—also tipped with nuclear warheads.

"Another angel will greet you now," Academia continued. "I am going to be relatively busy in the next few years, earth time. In Charleston, South Carolina at the Emmanuel African Methodist Episcopal Church, the oldest black church in the South, a young 22-year-old after a Wednesday night Bible study will kill their black pastor along with 8 others.

"Yet I will again be needed, where another massacre will soon happen on Fort Hood Army post in Texas by a Muslim Army psychiatrist who will open fire at a training processing center. He will kill 13 soldiers—

"Also, a man armed with a shotgun will kill 5 people at the *Capital Gazette*, a newpaper in Annapolis, MD."

"Academia, I've never seen such things I am now learning!"

"Yes, Iben, and you are about to discover even greater wonders than these!"

"Yes, the world is a mess, needing tolerance and Godly love. Someday, in the near future, God will once again reveal his Divine Spirit and the world shall become a better place. Farewell, Iben … God Bless you."

With this Academia evanesced into the vacuous unknown.

Chapter Fifteen

Ocean Exploration

Another scintillating Angelic Divine Counselor now appeared, Aqua Marina, the 'Divine Spirit of the oceans and the seas.'

With this, Aqua Marina and I plunged into the unknown entering that wonderland that few mortals have dared to travel. Then we sank deep beneath the white-caps of the ocean! I learned that earth contains 320 million cubic *miles* of sea water! This translates to about 50 quadrillion tons of water.

Submerging into the clear blue infinity of the sea, I had, as already stated, no fear of asphyxiation which was only a worldly trait. Also there was no fear from Caisson disease, the rapid accumulation of nitrogen bubbles in the blood or the pressures that such depths the ocean demanded. Again, I remembered the Great Lakes and Russia's Antarctica lake realizing another great adventure revealed itself before me as the wonder of a small child going to a movie to see Jules

Verne's *Twenty Thousand Leagues Under the Sea* for the first time!

Along the continental shelf we swam down into enormous valleys and swam through great subterranean canyons greater than any found on land. We crossed mighty abysses more enormous than the Grand Canyon. Mighty currents from unknown subterranean rivers larger than the Mississippi swept us along! These great submarine currents carved these magnificent gorges.

We entered the Marianas Trench—so deep that if Mt. Everest was submerged, it would still be a mile underwater! Here we discovered thousands of animals and plants no one had ever seen.

Next we spotted an amazing fish thought dead for at least 60 million years. A live one was actually caught off the southeast tip of Africa in 1938. It was the *Latimeria*. Yet, another fossil-fish we discovered was the *frillshark*, found over a mile deep in the ocean having similar features of sharks over 30 million years ago. It was totally unknown to the upper regions of the ocean.

Coming upon the North Sea we discovered a lost land submerged beneath these waters. We called it Dogger Bank and found the remains of Pleistocene life. Were we actually observing the bones of Stone Age man scattered along with the fossils of bears, wolves, hyenas, the woolly rhinoceros and the giant mammoths? We floated through huge dead ancient forests of willows, birches, mosses and ferns from another world and time. Were we witnessing the actual world that existed before Noah's flood?

We also discovered *Caulepa taxifolia*. Where this deadly seaweed survives, the sea anemones, starfish, crabs, shrimps and many fish abandon the area. Though not toxic to humns, most creatures stay away from it.

Aqua Marina and I now toured the deep abyss of the ocean. We discovered strange isolated flat-topped mountains existing a mile below the surface. These mesas were remnants of mountains that once towered above the ocean's surface and then suddenly sank beneath the waves before recorded history.

At these depths, I realized, the pressure would crush any mortal because water weighs eight hundred times as much as air. At 33 feet the crushing weight of water equals that of all the miles of air above you. At 33,000 feet the pressure is a thousand times greater than at sea level which computes to 15,000 pounds per square inch. I was now over a thousand feet down into its inky depths without feeling any pressure, no coldness either and then I realized that I wasn't even wet!

Also to mere mortals no sunlight can shatter this blackness—but we could easily see numerous exotic ocean life unknown in the upper regions.

We spotted a dark undulating movement coming toward us. This giant creature was the mighty sperm whale of Moby Dick fame. It glided through us totally unaware of our presence. We were all 3,000 feet deep and I couldn't believe such creatures could dive to this depth! How can these whales stand such terrifying pressures and once again surface without the terror of the bends (nitrogen narcosis)? This was one of the great mysteries Aqua Marina solved by us, but alas, I could not yet reveal this information to mortal humankind.

As each human dies ... these secrets will then be disclosed.

"For now we see through a glass, darkly;
but then face to face: now I know in part;
but then shall I know even as also I am known."
—1 Cor. 13:12

Strange exotic creatures swam all about us giving off their living light of *bioluminescence*. From the largest to the smallest particle of life—all were controlled by God in his infinite wisdom!

We studied the lantern fish as they strobed their beauty through the inky blackness of eternal night, and the hawksbill turtle. We learned, to our amazement, that it ate *glass* for its main diet. These turtles feed on sponges that are composed of sharp needle-like silica glass spicules. The hawksbill is also a wonder to science in that they can survive many types of poisons found in many of the sponges they eat. Strangely, some natives that have caught these turtles have actually died from eating them. Yet the turtles themselves are unharmed by the toxins they carry.

Fish Language

Besides all the light and color of these fish something else caught my attention—strange noises under the water.

I swam toward a really loud sound following it to a little fish known as the croaker—using its air bladder to make these loud sounds.

Then I discovered something wonderful. That I could actually *understand* all their languages! They were calls to their mates, or were warnings against predators such as sharks.

The whales and dolphins were the best at doing this than all the other species in the oceans. Though not actually fish, but mammals, they still had the best communication of sonar and intricate language.

Oh, what could the mortals do with this knowledge?

Aqua Marina cautioned that I could *not* release their secrets because humankind was not savvy enough for such enlightenment. Many countries are exploring the planets and the universe while the wonders in the oceans beneath them in all their awe and majesty, remain a great mystery. And the most important is the realm of the oceans whose health determines the fate of life on earth, that vital link between the survival—or the extinction of the human species!

We explored strange subterranean mountains thousands of miles long and the mysterious deep valleys of the Mid-Atlantic Ridge.

What did we find? Was there life at these depths? We encountered wonderful geysers on the bottom spewing hot water at temperatures 700 degrees Fahrenheit! Here we discovered shrimp, crabs and even bacteria living off these thermal vents swimming around in pressures of over 6,000 pounds per square inch!

Mounds the size of football stadiums were present, being giant mineral deposits created by these subterranean geysers. The sea floor, we discovered, was full of cracks and valleys revealing vast hydrothermal vents where cold ocean water is pulled under, heated and recirculated. Here resided strange life forms that had no use for photosynthesis and therefore contained no chlorophyll! The process of photosynthesis I knew, produces carbon dioxide as a byproduct. I learned that another process, *chemosynthesis*, was at work here, producing the byproduct of sulfur. So, we had discovered a new phylum of plant life! The incredulity of it!

We encountered a great variety of deep-sea creatures. One of honorable mention crawling across the ocean bottom about the size of an oak leaf—was an eccentric beast having 10,000 eyes!

The *Titanic*

Then I leanred something of vast interest. I could hardly wait. We journeyed on toward Newfoundland. Deep within the ocean we spotted a dark mysterious shadow. What was this thing, silent and still? What was this haunting specter covered with rusticles, barnacles and cockle shells submerged in this murky depth amidst the shrimp and sea stars forever in her watery grave? Here in her quiet destitution … resided the mighty *TITANIC*.

On April 15, 1912 the *Titanic,* one of the greatest ocean liners ever built, hit an iceberg, and sank in less than three hours. As she floundered, she split into two unequal pieces. Downward she slowly drifted into the dark cold ocean over two miles deep. She was silent, yet austere, keeping her secrets to herself pondering them in this sanctuary of cold and darkness!

The *Titanic* was the largest ship on the sea in 1912 and was claimed to be a ship that "God could not even sink," setting out from Southhampton, England on April 10, 1912.

Speeding toward New York the *Titanic* traveled through the perilous North Atlantic ice field. The mighty ship struck an iceberg slicing open its hull four days out on its maiden voyage. Seven hundred and five people were rescued and 1,523 perished. Only one-third of those on board were saved and many life boats were only half filled. Hundreds of survivors plunged from the ship into the icy waters but the little boats did not return to rescue them. It was only the matter of a few minutes before hypothermia set in and those who jumped overboard in the last seconds—all froze to death.

She had over 2,227 people including passengers and crew aboard her with uncounted immigrants ready to start a new life in America. The royalty of the industrial society was aboard her including John Jacob Astor, Macy's founder and U.S. congressman Isidor Straus along with the ship's builder, Thomas Andrews. The *Titanic,* cautioned about the icebergs, steamed "full speed" at 22 knots because the captain feared that a coal fire below deck could not be extinguish. They also wanted to set a new speed record. Shortly before midnight the ship struck an iceberg about 95 miles south of Newfoundland.

We decided to tour this great sunken ship. Over 2 miles deep we threaded our way through the ships interior visiting her passenger rooms, the grand ball room, the crew's quarters and mess hall. All was quiet now upon her deck where the band played while the ship was dying. Her regal library, containing thousands of unread leather-bound books, was now rotting away still in neat rows—untouched upon their shelves. Her grand stairway, brass and crystal chandeliers, still hanged from her ceilings … proclaiming her sovereignty of a golden age past.

Aqua Marina told me to touch the *Titanic's* hull. As I did,

I was whirled through a kaleidoscopic swirl of luminescence. I watched the scenario of the last hours of the ship's *coup de grace*. I sensed the panic and screams of men, women and children being placed into life boats. I observed the reality of all that took place that infamous early cold dark morning. I could actually feel the empathy of those left aboard the ship as they saw the tiny life boats leaving with their children as they set off into the cold frigid darkness.

I felt the pathos of those safely aboard the life boats. Their oars splashing way beyond the great majestic ship into the strangely calm icy waters. I could hear, even miles from the *Titanic,* the melodious sound of the ensemble playing music upon her deck, moving over the dark waters, giving comfort to the surreal scenario unfolding before them. The survivors now rowed off into the inky black unknown. They were leaving forever the world they once knew. We observed many survivors screaming and jumping into the icy waves only to perish from the cold. Those aboard the life boats were to have a future … but those swimming in the ocean and those still stranded aboard the *Titanic* … their fate was sealed.

In these boats the cold wind blew against their bare skin penetrating deep into their clothes. Many a mother's body hovered close to their children and babies to warm them as a mother goose protects her young goslings from the cold.

I could feel the empathy of those in the life boats as they left their loved ones. Husbands separated from their wives, mothers separated from their children as they were lowered over the side of the huge ship out into the inky blackness. Down and down other life boats came striking the water 60 feet below. Then they rowed away from the mighty ship in fear of being pulled under by the maelstrom when she sank. I could see the great ship listing with rows of lights now appearing above the surface with almost half of the great ship's bow disappearing beneath the cold unforgiving sea. As the pink incandescence of the distress flares shot skyward into the star-studded night illuminating the ship's death agony, we could see hundreds of passengers in their life vests floating in the icy water.

I heard what they heard—the faint music moving through the ebony night—the final hymn of her funeral pall. Then in my worst horror I watched as the stern or rear of the mighty vessel rose upward her massive props pointing heavenward and the sounds of explosions and hissing. Boilers were snapping like dynamite blasts as the downward momentum of the ship increased. Then screams chilled the air as her lights blinked off—leaving only a dark shadow as it slowly disappeared beneath the angry waves of a bubbling and frothing ocean. Here she was welcomed magnanimously into her silent grave for all eternity.

There was never such a quietness upon the sea. People in the life boats were stunned to silence and shock, their tears dried upon their stoic faces not yet comprehending what had just taken place—one of the greatest maritime disasters had just been witnessed and the mightiest passenger ship ever built up to this time—was but a memory.

Was some sort of psychometry from the ship revealing these events, or were its very ghost giving me this vision of things past I could not tell. I could see from my perspective that black sky opening. Rays from a brightly faceted diamond of Divine Light appeared. I learned this phenomenon of divine radiant energy was the grand manifestation of the

Shekinah Glory of God. Somehow I realized it to be that same radiant fiery illumination witnessed at the the Jewish tabernacle over 3,000 years ago.

Mighty angels now glided down from this light to minister to those lost on the ship while others ministered to those already treading water and to those in the life boats. Only the angels and I observed this—

"Are these angels going to save them," I inquired?

"No Iben," Aqua Marina spoke, "they are showing those aboard the ship how to be brave, how to take courage … and how to die. They are enlightening them how to attain total peace in the face of death. Really Iben, no one really dies alone! Other angels are comforting those that have separated from their family members and loved ones aboard the little boats.

"Iben, you can actually meet these lost souls, those that succumbed that eerie night to their final destiny … and also meet the survivors and how they felt abandoning their loved ones, family and friends. Those survivors, that have since died along with those that perished will be glad to relate their stories to you—when we return."

Through a time-inversion we now retrieved the present once again. We toured the whole sunken ship traveling through its many corridors, hallways and passenger rooms. We saw personal trunks of the passengers still intact and shaving kits still bearing their straight razors along with their personal eye glasses. In the wine cellar hundreds of bottles of vintage wine were found with their corks still intact, their contents still drinkable after all these years!

And then something glimmered on the promenade deck … a beautiful ring set with numerous diamonds from one of the wealthy ladies on board the *Titanic* … who stayed and perished with her husband. This ring, void of the finger which admired it so … gone forever into the abyss.

Then, the realization that I was dead and living in the afterlife hit me fully again.

The *Lusitania*

We now explored the mystery of another sunken ship which sank on May 7, 1915 torpedoed by a German U-boat 12 miles off the Coast of Ireland. Here under 295 feet of murky water we discovered the mighty British luxury liner, the *Lusitania*.

There were 2,057 people aboard her with 1,198 losing their lives. I wondered why it had sunk in only 19 minutes. Aqua Marina told me I could reveal the reason why it sank so fast.

We studied the gaping hole in its hull where it was torpedoed and we could see these wounds and another huge gaping tear in her hull from still another great explosion.

The *Lusitania*, Aqua Marina revealed, was carrying secret war munitions. These were ignited by one single torpedo which blew the ship apart. The ship in her death agony sank in less than 20 minutes. The German submarine commander was stunned at the massive explosion which destroyed her. Perishing within her bowels were some famous Americans such as the famous theatrical producer Charles Frohman, Elbert Hubbard, the famous writer and the millionaire, Alfred G. Vanderbilt.

"Why fear death? It is the most
beautiful adventure in life."
—Charles Frohman—Said to be his last words
before sinking on the *Lusitania,* torpedoed May 7, 1915.

For miles along the ocean bottom we encountered peculiar snow-like mounds of white icy sediments known as methane hydrates. They resembled water ice, being composed of a crystalline solid containing methane gas. We discovered this "ice" could actually burn like coal as the methane effervesced from it, and they could potentially be the world's next new alternative energy source.

Strange manganese nodules containing copper, cobalt and nickel also littered the ocean bottom whose origin is unknown to mortal man—but their many esoteric riddles were all solved by us!

We stumbled upon exquisitely beautiful diamonds of flawless pure carbon scattered across miles of the ocean floor beneath us. We found millions of them along the Atlantic deep coastal regions around Namibia, Africa. They will soon prove to be some of the richest marine diamond deposits ever located.

Then we saw a ghostly shadow in the dark crevasse of the ocean bottom moving along toward a tiger shark. It was a *KRAKEN*, the legend of superstitious seafarers of olden times—the true terror of the deep. This giant squid of the sea-monster fame bore tentacles hundreds of feet long with a marquee of lights blinking on and off in unison, changing colors in beautiful patterns. While we watched, it attacked a shark now twitching in its large monstrous claws instead of suckers as normal squid. Then it paraded its sparkling colors as proud as a peacock over its victory kill. Now the squid suddenly ducked into its lyre, the hull of another sunken ocean liner with the shark still struggling in its vice-like death grip. A moment later the kraken disappeared in the dark passages deep within the ship.

"Iben, you might think that the *Titanic* sinking in the North Atlantic carries the greatest loss of life—but almost four years later the French auxiliary cruiser *Provence* went down in the Mediterranean with a loss of no less than 3,000 lives! Here was that mighty ship that sank in 1916 resting thousands of feet beneath the sea—with this huge sea monster, the great kraken in her bowels!"

From here we explored many Viking ships, Greek and Roman ships full of wondrous marble statues, amphorae, and other archaeological artifacts. Then something very interesting caught my eye. I noticed a strange corroded bronze gismo lying at the bottom of the Mediterranean Sea, probably lost from a Greek ship during a storm. What kind of a structure was this? It seemed to actually have gears and cogged wheels as a modern clock! Was it a type of computer? What kind of strange mechanical device could this be? I could not really tell. Then Aqua Marina enlightened me upon its function.

"Iben," she continued, "such a device has actually been found that has stunned the archaeological world! It is known today as the Antikythera mechanism (a mechanical orrery). It was found in the sea off the island of Antikythera, Greece, in 1902. It is one of the most controversial discoveries ever made!"

It turned out to be a wonderful mechanical astrolabe or

an ancient armillary sphere. It had many interlocking gears similar to a clock. It was used as a computer to calculate the rotation of the planets and stars! And it was manufactured around 80 B.C.! Interestingly, the technology of this device wasn't thought to be known until the Middle Ages when ancient clocks started being produced. Yet, here we see that the ancient Greeks had created a work of genius and even had advanced technology this far back in time! And now we discovered that there were more than just one of these extraordinary instruments created for navigation!

The Bermuda Triangle

We now came to a dark strange vortex—

We had arrived at the Devil's Triangle or Bermuda Triangle, known also to seafarers as the Twilight Zone of the Atlantic!

Now appearing out of the inky black of nothingness were many lost ships and planes.

"What fate did these people encounter?"

"Iben, let the power of psychometry show you what happened."

What Aqua Marina related to me next even sent the very hairs on my neck on end! And it is more bizarre than mortal man can imagine. And this strange phenomenon, I might add, is of the preternatural order of unknown phenomenon.

"And the Lost Patrol?"

"Yes, Iben, also known as Flight 19 where five navy TBM's also called Avengers, on December 5, 1945, were on a routine navigation exercise when they suddenly just disappeared—"

This became one of the strangest unsolved mysteries of the sea and air.

"It will now be revealed to you, Iben, what became of these Avenger planes, along with many other planes and ships."

We solved the enigma of Flight 19.

Are there alternate dimensions within our universe that we are not aware of?

"What about these dimensions?" I asked. "Is the reality of a universe having four or five dimensions possible in a universe having only three dimensions?"

"Physicists," she continued, "have demonstrated that parallel and alternate universes can actually existence. For example, some atoms can change their orbit, while at the same time they still seem to stay in their same orbit! Physicists can't explain it! Certain subatomic 'waves' can pass totally through one atomic nucleus and *at the same time* pass totally through another one beside it. *Also, subatomic matter can also act as particles or waves at the same time!*"

Your soul, I learned, is like this. The living personality or plasma entity which is immaterial belongs *not* only to our three-dimensional world but to other more fantastic worlds. You will even encounter systems of universes yet unknown and actually travel through higher and more complex dimensions! Humans exists in a universe that can only be conceived by the five senses. This is why they are so narrow minded!

A fourth-dimensional universe is the one humans now live in — our three-dimensional universe plus the concept of time.

In a fifth-dimensional universe can have a person doing

his work at the office and at the same time enjoying his favorite hobby!

In a sixth-dimensional universe you could live in the age of the pyramids and in the time of the Romans simultaneously.

A seventh-dimensional universe you could be dead and alive at the same time (as we are now).

In an eighth-dimensional universe you could travel by thought.

In a ninth-dimensional universe you could get college degrees in dozens of subjects from biology to psychology, from math to medicine!

But Iben, I digress. You are wondering what all this has to do with these ships and planes which disappeared in the Bermuda Triangle?

Well, you can relate only the following to the mortal reader. But most divine knowledge must wait until their death.

When God created a multiple dimensional universe paradoxical interstices were formed. These interstices are demarcations between dimensions. When matter travels through them, it is caught between time and space—and the nether world. These strange barriers run in parallel lines straight through the Bermuda Triangle separating all these dimensions so they will not merge into each other causing chaos.

"It is also like the human eye," Aqua Marina concluded. "The retina contains a phenomenon known as the *blind spot* where it is connected to the optic nerve. You are not consciously aware of this spot, but, nevertheless, it is still there. In the same way this 'portal' is found in the Bermuda Triangle."

Chapter Sixteen

The Sharks

*S*harks were a wonderful study. They have lived in the oceans unchanged for over 300 million years, making them survivors equal to that of the scorpion, the cockroach, the horse-shoe crab and the Ginkgo tree! I noticed that some sharks had two separate uteri and before birth the stronger baby shark eats all the others. Therefore, at birth only one baby shark in each uterus is left to be born!

Yes, the world of the shark is a strange one! What a cruel ocean it seemed to be.

"Not so, Iben," Aqua Marina spoke, reading my mind. "You see, the human species kills his fellow beings for sport and pleasure and from rage and anger. This mass extinction of the human race is known to mortals as murder and war. Animals and sea creatures only kill for their food and in the protection of their mates and offspring."

We met Megamouth face to face! Also known as *Megalodon*, this shark was 60 feet in length weighing over 50 tons! It was thought to be a prehistoric extinct species, the largest shark to ever live! We discovered it was actually alive! It still swam deep in the lower depths hidden from all those mortals who thought it had died out millions of years ago!

"But can sharks get cancer?"

"Sharks do have *less* cancer than humans—but they are not immune to it. Yet, the species, *Chondrichthyes,* that includes the sharks, skates and rays, have indeed been cursed with some types of malignancies."

The sharks of the oceans, I learned, are true miracles of nature. They can detect an electric field 25 million times less than a human can. Their sensitivity is the most remarkable in nature. They can detect an electric field of less than five-thousandths of a microvolt per centimeter. It enables sharks and their relatives, the skates and rays to locate hidden prey such as fish hidden beneath the sand on the ocean bottom.

These electric fields guide sharks in their migration and navigation. They help locate their mates through a process known as *electroreception*. And these fish can even electromagnetically orient themselves to the earth's magnetic fields!

I could hardly believe that fish actually possess some of the mechanisms which the birds use in navigation! Then I learned also that butterflies, bees, turtles, whales ... and even many microorganisms such as bacteria and algae use *magnetotaxtis t*o find their way through the oceans, lakes and rivers!

Then we studied the poisonous stonefish and lionfish along with the striped sea catfish—all very deadly to mortals. We saw a strange sight indeed—an armada of venomous sea snakes many miles long swimming through the ocean. What a horrific sight, for their bite is excruciatingly painful and very deadly to mortals, being twice as poisonous as the king cobra!

Atlantis and Mu (Lemuria)

From here we traveled to an undisclosed island off the south equatorial current, miles beyond the coast of South America.

"Iben," Aqua Marina continued, "what now lies before us is a great haunting mystery of a strange remaining civilization, a lost metropolis ... which perished over 15,000 B.C., predating the Egyptian Empire by 10,000 years!"

ATLANTIS! The only surviving ruins of the lost continent of folk-lore and legend. No wonder human beings missed this city for much of it was under a deep stony cliff in a grotto or cave much like Petra, 70 miles south of Jerusalem, or the mysterious lost city of Mesa Verde, Arizona.

In this niche circling a submerged ancient volcano we discovered the center of the necropolis containing beautifully carved statues of solid marble. There were magnificent Acropolis-like temples more beautiful than those in Greece. Preserved from the millennia of time itself, they were mostly intact, though many had been humbled from the erosion of salt water, coral, algae and barnacles. This gave these wondrous structures a surreal effect upon me. The ocean currents moved the emerald seaweed upon them as a breeze would blow Spanish moss over the oak trees of Louisiana.

Yet other grand temples were inlaid with priceless silver and gold, built to honor their ancient gods and heroes—now toppled over in ruins ... from sheer age.

There were also pyramids grander than those of the

Aztecs or even Egypt. Here we found religious temples with wonderful solid gold spires crowning them, and towering ziggurats grander than that of the Babylonian Empire!

Here we realized that Atlantis was a complete conglomerate of all the major architecture of the world! It was as if all civilizations sprang from this one area and borrowed their perfect ideal of construction and promulgated it throughout all the continents of the earth! Then, suddenly and without warning, this complete metropolis succumbed beneath the ocean by a major subterranean sinkhole, and after a while, completely forgotten to history. It has only survived by strange legends and myths, told by imaginative survivors to an incredulous ear.

Atlantis was now lost to the mainstream of science. It was never more to be seen by humankind. Its grand buildings somehow survived drifting to the floor of this massive sinkhole. It crumbled to oblivion in only one day as legend proclaimed. Thousands of inhabitants perished in the deluge as it sank hundreds of feet into the Atlantic without a trace. And here, silently before us, resided this great majestic city, only somewhat worn and tarnished, her beauty and splendor slightly fading after all of these long long centuries!

"Did all the Atlantians perish within this city?"

"Iben, there were a few survivors on the main continent of South America in what is now Venezuela. They are a lost race of primitive peoples known today as the Yanomamo. They were the only survivors of this tragedy and they almost perished, having to go back to the stone age for survival!"

Alas! What a pity, but it just goes to show that the human race isn't as smart as it thinks. Sometimes events can be so radical as to alter the very infrastructure of our civilization or easily alter the total scheme of history. The pet theories that scientists now have as "absolute truth" may be totally disproved in the future!

> "Man is like to vanity; his days are like
> a shadow that passeth away."
> —Ps. 144:4

"Was there also a lost continent of Mu?"

"In fact, Iben, Col. James Churchward wrote his book, *The Lost Continent of Mu*, in 1926 stating that he decoded a secret collection of sacred texts, the *Naacal Tablets*, that he had found in Tibet which told of a series of islands that ran across the Pacific all the way to Easter Island."

Did we locate yet another race of people of olive skin and mysterious dark eyes known as the Muvians from the Lemurian Empire? We explored the depths of the Pacific Ocean to determine if this mystery was indeed factual. We actually discovered that it flourished for a time alongside Atlantis, coined currency and exchanged ideas and commerce not only of gold and silver but foodstuffs and plant seeds, textiles, spices and perfume oils.

The Lemurians did not possess the wealth and secular knowledge of the Atlantians and were somewhat happier because of it! They were a more peaceful society, being against war and capital punishment. The Muvians taught their children the rules of their society, how to love one another in a family environment and live in tranquility. The great world societies of the Twentieth and Twentieth-First Centuries could have learned much from them—but alas…

Aqua Marina informed us that a meteor hit this island

civilization completely vaporizing it into oblivion. The only survivors were those which drifted upon man made rafts to the mainland of North America. With their extraordinary technology lost for all eternity, they finally regressed back into the primitive tribes of the North American Indians!

Now I was shown a strange, mysterious book—*The Book of Dzyan* which allegedly survived the destruction these twin civilizations. It was an anthology of philosophy and wisdom from these ancient peoples, lost and incomplete, handed down verbally and finally written by hand thousands of years before Homer ever conceived of his great epics, *The Iliad* and *The Odyssey*!

I wondered if any other cities in more recent times were destroyed like these. I was instantly shown Port Royal, a busy seaport, located in Jamaica, where in 1692, an earthquake destroyed it. It sank without warning instantly killing 2,000 people and sent thousands of buildings to a watery grave. Coined the "wickedest city on earth" at that time, a haven for pirates, taverns and gambling dens—it literally disappeared on that infamous day many long years ago.

I heard other sounds, faint at first and realized they were coming from one of the Trident strategic submarines in our vicinity, the *USS Arkansas,* which carry long-range ballistic nuclear missiles. We were receiving their radio communications, but were cautioned not to reveal their clandestine messages!

But I knew once again—that the earth had just moved one step closer to imminent danger.

Chapter Seventeen

Jules Verne/H. G. Wells

*A*qua Marina introduced me to some eminent Supernalites. We were at the depth of 35,000 feet with six tons of pressure per square inch upon us. One by one they introduced themselves.

I recognized them to be Jules Verne, the French author; and H. G. Wells, the British author, both geniuses of science fiction. I was in awe and most impressed since I had read most of their writings as a youngster. They were in total ecstasy, their *reward* in the afterlife doing what they did in mortal life, exploring the oceans and the seas. The amity we felt toward each other was awesome—with our thoughts totally enraptured within our hearts and minds.

Then we encountered the *Trieste*—a modern underwater bathysphere. It was exploring the Marianas Trench, the deepest gorge in the Pacific Ocean. The oceanographers were looking out from their thick fused quartz windows, while we were looking back at them from the ocean bottom. But, of course, they were oblivious to us for we were now beings from another time, from another dimension, from literally another world, immortal beings, children of light, saints of the Almighty God, not made in the image of man—but made in the image of God.

We explored the East Pacific Rise, an underwater mountain range southwest of Acapulco, Mexico. I thought that the ocean would be a cold place, but here we discovered wonderful hydrothermal vents—fissures thousands of feet deep. These spewed scalding, acidic water where giant Jericho worms with red plums were undulating as wheat in a field to the ocean currents! They were subjected to extreme temperatures and horrendous pressures, thriving in total darkness at a depth of 8,000 feet! Here we discovered hundreds of new species living in these fervid waters.

Wells spoke, "These tube worms with the red plumbs, contain hemoglobin that combine with hydrogen sulfide. Hydrogen sulfide, emitted from these thermal vents, is oxidized by bacteria then converted into food. In other words, Iben, there is no need for chlorophyll or for photosynthesis for that matter. These species can live where no sun exists— off the heat of the interior of the earth! We discovered that these strange worms are known as chemoautotrophic organisms—metabolizing their food from carbon dioxide and sulfides from the bacteria living inside them."

Awesome! I thought chlorophyll was the precursor of life upon the earth because animal life depended upon it to produce all their food, and yet here—

Within the glassy lava spread along the ocean floor, small volcanoes spewed their super-heated minerals into the ocean forming chimneys known as black smokers. One we coined, *Godzilla,* over a hundred feet tall off the coast of Oregon.

We now explored these vents of super-heated water and found strange one-celled organisms known as the *Methanoccoccus jannaschii.* This species is known as an "archaea" meaning, "ancient." *Two thirds of their genes are not like any life form known today. These exotic creatures, found two miles beneath the ocean, do not fit into any known category or classification known to man.*

Mussels, shrimp, clams, limpets, sea anemones, snakelike fish with bulging eyes, squids and even crabs were all living around these vents. Here we discovered a strange species of shrimp with eye-spots located on their backs, *eyes without lenses* that could see beyond the normal range of the spectrum.

Then Wells revealed the animal life of the deep oceans, namely the Globe-fish, the Oar-fish, the the Albacore, the red deep-sea shrimp and the 'primitive' Horseshoe Crab.

"This Horseshoe Crab looks as if it has been left over from the age of the dinosaurs," I laughed.

Wells continued, "Iben, you are right. You see, the horseshoe crab, *Limulus polyphemus,* is not a crab at all but kin to land spiders and scorpions. It closely resembles the long extinct trilobites which flourished during the Cambrian period 300 million years ago. So it has actually lived *before* the dinosaurs and walked beneath the legs of these great saurians and even survived *after* their demise. Its blood is blue because of its high concentration of copper! It is one of the world's oldest surviving inhabitants. It has two odd pairs of eyes. One is a compound many faceted lensed eye which can see polarized, ultraviolet and infrared light (as found in bees). The other eye is quite small and simple."

Along the ocean's bottom we found an ugly fish having snapping jaws with greenish-yellow eyes and overlapping scales. Its dorsal and pectoral fins were set on stalks of vestigial limbs which looked like it once lived on dry land. What was this fish—unlike anything we had seen up till now?

Wells stated, "Iben, can you tell us what it is?"

"Maybe," I replied. "It looks like a *coelacanth*, a fish believed to have vanished completely from the oceans more than 50 million years ago. One was caught around the Indian Ocean, I believe, in 1938!"

"Right you are, Iben! Evolutionist are still baffled about the origin of this fish!"

I observed the euphoria in the faces and eyes of Verne and Wells alight with the wonders of the deep and they now *knew* why they had been born—*and why they died.*

The camaraderie and interactions of Aqua Marina and all these ocean Luminaries were fantastic! The things they taught and the drinking of pure unadulterated divine knowledge of the oceans of the world was beyond my wildest dreams! Not one person among us being more pompous or pedagogic than the other—all teaching and learning on the same level! Pride and arrogance of the pedagogue had been vanquished between pupil and teacher. What a fantastic thing! Too bad the high schools and universities of the earth couldn't observe and learn much from this mentor/student relationship!

We now encountered a warm Pacific Ocean current discovering an unsettling and chilling phenomenon taking place. The demise of the colorful corals along the Florida coastline that were caused by the reef-killing bacteria, *Sphingomonas*. These bacteria can advance nearly an inch a day leaving behind only bleached coral skeletons. It has, to date, killed over one third of the corals along the Florida coast.

Onward we traveled to the Pacific Atolls, namely the Marshall Islands, Bikini and Eniwetok. Here we witnessed the awesome destruction of the hydrogen fusion weapons of the H-Bomb. We learned about their dire effects upon life species, now only survived by mutant giant rats and radiation-immune cockroaches—another precursor of the end-times.

I learned that from 1945 until 1992 the United States detonated 1,051 nuclear bombs: 210 above ground, 5 underwater, and 836 underground. The vast majority were held in Nevada at Yucca Flats, but over 100 were tested in the Pacific Atoll. There was enough energy released by the Bikini atoll tests to the equivalent of 1 Hiroshima bomb detonated every day… for 25 years!

The USSR, who exploded its first test atomic bomb in 1949 had, by 1989 tested 713, including one in 1961 which was the largest ever detonated—yielding 58 megatons of energy.

What other wonders lay yet for me to discover in this enhanced state of being that mortal man calls only death!

Evolution vs. Creationism

We now found ourselves in the 1850s and have just boarded the sailing ship *H.M.S. Beagle* on which a naturalist kept stating to the members of his crew. "Survival of the fittest" over and over and other redundant phrases of natural selection that seemed to preoccupy the mind of this great scientist.

Wells continued, "Iben, his name is—

"Charles Darwin," I interrupted.

"Yes!" Wells confirmed.

We all set sail across the oceans aboard the *Beagle*, Darwin's ship. We visited the Galapagos Islands, Australia, Tasmania and New Zealand. After five years Darwin returned to England, and wrote his book, *The Origin of Species*, published in 1859.

"So, evolution is true? Life really did evolve into various species?"

"No, no, no, dear Iben!" Wells confirmed. "Far from the truth! Let me tell you the real story of creation. Remember in the Holy Bible … Genesis 1:1, 'In the beginning God created the heaven and the earth.' It seems many scientists have overlooked this important bit of information and developed their own personal theories about earth's creation, leaving God totally out! Many scientists should really be ashamed of themselves!"

Does the Theory of Evolution attack the Christian belief?

Wells continued, "Hitler's system of Nazism and Marx's communism originated from naturalistic philosophy. These ideologies, in turn, cause apostasy, atheism, humanism and liberalism. All these doctrines have proved to corrupt America and helped erode the morals of modern society.

"Were you created only by a freak of nature, Iben, or by a lucky, mindless randomness—or were you created by God?"

"About this Theory of Evolution," I asked? "Is some of it not true?"

"Iben," Wells continued, "even now the Evolutionary Theory still cannot be proved! Evolution is only a *hypothesis* of how life originated and evolved into more complex species. This theory is based on pure faith! Evolutionists state that one simple cell of protoplasm (without a mind to guide it) puts itself together, so they say, forming tissues, organs and the systems in the body of all living things. Yet many scientists proclaim that this *simple indefinable substance* of protoplasm is the *most complex substance known to humankind*! No human has ever come close to manufacturing any of it in the laboratory.

Synthetic Biology/Miller-Urey/ Rebek Experiments

"Also, scientists, in a process known as *synthetic biology* are experimenting with recombinant DNA trying to produce artificial life in the laboratory. Artificial life is defined as being produced totally from non-living materials, i.e. totally man-made.

"Bioengineers are splicing genes into bacterial cells creating new cells known as *synthetic cellular reconstruction*. In this process, known as DNA sequencing, the genes of one creature are spliced into another cell's genome, producing new colonies of the same bacterium. Thus synthetic biology is really only a *recreation* of existing life—not a *totally unique life form*. But are those scientists in charge of such bioengineering ready for the responsibility of such knowledge and it dire consequences upon the environment? We can just look at the oil crisis, atomic energy and the burning of coal and all their pollution, including the process of fracking (wastewater injection wells) to produce natural gas … causing earthquakes ... to learn how environmental issues can effect everyone upon our fragile planet.

"Was Mary Shelly, who wrote *Frankenstein*, actually warning us way back in the 1800s about attaining such inauspicius knowledge?"

"How about the Miller-Urey experiment?" I questioned, learning about it in my old chemistry class in high school.

Verne now spoke, "Oh, that! This experiment, as you know, is where a flask of inorganic chemicals is charged with electricity to resemble lightning. This does produce some macromolecules resulting in the formation of some amino acids. But, if the experiment continues, these large molecules (polypeptides) will actually break down into simpler molecules thus destroying all hope of producing the phenomenon of life."

"Wasn't there an experiment that someone created a synthetic living molecule from scratch?"

"Yes," stated Verne, "this is known as the Rebek Experiment. Scientists used the processs of *molecular recognition* in creating the *first synthetic organic molecule* that can reproduce itself. Julis Rebek, an MIT chemist, combined the basic building blocks of some amino acids.

But was it actually alive? Do snowflakes or many mineral crystals replicate? Are they considered *alive*? Just because a substance replicates does *not* prove that it is actually alive. Biologists have many criteria to define life and the *ability of replication* is only one of them and life must be defined *if* a substance meets *all* of these criteria at the same time. Some of these criteria are: respond to stimuli or irritability, movement, growth, nutrition and reproduction. So the riddle of life continues … when do amino acids actually combine to form a living entity?

"Iben, ever heard of the phrase *ontogeny recapitulates phylogeny*?"

"Yes, isn't that where embryologists state that the gills in the human embryo develop into lungs?"

"That is what they believe," Verne continued. "Evolutionists have stated that the human embryo passes through a gilled stage in development to the fetus. This is *not* possible, for the human embryo does *not* have any gill-like structures or vestigial organs like gills that later become lungs."

"I thought the human embryo passes through an evolutionary phase as a kind of sped up evolutionary process?"

"This accelerated process of evolution is totally false. This theory, created by Professor Ernst Haeckel in the late 1800s, has already been *disproved*! Yet, college professors teach it as *fact*!

"Also, Lamarck's theory that giraffes have longer necks because they had stretched their necks trying to reach higher greenery and over thousands of years their necks expanded to reach these leaves. This has also been *discarded* years ago even by the evolutionists! Yet, the same conclusion is reached if rats jumped into water and tried to grow gills, how long would it take them to succeed? So, if evolutionists believe this, let them start jumping off a high cliff and see how long it takes them to learn to sprout wings.

"Another thing, Iben, is the mystery of the bombardier beetle. Inside this insect are two chambers which produce two harmless chemicals, hydrogen peroxide and hydroquinone. When they are mixed together there is an explosive reaction which deters any predator from eating them. If those chemicals were not mixed correctly, they would blow themselves up! So how, without Divine Guidance, could this little beetle ever succeed in accomplishing this miracle of nature?

"Also, a complicated watch could never, even in a 100 million years, be formed from randomness. It takes a type of intelligence to make it. You see, it has a *purpose*, and that is to tell time to a higher being (the human). So how could it form unless an outside force created it for a *specific purpose*? In other words, *a watch would not just compose itself without some entity wanting to track the concept of time.*"

Verne now explained that the Evolutionary Theory is like believing there could be an accidental explosion in a printing shop and come out with the works of Shakespeare!"

Therefore, I concluded, that all life was created by the wisdom of an *Intelligent Designer.*

"One other thing, Iben," Verne concluded, "evolutionists believe that whales even have vestigial legs and surmise that they, instead of leaving the ocean to live on land, *left the land and returned to the ocean*!"

A hundred other facts concerning evolution as being a

false belief were expounded before me, proving without a doubt that *Divine Intelligence* created life and giving it that DIVINE SPARK separating mankind from the animals. And true wisdom begins with the "fear of the LORD."

Theomorphic Ubiquity

The Supernalites and I could transverse through time and enter a strange state known as *theomorphic ubiquity*. In this reality we can converse with a hundred people in a moment ... or travel through all the oceans at the same time! It is like a total dream but a reality I know to be true. Yet, it made perfect sense. Let me explain. When I was a mortal I can remember waking up having dreamed two dreams at the same time! I believe that since the brain is composed of two halves, both halves can dream separate dreams at the same time, thus the person can remember both dreams as if he were doing two completely different things (like taking a bath and riding a horse) simultaneously! So this, traveling back in time observing the ocean explorers and exploring these exotic dimensions is becoming more commonplace and thus, more normal for me.

We studied all the prolific toxic pollution at the bottom of our oceans. There were hundreds of fifty-five gallon drums containing highly poisonous nuclear wastes, many low-level radiation wastes buried on military reservations and dumped into the ocean. Even Russia has dumped tons of plutonium wastes from atomic research labs into a prime squid fishing area in the Sea of Japan.

We now proceeded to the Alaska Peninsula where the *Exxon Valdez*, a supertanker, spilled over 11 million gallons of crude oil into Prince William Sound just below Valdez, Alaska causing a great ecological disaster.

Then we went to the North Sea where the Piper Alpha oil platform exploded killing 166 people. This rig was producing 140,000 barrels of oil a day causing untold environmental damage to the area.

Prophecy was revealed that yet other oil disasters will occur in the near future. There will be British Petroleum (BP) oil spill in the Gulf of Mexico, drilling rig known as Deepwater Horizon which will explode...

We learned that the fishing industry of the world has been ruined by toxic chemicals from pesticides and fertilizers. Many deadly chemicals such as PCB's (Polychlorinated Biphenyls) have been discovered in fish—rendering them sterile.

We learned that the oceans of the world are becoming acidic. This acidification of the oceans is threatening its marine life.

Alternative Fuels

I also realized how the human race could alleviate some of the world's pollution. There are many plants which can be made into alternate fuels, such as many varities of corn, *Jatropha curcas* (a weed from India), the common switchweed, and the giant Miscanthus. Coastal Bermuda grass, along with numerous weeds such as camelina and pennycress, can be used. Even coconut oil, pond scum, seaweed, ocean brown kelp, sunflowers, and bamboo can produce biofuels.

But, of course, I learned, that hydrogen will be one of the most efficient fuels for the future of mankind."

I learned that water separated by hydrolysis can produce a very proficient non-polluting source of energy.

But scientists, I learned, may be looking at the problem incorrectly of splitting water into its components. They should, instead, be thinking about *combining hydrogen and oxygen together*! You see, when oxygen and hydrogen are combined, explosive energy is produced. The by-product made when this happens—instead of polluting the environment—forms only water! You see, 20 cubic feet of hydrogen gas combined with 10 cubic feet of oxygen gas, when ignited by a spark—produces *energy* and *one pound* of water!" The hydrogen car is now being developed throughout the world. These models, known as *zero-emission technology*, take compressed hydrogen gas to produce electricity, and as stated earlier, leaves only *water* as its exhaust!

"At the rate of pollution," Aqua Marina concluded, "we are seeing now, unless something is done real soon, our oceans will be a filthy cesspool of stinking and dead carcasses. And without our oceans—the human race is doomed."

It was now time to bid the Supernalites, Verne and Wells farewell. Such amity we shared! Then they evanesced back into the mysterious oceans.

Rising upward, Aqua Marina and I were now tossed from a wave much as a cork is blown from a bottle. I caught a cross wind arriving in a tropical rain forest along the coast of Malaysia!

We encountered beautiful herons, egrets and white

albatross. There were tapirs and tree monkeys all agitated by a thick smoke—

Forests were aflame from plantation owners clearing their land in Indonesia over 100 miles away. This ash-filled smoke had spread on to Singapore, Brunei, Thailand and even to the Philippines, disrupting air traffic and closing schools.

It seems strange that I can be learning so much as my curiosity was limited before, either by myself or by my circumstances. But now the more I observed the natural world—the more I wanted to study and learn. The enhanced human mind of the Supernalite is insatiable in its curiosity and unfathomable in its comprehension.

The tropical rain forest was alive with wild orchids, flowering trillium and blue phlox with their redolence filling the air with perfume, while wild bees, exotic insects and colorful butterflies swarmed all about.

Here we studied a strange butterfly known as *Heliconius sara* whose caterpillar eats only passion vines of the genus *Passiflora*. The anomaly is that these vines contain deadly cyanide to protect the vines from predators. We learned how these caterpillars eat these vines and and yet survive this deadly poison.

Now Aqua Marina stated she must be leaving, and effervesced back into the oceans of the world.

I became mesmerized with all I had seen which left me with some profound maxims:

"Why can't humankind learn to live in peace,
for life is short, but life's potential is illimitable.

God has everything under his control —
no matter what the circumstances fate has brought you —
God is in the midst thereof.
—The Author

The Choice

We are our own worst enemy.
We have the choice to direct our lives
for Good or for Evil.
We put poisons into our bodies:
alcohol, cigarette smoke, drugs, etc.
and wonder why they sputter, backfire, and die.
Yet, we each have within our grasp
the Spiritual Wisdom to direct ourselves
to a Greater Potential—a Divine Purpose
to become all we are capable of—
to sprout the Seed of Destruction,
or sprout the Seed of Deliverance.
—The Author

And a lesson to myself about being so blind and disinterested in nature and the beautiful things around me before I died. Here are some platitudes I pondered…

"Live the day to its fullest for each passes but once, remembering that life is a precious gift, a sparkling diamond imbued with divine love,

a grand miracle of supreme wonder —
yet only a tiny moment formed by the infinity of God."
—The Author

"We cannot hold a torch to light another's path
without brightening our own."
—Ben Sweetland

"You cannot go back and have a new beginning—
But you can start now to go forward
and have a new ending."
—Carl Bard

In addition, the lesson to be learned by those people
which find life dull, prosaic and boring…

Lost time is never found again.
But I learned after death…
TIME IS DESTROYED BY ETERNITY,
FINITE IS DESTROYED BY INFINITY,
AND MORTALITY IS DESTROYED
BY IMMORTALITY.

CHAPTER EIGHTEEN

Welcome to the Inner-Cosmos— the Human Body.

At treetop level we were now enjoying the close up of view green leaves shining in the sun. I realized that I had no fear of falling. Falling was a worldly instinct and it is odd how quickly I forfeited it. Gravity had lost its power over me.

I now realized the awesome potential of my spiritual body. I could travel subsonic (as we had been doing in the oceans), supersonic (faster than sound as on the space station) or hypersonic, as fast as light (as I did earlier to Alaska) or superhypersonic (travel faster than the speed of light)!

Another refulgent Angelic Divine Counselor now appeared.

"My name is Micronia. I will be your next guide through more great wonders."

I had always had a great passion to travel into the world

of the minute, the small microscopic world of nature and of the universe.

"How shall we start?" Micronia questioned. "Want to travel into the realm of the atom, the building block of the universe or through the human body?"

"You mean we can actually travel through the—"

"Through the human body, Iben, yes. That is your choice?"

"Ever since I received a microscope at the age of eight, and after reading *Fantastic Voyage* by Isaac Asimov, I have wanted to study the mystery of the inner cosmos. Yes, the human body would be an awesome quest," I answered, surprising even myself.

With this Micronia and I began to drift over a small community in Oklahoma City. I hadn't realized it had now been many years since the Oklahoma City bombing. It seemed like only yesterday and in Eternity it is!

> "But, beloved, be not ignorant of this one thing,
> that one day is with the Lord as a thousand years,
> and a thousand years as one day."
> —2 Pet. 3:8

We entered Seminole County and arrive at Sacred Heart, a small community about fifty miles southeast of Oklahoma City, a habitat of mostly rural farms. Here we stealthily entered a small farm house, being invisible to any mortal who happened to be inside.

Micronia spoke, "Iben, this woman before us will be our subject for the exploration of the human body — a complete universe within a universe!"

Even before her face became visible—we began to shrink smaller and smaller. As the room greatly increased in its size, a mosquito buzzed by as big as a car with its proboscis as long as a sword!

Still smaller we shrank until the dresser drawers and bed became unrecognizable, the snow-white top sheet which covered this lady towered above us as a massive snowy mountain a thousand feet high containing canyons and crevasses hundreds of feet deep.

At this moment I came eye to eye with a ghastly looking creepy crawler, a giant bug as big as a house, bloated with the blood of its victim!

"Iben, these monsters are commonly known as bed bugs!"

"But this is an isolated case, right?"

"My dear Iben. I wish it were so. These parasites are brought into our country on passengers from ships and planes coming into the United States."

As we grew progressively smaller I could see much tinier creatures looking like little bears moving across this "mountain," being only a wrinkle in the bed sheet. I learned that these were tiny dust mites! As we neared this huge wrinkle, it became a convoluted material of knots, turning and twisting in large circles and swirls—the threads of tiny cotton fabric which looked like a veritable jungle of twisting vines of some alien world. These dust mites, their red hairy jointed legs and their roving red eyes lived in colonies upon these sheets, as mountain goats upon an Alpine tundra. They were eating tiny pieces of her dead skin that shed from her body. These mites, to us looking as big as cattle, were grazing upon these flakes of skin.

The once narrow decorative blue stripes on her bed sheets were now as large as interstate highways. This lady in relation to our diminutive size stretched many miles long!

I realized we were one ten thousandth of an inch in diameter. Smaller and smaller we grew, drifting into great cords of hair seeming to us now bigger than oaks.

From her scalp we entered a pore in her skin following a single hair down into the live dermis. Here we encountered a bizzar creature identified as a follicle mite. Then we traveled on through the subcutaneous layer. Total darkness. Then, as our hypervision adjusted, strange formations came into view ... such as the skin's sweat glands.

I realized that we were now one millionth of an inch in size—or about the size of a tiny microbe.

The moved on through the bony structure of the skull penetrating through it entering the dura matter, the arachnoid membrane and the pia matter. We plunged through a force field or barrier shrouded as in a thick opaque teleplasmic mist or fog.

The Human Brain

"Iben," Micronia announced, "behold, the human brain! *That great raveled knot*, as proclaimed by the neurophysiologist Sir Charles Sherrington. The human brain is the greatest enigma of all containing strange dreams, hidden memory and cosmic thought. That one fantastic organ above all others that produces a rational being, having an awareness and consciousness. Molded by Almighty God, the mind has that spark of divinity, that unbridgeable chasm between man and beast."

"A triunity, made up of body, soul and spirit, placed in
sovereignty over the earth, crowned with glory and honor."
—C.I. Scofield

"So God created man in his own
image, in the image of God
created he him; male and female created he them."
—Gen. 1:27

Through this dense fog we discovered the living human
brain in all its magnificence. Micronia and I stood in awe
of it. It was only a little over three pounds of cellular tissue
creating a major split in the animal kingdom, separating the
human species from the lower forms of life.

Micronia explained that God created *Homo sapiens*
with the largest brain mass to its body weight—around
2%. The cerebral cortex, the thinking part or outer brain
makes human beings totally unique. Here were billions of
neurons in a vast wonderful spider web or network of tissue,
a delicate, yet fabulously complicated computer having
trillions of bytes of information processing 100 million
messages every *second,* having a storage data bank larger
than some libraries have books. It also uses, I learned, about
25% of the body's oxygen intake and 20% of the blood
supply, generating 0.07 volts or about 70 millivolts (one
thousandth of a volt). Yet, we observed the brain utilizing
about 20 watts of power when alert.

Micronia continued to reveal this wonder of the human
brain, more complex than anything I had ever seen. We
passed through its cerebral hemispheres and entered the
frontal lobe. Here we encountered electrochemical energy,

the current of human thought. We learned all about the electrophysiology of the human mind. The frontal lobe, I learned, controls motor functions of the body, the eyes and mouth, arms, neck and head. From here we traveled to the thalamus, which controls temperature, pressure and the sensations of heat, cold, pain and touch.

We encountered the cerebral cortex, the outer and most complex section of the brain, containing the hyper-cognoscere—the magnificent thinking mind.

We were now so small each neuron was larger than a rail-car, where we could observe the firing of the efferent and afferent dendrites and axions of each nerve impulse. We could actually feel the surge of electrical brain waves as electricity surges through a wire!

Micronia informed me that this lady was in a deep sleep mode. I realize that we could tap into her electro-magnetic energy field and actually see into her dreams. She was having a strange nightmare!

I spotted an evil specter distorting her brain waves. Micronia unleashed his scepter as powerful as a bolt of lightning, just as the homunculus raised its tiny red eyes and let out a hiss—it was blasted into oblivion.

Prayer defined

"Be cautious, Iben," Micronia continued, "for there are all sort of these mendacious demons present in her mind. For years, psychologists have stated that prayer is nothing more than a person influencing their subconscious mind through self-induced hypnosis."

"I have always wondered about the mystery of prayer and how we can communicate with God."

"My dear Iben, is prayer just a brain-altering state as those of transcendental meditation proclaim? By thinking such we are leaving out its most important concept—*contact* with the Almighty! Psychologists have proclaimed that prayer is nothing more than a person influencing their subconscious mind to seek its own selfish goals and desires. The physiology of prayer can actually alter physical brain-cells and neurons. This can cause euphoria and actually cure depression by blocking monoamine oxidase, an enzyme that presents the build-up of neurotransmitters such as serotonin, norephinephrine, dopamine and enkephalin.

"Prayer, can be defined as the ability to communicate via psychotronic processes (receiving divine knowledge from an outside source) with supernatural omniscient Cosmic Intelligence (God) having vast spiritual wisdom and divine knowledge way beyond our natural mental realm. There is also an *unknown factor* ... beyond the electro-magnetic realm past the hectometric waves ... known to science as *radionics*—or ultra high frequency waves. These *spiritual waves* which prayer utilizes can be defined as D*ivine Telepathic Communication*.

"Prayer is a *communication conveyance system* of divine origin incorporated by phenomena not yet perceived nor comprehended from ESP (extra-sensory perception) to telesthesia (information beyond the natural five senses)."

I now understood the living brain, its awesome functions and saw how through the effort of systematic prayer and faith—we can converse and commune directly with the Grand Designer of the universe!

"Prayer, through the phenomenon of supersonics or the utilization of ultra-frequencies from God, can cure asthma, high blood pressure and anxiety. It also produces *delta* and *theta* waves throughout the brain caused from pacification, where the brain becomes tranquil, calm, serene and peaceful. Prayer can have a positive effect on fungi and even make plants grow healther! People who pray don't die as often in the hospitals and need less drugs for pain. The risk of dying from entering the hospital is much lower for those who attend church. Prayer calms the nerves, prevents depression, and also prevents suicide. Another way of thinking about prayer is that it can also trigger the happiness gene of the human genome, activating *eudaimonic processes* of wellbeing. Through prayer we can become so positive and confident that our body fights off diseases, reinforces antibodies, stop arthrisis pain, and can even destroy harmful viruses and cancer.

"Prayer and faith, Iben, have been shown to speed recovery of alcoholism, bone surgery, drug addiction, stroke, rheumatoid arthritis and heart attacks. It lowers the level of the harmful stress hormone cortisol which helps the body live longer. Prayer helps fight off diseases and has even been proven to heal bones and cure depression. Love, amity and compassion are the positive aspects to this healing power. Also, *prayer is not just a physiological phenomenon* which affects the human brain. It can be defined as a direct *mind-link* with God. *Prayer is a portal to God's healing power, divine revelation and guidance.* It can also lead to a *divine anointing*, or a *direct manifestation of the Holy Spirit.* You see, prayer, through the blood of Jesus, opens up a bridge between man and God just as it opens up the path to the Holy of Holies into God's glorious Kingdom. We can *now* communicate to God and God can *now* communicate to us."

It is sad that many people just don't utilize this opportunity of Divine Infinite Power to actually converse with the Ultimate Supreme Being, the Comforter, the Creator of the Universe. Yet, prayer is not used to its full potential, being far greater than mortal humans could ever understand. It still exists, nevertheless, to show the Way and the Truth and guide those wise enough to pray to God, to thank Him for their many blessings and to SUPPLICATE HIS ULTIMATE POWER AND WISDOM IN THEIR LIVES!

Micronia continued, "Through the power of prayer most of these homunculus, incubus or imps can be eliminated, though there are some very resilient impostors known as Chupacabra which are much stronger. The one I just zapped with my scepter was from the suborder of evil Archangels, called Envy."

This lady, I learned, was envious of another lady where she worked and so let this evil entity into her mind.

"Mortals acquire these evil beings via bad movies, diabolical friends, impure music, drugs and being bullied when young or at work. The minds of most humans are infested with such demons.

"Remember, Iben, when you were killed, that shadowy effluvium which was released at the time of your death? That was these incubus being released from your mind and body. I didn't really destroy it, it just fled away into space, searching for another victim's mind to enter at the right moment when their attention is diverted from God's Will. It should be known that this woman had just prayed before she went to sleep, otherwise I wouldn't have had the divine power to confront this demon. To chase some of these incubus away is part of our Spiritual Divine Mission here on this fantastic journey through the human brain."

I now knew why there was so much evil in the world. These evil incubus, were ubiquitous in all the minds of the earth, no exceptions (except one—Jesus Christ). We have witnessed many deaths since we began our odyssey and I had noticed some strange evil effluvium separating from the souls at the instant of death but only now realized what it was!

"This incubus exists within a different plane than us. These imps live in a different level of reality and dimensions—a strange world of distorted thoughts and dreams of which they are very comfortable. Out of the human body they exist in accursed ellipsoid and polygon dimensions. Entering these dimensions would be like nothing the human mind could fathom, a total impossibility in the space-time continuum as mortals comprehend things."

The human brain producing electrochemical reactions actually creating thought and reasoning. Totally incredible!

The cerebral cortex, I discovered, is the seat for higher learning and critical thinking. The left brain, neurologists used to think, contained the logic and talking and the right side controlled the creative and emotional aspect of thought. But we discovered the mind to be much more complex than this—that impulses are carried all across and inside the brain in complex thinking.

The cerebral cortex, I learned, is divided into two main halves by a large bundle of nerves known as the corpus callosum. Ambidextrous people (those that use both their right hand and left hands equally well) have a larger corpus callosum than those that don't. Interestingly, the total brain volume contains more white matter extending from the front to the back of the brain, while the female brain has more of these connection running between the two hemispheres of the cerebral cortex.

"The whole human brain consists of over 100 billion nerve cells. These neurons are connected by synapses, dendrites and axons. These neurons 'fire' their electrical charges causing data to move along from cell to cell in one thousandth of a second, the precursor of a tiny thought. When hundreds of millions of these fire all at once the phenomenon of consciousness or awareness is born. This is known as *hyperneuron activity*."

Along our journey, we encountered some effulgent Supernalites, all dressed in the period of their times, reaping their rewards in the Afterlife. Deep within the *basal ganglia* of the cerebrum, we encountered Sigmund Freud, who was the Austrian physician, the "Father of Psychoanalysis." Next to him was Carl Gusgtav Jung, a Swiss psychiatrist, who developed "analytical psychology." Freud believed that dreams were mostly romantic, while Jung thought dreams were of a more religious nature. Both realized now that their petty theories evaporated into scientific myth as they were awed by the human mind—humbled by its vastness and complexity.

Later, across the *fissure of Rolando*, just within the temporal lobe, we discovered Ivan Pavlov, a Russian physiologist, who coined the term, "conditioned reflex." He was conversing with William James, psychologist, "father of American pragmatic philosophy," who also delved into the religious aspects of the mind, and was interested in extrasensory perception such as clairvoyance, telepathy, and hyperkinesis (known collectively as "*Psi* Phenomena). They were studying the brain as they did in their past lives, still learning the secrets of neuropathology, cognitive thinking and latent memory.

We didn't disturb them, but continued on our way... now encountering the brain's chemical transmitters. There were millions of amino acids, endorphins and their components enkephalins that reduce pain or even block it. Then we discovered dopamine and oxytocin. They can be released by a hug, a kiss, a word of praise or even by touch releasing the feeling of love and euphoria. Dopamine is considered the master molecule of addiction. I learned that chocolate contains similar chemicals that affects the brain and are called the 'love' chemicals. This hormone, along with oxytocin, combined to produce the "mother and child bond" and the *cuddle-syndrome.* The lack of dopamine, I learned, causes Parkinson's disease. Oxytocin triggers the bond that couples have when they fall in love.

In the pituitary gland we found natural pain killers which behave like morphine. We located *norandryalin*, the mood, appetite and learning chemical. This chemical gives a person the feeling of bliss, euphoria or pain. We discovered serotonin throughout the brain and learned how the LSD molecule is a close copy of this chemical and therefore causes hallucinations. Even laughing increases catecholamines and cytokines (both linked to alleviating depression and lowering blood pressure) which reduces inflammation by activating the immune system.

I spotted some interesting polypeptides.

Pointing to each of them he stated, "This one is cortisone and that one is estrogen and this one is testosterone."

Testosterone is a male hormone. What is it doing in a female body?

"Right, you are Iben." Micronia continued, "there are female and male hormones, which regulate both the female and male bodies! The woman's libido (sexual desire) is regulated by small amounts of testosterone!"

Another protein we found was *cholecystokinin tetrapeptide* (CCK-4) which the female brain releases in times of stress or premenstrual syndrome. It can cause panic, nausea, irritability and even induce headaches in women during their "periods," or menstrual cycles.

That's a very important one! I thought.

Blocked by a somewhat thick fog we finally located the hippocampus, the brain's center for short and long term memory. We now entered the cerebellum. I learned that it contains half of the brain's neurons and processes memory. Besides regulating the speed, intensity and direction of movement, the cerebellum has a massive cable of fibers consisting of over 40 million nerves traveling to the cerebral cortex. (I learned that this was 40 times as large as the optic nerve). Located in the cerebellum we found the *neodentate nucleus.* It is present *only* in humans and controls the processing of language.

I now realized that this lady under our scrutiny will start to have some memory problems when she reaches 85 years old. But now we see only a hundred or so cells affected by it so it will be many years before other cells become involved, degeneration occurs and the symptoms of dementia materialize.

We next studied the amygdala, Greek for "almond shaped." I located both of them, one on each side of the brain.

Besides being the waking and sleeping center of in the brain, the amygdala protects a person from the threat of danger. If danger presents itself they trigger the autonomic (subconscious) nervous system, alerting the body. The amygdala is also the seat of aggression and fear. Here the amygdala determines if a person will become an introvert or an extrovert, temperamental, shy or bashful. It is the supersensitive thermostat of the brain. The amygdala makes the hyper-fast blink of the eye without thinking which can save one's sight in an instant! But if the amygdala overreacts and gets overloaded it can cause phobias, panic attacks and the Post Traumatic Stress Disorders (PTSD) afflicting war heroes and rape victims—inducing violent nightmares"

We learned the mystery of how meditation and prayer actually increases the blood supply sending more oxygen altering the brain's neurons thus increasing mental prowess, clarity of mind and enhancing social behavior. *Christian prayers do much more—they actually contact the True Source of wisdom, the Divine Power of miracles, healing and peace of the Holy Spirit.*

Sleep

Through this fog we now entered the hypothalamus. Here we found the *suprachiasmatic nucleus* which is the master clock of the brain. It regulates the day and night cycles, the circadian rhythm of the brain. It determines if you will be a morning lark or a night owl. It controls the male and female personality and the development of a heterosexual or a homosexual person.

Next, we learned why both sleep and dreaming are necessary. Sleep is vital for our body to function properly. It is necessary for its steady growth, tissue repair and cellular regeneration. Sleep also helps the brain to process information. Lack of sleep, I learned, promotes obesity and accelerates the aging process. It raises the risks of high blood pressure, heart disease, diabetes, depression and anxiety. It increases amyloid-beta protein, along with beta and gamma-secretase, that mutate into sticky clumps forming plaques. These plaques can lead to the death of brain neurons. Older people lose acetylcholine, a neurotransmitter crucial to memory function. Noteworthy, it is little known fact that most of the Cherokee Indians do *not* get Alzheimer's disease! Could there be a gene that prevents this in these Indians? Also, the lowering of your blood pressure back to normal reading of 120 can result in fewer cases of dementia.

Next, we entered the insular cortex where stress here can actually stop the heart. Stress can kill a perfectly healthy person who otherwise eats right and even works out!

Aspirin

All the chemicals within the brain we now identified.

"What is that chemical," I asked, floating by—

"Iben Jair, that is acetylsalicylic acid, the miracle compound aspirin. This lady has taken some hoping it will alleviate her headache pain."

The mystery was solved on how aspirin works. It acts as an analgesic by blocking the enzyme and hormone prostaglandins which inhibits the firing of the electrochemical signal running across the synapses between the neurons. Aspirin, I found, also acts as a blood thinner and keeps the blood platelets from clumping together, thus preventing deadly heart attacks. It can also cure certain cancers such as those found in the stomach, esophagus, colon and rectum.

Next we enter the *labyrinth of cognition* lying hidden in the mist of this fog close to the hypocampus, the harbinger of dreams and intuition, of latent talent and many times of unrewarded genius. I now realized just how complex the human mind actually is ... and that—

"We are made in the *image of God*!"

Made in the Image of God

"What does this mean, Micronia?"

"What did God mean by—*made in His Image*? Iben, this statement can revolutionize human relationships! Is this merely the physical (anthropomorphic) resemblance of humans to God? Or does it mean grander things? Of all God's creation humans are truly unique upon Earth. Man has been endued with creativity, imagination and purpose. Mankind is the crowning masterpiece of God's creation. Again, upon the planet Earth humankind is the Creator's peak of opulence of achievement. *And the Christian, through the atoning blood of Jesus, is the offspring of God with unfathomable potential!*"

This lady's emotions triggered from her day's stress has given her a headache. Depressed people develop more heart problems and those that repress anger get cancer more often.

"Iben, there is a major link to emotion and cancer! Yet, those people that attend church get less cancer and heart attacks! Another good reason to attend the Christian church of your choice. The Holy Spirit has a positive effect upon the mind and the physical body. And negative emotions weaken the immune system while positive emotions actually strengthen it."

I learned how good attitudes and a strong belief in God can relieve stress and actually prevent disease! Also those who are in love have a more responsive immune system. Even men who are happily married have a lower risk of chest pain! Human companionship has a marvelous effect upon the well-being of a person. Visiting patients in hospitals can speed their recovery time. Married people have fewer diseases, survive cancer better and can actually live longer than the unmarried. Faith can even prevent depression!

From here we passed on through the mysterious fog exploring the great arteries and veins of the brain. What a magnificent structure is the human brain, a total unique miracle created from the Mind and Image of God himself!

Einstein's Brain

Here we entered the cerebellum and pons discovering many oligodendroglia helper cells. The smarter you are and the higher your I.Q., the more of these cells you have. These cells form a vast, complicated neural network more than those that do not utilize their minds to their full potential. It should be noted that Einstein's brain had *four-times more* of these helper cells, along with a profusion of glial cells and astrocytes, all of which increase intelligence.

Dreams and Nightmares

We could observe her brain waves much like watching a TV program and actually probe her dreams! We could interpret these waves and see how her stress and trauma was affecting them.

Dreaming, I learned, was not only a way for the mind to purge itself by processing new information received each day, but a *device to penetrate into the depths of alternate worlds.* When you are in tune to God's blessings and favor, you can partake in *special divine dreams* that reveal the heavenly realm. Some have vivid dreams of being in Heaven each night. Yet others visit the dimension of Hell—experiencing evil nightmares. And many people in their dreams—sometimes visit both!

Some of the things she dreamed seemed rather familiar to me in my past life. I also had vivid encounters with the subconscious mind where reality and fantasy mingled together.

The Strange Bridge Dream

Night terrors crawled forth. We encountered stranger dark veiled phantoms with shadowy bodies, deep cold dungeons and twisting stairways going nowhere and massive deep dark open wells to fall into. There were also rats and spiders, sinister snakes and creepy crawlers and other horrible specters that go bump in the dark resided in these extremely realistic, colorful and panoramic nightmares.

Horror and the macabre played out before us during her rapid eye movement (REM) sleep. Other dreams were of a long suspension bridge spanning high over some vast unknown abyss. She and her friends were walking across it, their final destination upon the other side shrouded in a Stygian darkness. This abyss was an immense cauldron of swirling clouds far below, miles in diameter as a huge hurricane with this gaping hole in the center. Larger and larger it loomed before her and she watched in great trepidation a suspension bridge began to sway upon its side with large numbers of helpless people sliding and falling from it screaming and inexorably disappearing into this deep strange pit of dark oblivion. She was on the verge of being caught in this hellish vortex herself ... almost awoke, shifted and turned upon her side. This finished the dream as she almost regained consciousness. Once again she settled into another dreaming state but that last nightmare of the bridge and maelstrom was gone, to be replaced by a much tamer fantasy.

I couldn't place my finger exactly on it but some of the phantoms in her dreams seemed vaguely personal and familiar. It was some type of *deja vu* I felt toward this lady and her life. I was beginning to have more than just a passing interest in this woman of whose brain I was coursing through whetting my interest to learn more about her.

With her asleep, I figured, the brain was asleep also. I now realized the mind was just as active asleep and it was awake! Even while sleeping the brain continues to handle enough neural impulses to run the entire world's electrical grids!

We learned about the cause and cure of schizophrenia. We recognized other macromolecules in the blood. I recognized one as *docosahexaenoic acid* (DHA). Remember, Iben, that fish oil and those sardines contain this DHA.

It inproves the infant brain's development and prevents Alzheimzer's disease (*senile dementia*) and Huntington's disease.

Learning actually forces the corpus callosum to grow thus connecting both halves of the brain with better communication. And smoking, besides reducing blood flow to the brain, also raises the possibility of a blood clot here. Smoking, I discovered, actually *increases the risk of cognitive degeneration* as humans age.

Then a rather strange substance floated by.

Micronia now pointing his finger, "Iben, this is histamine, a brain transmitter, which produces hyperactivity and a high tolerance for pain. The male brain has more histamine which is the reason men commit suicide more than women."

What a buzz of activity was the human brain! We counted over five thousand enzymes with over two million chemical reactions per minute! Awesome!

The Mystery of Latent Genius

Near these areas we found another mystery. I always wondered why some people did not do so well with menial jobs such as working as a teller in a bank, stocking groceries, or sorting mail. They were always making mistakes and were not considered very good at their jobs. Some even considered them to be "slow" at their work. Then I found out the reason. Many of these people were actually very smart but were focused upon more pertinent matters, having their brain wired differently than others. Einstein, when he was young, was like this.

Then we discovered a few completely unknown areas in the brain. We realized them to be esoteric nerves that regulates the "focused desire" of a person. Those problem-solving thoughts that the average person does not normally think about — but *these* people do. Many of them who have trouble at their jobs seem to have a short attention span, when actually they are just interested in other areas of endeavor, a *digressive mentality* which affects their short term cognitive thinking. These people, usually highly intelligent, have not found their true interest to really motivate them and they are working in an environment of which they are not suited. Many never discover their true abilities or penchants in life. Therefore, they are usually moody, morose individuals that many times seem lost, melancholic or depressive. Yet other employees do a good job by suppressing these emotions by becoming jovial or happy-go-lucky at work. Yet others commit suicide.

The Methuselah Factor

We discovered the Methuselah factor in cells or the *telomere* enzyme, also called the *Fountain of Youth* enzyme. This enzyme controls the division of cells that cause aging and resides in each chromosome. It regulates all cell division and reproduction. If this telomerase weakens, a cell could divide indefinitely. But *without* the action of telomerase, cancer can form in the cell. So the body has made a choice. Live a shorter life and die without cancer or live longer and develop cancer.

We learned the secrets of Down's Syndrome, Alzheimer's disease, Cerebral Palsy, Muscular Dystrophy, Multiple

Sclerosis, Parkinson's disease, postpartum depression, bipolar disorder, epilepsy, schizophrenia, Post Traumatic Stress Disorder (PTSD) and Attention-Deficit/Hyperactivity Disorder (ADHD), and many other maladies of the mind. Notably, those with ADHD are twice as likely to get into traffic wrecks and are more prone to drug and alcohol abuse and have trouble keeping a job. We also studied exactly what strokes are, those insidious blood clots stopping the flow of blood to the brain.

We noted that over 100,000 brain cells or neurons die each *day* after a person reaches 25. Neurons usually do not reproduce themselves. Yet, we found nascent nerve cells just waiting for the right growth-stimulating hormones to once again become active. If scientists just knew how to trigger these brain neurons, the condition known as Alzheimer's disease might easily be cured!

I learned how drinking alcohol damages brain cells. For every ounce consumed it destroys 100,000 irreplaceable cells. Drinking can cause cancer of the tongue, mouth, esophagus, larynx and even the liver. Notably a person that smokes and drinks has a higher risk of head and neck cancers. Alcoholics have higher rate of developing esophageal cancer.

Drinking alters the brain, namely the pleasure centers, affecting the attention span and judgment. The frontal cortex which controls memory is slowly erased, along with the basal ganglia which controls obsessive/compulsive behavior gets confused. Again, all addictive drugs affect the neurotransmitter dopamine (the pleasure chemical), and stimulates neurons. This is the reason people feel high, and become sleepy and depressed. Alcohol causes inpaired concentration, slows reflexes, disrupts sleep, and causes high blood pressure.

A flash of light transpired between two dendrites. Then other flashes occurred in a lightning-fast salvo causing millions of neurons to fire, lighting up their cells like fiber-optic cables. The magic and wonder of actually *seeing* human thought! Another miracle imbued by God in his infinite wisdom! Millions flashed at once! The seat of the human mind! Awesome! How can I describe the feeling that came over me? I was overwhelmed!

All that a human being thinks and says—all that he is—his memory and his consciousness—lies in these flashes of electrochemical energy—the hyperneuronic activity of human consciousness!

Could the mind actually be separate from the brain? If so, then why couldn't the mind survive after the death of our brain? Can the mind be considered the personality or soul of the individual? If this is true, then we of the human race, without a doubt can survive death. I realized that I am now the living proof of this phenomenon!

(*The mind of the Supernalite, those Beings as myself beyond the grave, have a different bioplasmic mind connected to God, a totally different concept of reality in a foreign alternate dimension of time and space*).

The human brain, I learned, is composed of over 500 trillion synapses, which when millions fire at once produce a single thought. These synapses link the billions of neurons with the others. And they fire in about one thousandth of a second and travel through the brain at about 400 mph."

B*ut there is still something missing in the brain—there must be something else?* I pondered, being silent for a time. We found ourselves at the back of the brain and through this dense fog we could just make out the occipital lobe, the seat of vision.

"Our Second Divine Mission into this woman's brain will now transpire before us."

Harmful Effects of Smoking

"What will she die from then, Micronia?"

"Lung cancer, unless I can stop or prevent her from smoking herself to death. You see, this is my Divine Mission, to reveal the harm she is doing to her body by smoking two packs of cigarettes a day!"

As I watched, Micronia held up his scepter and at this instant a bolt of lightning permeated from his awesome weapon as a lightning strike upon her *nicotine addiction center*. Then these neurons glowed and fired off their synapses causing a stirring of current throughout the brain for an instant. Then all was quiet again with normal brain wave activity.

He stated that he had just communicated with the Source of all Divine Miracles, releasing spiritual power giving this lady before us the tenacity to stop smoking.

"But all this would be impossible unless she had prayed to God to help her stop. This she had done many times."

"Will this cure her of smoking?"

"*Instantly*, if she is receptive. But I can't change her mind. I can only send a seed of good wholesome thought (Divine Thought and Wisdom) into her. She, and only she can make up her own mind on what to do. For you see she is also pregnant! I have merged my mind into that of the Almighty and saw into her future a healthy baby, free of disease! Usually a mother who smokes will have a baby weighing about 2 pounds less than a mother who does not smoke.

188

"You, Iben can also pick up on these wave-links from the Almighty much as two tuning forks vibrating at totally different frequencies. When they touch they will automatically adjust their frequencies and come in sync with one another. They will, in turn, produce the desired mental attitude in this lady enabling her to stop smoking."

"With each passing day it seems that my abilities and interests are increasing."

"And this is just the beginning! Think of what Eternity must be like in another thousand earth years of living to your full potential?" Micronia confirmed.

Completely awesome!

"So, Iben, what have you learned on this journey through the human brain and mind!"

"Well, let's see. I have learned that the brain is the very best example of God's crowning masterpiece. A three-pound mass of gray and white gelatinous matter being the most complex substance in the known universe! The brain contains some 100 billion neurons. It is all that a person is, the total mind."

Divina Particular Aurae

"Not so fast, Iben. Something has been left out. That teleplasmic mist or fog which you have ignored until now permeating throughout the mind of this woman. We call it the D*ivina Particula Aurae.* Have you ever wondered what that is?"

An instant of intuition struck me and I recognized it

to be her SOUL, living independent of the brain and yet connected into the mind, her *total personality* and *total inner being* as a house is related to the home, as books are related to reading, as water is related to snow, as light is related to sight, as love is related to marriage and how God is related to the universe!

"That is very good Iben. You must remember one more thing. That all you learn while upon the earth is stored in your soul. Just as Jesus Christ was part man and part God. After death the soul is freed, much as the butterfly is release from its pupae. The human body, likewise, can be likened to a rocket. After this rocket (your body) has been spent launching its satellite (your soul) into space, its fuel is used up and discarded. But the satellite (your soul) survives and continues upon its Divine Mission.

"Iben, "what you learned in your earthly form before death is redeemed after your resurrection in the afterlife. This explains why you should learn as much as you can before you die. It is not learned in vain because all your positive learning, treasured memories, and beneficial education will be carried over into your next life."

"And as we have borne the image of the earthly,
we shall also bear the image of the heavenly:"
—1 Cor. 15:49

"The goal of all life is death."
—Sigmund Freud

Chapter Nineteen

Paranormal Abilities

We watched in amazement as impious incubus fought for recognition and control of the thoughts of this lady asleep before us. No wonder her dreams were vivacious and sometimes violent with all this going on! But let's first digress a little and define the use of this power known as paranormal phenomena.

"As beautiful as the flower is,
Its fragrance as perfume…
No plant has ever seen their beauty,
Nor smelled their scented plume.

The plant creates the nectar it will never taste—
But for the honey bee it shall not waste,
And now the bee will feed its hive,
and keep its thrifty family alive.

The plant has no concept of pollination,
Yet fertilizes its flowers with total variegation."
—The Author

Micronia continued, "Iben, you see, before the fall of humankind, Adam and Eve used divine spiritual powers to communicate with God and to each other. Then, after they sinned, they were lost to the human race. God, in his infinite wisdom, chose to suppress them from mortal man. Sometimes God *still* does imbue these *divine gifts* upon those that seek him in earnest.

"Examples of these divine miracles in the Old Testament are Noah building the ark and in Joseph's interpretation of the Pharaoh's dreams. Yet others were the encounter of the angel with Balaam, the encounter of Moses with the Pharaoh, and the angel's contact with Gideon.

"In the New Testament, divine powers were manifested when Peter, James and John healed the sick and saw the vision upon Mount Hermon (the transfiguration), at Paul's conversion, and God's message in John's visions of the future fate of humankind in Revelation.

"So, paranormal abilities or extra-sensory perception (ESP) are all a natural function of the higher senses, but have been suppressed, and their ability has since atrophied. Since the fall of Adam, they have been forbidden by the Divine, guarded by the angels, forgotten, became latent, left undeveloped and finally all but disappeared from the human race."

"Micronia, I have noticed that the longer I am in my new glorified body I am now communicating with fewer and fewer symbols in our divine language. It seems that our symbols are becoming more refined and concise."

"This is true, Iben. The longer you are in Eternity the more precise it will become. Later, you will communicate a whole complete thought with a lot less symbols with much more concise and exact meaning. Just a few symbols or words will communicate divine wisdom as many books do now! Similar to the perfect communication of giving a diamond ring to the one you love, or that special rose at anniversary time, or having your love just touch your hand states thoughts that mere words cannot express. So it is with our divine language. But very gradually you will lose the ability to communicate with the mortals for your intelligence and mind will expand past their paltry conceptions and macaronic language.

"Also, you shall learn that the universe is what we comprehend. The more we comprehend, the bigger our universe becomes. Then we ultimately link with what is known as the Universal Spirit, Divine Mind, Cosmic Consciousness or Absolute Truth.

"The same is when we could perceive the whole of humankind aging. Here in the eternal realm everyone immediately reaches their peak of opulence, that is, their perfection in their spiritual bodies. You see, Iben, the *mortal* body has cellular degeneration. The human body eventually starts decaying and winding down into old age and death. We, in Eternity are also not aware of time as mortals know it. We are on a different time scale altogether known as the phenomenon of Translinear-Chronometry. God's time-measurement is beyond that of mortal man and transcends into the realm of the angels and divine beings. Therefore, we have the ability to travel into the past and see things that happened long ago."

I learned that many of man's problems, would be solved if they would only listen to their *inner voice*, what their subconsciousness from God reveals. If they would only meditate upon the Word of God. It is a shame that humankind, mortal man, lives just *outside* this threshold and cannot explore, nay even fathom that realm of *greater knowledge* which lies a little beyond his perception. Divine Psionics is a doorway through which those deeper aspects of the creative self can be approached, that fantastic portal to universal consciousness of which all men are a part but after the fall of Adam and Eve, so few are aware. It is a shame that the world today is taken up with the gods of the Monetary System, corrupt CEO's that worship money, the corruption of organized religion and rejecting the Holy Bible as the inspired Word of God. It is sad that the human race is faced with annihilation through apostasy, and that even our great nation is deteriorating by evil forces mainly from *within*. It is regretful that we can place a man on the moon, send a probe to the far reaches of outer space, or fight a war costing the taxpayers billions of dollars, but we can't even feed our poor, homeless and starving within our midst.

The human race, I now realized, will *never* be able to solve all its many and complex problems by itself. It will definitely take an *outside force* to keep humanity from destroying itself. Yes, Iben, we need is a new divine heart to replace the old sin nature, carnal mind and malicious motives. We need a synergetic approach to the human race, a renewed mind and divine anointing to take out the seeds of bitterness, hate and hurt replacing them with divine love, caring and respect of all people and all races.

We now bid farewell to *that great raveled knot*, the humah brain—the most complex substance even known.

> "Wisdom lies in thinking about the future
> consequences of our actions."
> —American Adage

Chapter Twenty

The Eye and the Ear

*M*icronia and I once again continued our After Death Odyssey through the human body, learning all about its grand wonders and mysteries.

Still near the human brain of this unknown lady, we plunged into the depths of a strange inland sea.

We entered a vast salty ocean of the vitreous humor of the human eye and observed the red blood cells actually feeding the retina! Here were strange patches, odd spots looking like ruptured blood vessels. Micronia informed me that people who smoke are *two times* more likely to develop macular degeneration. We studied the optic nerve with its mysterious blind spot and swam through the vast ocean of the vitreous humor, a vast salty sea between the retina and the lens. We stood in the anterior chamber between the lens and the cornea known as the aqueous humor and it seem to us as being more capacious than any large football stadium ever built. Also there was some cornea damage caused by the herpes virus (the same virus of fever blisters and cold sores) known as ocular herpes, or *stromal keratitis*. Then we studied the lens, then the iris—and stood in awe of yet another miracle of God's divine masterpieces.

We passed the vestibular nerve entering the inner ear. Spiraling through the cochlea, we traveled into the organ of Corti. From here we toured the semicircular canals, the *ossicles*, exploring the stapes (stirrup), the incus (anvil) and the malleus (hammer) of the tympanic cavity. We soon discovered those strange ear stones, those little rocks of carbonate of lime that give morals the sense of balance and their gravity sense to determine "up" from "down."

We studied the tympanum or eardrum, and all its nerves, now realizing just how sensitive they are. We learned that the *lowest note* we can normally hear is about 18 cycles per second; *the highest* is about 18,000 cycles per second!

Then we plunged downward through the neck of this wonderful enigmatic woman. Her mind, still swirling in fantastic dreams, was completely oblivious to us as we coursed on through her blood stream, now on our journey to the human heart!

So we entered a capillary leading to the internal jugular vein which directly led to the superior vena cava, the largest vein in the human body.

The Circulatory System

Harvey/Pasteur

Micronia revealed the strange world of blood—yet another miracle of the divine. After a short duration, he introduced some radiant Supernalites, eminent physicians and great scientists, doing what they so loved doing in mortal life — studying the human body!

Before me appeared William Harvey, an English physician. He discovered how blood travels throughout the circulatory system. He was accompanied by Louis Pasteur, a Frenchman, who was one of the greatest bacteriologists of all time. He developed the vaccines against rabies and tetanus (lockjaw), and developed the process of pasteurization of milk.

William Harvey started our disquisition. "Iben, we have been waiting for you! The human brain is fantastic but so is the heart and blood! One couldn't exist without the other. So let us begin!

"There are 25 trillion red corpuscles containing hemoglobin in the average human. The red cells perish in about 120 days and must be replenished. Five million red corpuscles are manufactured *each second* in the bone marrow to replace those that die. White cells and platelets make up the remaining volume of the blood."

I was traveling with the blood back to the heart, now turning blue from releasing oxygen and gathering carbon dioxide from the billions of cells throughout the body. We then came through a narrowed flap in the vein wall.

Louis Pasteur spoke, "Iben, this is a hinged flap or a valve in the vein—preventing the back-flow of blood. If this woman stood up quickly these valves would prevent the blood from puddling in her feet. Another reason to refute the concept of evolution. How did these valves form if we evolved from the animals to survive in an upright position?"

Yet thousands of other complex proteins and vitamins

were explained beautifully by Pasteur. Estrogen (the female sex hormone) and along with antigens and all sorts of enzymes and steroids were turning and twisting in the blood's current along with the red and white blood cells.

The blood was a much more complex substance than I ever imagined! A real *living tissue* though it is a liquid.

I learned why taking care of your teeth and gums was important. Gingivitis and pyorrhea can both lead to an accumulation of bacteria in the bloodstream producing dangerous toxins. This makes arteries thicken and harden causing the buildup of plaque. This can, in turn, lead to diabetes, kidney failure, osteoporosis—and Alzheimer's disease.

The secrets of hemophilia, leukemia, uremia, diabetes, embolism, sickle-cell anemia, along with hundreds of other blood diseases were now revealed.

"Could you please explain the mystery of hemoglobin?"

"Yes, Iben, I would love to," Harvey proclaimed! "You see, this hemoglobin is a very complicated protein, composed of thousands of individual atoms of six different varieties. This complex molecule has a molecular weight of 68,000! See those four little iron atoms it contains? Without these four tiny atoms, hemoglobin could not carry oxygen to all the vital cells and life as we know it would perish.

"Noteworthy, Iben, is that the blood-clotting mechanism involves more than a dozen proteins and definitely could *not* have been created by evolution. The mechanism of blood clotting is very complex involving more than a dozen enzymes and proteins. Clotting could never happen if even *one* of these above blood proteins were missing."

Harvey now explained all the Rh factors. I learned

how low-density lipoprotein LDL (bad cholesterol) creates plaque build-up in the arteries and that the high-density lipoprotein HDL (good cholesterol) actually removes this bad material from the blood, thus preventing a heart attack and hardening of the arteries.

As we traveled through these arteries I observed the buildup of cholesterol, known as atherosclerosis, which is the narrowing of these vessels. If a blood clot (an embolus) clogs one of these arteries supplying blood to the heart or brain, an embolism occurs. This is known as a heart attack or stroke.

I watched in fascination as some weird conglomerates of protein undulated past us turning and twisting through the blood stream.

"What are these strange orbs?"

Harvey continued, "Iben, these strange globular masses are deadly viruses artificially introduced into the body. Follow them and you will discover their source of entry."

I did follow them and saw hundreds whiz pass me, their surface membranes quivering, getting used to their new environment. Then I saw another strange thing I couldn't understand at first. Then it struck me what it was.

On her outer skin I could see a large circular shaft penetrating into an arteriole with blood being sucked up through it while these viruses were being released into the blood. I further investigated this phenomenon and discovered it to be the proboscis of a mosquito sucking the blood of this lady!

"This is no ordinary mosquito, Iben. Remember that mosquito buzzing around this lady's bed when you began to shrink in size? Now see it upon the surface of her arm? This mosquito has somewhat striped legs and is an import from Southeast Asia, called the *Aedes albopictus* or the Asian tiger mosquito. It arrived in tires shipped into the United States from other countries. It also carries the harmful viruses—dengue fever, chikungunya and Zika."

In a few seconds the immune defense system, though weakened from this lady's stress at work and lethargic from years of smoking, finally released white killer cells, macrophages, to attack these invaders, releasing antibodies. Now these antibodies, proteins known as interferons and cytokines, attacked the outer protein shell of the invaders. What a battle ensued! As crevices appeared in the dengue virus' membrane, it went into its *coup de grace*, its death agony, blowing its insides out, trying to rid itself of the irritating chemicals eating away on its surface membrane—just as a popcorn kernel, when heated, pops open! Then the white blood cells tore this remaining debris apart digesting them completely!

Another virus attacked a cell injecting its DNA. Soon the cell exploded spewing thousands of tiny spores into the blood. Many macrophages and antigens were alerted into battle, yet some viruses were escaping. For a while it looked like the viruses were winning.

Silently the war of dengue fever rampaged inside this lady's body.

Dengue fever in the United States! Isn't this a foreign disease?

Pasteur spoke, reading my mind, "So it *was*, Iben. Remember malaria has been discovered in Arkansas along with Yellow Fever in the recent past. So other diseases will come forth as the plight of the human race worsens. It is the beginning of the end. God will soon come to purge the world. And yes the Asian tiger mosquito has now spread dengue, the harbinger of even more deadly viruses soon to come. This, along with the AIDS virus and Hepatitis C viruses are here to stay. Things will eventually get worse as people travel between countries."

All these famous doctors of medicine were watching this battle of her miraculous immune system in action against these foreign invaders, enraptured in awestruck wonderment with complete ornate expressions upon their faces. They were all in total ecstasy!

Still other strange cells passed by us—

"What are those?"

Pasteur continued, "Those are insulin. Insulin produced by the pancreas regulates sugar in the muscles and liver. Estrogen (female sex hormone) can slow the development of osteoporosis (thinning of the bones) in older women. And that one I'm pointing to is prolactin, a pituitary hormone, necessary for lactation and is secreted in large amounts during pregnancy.

"See that over there, that is a dangerous blood clot, an insidious free-floating monster in the blood. If it grows much larger it could clog an artery in the brain or in the heart causing a massive stroke or heart attack. See those chemicals attacking the membrane of this clot? Those are the remnants of that aspirin she took before lying down to help her headache. As stated earlier, it may eventually save her life by dissolving this clot as aspirin is a known blood thinner. Aspirin can actually prevent strokes in this way."

"Aspirin?"

"Sure, Iben, the common aspirin can dissolve these clots if used regularly."

Behold! The Human Heart

We now grew closer and closer to the human heart. The steady thumping grew louder as we neared the superior vena cava, the largest vein in the body. In our small state of being, the heart was only beating, it seemed, at a much slower rate than its normal 70 beats per minute.

Looming before us as large as a shopping mall was the majestic pulsating heart! With blood flowing through it, each heart cavity seemed as large as an auditorium with blood vessels as huge culverts connecting it to the rest of the body. Totally awesome!

Micronia now revealed that the human heart beats over 2 billion times in a 75-year lifetime. It pushes 2,000 gallons of blood through 60,000 miles of blood vessels, beating 100,000 times *each day* of her life. And it even started *eight* months *before* she was born. It pumps 5 quarts of blood a minute to every cell in the body causing the blood to flow about six inches each second. So far, her heart has pumped approximately 350,000 *tons* of blood! Only God in his infinite wisdom could have ever conceived such an overwhelming design. Hugh veins and arteries pulsed with life. It appeared before us in all its radiant glory, another glorious design and miracle of God's great masterpieces!

Harvey in his glory, spoke, "Iben, note the muscular band connecting the heart chambers together. This is known as the bundle of His, named for the German physician Wihelm His, Jr. The sinoatrial node in the right auricle controls it beating, also known as the *pacemaker* of the heart. This node fires an impulse into the heart synchronizing the beats."

We passed right into the right atrium. Here I noticed an oval depression. Harvey stated that this is the remains of the foramen ovale, known now as the *fossa ovalis.*

Harvey continued, "Iben, remember the fetal heart and its foramen ovale? This is what is left of it after birth and after it closes off properly. If it doesn't close at birth it is known as a 'hole in the heart,' a congenital heart defect known as *atria septal defect.*"

Here I noticed another malfunction. I could see in the aortic valve that separates the left ventricle of the heart from the main body artery, the aorta.

"Iben, this is known as a heart murmur. Remember we mentioned that this woman had something else wrong with her? When the valves become diseased they no longer close completely and allow some back-flow of blood in the left ventricle. Heredity was the cause of this malady but stress from the years at the office and again her smoking has worsened it."

Heart Disease and Smoking

"In a single year," Pasteur now spoke, "diseases of the heart kill far more Americans than died in World Wars I and II, the Korean and Vietnam wars—*combined*! *Fifty percent* of the deaths in the United States are due to heart disease. Benzopyrene, one of the dangerous chemicals in cigarettes, is now known to cause lung cancer. The nitric oxide and nitrogen dioxide in cigarette smoke *increases* your blood pressure and *decreases* your tolerance for exercise. Smoking also *increases* the chances for a blood clot which can lead to a heart attack. Smokers can have as much as 5% deadly carbon monoxide already absorbed in their blood reducing the amount of oxygen intake from their lungs. Carbon monoxide is so dangerous that only 1 part in 100,000 will cause illness, and one part in 750, will cause death within 30 minutes. Smokers also have higher LDL (bad) cholesterol levels and lower HDL (good) levels. Thirty percent of all coronary heart disease deaths in the U.S. are attributable to cigarette smoking.

"Smoking, without a doubt, kills 420,000 Americans each year through heart disease, cancer and emphysema. Since 1980, *three million women* have died prematurely from smoke-related illnesses. The result of smoking has caused as many deaths as the great epidemic diseases such as typhoid, cholera, tuberculosis, AIDS, alcohol, car accidents, murders, suicides, drugs and fires—*combined*!

"Nicotine mimics some of the effects of the neurotransmitter acetlylcholine to increase the heartbeat fifteen to twenty-five times per minute while constricting blood vessels in the extremities causing *hyperplasia* destroying the fine cilia in the lungs that is needed to clear the lungs of debris and mucus. Smoking, besides containing nicotine, has deadly carbon monoxide which promotes coronary artery disease. *Also people that smoke one pack of cigarettes a day are twice as likely to have a heart attack; and for each pack smoked, subtract on the average 3 to 5 hours off your life!*"

"I have heard that smoking cigarettes can cause women to have cervical cancer? Is this true?"

Harvey spoke, "Smoking has been *proven* to cause

cervical cancer in women. Women that smoke have *four times* as many cervical cancers as women who do not smoke. It should be noted, Iben, that women who smoke one pack a day or more for 12 years or longer increase the risk of getting cancer of the cervix *12 times* as great as those women that don't smoke at all.

"Smoking is the largest preventable cause of premature death and disability in the United States. It causes lung cancer, disability and death more than any other single known factor. Smoking worldwide has killed 70,000,000 people in the 20th Century.

"About three million people throughout the world die from smoking each year. Oddly, in China tobacco causes more deaths from chronic lung disease than from lung cancer. In India smoking mainly kills through tuberculosis rather than lung disease. Cigarettes contain over 4,000 chemicals, including trace amounts of known poisons such as DDT and formaldehyde. Cigarette smoke hardens the arteries, produces a higher death rate from coronary heart disease and even causes lumbar disease of the lower back. Younger women who smoke often have trouble getting pregnant and have higher incidences of miscarriage, placental problems and low birth-weight babies. It even effects cholesterol fighting factors in the blood. Smoking also causes liver, colon and breast cancer, Type 2 diabetes, erectile dysfunction and deadly ectopic pregnancies where the embryo implants in the fallopian tube outside the uterus causing massive complications to the growth of the fetus."

Pasteur spoke, "Iben, smoking cigars are no better for you either. Cigar smoking increases the risk of pancreatic cancer, bladder cancer, heart disease and lung cancer. They also have more toxins and irritants than cigarettes. Carbon monoxide is one of the toxins contained in cigars (as well as in cigarettes). Cigars contain the toxin nicotine also. In some cases, cigars can contain up to 23 *times* the amount of nicotine found in cigarettes."

Marijuana/Oriental hookah/E-cigarettes/Exercise

Micronia confirmed that Marijuana smokers fair no better. Marijuana contains 33 of the same harmful chemicals as tobacco and is a carcinogen (causing cancer). It contains the psychoactive ingredient, *tetrahydrocannabinol* or THC, a mind altering drug that *alters the structure of the brain* causing *personality changes and even brain damage.*

She related that marijuana and hashish can harm your chromosomes and even break down your immune system. It can also cause *impotence* and *temporary sterility, producing female-like breasts in men.* There are 61 potentially dangerous cannabinoids which make up only a fraction of the 421 known chemicals in the cannabis plant. We discovered that *benzanthracene* and *benzopyrene*, two known carcinogens, are 70% *greater* in marijuana than in cigarette smoke. Marijuana is addictive and is a *gateway drug*, leading to more dangerous and powerful drugs. One in 11 who use it become addicted. It also causes impaired memory and leads to eating disorders, slows learning, and slows metabolism. Marijuana can even be more dangerous than cigarette smoke producing sinusitis, pharyngitis, bronchitis and asthma.

"How about edible pot?"

"Oh, that!" Micronia continued, "Marijuana-laced

cookies, brownies, candies (such as lollipops), sugar-free vegan bars, cough syrup, white chocolate peppermint squares, cannabis lemonade, cannabis coffee, cannabis hot sauce, cannabis sodas, cannabis spiced peanuts, even marijuana-infused wines, *et al*, have been designed to *deceive* the public. Food impregnated with marijuana can still cause a "high" and lead to anxiety. *Eating or drinking it is as dangerous as smoking it.* Many of the same psychoactive drugs and dangerous chemicals are still present whether you eat it or smoke it. All these drugs are still ingested within the human body.

"Also, a medical marijuana patch can now be place upon the body, or marijuana-oil rubbed into the skin, or even cannabis oil drops containing THC can be placed upon the tongue to regulate epilepsy."

"Could animals benefit from marijuana?"

"Iben, that seems like a strange question, but scientists are actually developing CBD oils derived from marijuana designed especially for dogs. These oils contain cannabidiols (CBDs) *nonpsychoactive* components. They can be used to relieve a dog's joint pain, epilepsy, arthritis and even sooth their anxieties."

"How about e-cigarettes? That new concept of "vaping? Could this be harmful?"

Pasteur now spoke, "Oh, those modern smokeless devices? Well, tobacco-derived nicotine may contain diethylene glycol, a toxic compound found in antifreeze. Its cancer-causing vapors contain at least 26 harmful *radioactive* metals such as lead, tin, zinc, nickel and chromium. These e-cigarettes also contain nicotine thus making another nicotine addict."

Micronia informed us that smoking moist tobacco through the Oriental hookah is also dangerous. This smoke contains benzene, known to cause leukemia and other cancers. The hookah smoke, even though it might contain fermented fruit and molasses and even smell real nice, is still very harmful, containing just as many heavy metals as the e-cigarettes.

I now addressed Harvey, "I have heard that exercise is good for you. Could you expound upon this?"

"Sure, Iben," Harvey beamed. "Exercise improves the body's immune system and can relieve headaches. Walking makes you breathe deeper and cleans the lungs. Even menstrual pain and depression are both alleviated by exercise. Walking promotes creativity and strengthens the lower back. *It can affect your brain chemistry by helping it grow new neurons— reversing dementia.* Exercise can even postpone the onset of Alzheimer's disease, increasing your life-span. Walking and jogging for only 20 minutes each day, enhances sexual desire and increases your vitality by releasing beta-endorphin, an opium-like chemical to relieve stress giving you a natural high! It even increases your levels of HDL (good cholesterol) and reduces the triglycerides in your blood. Walking and exercise also activates the protein *brain derived neurotropic factor* (BDNF) which helps repair and protect the brain, even promoting a cognitive and acute mind.

"Also, the hippocampus, the brain's memory area, shrinks with age. Exercise makes it grow healthy once again, helping dementia stay away."

CHAPTER TWENTY-ONE

Behold, The Human Lung!

*M*icronia, along with the Supernalites and I were on our way toward her lungs. We entered the pulmonary artery and headed through the blood stream once again moving with the current to one of the twin lobes of the breath of life.

In less than a second we entered a capillary plunging almost immediately to the place where the carbon dioxide/oxygen exchange occurs.

Harvy spoke, "Iben, the human lung consists of 100 square meters or 50 times the area of the skin. Pumping at the rate of 75 gallons an *hour*, the heart pushes *its total volume of blood* through the lungs every *thirteen seconds*! The lungs, like the heart, never stop moving and utilize about 12,500 quarts of air a *day* metabolizing oxygen!"

Harvey proclaimed that the heart pumps 17 pints of blood each *minute* through the lungs taking less than *one second* for this blood to release its carbon dioxide and replace it with oxygen! The expired air contains from about 4 to 7% carbon dioxide.

Micronia now revealed the miracle of *perfusion*. Here, bluish blood full of carbon dioxide was going in one part of the lungs, soon emerging cherry-red replenished with life-giving oxygen.

Micronia related that if she would only stop smoking *now*, her lungs would start improving immediately. If she continues smoking she risks dying of lung cancer.

Micronia related that s*moking is like being in an atmosphere 92 times as polluted as the air we now breathe!* Smokers are from 3 to 4 times more likely to develop *squamous cell skin cancer. Tobacco* also suppresses the immune system and can cause blood clots, leading to heart attacks and strokes. He further stated that cigarette smoke reached 600 degrees F. So this further destroys her delicate lungs as it travels down the trachea.

"Remember, Iben," Harvey spoke, "that *nicotine is one of the most poisonous substances known to humankind. One concentrated drop is enough to kill a person!* It also constricts the oxygen intake to the unborn child. Even some of those in the fields that pick the tobacco leaves, many times come down with *nicotine poisoning. The human body is the temple of the Holy Spirit.* So why contaminate it by smoking cigarettes."

The Kidneys/Digestive Tract/Breasts/Laminin

From the lungs we all traveled to the kidneys. We studied their nephrons by convoluting through the Loop of Henle and we learned how they worked as a filtering system.

Here I discovered some kidney stones composed of calcium oxalate, huge boulders to us, but these consisted actually of only tiny grains of sand. But, if they grow any larger they could clog the urethra—becoming excruciating painful.

Micronia revealed the function of the pancreas as we toured the Islets of Langerhans. I learned it produces and regulates insulin and glucagon (animal starch). This, in turn, manufactures sugar, thus aiding in the oxidation of carbohydrates—giving the body its energy. Then we arrived at the liver. I learned it works filtering the blood by extracting wastes, turning bile its greenish color.

Pasteur now gave me a personal tour of the digestive tract. I learned the secret of how the friendly *E. coli* (the good bacterium) can actually create Vitamin K in the intestines!

Micronia revealed the miracle of lactation. I learned that her breasts are actually modified sweat glands! Milk is a specialized form of sweat, enriched with proteins!

Pasteur taught that breast milk has the perfect enzymes, the long-chain fatty acids and proteins that could never be reproduced in the laboratory. I learned that breast fed babies have less respiratory infections and allergies than bottle-fed babies, fewer ear infections and even fewer rashes. *Breast-fed babies can increase their I.Q. status, having all the necessary vitamins and nutrition for the developing brain!*

I noticed a strange molecular substance interwoven and omnipresent in *every* human cell. Micronia revealed it is a type of protein known as *laminin* and it is found in all life forms—every living animal cell, large or small. This laminin is the adhesive that holds all the organs and tissues together, the "glue" of the human body. Without laminin a condition known as *congenital muscular dystrophy* results. In its molecular form it is usually found in the configuration of the Christian cross. As Christ, the creator of all life, laminin is seen in the symbol of this cross, a subtle reminder of the divinity of life.

A thousand medical books could not hold all the marvels that Micronia and the Supernalites revealed to us! Such wisdom I was learning! The most important thing is that the human body is the most technical and wondrous comprehension and miraculous creation by Divine Mind.

CHAPTER TWENTY-TWO

Behold! The Human Uterus

*M*icronia, our eminent physicians, and I now entered a large cavern in the human female body. It should be remembered that we're still existing at the level of a tiny microbe.

Now looming before us was this capacious room. I stood in awe as we traveled up the fallopian tube as my excitement intensified. Miles later, it seemed, we came upon—

How can I describe this wonder? A divine epiphany? At that moment I realized what I was looking at *the human ovary*! There inside it were hundreds of tiny unfertilized eggs in various stages of maturity, the nascent origin of the vestiges of a human life!

Micronia taught us that at birth this lady's two ovaries on each side of the uterus contain 500,000 undeveloped eggs. Yet between puberty and menopause *only* about 400 will actually reach maturity!

We learned that sex is determined by just one tiny gene of the 46 chromosomes. This gene turns the fertilized egg (zygote) into a male. A zygote without this tiny fragment of genetic material, turns into a female.

> "The male is a biological accident:
> the Y (male) gene is an incomplete X (female) gene...
> In other words, the male is an incomplete female."
> —Valerie Solanis

Pasteur now explained that the human embryo at the zygote stage (beginning of fertilization in the union of a spermatozoon and egg) has *both* male and female sexual traits.

I questioned why after one spermatozoon enters the egg or ovum, other sperm can't penetrate through.

Pasteur answered, "You see, Iben, if more than one spermatozoon were to enter the already fertilized egg, it would destroy its DNA as a fail-safe mechanism. So the first spermatozoon to arrive through the cell wall at the moment of conception, hardens its zona pellucida of the ovary's outer surface. This switches the egg's electro-magnetic field of calcium thus preventing any other sperm to enter. If more than one sperm enters, a condition known as *polyspermy* results—leading to a miscarriage. The rejection of this malformed zygote protects the mother from giving birth to a deformed child."

Notably, we learned all about twins and the miracles of birth. We studied Hellin's law which states that twins occur once in 80 pregnancies, triplets once in 6,400 pregnancies, quadruplets once in 512,000 pregnancies.

"Is there a link between genes and homosexuality?"

Pasteur continued, "There is a cluster of brain cells that

guide men's sex drive that is twice as large in the heterosexual male than in the homosexual male. Having this propensity toward homosexuality is known as *gender identity disorder* or in extreme cases, *gender dysphoria*."

Pregnancy/Ovarian Cancer and Talc

Traveling through the uterus into the area of the ovary we discover something rather strange. There were hundreds of large rocks the size of beach balls, round, with irregular surfaces.

"These rocks Iben," stated Harvey, "are talc granules. Women that use talcum powder which chemically is related to asbestos can work its way up the birth canal causing ovarian tumors and cancer of the uterus! Oral contraceptives which halt the release of eggs can cut the risk of ovarian cancer by as much as 50% if taken for many years. Tying off the fallopian tubes lessens the risk of ovarian cancer. This is because the ovaries are sealed off from foreign substances and environmental contaminants.

"Women having none or one child have a better chance of developing ovarian cancer. Having two or three children will lower the chances greatly. This is because pregnancy interrupts the constant flow of eggs and gives the ovaries a chance to rest. Fertility drugs stimulate the ovaries producing more eggs, irritating the ovarian lining and potentially increasing the chances of cancer. This also causes multiple births. Up to eight babies at one time of different sexes can be produced using this method."

A whole litter at once, like a cat, I thought.

I remembered that a 27-year old mother on December

20, 1998 gave birth to the only known living set of octuplets. Nkem Chukwu who had taken fertility drugs gave birth to six girls and two boys at one time!

I began to smell something. I couldn't make it out exactly—something I had smelled before. Strange, but very fragrant and soothing like the smell of a rose or maraschino cherries.

"What is that smell?" I inquired.

"Iben," Harvey continued, "ever wonder how the sperm finds its way through the uterus to the egg? Well, what you are smelling is the *cyanidin* molecule, the smell of wild cherries released as a pheromone by the human egg! The ovary acts as a beacon giving off this pheromone-type substance to attract sperm toward it. In other words, Iben, the sperm actually *smells* the ovum and swims toward it!"

So that's the reason maraschino cherries smell so good! That smell takes us back a long way!

"The sperm also contain other chemicals which act as an aphrodisiac producing the ardent desire to procreate, thus empowering them forward, seeking out the ovum. And yet, even after conception, one in four pregnancies end in miscarriage. So the odds are a lot smaller than you think of being born. Yet, here you are! Lucky you!"

The Unborn Child

Micronia revealed that God determines who should be born, which tiny spermatozoon will unite with just which egg in the mother. He stated that it is NOT predestined, just guided by God's Divine Purpose.

Now incredibly we encountered the human fetus living

inside the womb. We penetrate the amniotic sac and observe this living human baby at thirty weeks old.

We could easily tell that it is a little girl. At this stage in her development, I learned, she could frown, swallow and her vocal cords are complete. She has tiny soft lanugo hair upon her tender little body and she has eyelashes and eyebrows. As she moves around in the amniotic sac we see her jerking. She has the hiccups! She is hyperactive and is having an allergic reaction due to the chocolate bar her mother had before she went to sleep. Her little face, red and wrinkled has the sweet countenance of wonder, floating weightless in the amniotic fluid. Her eyelids can open and shut though she cannot yet actually see. Now she begins to suck her thumb! Her little heart (*formed at 21 days after conception*) is already pumping blood at 600 pints a day!

Micronia further explained that the embryo can actually hear things outside the womb. She can hear her mother's heart beat and she can recognize her mother's voice and can even tell if she is angry or tense. The baby, before she is born, should have gentle soothing music such as religious, classical and nature sounds played to her, for she can actually *hear* this music which can soothe her moods while still in the womb!

Pasteur confirmed, "Also, Iben, the unborn feels very secure in the womb and when the time comes to be born goes through trauma and shock into an unknown harsh world, from one of warmth, tranquility and peace to one of pain, bright lights and hunger."

This could be an allegory of the death experience, I thought. *Birth means 'death' to the place where you were conceived, the protective womb. Oddly the baby is created to live a life beyond* the comfort of the womb—just as we are created to fulfill a life beyond our known existence of the grave!

"How can the embryo survive? I mean, it is a foreign tissue to the mother's body isn't it?"

"Pasteur continued, "It is a great mystery that the fetus ever gets born! The mother's immune system regards the fetus as a foreign tissue, an invader—"

Harvey cut in, "Pregnancy, Iben, is a paradox. The baby has genetic material from both parents, its tissues therefore could be rejected much as a transplanted kidney, liver or heart. There are a number of reasons why it is not. At the beginning of pregnancy one certain protein masks the foreign antigens on the surface of the embryo rendering it 'invisible' to the body's immune system."

Strange, I pondered. *This baby looks a lot like me! How did I perceive this? In my new enhanced state of being I could see deep into this precious unborn child's eyes into her inner being and somehow knew that this baby was part of me.*

"Right you are," Harvey confirmed. *"Iben, this baby girl is your child and her name will be Cassandra!"*

"How could this be," I questioned. "I have been dead for many years now! How could I father a child?"

"Cryogenics, Iben," Harvey stated emphatically. "Remember, your sperm were preserved and frozen just weeks before your death—and your wife, Faith, wanted another child to honor *your* memory! And Ambrose, her new husband, was found to be sterile."

Now I knew! What ecstasy overcame me knowing that this woman we were traveling through was still the love of my life, Faith—and she was carrying my child! Now I realized why I had *deja vu* when I encountered her dreams.

She was my mortal wife in another reality! How wonderful and fulfilling this *afterlife* can be. God bless her! I am the father of another child—and I have been *deceased* for many years. Just incredible!

Mortal mind could never perceive any of these wonders the way I now have!

We found ourselves once again outside the body of my beloved wife, Faith.

We now bid farewell to Harvey and Pasteur, who were in total ecstasy doing in the afterlife what they so loved to do while on earth… to contine the divine mission guiding others through the human body—and in a flash… they were gone!

> "Statistically, the probability of any one of us
> being here is so small that you'd think the mere
> fact of existing would keep us all in a
> contented dazzlement of surprise."
> —Lewis Thomas, *The Lives of a Cell*

Micronia, my guide, stated that we have now ended our tour through the human body. We needed to make yet another journey—this time into the realm *beyond* the tiny microbe. You see, humankind lies between the infinitely large and the infinitely small. We will not stay this size any longer, but will grow steadily *smaller* and *smaller*. Micronia wanted me to experience the action of the universe beyond anything that I had ever comprehended!

"It is impossible Iben," stated Micronia, "to tell what wonders still await you upon this fantastic After-Death Odyssey, beyond the reality and comprehension of mortal imagination, as we now continue into *The Great Unknown.*"

(THE END OF BOOK I)

Thus concludes Book I of the Trilogy,
Eternity.
Continue the exciting After-Death Odyssey of
Iben Thayer in Book II:
Mysteries of the Unknown,
and enter God's Kingdom of more amazing
and miraculous adventures.

Now continue the After-Death Odyssey...
Mysteries of the Unknown,
that miraculous dimension beyond death.
Encounter the fantastic world beyond the atom,
and witness the creation of our universe!
Journey to the Earth's core, exploring a domain
of strange beasts and a mysterious Lost Kingdom
as recorded in the ancient texts of the Bible.
Travel back in time to witness the birth,
death and resurrection of Jesus Christ.
Witness the horrors of the great world wars
and discover many new spheres of fantastic wonder
too numerous to mention.

Book TWO

Mysteries of the Unknown

Now continue the After-Death Odyssey...
Mysteries of the Unknown,
that miraculous dimension beyond death.
Encounter the fantastic world beyond the atom,
and witness the creation of our universe!
Journey to the Earth's core, exploring a domain
of strange beasts and a mysterious Lost Kingdom
as recorded in the ancient texts of the Bible.
Travel back in time to witness the birth,
death and resurrection of Jesus Christ.
Witness the horrors of the great world wars
and discover many new spheres of fantastic wonder
too numerous to mention.

CHAPTER ONE

*L*et us continue the unique adventures of Iben Thayer and his After-Death Odyssey. We are leaving the Oklahoma City bombing holocaust, the wonders of the ocean, and the miracle of the human body. Our strange voyage now leads us into t*erra incognita*—directly into the Mysteries of the Unknown.

"Micronia once again appeared before me. Iben, I will continue being your guide through this phase of your journey, your host through our infinite voyage—this time into the very minuscule ... encountering the elementary building blocks of matter, the tiny atoms and entering the strange intrinsic dimensions of their atomic structures."

We found ourselves still in the farm house where we toured through the blood stream of my wife, Faith. In the bedroom we traveled through the wall and before I could get outside, I smelled a fetid odor.

The Tenacious Cockroach

"Yuk! That smell? What is—"

"Iben," Micronia answered, "that is the odor of a female cockroach's pheromone meandering through these walls!"

I bravely followed this scent. Since we were still the size of a microbe, this female cockroach seemed as large as a passenger jet.

What in inferior species of life! I pondered.

"Did you know that the cockroach can taste with its legs as the common housefly? It can also survive up to *ten times* the radiation of a human! This means that after a nuclear war the roaches will still be living while humans will be dying from radiation poisoning. They've survived for 350 million years roaming around the feet of dinosaurs and watched them perish. They have also been around seeing the birth of the human race and will undoubtedly be around to see its demise.

"Their little bodies can adapt to many poisons and pesticides for they have built-in enzymes that can mutate (as many bacteria and viruses do), building up a resistance to them. Many species can also fly away when threatened! Many roaches can spring across the floor from 0 to 100 mph in one second! Iben, even if a bear attacked you, you couldn't run that fast! Could you withstand the pressure of a smack of 2,500 pounds of pressure per square inch? The cockroach can! Some can survive and still run away if a fly swatter hits them! That would be equivalent of being hit by a car traveling over 120 mph! Some species can even hold their breath under water for over 30 minutes!

"The human does have one ability that is *superior* to

the cockroach. The cockroach carries at least thirty-three disease germs in its body that can affect humans, including salmonella and hepatitis. Yet the human body can be a carrier to *thousands* of different disease germs!"

I may have to change my attitude about the lowly cockroach.

I noticed how complacent this insect was, roaming around making this wall its home. In its little primitive brain somehow it cannot think past its limited existence, that of being a cockroach! Of course it can't understand as humans do, but they also believe that the lives they're now living in their mortal bodies are *their* ultimate existence! (A cockroach has never murdered, committed suicide or sinned either!)

Each life entity, I mused, *thinks this about themselves as being the complete and perfect life form. Dogs, cats, elephants, giraffes, monkeys, snakes, spiders, and even the lowly single-celled, amoeba. They can't fathom any other existence than the one they are living. So if they cannot comprehend being in any other form, how could they "think" their way to evolve into a more complicated species as evolution states? Human beings are no different. Being born human, we think we are the only superior race in the universe! Also the male thinks that his body is the ultimate shell of life and so the female thinks the same. They just can't comprehend how the other sex thinks, acts and experiences reality! Or conceive of evolving … physically or spiritually.*

"Can you find the lesson here?"

I was pensive for a moment.

"Yes, Micronia. It is that human beings believe that the life they are now living is the ultimate existence and when they die want to be resurrected and placed in that filthy old shell of their body once again because that is the only existence they know! If they would only think BEYOND the life they now exist in on a new plane or a different dimension they could see BEYOND their paltry existence upon the earth and be at peace with this phenomenon, that metamorphosis collectively known as DEATH! Also, the *Spiritual Body* is still a mystery to the mortal and they do not understand the difference between that and the physical body … or what the *Image of the Heavenly* means. It still is a total enigma, for the Bible states, *flesh and blood cannot inherit the kingdom of God; neither doth corruption inherit incorruption.*"

"Wow! Very good, Iben!

The Tiny Atom

We now traveled through solid sheet rock, insulation, plywood and brick of this house and were once again outside in the cool fresh air. Here our adventures continue to those unknown lands and uncharted dimensions aspiring us onward toward our Ultimate Destination.

Micronia stated, "Iben, we are going to have a wonderful time. We are going into the realm of the minute, beyond the imagination where never mortal mind nor human eye hath seen, to the molecular structure of the universe and see actual atoms face to face!"

When we left the world of the living human body we were still very tiny in size. We now shrank beyond the world of the microbe, even way beyond the virus and stopped at one angstrom. The angstrom is one hundred millionth of a centimeter (about the size of a light particle known as a photon). Then we plunged *beyond* the angstrom. We stopped again to minus 100 angstroms and then minus 1000 angstroms!

The things I once knew and could identify were no longer to be seen. I entered a totally foreign and unfamiliar landscape beyond known reality. We even traveled beyond this to the surrealistic land of molecules, twisting and turning, miles and miles of them spreading outward into infinity!

"We are now ten billion times smaller than the average human!" Micronia proclaimed.

Behold! The Cosmic Dawn

"Iben Jair," Micronia stated, "we are now proceeding back into the beginning of time. We are now going to observe the universe as it was when the embryonic pinpoint-size cosmos, the cosmic egg, was held together by the very hand of God and behold its birth in less than one nanosecond, or a billion billionth of a second!"

Micronia revealed the existence of an antemundane universe—a tiny flicker of light glowing intensely pure and bright as nothing I had ever comprehended. Having the divine energy of 1000 trillion galaxies in a black void of nothingness—it was suddenly released from God's mighty hand!

"Stand back and behold the omnipotent power of Almighty God!" Micronia proclaimed.

A microsecond later this hot mass of plasma exploded in an incomprehensible shock wave known as the "Big Bang. This intense glowing energy now underwent *phase transition,* time began, and energy coalesced into matter. Then in only a fraction of time this massive blast generated cosmic strings of particle waves giving birth to exotic atomic exotics as the MACHOs and WIMPs. These then cooled into tiny bright blue galaxies full of stars sparkling all magnitudes and colors within a nascent universe!

We learned that Massive Compact Halo Objects, or MACHOs now coalesced along the edges of the galaxies forming a phenomena known as "gravitational lensing" where stars are brightened and magnified. They, along with the WIMPs (Weakly Interacting Massive Particles) now were combined together forming the Theory of Everything (TOE) or the Theory of Supersysmmetry (SUSY) and the Superunification Theory which is an extension of the Grand Unified Theory (GUT). God designed these MACHOs and WIMPs to hold the galaxies together, keeping them from contracting again into another nascent universe!

We learned that only 10% of the universe is lit with stars, the rest consists of *mysterious enigmatic dark matter*, the X unknown of the universe.

From here we encountered the universe's background noise, that ancient reverberation of that first spectacular explosion. We realized it to be the distorted static from God's actual *Voice* when He spoke the universe into existence on that first magnificent day … long, so very long ago.

As the universe cooled, all these atomic forces solidified into "cosmic strings." Around these strings now condensed massive galaxies and nebulae. God now guided this matter to form suns, planets and moons continuing his divine wisdom and magnificent genius of terraforming many of these planets, sowing them with the mysterious seeds of organic life.

I learned there were many strange and mysterious things in our universe—*beyond* the shallow imagination and limited mind of the mortal human species!

Magnificent Luminaria, renowned scientists, appeared before us, all dressed in the period of their own times. One by one these great Supernalites introduced themselves. I was much impressed, for I had studied them in my science classes.

Before me were Galileo Galilei, of Italy, the father of modern experimental science, expounding upon astronomy, physics and mathematics; Benjamin Franklin, American author and inventor; Marie Curie, a Polish physicist, discoverer of radioactivity; and Buckminister Fuller, an American architect, discoverer of *fullerenes*, those mysterious atomic molecular structures resembling geodesic domes

I was awestruck! I had never seen such eminence in one place. Yet here these Illuminati are as alive as I am, still studying, conversing and debating with one another the mysteries of the atom, quantum chromodynamics and quantum electrodynamics.

Here resided their grand laboratory—being as large as the universe itself! What wonders these Supernalites relayed to me!

"Micronia," I inquired, "why isn't Einstein here?"

"Well, Iben which Einstein are you referring to? There are many 'Einsteins' in the hereafter."

Micronia then scanned my mind, "Oh, Albert, the

physicist?" Regretfully he couldn't come. He has been extremely busy lately working on—"

Franklin interupted, "Iben Jair, 'the wise one,' welcome! We will be your guides through the ultimate quest, the very building blocks of matter, the structure of the universe as you have never imagined!"

Snowflakes

Being this small the first thing I noticed was strange exotic crystals of atomic structures dotting the vast landscape. Beautiful patterns of snowflakes loomed before us as large as great delicately laced "ferris wheels."

We balanced ourselves upon a space lattice as a construction worker would upon a newly built steel skeleton of a skyscraper. I could make out individual atoms as a spider web shimmering in the sunlight.

I could see trillions of them falling—and each one unique from all the others, *ad infintium*!

Their lattices were almost as if they were alive as they kept growing as molecules were being added to them second by second making them expand larger and larger!

Galileo spoke, "The changing of water into a snowflake is so complex that computers have only begun to piece together this puzzle. Water vapor gives off heat as it changes, producing dendrites. The crystal then grows determined by temperature and humidity. These ice crystals keep expanding producing a beautiful array of patterns *all* having a six-spoke symmetrical configuration.

"Look into their centers, Iben, and tell me what you see. All snowflakes have this.

"All these snowflakes contain particles of debris in them like a flaw of carbon in a diamond. These particles are what the water crystallizes around. The debris you are seeing, is the dust from a micrometeorite! It came from a meteorite when it vaporized entering our atmosphere.

"Even bacteria high in our atmosphere can produce snowflakes! You see, these bacteria, such as the exotic *Pseudomonas syringe*, *Actinomyces* and *Deinococcus radiodurans* can cause this crystal formation. These bacteria can withstand UV radiation 5,000 times more than humans and even survive dehydration for months. Some of these bacteria can even create their own snow storms upon the earth!"

"Mortal man," Marie Curie proclaimed, "hasn't yet begun to understand the wonder of the snowflake, one of God's most beautiful and intricate masterpieces, yet but a very tiny wonder of our universe!"

Then, for one brief moment, I thought I caught a glimpse of an exotic magical city in the twinkling prism of a tiny snowflake. A minuscule world, an island metropolis existing only a million times smaller than a normal precarious speck of dust, drifting silently in this frozen fairy-land of wonder! We named it "Whoville" in honor of Dr. Seuss' *How the Grinch Stole Christmas*.

Could a type of life be composed of substances beyond the atom unknown to physicists? I wondered. I then thought about the life after death that I was now living!

This reminded me that mortal humankind should learn to live in peace because the Earth was also floating as a tiny particle of space debris, and all its inhabitants were created from a tiny speck of dust, each person a tiny miracle, all orbiting a minuscule sun, a mere pinpoint of light within a gigantic island universe floating through unfathomable space.

Now we shrink to minus 10,000 angstroms, small enough to study the structure of the atomic nucleus! It now appears about as big as our moon! Its electrons were spinning in orbits thousands of miles into space!

"Iben," Fuller spoke, "look closely and you can see strange wondrous crystal-like structures, not diamonds and not snowflakes but strange zeolites, lattice-like hollow atomic structures just now being studied carefully by physicists.

"Look Iben, from here you can see the nucleus' electrical charges, along with its protons and nucleons!

"You can actually observe their electromagnetic forces that bind these subatomic particles together. These binding particles are known as *gluons*!"

The neutron changed into a proton, with an electron blasting off into space in a flash of heat! Was I seeing things?

"What you have just witnessed Iben," Marie Curie explained, "is one of the great wonders of the universe, the actual TRANSMUTATION OF MATTER! One element actually changing into another right before your eyes!

"You are witnessing free neutrons breaking down— changing into protons. Each time a neutron undergoes such a mutation, an electron is emitted. This is also known as *radioactivity*."

We learned why these nuclei disintegrate and solved the mysteries that had puzzled physicists for a hundred years!

Then an awesome bolt of lightning flashed near me, hitting the very center of an atom!

"Iben, you have just witnessed a gamma ray hitting the nucleus of an atom," Marie Curie explained.

With this explosion, a tiny atomic particle was released.

"The birth of a pentaquark, Iben! Look closely and you will see another particle, the quark and yet inside the quark was another particle, the exotic antiquark!"

Next we watched radon scintillate and release its energy changing into radioactive bismuth and polonium!

"There is a positive charged particle less massive than a proton. The mystery is that an electron can exist in two different forms. The first one is the ordinary electron, and the other one is known as a *positive* electron, or *positron*. This positron is the antiparticle of the electron, its reverse, so to speak, and anything the electron can do, the positron can do—only in reverse!"

"This," I sighed, "is almost beyond my comprehension."

"Nonsense Iben, you now have the enhanced intellect of a Son of God, a Saint of the Divine."

Marie Curie explained the heart of the atom. That besides the positron, I learned, there is a negatively charged proton, an antiproton! The electrons and positrons when they meet can annihilate each other and so can the protons and the antiprotons.

Another mystery of the universe opened up. There it was and I cannot explain it in mortal words. There lay before me a foreign world as life is to death, an anti-universe, composed of antimatter consisting of atoms with nuclei built up from antiprotons, antineutrons and the strange antipositrons!

Such things do exist! I pondered.

"Iben," Marie Curie concluded, "we shall travel into one of these anti-universes and seek divine knowledge on how they are formed at a later date. These alternate and parallel universes are totally like nothing you have ever imagined or seen!"

I discovered that for every atomic particle their existed an antimatter counterpart like a mirror image. Matter and antimatter are collected into separate galaxies and enigmatic multiverses.

I surmised if ordinary matter produces radiation consisting of photons, might not anti-matter produce radiation of antiphotons?

"This secret, will be revealed unto you, in God's due time. Also, you will soon see the annihilation of a whole universe before your very eyes."

Now we learned all about the neutrinos, alpha particles, and photons of light. A typical photon of visible light has a wavelength of about 1/20,000 of a centimeter and this is about as wide as a thousand atoms. Since we are as small as we are it flashed across our sky brighter than a thousand suns! They travel, as all light does, in tiny bursts of energy known as *quanta*, similar to a spray from a water hose.

All the Supernalites and I watched the transmutation of matter with utmost awe. Then a neutron hit a uranium nucleus, instantly exploding in a tremendous flash of energy! This resulted in barium and krypton.

Franklin explained that this phenomenon was how the theory of the atom bomb came to light. Now I was seeing the inner working of how these atoms make up the building blocks of the universe!

I watched as a uranium atom was hit by a neutron transmuting it into the new element, neptunium. Then once again its nucleus rearranged itself, changing into the element plutonium!

The transmutation of matter, elements changing into other elements. What a wonder this universe is! I learned that with our enhanced senses we can see that other clandestine forces are active in the universe, strange forces scientists are not aware and as yet have no known instruments to detect.

Then we studied the subatomic particles, the quarks and the gauge bosons. All these particles are the wonderful "building blocks" which create all the known universe.

Thus the very *secrets of cosmology and astrophysics* were manifested before us!

We witnessed a phenomenon never before seen by mortal man—the *graviton*, that mystery sub-atomic particle only guessed at by scientists to exist—and it whizzed around our heads as if it were trying to comprehend *us*!

The Illuminati and I unraveled the Theory of "Heisenberg's Uncertainty Principle" or the "Uncertainty Theory of Matter!"

Franklin and Fuller expounded wonderful new theories such as Electrodynamics, the Grand Unified Theory (GUT) and the Loop Quantum Gravity Theory. These, along with other mystifying theories we meticulously unraveled and solved.

Still at minus 10,000 angstroms I saw unfamiliar substances, strange geometric puzzles, dazzling complex structures—

They futher explained the crystalline structure of the carbon atom! This is the lattice work of the hardest substance known to humankind having the shape of tiny pyramids, the diamond! These other four-sided structures flattened into hexagons is soft graphite which is used in pencil lead.

And now Fuller was in awe as we discovered another structure, a particularly elegant and resilient configuration composed of 60 carbon atoms (C60), resembling a geodesic dome.

"Behold Iben," Fuller commented, "the THIRD STATE OF THE CARBON ATOM! I have coined it a *synergetic geometric cathedral* and it is the strongest form of matter in the universe! An edifice formed from such a design could withstand even an atomic blast or any power the universe could throw against it!"

"Iben," Franklin cut in, "you will be introduced to this exotic carbon atom once again in the near future. And believe me, it will be something beyond your wildest imagination!"

I learned all about nuclear fission and nuclear fusion! In the sun helium is the by-product of burning hydrogen. The sun converts hydrogen into helium. One-fourth of our sun is now helium!

Then I realized our universe to be a great pulsating kinetic automation with a Divine Purpose, to produce life as its ultimate or teleological goal!

Our cortège of Intelligentsia now welcomed me into their camaraderie of enlightenment as we all studied the exotic elementary particles of the atom, namely the fermions, mesons, gluons, neutrons, leptons, baryons and a hundred others. Deep within these particles vacuum bubbles and strangelets existed… that could ultimately alter, tear or shred our three dimensional universe into multiverses that the mundane mind could never comprehend.

We studied all the aspects of quantum mechanics, *and then absorbed ... all mundane and mortal knowledge!*

I was totally stunned and awe struck!

"Was there anything beyond this," I questioned.

We plunged from minus 10,000 angstroms to minus 100,000 angstroms, then to minus 1,000,000 angstroms, then minus 10,000,000, then minus 100,000,000 and *beyond.* We entered into strange alternate worlds as alien to a human being as a fish is to realizing that life can exist outside his realm of reality, the little pond in which it dwells.

From here we observed only from a far distance another prismatic ingress leading to a strange convoluting anti-matter universe, a totally foreign concept to a human being, a complete paradox of reality which we only observed but dared not enter, an anomaly which cannot be comprehended in a three dimensional reality!

Fuller asked me if I could ever conceive of living in such a place as an anti-matter universe! I knew not the answer.

Can I go on? We are standing at the threshold of the human spectrum of knowledge *beyond* which to mortal mind is but a *cul de sac. What we have discovered in so short a time is that mortal man will never be able to enter into this realm of the universe to get "Divine Enlightenment" except that of being purged through death.*

I reflected upon the majesty of the universe,
its organization, its power never ceasing,
always vibrating, pulsating, moving,

forever constant and forever changing.
What a miracle! No wonder mortal man has doubts,
for he cannot see—
nay comprehend the infiniteness
of the creation he exists in,
nor the wonder of its Creator, God.
—The Author

What a strange and wonderful thing life is, I thought. *And yes, even DEATH!*

At this last statement, our renowned Illuminati, Galileo Galilei, Benjamin Franklin, Marie Curie, and Buckminister Fuller, all evanesced back into the great unknown from which they came.

CHAPTER TWO

Strange Amoeba and other Protozoa

*A*s we increased in size once again to the world of the microbe, Micronia revealed the variety of microscopic life. We solved the mystery of the amoeba *Proteus* and taught how this protozoan reproduced and fed. Not even having a brain or ganglia as most creatures, we learned how this fantastic creature, a mere "blob" of protoplasm can actually *think* without a brain!

We witnessed this fantastic creature undulating and creeping along in the bottom of a creek with its pseudopods stretching and flowing forever forward—searching for its next victim. We learned how it reproduced and then we solved one of the great riddles of the microscopic world. Whether it could, by dividing, become *two new organisms* once again? Did it hold the secret of immortality? Yes, only we were allowed such esoteric knowledge.

We located yet another amoeba. This deadly plasmodium before us was *Naegleria fowleri*, an insidious protozoan usually found in fresh-water ponds and shallow lakes. This microscopic "blob" can enter into a swimmers nose, crawl through their sinuses—eating the brain causing deadly meningitis, usually fatal in almost 100% of its victims. This deadly organism has been found just south of Little Rock, Arkansas in a small recreational lake used for swimming.

We also discovered that the Euglena, along with the blood parasite trypanosome (that causes African sleeping sickness) and the human sperm, all have a whip-like structure (flagellum) that is used for locomotion. We were amazed to find that the human sperm, consisting of both a head containing the DNA material, and its long tail, were actually *two separate organisms* actually living in a *symbiotic* relationship with each other!

In a supernatural intuition, I recognized some eminent Supernalites, dressed in the period of their time. Here were Leeuwenhoek, "The Father of Microbiology," a Dutch amateur scientist, designer of the first microscope; Lazzaro Spallanzani, an Italian biologist, who taught that microbes did not spring from inert matter; Robert Hooke, an English experimental scientist, inventor of the first compound microscope, who first published his *Micrographia*, the study of microscopic animals and plants; and John Snow, "The Father of Epidemiology," who expounded first and foremost that Cholera deaths were caused from their sewage-polluted Thames river in England.

I also spotted Battista Grassi, who was once an Italian authority on the nature of worms and ants, who was conversing with Ronald Ross, a British physician, that proved the *Anopheles* mosquito transmittes malaria. They were both conversing with the renowned German physician, Robert Koch, "Father of Modern Bacteriology", who isolated the microbe, *bacillus anthracis*, that causes anthrax and also discovered the bacterium, *tubercle bacillus*, that causes tuberculosis.

Grassi, Ross, and Koch were great rivals in their old lives, jealous of each other's work and full of arrogance and pride, but here in Eternity, have become the best of friends, having great rapport and camaraderie, still studying the microscopic world up close and personal of which they all loved so much. Such are their rewards in the Afterlife!

Our menagerie continued as we encountered the mayfly and dragonfly nymphs. We also studied the mosquito larva, fish, frogs and snail eggs were all in abundance at the bottom of this creek.

I could talk about these creatures for a hundred years and not exhaust their wonders. What a magnificent God to create such complex tiny animals that were completely unknown before the invention of the microscope! The thousands of other animalcules we studied must now be abandoned because of the time and space of this book and because mortal man could not even grasp the nature and complexity of all I had seen.

The salamanders, turtles and fish that were so large as to be invisible before, now came into view as we increased to normal size once again.

Also, Micronia stated, it was time for her, along with all those eminent bacteriologists, to leave. With this, they instantly vanished!

The Lakes and Ponds

I now increased in size to normalcy and the world of the minute evaporated before me as I returned to the world of which I was accustom.

Another Celestial Immortal Infinite, Aqua Pura, came forward to teach me the wonders of—

So, I now explored all the freshwater fish that reside in the lakes, rivers, ponds and streams.

I was told to write down only a TRACE of the things we accomplished, for humankind would not believe it. This reminded me when Marco Polo returned from his voyages and only a few believed him. Jesus Christ also told of the mysteries of God and few believed him.

The Lungfish and the Coelacanth

Just then there was a strange movement. A mysterious creature undulated toward me left over from the age of the dinosaurs! A weird creature, but alive as any I've seen.

"Behold, Iben—the Lungfish! A hundred million years later and the lungfish were still living while all the dinosaurs had long since perished. Strange as it seems, it is a survivor, along with the horseshoe crab, the cockroach and the coelacanth. Oddly, there have been found fossils of them as old as 400,000,000 years! Presently, there are only five species of lung fish living today in the rivers of Australia, South America and Africa. They all live in fresh-water rivers that sometimes dry up. And yes, they all have both gills and *lungs*!"

We also learned about the strange two-foot Asian walking catfish residing in Miami Florida's waterways and the Biscayne Bay area. These strange catfish escaped by actually crawling from their ponds into canals and creeks. It also has a primitive lung that absorbs oxygen from the air!"

I found myself twisting and turning through a vortex. In an instant we found ourselves in the highlands of Scotland!

Lock Ness

We encountered a shadowy dark fresh water lake, over a thousand feet deep. What secrets will we find within these strange waters?

All of a sudden the surface of the water began to churn and boil as if stirred up by the hand of some giant Titan. An object moved toward some fish and snatched up one in its massive jaws. I took it to be part whale but we were in fresh water. What could it be? It moved at a high rate of speed through the fog and vanished below the water's surface in an instant!

"Iben," stated Aqua Pura, "you have just seen the Morag monster! You probably don't recognize it by this name. How about Naitaka? Or better yet, Ogopogo?"

None of these names sounded familiar.

"How about the 'Loch Ness Monster,' Iben!"

"Wow! We were in Lock Ness, and had actually seen the fabled monster of yore!"

"Iben," Aqua Pura continued, "it is a type of *Eleasmosaurus,* a member of the plesiosaur family resembling an aquatic dinosaur! This creature now survives in the waters of Loch Ness, sealed off and trapped here for eons from an ancient natural disaster. Even Arthur Conan Doyle accurately described one in his book, *The Lost World*, written in 1912!"

We actually saw other leviathans which were direct descendants from these species swimming in the Loch! No wonder the scientists are confused! They thought all those pictures were of *one* animal when really there were many more species here to baffle the world!

Aqua Pura explained that I could travel anywhere I wanted. Just think of it and behold, it will come to pass. So I began to think of different places to travel and behold we were bathed in a labyrinth of warm, glowing and peaceful colors. Vertigo engulfed me as I fell as into a deep variegated abyss—a swirling tornado of a kaleidoscopic light—

Piranha

We found ourselves at Lake Calion, just north of El Dorado, Arkansas. Here I saw a strange creature. It reminded me of an ancient fish only found in the warm waters of Africa.

Oddly, the fish we discovered in Lake Calion was the red bellied piranha, a native of the Amazon River. A similar species has also been discovered in Mattocks park not too far from here. These exotic species are now thriving throughout the warmer lakes and streams of Arkansas and Louisiana.

In Lake Calion no less! Wow!

Naturalists will be in a quandary for a long time trying to figure out just how these fish relocated themselves here in Arkansas.

This is bizarre and scary to realize that these insidious creatures are actually thriving in lakes in the United States!

As Aqua Pura began to fade away, she stated she must now go and protect the many endangered species that are in our ponds, lakes, rivers, and fresh-water streams against pollution and their extinction.

"The wonders of nature
imbued by God in his infinite wisdom."
—The Author

I was now introduced to the Spirit, Phosphoria, "the light of life," and the Supernalite Leonardo Fibonacci. We learned all about the birds, their nesting rituals and their habitats. We were enlightened about the great "Bald Eagle die-off" in DeGray, Arkansas, where birds have perished from unknown causes. This strange disease causes paralysis, even eating holes in their brains! It wasn't a bacterial or viral infection. Could it be kin to mad cow disease or a type of deadly neurotoxin?

We learned about the Arctic tern, having the greatest migratory route of all birds. They travel from the Arctic to the Antarctica and back each year, a round trip of over 22,000 miles! We learned of their best kept navigation secrets, that which keeps them from losing their way across miles of ocean. We discovered magnetite in their beaks and brains which help them align to the magnetic fields surrounding the earth.

We discovered that their eyes contain a light-sensitive protein known as *cryptochrome* which can also sense the magnetic lines of force guiding these migratory birds. They can even orient themselves to the stars, navigating across vast distances of land and ocean.

We learned that many birds can hear infrasound, ultralow frequencies of long wavelengths way below those of the human ear. Many birds live in a foreign world as dogs and insects do, where their senses are expanded far above and below ours, in a hyper-reality existence that humans cannot begin to comprehend!

Phosphoria further taught me about the lives of the reptiles, namely the turtles, tortoises and terrapins, along with the lizards and snakes. We discovered that the majority of the snakes were benevolent and harmless— yet others we found to be very dangerous—the rattle snakes, the cobras and the extremely deadly black mambas. I learned that there were 36 species native to Arkansas—and only 6 were poisonous! We studied the poisonous copperhead, coral snake, the water moccasin (cottonmouth), and the rattlesnake. We also studied the benevolent corn snake, hognose snake and the coral king snake. He stated mortals should remember the succinct adage:

"Red touches black, venom lack; red touches yellow, kills a fellow."

Amphibian Extinction and Pollution

Phosphoria revealed a Great Unsolved Mystery, the mass extinction of a major phylum of the animal kingdom— the amphibians. These little creatures, which includes the caecilians, frogs, toads and salamanders of the world have major genetic deformities when born. They are all dying as a species on a grand scale unprecedented in recent times. Biologists have now discovered an insidious fungus

Chytridiomycosis that has caused the extinction of over a hundred species of amphibians and frogs.

Are these extinctions a precursor of more serious things to come? Is pollution of God's great beautiful world starting to play havoc upon her living species?

Now he revealed the secrets of the spiders, chiggers, ticks, mites and scorpions. Why did God place these insidious creatures upon the earth? Was it just to torment humankind or did God have a grander scheme? I learned how they fit into the ecological niche and that in his infinite wisdom God created these creatures for a purpose other than to just curse the human race. Here I learned that the little black widow spider has one of the most virulent poisons of them all. Her bite contained a deadly neurotoxin being 15 *times* more poisonous than the rattlesnake and as dangerous as the King Cobra!

Now we learned all about the insects, including the beautiful butterflies and moths, wasps and bees of the world. Interestingly, I learned that there are about five times as many moths as butterflies! In North America there are a little less than 700 different kinds of butterflies—and about 9,000 different kinds of moths!

Then we studied the honey bees, discovering they were all in serious trouble with a phenomenon known as colony collapse disorder. This disorder is caused not only by the varroa mite but dangerous pesticides, namely the neonicotinoids used to control insect pests sprayed over farmlands. In the near future the neonicotinoids may prove to be as dangerous as DDT was decades ago when it was banned preventing another ecological disaster.

We learned all about the plant kingdom and the secrets

of chlorophyll and pollination. Then we studied all the trees, the pines and oaks along with thousands of other species—

Yet another Supernalite, the Italian mathematician, Leonardo Fibonacci, now revealed the most wonderful geometric patterns found in nature. We studied the sworls in pine cones and sunflowers, and thousands of configurations involved in a myrid of animals and plants, from the star fish to the bee hive—all utilizing complex mathematics embued clandestinely in the natural world.

With this, Phosphoria, along with all the others evaporated —

Cognitive Perception

In Eternity, I was learning that we now have a much larger perspective of the universe. Mortal man can only see that lighted portion of his world that they can conceive or perceive, that which is relative to our senses, and limited to our finite minds. The more humans learn—the more their reality is altered and enhanced.

Humankind must die to shed this mortal shell and put on immortality to break through this barrier of myopic vision which narrows his limited life. Death is not the end but a *reawakening of our spiritual minds*, enlightening the psychic and cosmic realm, revealing the magnanimous forces of the Unknown, empowered by the Creator of the Universe.

Death has become such a—how can I describe it to mortal humankind? It is like telling a fish about living upon land. It is like trying to relate to a dog what driving a car is like or what reading a book is like to a bird!

The greatness of God defies the limitations of language. Language is God's gift to humankind. Only humans have the brain and mental capacity to understand a *written* language and the greater things of life, the concept of love, truth, justice, life after death and the enlightenment of the soul.

Observing nature in all its wildest, raw environment is such an experience! Are you a nature lover? I wasn't—until Eternity overcame me. Now I can't seem to get enough of it! I can see God in nature, in the land, in the forests and in the rivers. I can see God *everywhere*! How strange it took death to show me what real living is!

I must now continue my many experiences in the Hereafter. Lack of time and having to make a living seem to limit the rapport and ardor and camaraderie upon the earth, and making a living suppresses many relationships. Here in Eternity it all is so different. Friends here don't just last a lifetime. They last *for all eternity*! Strange, how one phrase can mean such a great and unlimited thing. ETERNITY! What human life was made for!

Why can't human beings upon the earth learn more than they do? Why can't they study more? Why can't they love and have compassion more? *Why can't they see that death is only a gateway, a portal to the greatest and the most ultimate experience that God has for Homo sapiens?*

I became enlightened to the folly of humankind. They can't seem to learn from their mistakes because their carnal minds are geared to the things of the world. They must survive. To do this they think they have to cheat, steal, lie and kill to accomplish their goals to attain happiness. They just don't have the confidence, hope, faith or wisdom to understand what existence is all about. *They just can't see beyond the grave.* Therefore, humans can't possibly relate to being the best they can be while upon this old earth. Humankind is in a hopeless situation, a cul de sac with no way out. *Only through death, will the human race be illuminated and find the teleological destiny it was meant to live.* Many people think they are better than others and fail to realize that each of us is a *unique creature, created by God* for a *Definite Purpose* in life.

"Don't let college get in the way of your education!"
—The Author

"The heart of the prudent getteth knowledge;
and the ear of the wise seeketh knowledge."
—Proverbs 18:15

How can a mortal being live with himself and never want to learn about the world in which he lives? He leads a life of "quiet desperation," never wanting to expand his mind by reading past the sport's page, or even reading a great classic of literature. Yet, to really live means to really *think*, expanding your horizons, keeping an open mind.

You must learn new things and pray for those in need and thank God for all your blessings. *This is the only road to real fulfilled happiness and completeness which leads to the more abundant life.*

I must make note about my existence once again. I can't seem to really get over it. My mind—an insatiable appetite for academic nutrition, the *Knowledge of the Ages*, forming profound Godly wisdom of such I could have never attained while upon the earth in mortal form. My new way of looking at the world is so *different,* and my old body limited my perception, my imagination and all my thoughts. What a wonder to be utterly freed from mortal fears and all their egotistic derivations, wounded pride, hurt feelings, unrequited love, squelched rage, humiliation, failure, the vanity of ambitious strivings, abandonment and loss and worldly stress, not to mention the more insistent demands and limitations of the body itself.

The Concept of Reality

I studied the phenomenon of the Fourth Dimension, and realized that time travels in a straight line, and moves along as a recording tape or a disk. The tape can become twisted and time will be distorted, or the disk may contain a virus, be misread and at times may jump its track.

Take a flashlight and shine it down a dark street. Only what is seen in the spotlight is what the mortal knows as their reality. Now move the light from side to side and only that which is illuminated is known as reality, and its movement is known as time. All the person knows as reality is what the light shines upon—that is the present. As the light brightens or dims (perception), and as the field of view widens or narrows (concentration), and what the light has illuminated in the past (memory) … nothing more.

If the sun came out all our reality could be seen. This is what the "enlightened" mystics, prophets and those having "extrasensory abilities" are blessed with. They have *seen beyond* what the average mortal has seen and are therefore ridiculed and harassed because of it! Yet their epiphany or theophany can, not only be a unique experience, but illuminate with a divine light, the truth that lies just beyond the horizon of secular knowledge. *Few are blessed with this ability ... and even more tragic, few believe it when this knowledge is finally revealed.*

What kind of an unknown existence will I be living? I realize it is now a wonderful "after death" ethereal and incorporeal reality way beyond the realm of the physical world in which I was conceived. I also was realizing that the longer I stayed in these alternate existences, the three-dimensional world I once knew—was slowly fading away.

What other wonders and miracles will God unravel before me in this vast universe of His!

"There are more things in heaven and earth,
Horatio, than are dreamt of in your philosophy."
—Hamlet, Act I

"Would you waste time trying to explain
rainbows to an earthworm?
... an earthworm can't even see—
much less have a color sense."
—Robert A. Heinlein, *Space Cadet*

"Science without religion is lame,
religion without science is blind."
—Albert Einstein

CHAPTER THREE

Vesuvius and Her Secrets

*A*nother scintillating Angelic Divine Counselor now appeared.

"Fear not, Iben, for I am Torchere. I bring light out of darkness, and knowledge out of ignorance. I will now be your guide into—"

Oscillating our reality, we once again hurled across the ripples of time as a needle skips across a record to find another song. And this song was the forlorn song of Pompeii.

On a hot summer day of A.D. 79, we witnessed the ancient city of Pompeii, Italy, a beautiful metropolis of 25,000 people, south of Rome. Pompeii's inhabitants, with all their wealth, did not realize the extreme danger of living so close to Vesuvius!

I could hear the rumbling of thunder as we wandered through the cobblestone streets. Then I noticed a wispy effluvium shroud over Pompeii as it cast its dark shadow, blotting out the sun. I realized it was Thanatopia—

Then suddenly and without warning, Vesuvius

thundered and exploded with her wrath of judgment! Fiery cinders of pumice were blown from the volcano setting the city ablaze as heavy black smoke filled the sky.

Then a pyro-plastic shock wave of superheated air blasted through the city faster than the speed of sound scorching all in its path. Deadly carbon dioxide spewed from the volcano, stealthily and silently snuffing out all remaining life.

I wept for the inhabitants of Pompeii.

I was jerked from my reverie by Torchere.

"There could be no doubt that this was all
this terrible Saknessemm had done.
As to the existence of a gallery, or of
subterraneous passages leading
into the interior of the earth, the idea was simply absurd,
the hallucination of a distempered imagination."
—Jules Verne, *A Journey to the Center of the Earth*

My mind whirled into unconsciousness and my body was seized into the clutches of vertigo. I had the sensation of spiraling down into a great abyss—and was shocked back into the present.

"Torchere," I proclaimed, "I don't think I will ever get used to this time travel."

"Sure you will, Iben. Soon you will be a real *terra incognita* traveler, transversing through multiple dimensions as if you have done it all your life! We are here on another Divine Mission from God."

So we left the horror of Pompeii to its silent fate and moved toward the now extinct volcano of Vesuvius. How different it looked two thousand years later. No bubbling caldera full of boiling lava or smoke issuing from her silent stack. All was peaceful. All was quiet.

We ascended to the crown of Vesuvius. Upon her summit I stood for a time gazing outward toward the skeleton city of Pompeii, and then turned inward toward her haunting crater. We began our journey downward into her dark forbidden chambers and plunged straight into the unknown ebony depths of the earth!

We jumped from the precipitous ledge into the blackness of infinity ... and floated downward slow motion, time slowed and we descended lower and lower into the hollow dormant lava shaft.

How can I describe this exhilarating delight descending into her very depths with only a trace of sulfur dioxide in the air! Then we came to the old lava plug preventing further descent.

"Well, Torchere, "it's been fun—but we are at a dead end, the dried lava has plugged this vent preventing further progress."

"My dear saint, stand back and watch the power of Almighty God! Remember, Iben, our immortal bodies cannot be touched by mundane phenomena. Breathing is now a foreign trait to you. The pressures of our underwater adventures did not bother us either. Therefore, our spiritual bodies are immune to the physical forces of nature, whether it be heat, cold, extreme pressures or any other attribute of the physical nature of the universe! We are still in the state of *Interdimensional Transposition*. So, Iben, you won't have the problem of breathing when traveling through solid rock, or the trepidation of asphyxiation!"

Odd, I didn't even think of that! As Torchere proclaimed, I had no fear of suffocation when I sank into the dried solidified lava! As in the ocean, I had no sensation of breathing at all! How easily and gladly I forfeited that earthly trait! Odd also is that I could smell without breathing—

So we began to sink into the very lava tube that was plugged by solid stone a moment before. Down we sank into impermeable basalt! What did it look like traveling through solid rock! It is an indescribable mystery to mortal humankind but I will try to relate it to those interested in such things.

Well, it was dark at first, then as our eyes adjusted, I realized that I could actually see! He explained that this light was from their radioactivity producing this phenomenon of light known as Cherenkov radiation to see beyond man's paltry 400 (violet) to 700 (red) nanometers of visible light, or only 3% of the electromagnetic spectrum. And where the light was dim, the aurora of our glorified bodies radiated luminosity as a torch, lighting the way through the Stygian blackness of solid rock!

We began to feel the heat of the underground as we descended lower and lower. We neared the hot lava, an incipient red color, boiling and hissing and spewing steam.

Many times these angels would stop and comment about something we observed or noticed out of the ordinary. Strange how I could examine minute details of different minerals in the strata we were passing. I could even see soil bacteria living near this excruciating heat!

"*Pseudomonas aeruginosa* bacteria—a hospital's nightmare!"

"I can't believe that this heat doesn't kill them!"

"This bacterium has the astonishing ability to survive these harsh conditions. They can even live and thrive in distilled water!"

He enlightened me that hospitals actually dissolve penicillin in it to kill these bacteria. Many *P. aeruginosa* have even become immune to penicillin!

I then noticed hundreds of pieces of dull glass sown all through these lava layers. He explained that they should have looked familiar, in that I had studied them before.

"Look closer at them and tell me what you see!"

My eyes adjusted to the tiny building blocks of matter and then I jumped with delight!

"These are diamonds!"

"How right you are, Iben. The pressures inside the earth has produced them and the lava has carried them up from the interior of the earth and deposited them along this subterranean lava tube."

We continue through the lower depths of the volcano, straight down the hot magma tube. The temperature now reached thousands of degrees F.—with pressure building. Torchere explained that in the next hundred years, Vesuvius will again explode. Only this time, Naples, not far from the ruins of Pompeii, will be erased from the earth!

It is a good thing we are in a parallel universe or we would have burned up long ago!

Then we came to a hollowed out area with steep cliffs, the lava and magma lake boiling below us, exuding a most noisome stench. Upon this precipice was the most massive structure I had ever seen! Huge granite stone blocks were stacked upon each other, as some great Titan had directed a massive brick wall to keep out who knows what.

"It looks man made, but, how could that be, so many miles below the surface of the earth?"

"Iben, these quarried blocks were built to deflect the intense heat of the volcano! And there are more giant blocks here than it took to construct the Great Cheops Pyramid!"

"Then these carved blocks were really cut and stacked in place by human hands?"

"My dear saint, you have so much to learn! These granite blocks seal off the old subterranean lava tube which is now hollow. Come, I want t show you something."

The outside of these quarried stones erected upon each other were glazed over from the heat of thousands of years.

I learned that these stones were quarried and stacked here eons ago to keep out the subterranean heat when the volcano first erupted. Then the natives that lived in this ancient lava tunnel liked the heat and set up their dwellings. They resided here for hundreds of years until the volcano finally erupted and the surrounding area became unbearable for habitation. Finally, in desperation, these troglodytes sealed off this section of the tube and made an artificial exit a few miles farther down.

These stone blocks were terribly massive, being the largest ever quarried, even greater than those at Stonehenge, England! The temperature here was many times as hot as your kitchen oven!

Traveling through solid stone was such a fantastic thing! It is a phenomenon which must be experienced to be understood.

"As death," I surmised.

"How perceptive you are, Iben!"

Through the other side of these huge blocks we came to

a lava tube where once hot magma had formed a parasitic cone to the earth's surface. The temperature here on the other side was rather cool to us.

We entered into a capacious room having a high vaulted ceiling wet with dripping water. Oddly, I could see a glowing from this canopy, a strange luminescence as if the stars were out on a clear night! Then, by my surprise, I realized they were not stars—but insects! Gnat larvae using bioluminescence. The common lightning bug, the creatures under the ocean floor, those in the human body, and these creatures in the depth of the earth, all shared a common bond, that of the mystery of bioluminescence!

Another truth entered my mind. God, in his infinite wisdom, will not let life come into being without light. So no matter how dreary or dark your life gets, having God by your side can mean that you will have that shinning, divine Light to help guide the way for you.

"Is this unique upon the earth?"

"Some caves in New Zealand, "Torchere answered, "are so bright from the light of insects that guided tours are conducted to show off their glow worms on their ceilings! And Iben, you will see still *greater wonders* than these! Millions of gnat larvae can exist because these stones block the heat of the inferno only yards away!"

Miles and miles we descended, twisting through lava encrusted chambers as we moved deeper and deeper into the interior of the earth. We entered another long hollow lava channel and weaved through its smaller labyrinthine tributaries, rendering nightmares of random, chaotic tunnels carved by molten lava eons ago.

The Zamzummim

(Gen. 6:4, 14:5; Deut. 2:10-23)

Now we crossed under a massive archway carved from black granite etched with cabalistic symbols of a lost unknown language. Entering through this massive triforium was the entrance into a capacious cathedral chamber, hot and arid, with little or no humidity.

I encountered numerous slabs of basalt, polished with the glassy look of agate, their sides painted a faded yellow. Within this yellow background were more of these strange unintelligible markings etched in scarlet and ebony.

As my eyes adjusted to the darkness, I became aware of menacing silhouettes of numerous giant statuesque beings. Unlike normal humans, these beings had strange elongated heads prostrated side by side, rigid and unmoving. Each were resting upon their own personal butte. Unlike the Egyptian mummies, these were not wrapped in cloth, but wore only animal furs. Each of these creatures had a series of pagan tattoos upon their bodies, representing nature worship and their false gods. Their necks, arms, legs and faces were etched with strange cryptic symbols of their tribal status. On one butte rested a male figure that had markings etched in gilded gold—the signature of royalty. He also wore a necklace composed of a rare meteoritic crystalline quartz—the symbol of a king.

Yet others, mainly the females and their young children, were found wearing beautiful seashells and numerous teeth with tiny holes bored through them where a thin thread joined them together, known as "rococo" necklaces.

Statues, I thought at first, but—then I saw their large luminous eyes, staring at us from the unknowable beyond. These creatures, both male and female, along with their children, were all buried with their eyes opened!

How unsettling, I mused.

Then I noticed something else very strange. Besides their large enlongated heads, each had six fingers and six toes!

As I closely studied these strange hominids, I realized their true size. They were over twice as large as any human's in the upper world. What strange perceptive eyes and large massive mouths these creatures had! They could see better than humans ... and could probably eat an elephant in one meal, I surmised.

"An *Amebelodon*, Iben! They did not have elephants in those days. You see, these giants lived before the elephants roamed the land, so they ate a menagerie of strange creatures indeed."

Besides the mastodon, I learned, they ate the Goya, a type of giant guinea pig, another one of their main food sources.

"See that body wearing the necklace? It is known as an *ansate cross*. The precursor of the ankh of ancient Egypt! It is their symbol representing life. Anthropologists would be shocked to learn that the early Egyptians *copied* them from these ancient antediluvian giants of the Eocene Era!"

Carved on the stelae behind these ancients were a strange undecipherable pre-Egyptian language that I had never seen.

I now asked God for the gift of deciphering these strange

writings. As this unknown language began to unravel itself, Torchere pointed to one interesting hieroglyph.

These dead humanoids rested upon these ceramic stone slabs, painted with a yellow and red ochre, colors from the iron found in the clays of the earth. Upon the surface of these slabs of polished agate were painted symbols known to paleontologists as macaronis, similar to carvings found during the Bronze and Iron Ages of the past. Then I realized that we were looking at the very first symbols used to record history ... the beginning of the human languages!

They were similar, I learned, to the diminutive form of the *Devanagari* alphabet. Then I realized that I was looking at the forerunner of the ancient Sanskrit writings of the ancients of Akkad, old Semitic inhabitants of Southern Mesopotamia who founded the magnificent cities of Babylon and Assyria!

I now brushed away the dust of uncountable millennia from the sides of this tomb and interpreted the strange prehieroglyphics spelling one letter at a time:

"NAHSABFOGNIKEHT."

Reading from right to left, as most ancient writings do and without spaces separating the words:

Translating this to: "THE KING OF BASHAN."

I realized at this moment we were actually looking into the very face of the King of Bashan, whose name was not only etched on the base of his sarcophagus, but also in the pages of the Holy Bible. We had stumbled upon the remnants of the Lost Kingdom of Og, and this was the burial place known as the Valley of the Giants, the royalty from the land adjacent to the land of Edrei. Here in these olden times God first destroyed the Rephaim known as two races of giants, the Emim and the Anakims. Then their relatives, the Zamzummim, inherited the land of Og.

These humanoids, I learned, were from another place and time in the unrecorded history of the earth. They were known only in obscure biblical passages as the Rephaims, residing in Asheteroth Karnaim; the Zuzims, residing in Ham; and the Emims, residing in Shaveh Kariathaim.

These beings entered these lava tunnels, I learned, mainly to bury their dead and observe their burial rituals. These Zamzummim you are witnessing were mummified mainly by this heat, drying out their bodies so well that even the flesh, visceral organs and their skin were preserved, almost as fresh as the day they died.

Torchere explained, that in 1941, anthropologists found in China a jaw bone that surpassed the gorilla's in size, and named it *Meganthropus palejovanicus* (*Mega*, meaning "great," *anthropus*, "man"). These bones were carbon dated to be the oldest remains of man yet discovered and are well over 500,000 years old! This indicates that man's ancestors could have actually been huge and that —

> "There were giants in the earth in those days;
> and also after that, when the sons of God
> came in unto the daughters of men,
> and they bore children to them,
> the same became mighty men who
> were of old, men of renown."
> —Genesis 6:4

There weren't any Coptic jars that held the intestines, heart, liver and brain of these creatures, which meant that these bodies, unlike those of the ancient Egyptians, still contained all their organs.

"Even the brain?" I questioned.

"Yes, the brain can even be preserved if the right conditions exist. In Titusville, Florida, there has been found the skull containing an actual brain from ancients that roamed the area in 5,000 B.C.! Yet, other brains have been discovered—that exist over three times this old!"

Egyptian mummies, I realized, have been preserved, but only by extracting all their organs and using apothecaries, I could understand. But whole bodies, so that even their brains, stomachs and all their inner organs were intact! Even the eyes were preserved down to their eyelashes, finger prints, skin and hair. Even the fabric of their clothing and its colors were preserved down to their last detail!

These "chimera of the darkness" were truly a wonder of the subterranean world. There were dozens of them in this burial chamber, all lying beside each other in their best tribunal apparel, untouched by insects. This attire they wore consisted of a type of fur, their colors still bright and pristine as the first day they were made! These garments, all finely woven, would have rivaled any found in the royalty of the upper Nile in the Valley of the Kings!

What thoughts must have entered their minds when they were alive. And what strange thoughts now entered mine.

These hominids or bipedal primates, I learned, belonged to the pre-biblical period long before the antediluvian era. They existed even before the deluge of the Bible. These troglodytes were part of the first race of humanoids, whom

God destroyed. Later, God almost destroyed the complete human race, except for Noah and his family.

What was left of one of the first civilizations upon the earth were before us. Remember in the Bible that Cain was banished to the land of Nod, east of Eden. These Nephilim, sons of Anak, were the few nomadic survivors living until the last ice age finished them off, residing in the city of Enoch, named after one of Cain's surviving sons.

Then in a nearby grotto we discovered a mysterious menagerie of animals that also resided here. As the ancient Egyptians, they buried their food and all the things they might need to survive the nether world of the dead.

These were strange creatures indeed. These animals had mummified, perfectly preserved as the Zamzummim were, only these animals had been standing upright for eons as though still alive!

Food of the Giants

Mummified mastodons, and other giant bear-like creatures—long extinct from the modern world, were also present. Here resided a miniature four-horned "unicorn" horse, kin to the *Pilohippus* family, along with giant flightless birds that towered above all the other animals. Standing between all of these creatures, were the *Unitatherium*— the first rhinoceroses.

As I stated earlier, there was also present a giant species of rodent, the Goya, having little eyes, small ears and a large tail used for balancing on its hind legs. Smooth fur covered its entire body. It was akin to the guinea pig. Its fur was used for clothing and it was one of the main staples of their diet.

Then we saw the *Poebrotherium*, another food source, the very first camels to appear upon the world! And other strange carnivores such as great marsupial cats—

Here in the intestines of these long dead mummified creatures, I made an important discovery. Living bacteria were still alive but inert in these animals. Living single-celled organisms which were the remnants of their last meal resided inside these ancient mammals. If the right temperature ensued, these micro-organisms could very well come alive once again, and yes, one was the insidious smallpox virus! What a scourge this could cause if released, this strain being the precursor of the infamous variola strain which decimated Europe in the Dark Ages!

"My dear saint, Iben," Torchere stated, "don't be so overwhelmed. This is a great wonder, yes, but scientists have actually found *live* bacteria inside an 11,000-year-old mastodon carcasses in 1989, by workers turning a peat bog into a lake in a golf course in central Ohio, about 25 miles east of Columbus."

I then realized that these bacteria and viruses were, none-the-less, some of the most tenacious and oldest living organisms upon the earth!

Then I spotted a—mummified rabbit?

"Yes, Iben", Torchere continued, "this species is the precursor of the domestic rabbit! They were used for food, but more so, to clothe these giants only for their special days of celebration. The beautiful coats which these Zamzummim are wearing were made especially for their ceremonial rites and funerals created from their fur!"

All these mummified animals were killed and eaten for

food. How they made those beautiful clothes they wore, still, even to us, remained yet another intriguing Mystery of the Ages.

Yet the Zamzummim were destroyed. These nefarious troglodytes sinned against God and nature in interbreeding with the fallen angels and with a strange hominid apelike subspecies. Then God realized the evil they had become—a corrupted genetically modified organism, these strange mutants you now see. So God *uncreated* them. When these Zamzummim perished, they were gone forever. The way God has ordained it … And so shall it be—for all eternity.

A deep profound silence fell upon me.

"Try not to feel pathos for them, Iben, for they were iniquitous beings, sinister and evil, having no future with the things of God. Again, they were free to do what was right or wrong, good or evil, but chose to interbred with the fallen angels of Lucifer thus creating this chimerical hybrid. So God destroyed them in a cataclysmic event of such magnitude it reversed Earth's magnetic fields, tilted the Earth's axis, and even annihilated many of the larger dinosaurs.

"Then God bioremediated the earth and created the human race."

> "So God created man in his own image, in
> the image of God created he him;
> male and female created he them."
> —Genesis 1:27

"And the Lord God formed man of the dust of the ground,
and breathed into his nostrils the breath of life;
and man became a living soul."
—Genesis 2:7

The Ringing Rock

Wandering among these Zamzummim, I came to realize that this burial ground was connected by stairs leading down to an amphitheater where a strange rather large stone was placed, rough and sharp untouched by chisels or stone tools. This odd metallic mineral was paraded upon a sturdy solid butte. It was left exactly as it was found.

"Does it look familiar to you, Iben?"

Inside this stone I discovered a composite of nickel and iron. I realized it to be a huge meteorite which had fallen from the sky eons ago.

Around this meteorite, I discovered all sorts of smaller stones.

"This, my dear Iben, is a special, sacred boulder known as the *ringing rock*."

I was awe-struck just being in its presence. I visualized what it must have been like when prehistoric medicine men played their ancient songs upon this rock before large gatherings.

I picked up one of those sharp stones and struck it gently, the sacred boulder chimed like a bell. When I struck it in several places or with various-sized pebbles, actual songs could be played. This meteorite, I learned, was the central focus of their elaborate cultural burial ceremonies.

I played the song of mourning for these strange beings.

The melody echoed off the walls of this "cathedral" leaving me with a sense of tranquility and wonder. A nostalgic song that these sacred walls had not heard for—

"Iben, a few years ago, a similar ringing rock was found in Riverside Country's Minifee Valley, southeast of Los Angeles. There are only seven such rocks known in existence—all in the southwestern United States!"

Such wonders I was learning! Death wasn't the end as most people think. *It is only a DOORWAY into which real complete life is only an enigma to mortal mind.*

So we left the Gigantes and wound our way through the ebony darkness, journeying across their silent footsteps … uncountable centuries gone.

"Iben, I want to show you something extraordinary. All of this seems chimerical enough, but still greater wonders await you!"

Strange Prehistoric Art

We continue our dissension under Vesuvius finally arriving at a great chamber. Upon these walls was another great wonder in the Lost Valley of the Giants. A colossal painting of wonderful eerie creatures that must be described to be believed! In fact, this mural before us was almost as brightly colored as the day it was created.

Etched in bright pristine colors were hundreds of prehistoric animals of a long lost era. There were the long-extinct *Brontotherium,* strange giant North American mammals residing with huge Pliocene elephants, with arrows and spears sticking into their sides. Others included extinct herbivores and the monstrous *Cynognathus,* a giant mammal-like carnivore, along with many crocodiles with narrow snouts akin to the gavial. Here painted in rich browns were also the now extinct species of the steppe bison, ancient cattle, and even a type of woodland bison, with a long extinct species of the addax antelope!

The radiant colors of this panorama continued. Long-extinct birds were flying through a painted sky of angry clouds from which below rose strange tree-like plants, the fan palms, towering above smaller bushes and dwarf trees.

There were painted among the green and brown grasses of this mural, the brightly colored moas of a lost age. Standing over twelve feet tall, these flightless birds were the largest that ever lived. Their bones have *only* been found in New Zealand and they were hunted to extinction in 1310 A.D. Moas were an anomaly indeed, for they didn't have tiny little wings as the ostrich, but these birds had no trace of wings whatsoever!

These great walls contained giant armadillos and a number of giant sloths—some of the largest mammals ever, towering high above all the other creatures! All these extinct animals were painted upon this cave wall in bright and realistic colors—almost looking alive!

Composed upon this magnificent mural were numerous other creatures, beautiful, wondrous creations of prehistory. We then realized that we were actually looking at the ancient world *before* the Zamzummim went underground!

They were painted with ancient paints of hundreds of colors, never believed obtainable by ancient cavemen. Rich, beautiful pigments derived from red ochre and manganese black, forming the true greens of the forest, the azure blue of the sky, shimmering aqua-greens of the lakes and light purple, creating the majestic mountains in the background. The panorama expanded above our heads as high as an eight story building covering a massive wall many times the width of a football field! At the lower right corner of the painting I could see a few huge hand prints each having six fingers pressed into the wall, the artists signature of this magnificent work of genius.

What a fantastic painting this was in the depths of Vesuvius! This great panorama of a long forgotten and forsaken world, lost to eternity buried in the abyss of the earth!

How did all these creatures die out?

"Iben," Torchere explained, "these Oligocene giants died out as swiftly as the dinosaurs and as mysteriously. A Great Ice Age ensued, forcing them, along with many of the huge animals portrayed in this mosaic to migrate from these harsh climates to travel deep within the earth."

"But," I asked, "what actually happened to the Zamzummim? Why did God curse these giants?"

I learned there were *three reasons:*

The first, I learned, was for sinning with the angels producing strange hybrid offspring, adulterating their species. Could this be another reason for Noah's flood?

The second reason was —

We discovered shallow bowls or goblets stained black. These contained dried blood from pagan ritualistic ceremonies where these Gigantes drank the fresh blood of their victims just after they were slaughtered. We were observing the very first culture ever to use vampirism!

I then learned a third reason. Further into the dingy cavern we discovered mounds of human bones that had been the grisly remains of an ancient feast. These dismembered bones had been stripped of their flesh, then roasted and cracked open for their fatty marrow. Their skulls had been baked then beaten open exposing the brains. They were cannibals, I learned, who ate their own kind!

We stared at this bizarre sight before us. He stated that many ancient cultures have eaten their dead in quasi-religious ceremonies, namely the ancient Anasazi those early Pueblo people in the American Southwest in the state of Colorado and a settlement in southern Germany, near the village of Herxheim.

"Were the Aztecs, Mayas and Incas of central Mexico and South America cannibals?" I asked.

Torchere was strangely silent upon this question— but continued with a stern warning that God will curse any culture or nation if they turn to vampirism or turn to cannibalism.

And so God cursed the Zamzummim altering the magnetic poles of the earth causing a great ice age to spread over the land, destroying their agriculture, forcing them underground and after a while—they were erased from the surface and finally from the depths of the earth.

From these mighty Gigantes I witnessed one of the greatest wonders of the world, never to be seen by mortals. I was greatly impressed by their strange ancient culture and these beautifully painted engravings and realized that only the saints of God could find and study such enigmas as these!

Thus ended our stay in these chimerical dwellings among these long dead Zamzummim, those strange beings of another world.

"My dear Iben," Torchere concluded, "let us now depart from these lost creatures of forgotten lore, and leave this infernal underground necropolis to its fate—someday to be purged by this volcano. Let us leave this dark underworld to these antediluvian Zamzummim lying in the depths of the earth ... that have perished into oblivion for all eternity."

Chapter Four

"All is not gold that glitters."
—Old Adage

"*M*y dear saint," Torchere proclaimed, "let us depart from these iniquitous humanoids of which the earth has kept no record. Come … let us exit these subterranean caverns sealed for all time and continue upon our fantastic quest."

Entering an old dormant lava tunnel we began to descend once again, deeper and deeper into the foreboding interior of the earth.

What is this string doing here running along the floor of this tunnel?

Like the ancient Mythian Ariadne, Mino's daughter, who gave Theseus a clew of thread to guide him out of the labyrinthine chambers, these ancient ropes of antiquity were weaved from hemp of uncountable millinnia! These malefic Zamzummim used these ropes to safely retrace their way out of these labyrinthine caverns!

So we now followed the stringed paths of these giants that

led to a forked passage. One passage led gradually upward with the rope, the other path sloped gently downward—containing no rope.

We decided to take the downward passage, slowly zigzagging deeper into the beguiling regions of the dark underworld—where no man had ever explored.

"Where does the rope, ascending upward, go?"

"To the outer reaches of the empty tunnel shaft," Torchere continued, "leading to the exterior of the volcano. But it has since been recently plugged by an earthquake around 8,000 years ago."

"Recently, *only* 8,000 years ago!" I proclaimed.

"Sorry Iben, I forget that human trait of keeping time in its rightful place. Zipping in and out of history as we do, it seems only yesterday to me."

The dark path of the descending tunnel lay strangely forbidden. We became curious spelunkers of our subterranean *terra incognita*, and began our descent once again through strange dark and tortuous caverns. What wonders awaited us I had no way of knowing.

Noting that we were now many miles below Vesuvius, we entered the downward spiraling egress and continued our odyssey into the unexplored fascinating depths of the earth.

"We are entering the Erebus, Iben."

"The Erebus?" I inquired?

"Where the Greeks and Romans thought the soul passed onward to Tartarus. This is where we are heading."

From here the lava tunnel intersected with a limestone cavern. A tiny tributary of a river was running through the cold, dark and dank tunnels—

We entered a subterranean fairyland of strange vistas,

shadowy and secret, never seen by mortal man. We found huge rooms, soaring cavern walls containing delicate calcite crystal formations. We came upon a veritable forest of towering stalactites and stalagmites, exotic formations of limestone, cave coral, along with flowstone and fiery scarlet curtains hanging from the walls.

Now, following the earth's fault lines we intersected numerous salt domes, then penetrated sandstone as we spiraled our way deeper and deeper. We then hit solid bedrock and moved slowly through solid stone as a knife slicing through soft butter.

We continued descending through solid granite and sedimentary rock formations.

Mohorovicic Discontinunity/The Big Crater/*Chlamydomonos*

Under these massive pressures, gold was actually squeezed from the rocks. Since gold didn't oxidize we were looking at the pure unadulterated element, in all its pristine colorful hues! There were within these cave walls a hundred times more gold than in Fort Knox, Kentucky! It shimmered along the walls of this cavern and beneath our feet in massive nuggets weighing hundreds of pounds upon which we walked for miles and miles, truly making the "yellow brick road" from the *Land of Oz,* a reality!

We discovered other oddities of nature. Torchere revealed various minerals and the soft light of living organisms covering the cavern walls and illuminating all its majestic wonders, even producing light beneath the ponds! How ultra-beautiful it was—a veritable fairyland of variegated colors irradiated by microscopic organisms, coruscating their ghostly iridescence throughout these magnificent caverns.

Then I saw something of interest embedded in the rocks. Blue crystals of vast beauty!

"These are blue star sapphires, Iben. The ones you see here are worth millions of dollars on the world market. Sounds incredible, yes, but an X-ray technician from Chattanooga, TN actually found a similar one paying only a few dollars for it to be used as a paper weight! A Dallas gemologist identified it as being a 3,500 carat gem worth about $4 million after it was cut!"

Thousands upon thousands of these gems were embedded in the cavern walls and floor and could easily be picked out with a pocket knife! Other gems we found just as impressive were topaz, carbuncles, rose quartz, chalcedony and beautiful aquamarines embedded in the rock fissures through which we gingerly passed.

"Oh to be mortal again!" I jested.

"Iben, riches are so mundane fleeting upon an evil earth soon to be destroyed by God and recreated by Jesus Christ himself.

"We have reached the Mohorovicic Discontinunity, named after Andrija Mohorovicic, a Yugoslav seismologist, the first to detect the ending of the mantle. And you thought that magma came from the hot interior of the earth! Not so Iben! It comes from around the Moho between 30 to 50 miles deep!"

Leaving these marvelous limestone caverns we continue descending into the unknown through mysterious fault lines and volcanic fissures coming in contact with an ancient volcanic vent. We followed this tube of kimberlite downward further to the earth's interior.

Torchere revealed vast sulfur beds which now intersected along our pathway containing many rock crystals along with hundreds of other exotic gemstones, many being much prettier and much more colorful than those old diamonds which have become quite commonplace by now.

Then we pierced a methane gas pocket. If a match were struck here, an explosion of untold proportions would ensue.

"Iben," Torchere spoke, "ever hear of the Big Crater, Anderson #1, near Norphlet, Arkansas in the Smackover Oil Field? One such gas pocket upon the earth's surface was hit when drillers, north of El Dorado, were drilling in the 1920s. As the well pierced a methane pocket, workers ran for their lives as the derrick, along with the drilling rig crumbled and disappeared beneath the earth.

"The next day one of the visitors, while looking at the gaping hole, lit a cigarette causing a massive explosion. Anderson #1 burned for a month shooting flame hundreds of feet into the air. Its plume of burning methane could be seen as far away as Hot Springs, 120 miles distant! The "Big Crater" still scars the area around Norphlet to this day!"

Penetrating into vast deep layers of coal we encountered massive anticlines and faults hitting numerous ancient marine fossils beds. Then we discovered—sweet crude oil!

"Oh to be mortal again!" I teased. "If I could have discovered this while I lived, I would be fabulously rich in material possessions, the envy of any oil man in Texas, or Kuwait!

"Iben Jair, really now, we know that riches are so

mundane. We realize that we are most happy and fulfilled in the possession of the Holy Spirit. Soon Jesus Christ will return to earth in the Second Advent that glorious day all the saints of God will rejoice when Christ returns. We also know *the abundant life* can be had while living upon this earth before His Second Coming by all who possess this Spirit of God."

We passed through this viscous liquid, then proceeded our zigzag course down into the hot earth. Much later we came upon a subterranean river, boiling from the fierce heat. The water in this cauldron was hot enough to boil vegetables!

Even here a strange type of organism, the *Chlamydomonos*, was found alive and well! These single-celled algae were actually thriving in these scalding hot waters! Actually, I learned, these strange bacteria have also been found in a geyser in Yellowstone National Park!

We were now many miles beneath the surface of the earth. Here the intense heat melts the tectonic plates, causing earthquakes. This is where the development of active volcanoes form.

"As Vesuvius?"

"Yes, Iben! This layer was composed of solid and molten rock, that caused the mid-oceanic ridges to form and the sea-floors to spread apart. It extends down to about 125 miles. The continents actually float upon the mantle and its edges are pulled under as in California, causing the San Andreas Fault. If they are pushed upward they form many of the mountain ranges such as the Himalayas."

Tectonic Plates and Pangaea

Torchere further explained that long ago there was only one land mass, known as Pangaea, which further split into two parts, the northern section known as Laurasia, separated by the Sea of Tethys. The southern part was known as Gondwanaland and one great ocean, known as Panthalassa. They began to drift apart and after eons of time formed the continents as we know them today.

What made these continents separate? These massive continents, I learned, are floating upon what is known as tectonic plates. When they collide and overlap, mountains are formed. Where one plate moves under the other, earthquakes happen. Where these plates slide beside each other, transform faults occur.

I thought the pressures a mile under the ocean were powerful—get solid rock above your head and you have pressures over ten times that of water! Here miles below the Red Sea massive forces were expanding, increasing it about eleven inches a year. Slowing it was turning the Red Sea into another major ocean though it will take a few more million years.

The forces equivalent to thousands of atomic bombs were at work here producing earthquakes and volcanic activity on an unprecedented scale!

Lystrosaurus/Labyrinthodont/Homo floresiensis

We could actually see pieces of continental rock left behind being indigenous to Africa but located in Arabia! This proved without a doubt that these continental plates were once a part of each other! Also we found fossils of the *Lystrosaurus*, a hippopotamus-like reptile and the *Labyrinthodont*, resembling an overgrown five-foot salamander, along with the *Mesosaurus*, a plesiosaur-like creature. They have been discovered in *all* the different continents, proving they were living on one land mass over 200 million years ago! There was even a fern-like plant known as *Glossopteris* which was also found fossilized within these continents. Many of these gondwantherians such as the salamanders, aquatic dinosaurs and mammals were all survivors of the ancient land of Pangaea of eons past! We also discovered Antarctic's 200 million year-old past contained warm oceans!

Then I heard something—a strange high pitched piercing sound.

I realized that I was hearing ultrasonics or electromagnetic radiation beyond the normal range of the human ear! These radio waves are produced from the strain of rocks being squeezed under tremendous pressure. Dogs, insects, birds and even fish can sense these ultrasonics and may have trepidation just before an earthquake or tsunami!

Deep within the earth we stumbled upon strange hominid fossils. These archaic beings were furry-footed, had a thick bony eyebrow ridge, smallish teeth and were of diminutive size (about 3 feet tall) having grapefruit-sized brains. Were they a new unknown species of humans or did they have a disease known as microcephaly? Scientists have coined such beings *Homo floresiensis* and based on the new thermoluminescence dating method were determined to be around 800,000 years old. Some of these bones have actually been discovered on the Indonesian island of Flores.

We named them Hobbits after J.R.R. Tolkien's trilogy, *The Lord of the Rings*. How they got here was a great unsolved mystery.

We witnessed the incandescent and bubbling fumaroles of Erta Ali, one of seven volcanoes dotting these plates, from a most impressive viewpoint—that from the bottom of the massive magma chamber over 45 miles *below* the earth's surface!

Here also we found the remains of the Isle of Thera, 75 miles north of Crete. When in 1450 B.C., it was totally destroyed when the volcano Santorini exploded. It was five times as powerful as that of the Krakatoa eruption of 1883. Santorini blew 25 square miles of debris from its crater! Incredibly we could still see the remnants from this massive explosion which obliterated the Mycean civilization!

CHAPTER FIVE

*W*e now discovered a beautiful yellow mineral, not gold, but fool's gold! How beautiful are the crystals of iron pyrite! Prettier than gold! Though not near as valuable. But to us it was more magnificent, with their huge crystals many feet across formed by the tremendous pressure of tons of rock! We were beyond the monetary value of such things and could appreciate these minerals for their intrinsic value alone.

Miles upon miles we journeyed downward while studying all the precious minerals comprising its interior.

"Fascinating!"

These gems were all beautiful but under our ultraviolet vision they became all the more sensuous!

To the Earth's Core

We transected the crust and entered the mantle, many thousands of miles deeper than the tectonic plates. Going through this we entered the "liquid outer core," consisting of a nickel-iron alloy. Proceeding through this we encountered the earth's solid iron "inner core." Here, the outer core interacted with the inner core—featuring a wild display of dynamic heat thousands of degrees.

> "There is a place within the depths of Hell
> Call'd Malebolge, all of rock dark-stain'd
> With hue ferruginous, e'en as the steep
> That round it circling winds."
> Canto XVIII—*The Divine Comedy* by Dante Alighieri

This phenomenon of energy we named, "Malebolge," in honor of Dante's great novel, *The Divine Comedy*. We have arrived at the Earth's core!

"Iben," Torchere replied, "we have answered another mystery of the Bible and of God! Remember Ecclesiastes 7:24? *That which is far off, and exceeding deep, who can find it out?* We now have our answer!"

Within the nightmare great prominences of ionic and kinetic plasma boiled and fulminated! Huge bolts of electricity sprouted forth all about us, known as the Ettingshausen effect. These kinetic electrostatic plasmas were energized from the movement of these two dissimilar substances revolving around each other.

It is impossible to describe the effect these tremendous pressures and heat have upon this huge pyroplastic mass. As arcs of piezoelectric dendrites pulsated they reminded me of a huge Van de Graaff generator. Strange effervescing plasmas affected by these extreme temperatures vermiculated and swirled about us producing a thermoelectron engine where the heat of the earth is converted directly into electrical energy! Huge bolts of electricity flashed and arced all about us as if we were tangled in some giant Wimshurst machine. This produced vast amounts of spider lightning creating a thermionic dynamo—the creation of the most horrible electric cyclone ever witnessed!

Blinding, superheated bolts of electricity and radioactive plasmas twitched, sparked, arced and flashed. Some were thicker and more powerful than tornadoes, creating a maelstrom of dendrites of super-heated lightning much more spectacular than anything ever seen in the upper atmosphere of the earth! All the largest dams in the world *combined* couldn't produce in a year, what this 'geodynamo' at the earth's core produces in only one short *minute*!

I stood in awe of such power studying the effects of the kinetic energy of the inner earth trying to comprehend the majesty of such a magnificent miracle! Too bad no mortal eye will ever be able to witness such things! If they could, they would never doubt the power and omniscience of the creator of the universe … Almighty God!

Geomagnetic Reversals

We started traveling once again upward through these many layers to the earth's surface.

"Torchere, please answer one more thing. Where is the magnetic pole of the north and south?"

"Excellent question, Iben! The earth produces galvanic jolts of electricity as inner cores move against each other in opposite directions. The north magnetic pole, then materialize under the Prince of Wales Island in Canada, one thousand miles from the actual North Pole! The south magnetic pole materializes near Wilkes Land, part of Antarctica, about 1,600 miles from the actual South Pole!"

I learned that there have been many geomagnetic upheavals, or magnetic fields that have actually reversed in times past. There have been some 300 reversals in the past 170 million years. Oddly, after 10,000 years or so, the magnetic field will gain strength but then switch polarity in the opposite direction! This means that the magnetic poles will shift along with these reversals. Known but to very few people, ten thousand years ago the magnetic poles were even in different continents than they are today!

"Could this be how the dinosaurs met their fate?" I inquired.

"That question will be answered at a later time, Iben."

Chapter Six

*T*wondered why I hadn't seen any of the souls of the wicked within these depths?

"That will be explained to you in due time, Iben," spoke Torchere. But you are right, there are no lost souls of iniquity in the flames of hell at the center of the earth!"

Pellucidar

Leaving the earth's fiery core, we once again traveled upward to the surface! Here it grew cooler as we intersected faults and fissures and zigzagged our way upward through unexplored limestone caverns.

Then we discovered an ingress and stumbled into a mysterious capacious panorama of extreme beauty, where two different shells, the upper mantle and the lower mantle separated, and collapsed into a giant bubble—miles across.

It contained a warm saltwater ocean surrounding wondrous high and low land masses. We could see a lower dark valley containing freshwater swamplands and freshwater lakes.

Mysterious and forbidding we realized this salt sea was being warmed by the earth's interior! Its green ceiling which vaulted many miles above us were held up by natural arches of solid rock. Peaceful clouds as on a summer day were floating under this canopy, with "stars" rippling and twinkling over our heads producing a soft greenish-yellow moon glow of light. As we watched a falling star streaked across this strange sky! I could also hear the faint roars from the forest's interior.

A peaceful environment?

There were many strange-looking creatures with large luminous eyes dotting this black volcanic beach.

I saw a sparkling object in the dark sand—living trilobites! They have been allegedly extinct for over 300 million years! This strange glowing species was a rare creature that had survived Noah's flood.

This swampland further consisted of a strange refulgent forest with variegated luminous mosses and ancient ferns all lighting our pathway. There were also many giant asparagus-like plants towering high over our heads, all scintillating a dim light such as solar luminaries! Other wonderful trees lighting up the dreary landscape were the giant palm and scale trees. Again, all these plants paraded their wonderful light, casting their own eerie halos and silhouettes upon the ground in the forever twilight that surrounded them! They have been extinct at the earth's surface for millions of years!

Then I saw a very intense greenish yellow light crawling upon the verdant mossy canopy many thousands of feet above our heads, and realized it to be a giant lightning bug! Thousands of them… all resembling stars! They could synchronize their light producing wonderful rippling kaleidoscopic patterns and 'chasing' motion effects that were hypnotic to us.

So, I realized that even in the dark deep regions under the earth our eternal God has produced light where there was none before. God *always* finds a way!

As I was watching this herd of trilobites some strange creatures came out of the dense forest and attacked them. These were giant horrible sea scorpions. A few trilobites fought back by thrashing with their tails aiming for the soft under bodies of these fierce creatures. One popped a scorpion full in the neck which seemed to contain a poison as the scorpion twitched with excruciating pain. It died in only a few minutes—its brightness dimming as it succumbed. The other scorpion flipped the trilobite over exposing its vulnerable underside jamming its sharp sting into the trilobite's tender belly—paralyzing it instantly with pain and venom.

The other trilobites scattered quickly upon the sand hissing and jumping into the water for safety. As the water churned with violence prehistoric fish were alerted to this herd of trilobites by their splashing. These attacked the trilobites like a school of sharks. The poor trilobites— escaping one terror only to meet another one face to face!

Then huge sea turtles swam into the fray. With a parrot-like beak, they joined these terrible fish in their feeding frenzy. Many of these trilobites were attacked but most escaped death by sinking immediately to the bottom burying themselves in the deep thick muck. Here the trilobites could safely hide from these fierce predators.

Dinosaurs

Then the air was filled with the screams of great reptilian bird-like creatures flying high above us. Spotting the trilobites thrashing in the water these huge pteranodons launched a downward dive. Swooping low over the water they snatched them up in their long serrated beaks. Twitching and turning to escape its death grip, one trilobite tried to sting the bird but couldn't penetrate through its hard mandibles. Then there was an audible crunch as it broke the trilobite's back and swallowed it whole!

Yet others raced into a nearby cave for protection. Evil crocodile-like pliosaurs, the greatest marine creatures to ever live, now attacked. They snapped up these trilobites in their immense jaws. I could hear the crunching sounds as the trilobite's armor was cracked open like a nut in a shell!

What strange creatures thrived in these waters upon the verdant swamps of this inland continent!

I realized that this land mass was divided by a precipitous cliff hundreds of feet high, separating a lower swampland from a geothermal active upper tundra.

As we neared the swamplands it was inhabited by the *Labyrinthodontia* salamanders who were here very much *alive*! If you remember their fossils we discovered lying miles under the continents. Also present were strange water dinosaurs having long-narrow necks and paddles along their thin bodies—all preying upon strange prehistoric fish.

We arrived upon a seashore of black obsidian glass. The upper tundra was composed of precipitous cliffs of hard black granite with cascading waterfalls higher and more massive than those of Iguassu! The upper plain was composed of geysers, mud pots and fumaroles blasting their scalding water hundreds of feet into the air, condensing into the canopy which rained water upon the lower swamplands.

Mortal scientists would be interested in these creatures for these beasts are somewhat *altered* than those fossilized bones found on the earth's surface, different and beyond anything anybody has ever comprehended in the upper crust! We have named this unknown land, Pellucidar, in honor of Edgar Rice Burroughs, who wrote, *At the Earth's Core*, published in 1914.

There was little wind on this part of the island, making it even more stifling and humid.

The roars I heard earlier were becoming louder now. I could feel the vibrations under my feet from some great creatures from the nightmares of youth, stalking and moving—

If I was a mere mortal, I would be extremely apprehensive about exploring this beautiful and intriguing lost world of Pellucidar! That mysterious land of unfathomable wonders and hidden dangers deep within the earth's interior!

CHAPTER SEVEN

Arkansaurus/Dimetrodon/Tuatara/Quetzalcoatlus northropi

Creeping their way through the thick brush were agile benign creatures having huge elongated heads with hollow chambers. They glowed with patches of green and blue and stood erect upon their hind legs.

I realized that they are eating the white flowers of trees that look just like Magnolia trees. Then I realized that the Magnolia actually flourished back in the time of the dinosaurs!"

We discovered some dinosaurs that were known as the *Parasaurolophus*; their hollow nasal passages and long crested crown produce very low sounds much like the elephant and their roarings could penetrate for miles inland. These wonderful creatures resided in a herd of about fifty, including their young. They trumpeted their "fog-horn" sounds as a warning to the others in their flocks against intruders such as—

Then a fast-moving dinosaur attacked! It leaped high in the air and snatched one of their new born babies. In a flash it slashed its victim with powerful claws then bit it behind the head. Then shook the little body with an audible snap breaking its neck. Blood squirted as it crunched down upon it. Now limp from death, it was carried off in the creature's mouth. I watched as he took it back to feed his young. This creature was a male *Arkansaurus.* The female was guarding their nest of hatchlings. Still, within this barbarism, they only kill for food. Even on a grand scale as this, 'murder' is unknown to them being indigenous only to the human race and the tiny ants. Mortal humankind along with many ant species, I learned, are the only creatures that kill in anger or for pleasure, creating slaves and wars in which to annihilate or control one another.

We discovered an egg nest and observed one little dinosaur with languid eyes just hatching out.

How cute—with its tri-facial horns, blinking its large innocent eyes adjusting to the light, this helpless little creature looked much as a turtle hatching from its shell. This dinosaur was similar to the triceratops and upon being grown will weigh a mere two and a half tons!

Now many meat-eating dinosaurs along with various pterodactyls arrived at the bottom of a high cliff as if waiting for something.

Then we heard a roar of thunder as thousands of smaller agile theropods reached the edge of the upper plateau, then hurdled themselves off the high escarpment. Now a fierce feeding frenzy ensued, a voracious free-for-all where the dead were eaten in a violent orgy where they fell. Full of greed for a free meal, tempers flared, dinosaurs trampled each other to death—killing even more, who were all eaten by the survivors! I realized this habitat of theirs is a closed habitat in that it only exceeds to a limited space. Their sky extends only a few thousand feet, while their shallow ocean extends less than a thousand miles creating a restrained ecosystem. Only a certain amount of creatures can exist here without a great die-off of species. Therefore, Mother Nature, or God has limited their breeding habits and their food supply. This being the reason that these creatures don't abuse their environment. They are not greedy. But if there is an over balance, mass suicide is the only answer! Remember the lesson of the Lemmings? Those rodents that live in Scandinavia that commit mass suicide every few years if their environment became too over crowded with each other.

Compare it to the earth's surface... also a limited ecosystem with only so much resources of food and minerals!

Then a strange lizard darted past us I finally identified as a *tuatara*. It is the *only survivor* from a long line of lizards that florushed 150 million years ago, during the Mesozoic era. It is still *living* in the upper crust of the earth even to this day! Remember the horseshoe crab? It has not changed for 300 million years! The Nautilus, a mollusks found in the Pacific Ocean, hadn't changed in over 400 million years! Also, the scorpion, the cockroach, the silverfish, the earwig, the alligator, the ginkgo tree and the Magnolia tree haven't changed in the course of time. Strangely, this strange reptile, the tuatara, is found living only in New Zealand today. Amazingly above its main two eyes is a primitive "third eye" or "pineal eye" (an extension of the pineal gland) which can detect infrared light and acts as a regulator for the creature's body heat. But the horse, the whale and many viruses have mutated, but only to a small degree. Oddly though none of these have 'jumped the gap' meaning that not any have actually *evolved* into another distinct creature. The horse is still a horse, whether small, as the *Eohippus* (a little horse) or large, as the *Protohippus*, it hasn't changed into another distinct creature. It is still a horse. The whale is still a whale, though evolutionists have stated that it got tired of the land and went back into the ocean! Most creatures, they profess, have left the ocean and learned to live on the land!

The viruses, I learned, have somewhat mutated in that their *enzymes* have made some of them immune to antibiotics, such as the cockroach or housefly, but no virus can survive without becoming a parasite to another cell.

Paleontologists have created the Geological Time Table to help explain these ancient periods. But there are two schools of thinking on this subject: *uniformitarism*, the doctrine where the forces of nature have been *uniform*, entombing creatures in ancient rock strata crushing them under tons of pressure in layers, the oldest fossils being deep within the earth with the more recent fossils being toward earth's surface; or the doctrine of *catastrophism*, where nature has acted more violently (as vulcanism and earthquakes) which may change the features upon our earth.

Further into this dangerous swampland we penetrated. Then I saw some shooting stars. A mass of about thirty of them landed not far off, splashing into the water, floating and dispersing upon its surface.

Then the water rippled as some giant crocodiles swam toward them.

I remembered those giant lightning bugs that live upon the green canopy or ceiling. In their *coup de grace* they flash their light becoming shooting stars as they fall in their death agony from the abode from which they have lived their whole lives!"

Then I witnessed a gigantic bird flying overhead. It was a giant pteranodon, the largest prehistoric bird to ever fly! It was larger than a small airplane—it being akin to the upper species which flew the skies of the Cretaceous Era over 68 million years ago!

This strange bird saw the stars fall and was searching for a meal. Sometimes they can catch these lightning bugs while in flight! They soar like large vultures high in the sky, sometimes snapping up the bugs from the mossy canopy high above. These birds can roost in the tall ferns, or build their nests in the cliff's ledges, and soar continually through the green tinted skies of Pellucidar.

Now we studied the massive predatory beasts that roamed these swamps. Roaming here in these massive jungles were five story meat-eating monsters even larger than the famed *Tyrannosaurus rex* of the movies!

The prehistoric creature before us was the rare *Carcharodontosaurus,* a third larger than T. rex. It's fossil was discovered in the upper world and actually dug out of an iceberg off the coast of Morocco north of the Canary Islands in 1995!

Here we discovered limited varieties of these creatures namely the mighty *Allosaurus*, the *Giganotosaurus* and the *Megalosaurus* all living, alive and well, here in this vast ecosystem!

Yet, I realized that many of these giant dinosaura seemed to be dwindling in numbers.

Limited space equals limited and dwarfed species, I pondered.

Were the smaller dinosaur species somehow replacing these giant creatures? There were many smaller dinosaurs than the larger ones. A limited food source equates that the smaller plant-eating and less violent species of dinosaurs will ultimately thrive and survive, thus thinning out these giant grander and more violent meat-eaters.

Finally, it was explained how all these beasts got down here—yet many were very different from the fossils in the upper strata. Worldly scientists did not have enough facts to extrapolate the truth of their diverseness and did not yet have enough pieces of the puzzle to figure it all out!

I wondered where all this water came from to form these inland oceans and swamps? Then I realized that after Noah's flood there was a massive wind and much of this extra water was drained back into the fountains of the deep, earth's interior, forming this inland ocean! Then God created all this variety of animal and plant life to thrive here to enjoy their environment *without* the perils of pollution and the destructive ways of mankind as upon the surface of the earth. So this is why and how the strange fantastic land of Pellucidar came to be!

We now moved beyond the swamp and traveled over the rocky part of the island, passing the precipitous cliffs, and once again plunged into the warm ocean.

Here many acquatic dinosaurs frolicked and played. All these unlikely beasts stayed within their own schools and herds respecting their own territories and boundaries seeming to get along with each other rather well.

Oddly, Torchere explained that this inner ocean rose

and fell creating "tides" along the shores here just as they do on the earth's surface. Therefore, all great bodies of water including that in Pellucidar was influenced by the moon's gravity! But the moon, though invisible, still influenced their circadian rhythm. Also, since the sun was so far away from the earth it had little to do with Pellucidar and the plant species here extracted heat from the interior of the earth as their energy source!

Interestingly, we spotted a couple of Supernalites, dressed in khaki pants with matching double-pocketed shirts, their heads covered with safari hats. They were in total bliss, studying all these eccentric dinosaurs. Somehow, I recognized them as Othniel Charles Marsh, once professor of paleontology at Yale University and the other was Edward Drinker Cope, the late professor of the American Museum of Natural History in New York, City. In their other life, they were bitter rivals, always in competition trying to out do each other in discovering and identifying different species of dinosaurs, but here they got along great, becoming the best of friends, studying all these creatures in rapt fascination.

Torchere informed me it was time to leave the mysterious *terra incognita,* the strange exotic lands of Edgar Rice Burrough's Pellucidar.

Mass Extinctions/Chicxulub Crater/Nemesis Theory

From here we exit this lost world, traveling up toward the earth's surface once again, zigzagging into a nightmare of subterranean faults.

We climbed massive fissures and crevasses and hardened magma chambers of extinct volcanoes lost to history. We explored many mysterious caverns following them for miles almost to the earth's surface.

We passed through a layer of limestone and found radioactive iridium. Tiny glass solidified droplets known as "tektites" formed from superheated sand and "shocked" (shattered) quartz.

I learned that about 65 million years ago a giant meteorite crashed into the coast of Central America on the Yucatan Peninsula. This resulting explosion created the 112-mile diameter Chicxulub crater. Thus iridium, a radioactive element, was scattered all over the earth and a deadly cloud of gases blocked the sun for decades creating a *nuclear winter* where the world's climate plummeted. The plants froze and died first, then all the dinosaurs succumbed as their food source perished. So, the world's largest predators which reigned for over 160 million years, were erased from the earth's surface for all eternity.

This meteor was about 20 miles wide, struck the Earth at 38,000 mph which vaporized and blew into space about 10% of the Earth's total atmosphere!

Also, just coming to light, is another anomaly that happened around the same time. Strange glass "spherules" also containing iridium have been found all around the Earth. These were caused from another giant meteor hitting Iowa creating a 30 mile-wide crater around the same time as the one that hit the Yucatan Peninsula. This *double* meteor strike caused this massive die off of species. This calamity marked the boundary between the Cretaceous and the Tertiary periods in the geologic time table.

Also Argentina had a meteor impact a little over 3 million years ago. This mile-wide asteroid exploded blasting out pieces of greenish glass containing radioactive iridium. It also cooled the earth's temperature a few degrees causing an ice age which erased many species, including the giant armadillos, huge marsupial sloths and some enormous flightless birds.

There have also been 13 other mass extinctions, I learned. One about 248 million years ago destroyed about 8% of all the earth's creatures. Many marine animals and early reptiles that inhabited the world during this time perished. Then the dinosaurs rose to power becoming earth's predominant life form during the Mesozoic Era (225-64 million years ago).

Other catastrophic events, I learned, caused mass extinctions that destroyed large numbers of aquatic bacteria and algae about 650 million years ago. The most recent mass extinction occurred about 11 million years ago causing many large rhinoceros-like animals to disappear from the North American continent. All these mass extinctions are collectively known as the "Alvarez Hypothesis." Mass extinctions have *not* occurred randomly but at intervals of about every 26 million years!

Occasionally a comet will come along that may be caught by Earth's gravity. This happens about every 26 million years. This is known as the *Nemesis Theory*, or the *Death Star Hypothesis*, formulated by Richard Muller of the University of California at Berkeley. This *Hypothesis* states that one of these meteors will again someday strike us possibly destroying *all* life upon our planet.

We encountered another oddity just a few feet below the surface. It was a thin layer of poisonous radioactive elements, namely that of cobalt 60, iodine 33, strontium 90, cesium 137, ruthenium 106, and carbon 14. It resulted from the above ground thermonuclear weapons tested in the 1950s. These noxious isotopes can produce cancer in less than one part per *billion*!

Then, a few yards from the surface, we encountered ancient fossils embedded in a layer of hardened mud.

I discovered I was witnessing the remains of a great global flood that Noah and his family survived, thus saving humanity from total destruction.

The Chinchorros

Then I touched something—realizing they were bones—

"What on earth?"

"Fear not, Iben! These bones are the remains of human corpses over 8,000 years old! They are known as the *Las momias*—the dead ones! The world's oldest mummies! Some of them predate the Egyptian mummies by 5,000 years!"

"Where are we?" I inquired, noting that we were about to break through to the earth's surface.

"We have the Pacific on the one side, and the Andes Mountains on the other. We have gone clear through the Earth, over 8,000 miles and finally arrived in Arica—in Peru, South America!"

I now realized that we were not far from the Atacama. This desert is the most arid place on earth. These mummies, known as the *Chinchorros,* were surrounded by food and personal belongings evidence of the belief in an afterlife.

We studied all their living habits and what they ate. We learned that many died from arsenic poisoning, pneumonia, syphilis and osteoporosis.

"Iben, look at this corpse closely and tell me how he died?"

I studied this body as a forensic pathologist would dissect a dead body. I examined the skull and brain, fingers, eyes, digestive cavity—including his lungs. Here were the results of *Mycobacterium tuberculosis,* or TB!

Tuberculosis, previously thought to have been carried to the Americas from Europe was found in these mummies thousands of years *before* Columbus arrived there, thus *disproving* that he brought this insidious plague from overseas!

Many of these corpses were still in fairly good shape unlike the Egyptian mummies.

We had now finally reached the surface of the earth! I looked around in the warmth of the sunshine and listened to the chirping of the birds. The nether world was interesting but the earth's surface and its fresh air were once again a thrill to behold!

Thus ended our odyssey into the very center of the Earth and back again. The journey of over 8,000 miles we made in what seemed like only a week's trip! I learned in reality took us many years to complete, starting with Vesuvius, Italy and ending here in Peru, South America!

"Volcanoes," Torchere continued, "near Mexico City, the Philippine Islands, Indonesia, along with those in

Guatemala and Ecuador will soon erupt. I must go protect their inhabitants along the the 'Ring of Fire,' volcanoes dotting the Pacific Ocean. We will travel to the volcano Mt. Nyiragongo, near Goma in the African Congo, causing uncountable people to flee the city as molten lava will virtually cut the city in half as thousands flee for their lives. The citizens of Goma are in bad need of God's angels and their prayers have been heard!"

"I shall continue to monitor dangerous volcanoes all across the world, including Mauna Kea, Mauna Loa and Kilauea, Hawaii. And earthquakes in Turkey, Greece, Mexico and Taiwan along with the volcanic eruption of Mt. Usu, Japan, and Mount Agung of Indonesia will beckon many of God's angels and Supernalites. We will gently guide all these victims into Eternity."

They related that soon great tsunamis will destroy thousands in Malaysia and Somalia. Even Indonesia will be hit by massive tsumanis where hundreds of thousands of people will be killed. And the volcano, Anak Krakatau (son of Krakatau), will once again explode, killing thousands more from its tidal waves. Also, Japan will soon have a massive earthquake resulting in a tsunami that will incapacitate their Fukushima Daiichi nuclear power facility. It will even be worse than the Chernobyl, Russia disaster.

"I will continue influencing the weather patterns controlling the El Nino and the La Nina which determine the hurricane activity in the tropical Pacific."

As I blinked, Torchere dematerialized—

Chapter Eight

Another divine Spirit, a great beacon of ethereal light, now appeared.

"Fear not, Iben, for I am Angelica, "the finder of lost lovers."

The Wayward Relationship

"Iben, you are aware you can go anywhere you want, see anyone you want and do anything you can. What would you, dear saint of God, enjoy now in Eternity?"

A million things raced through my mind. For some reason long ago in my freshman year at college a girl crossed my path and I wondered where she was, what she was doing, how life had treated her.

"Tell me the story, Iben. Why would you want to see this young lady?"

"Well, her name was Rachael Ann Crosby, and we were both attending Arkansas State University (ASU) in Magnolia before I decided to transfer to Oklahoma State after my Freshmen year. A little flaxen haired beauty she was—real sweet and congenial. We had a few dates to the football games and were getting along rather well. Rachael was very nice and we hit it off right away. I remember one cool night especially well after a concert at the Field House. We strolled across campus hand in hand to the Greek Theater and sat upon its concrete steps gazing up into the great sparkling void, a cool breeze upon our faces, our fates determined by that of which we had no knowledge. I was nineteen, she eighteen. The Milky Way spread before us as a canopy stretched across an infinite sky. What a perfect night. I can still remember the *exact* words she said to me, and what I said to her: *What would you say, Iben, if I told you I was falling in love with you? Rachael, I can honestly say that I am NOT falling in love with you!* I rudely and tersely replied back.

"Angelica, I was such a fool! At the time I was proud that I could honestly control my emotions—and my heart. I took life too cavalier. Falling in love wasn't my style. I had things to do, places to visit. My whole life hanged before me and I wasn't about to be tied up with anyone just yet! She scared me to death, if I might use the pun!

"It was as if she handed me her very special perfect pearl on black velvet and I callously tossed it aside and trampled it under foot. Then, I walked her in silence back to her dormitory in the cool air but the night and our relationship hopelessly and irreparably shattered. I kissed her on the cheek, turned, and walked out of her life forever. I never saw her again. I often wondered what ever became of her, what she ever accomplished in life.

"Less than a year later after my freshman year, I

visited the campus again and asked about her. Personnel in Registrar's Office told me she had been killed in a car crash the summer before. I was crushed. You see, Angelica, she was the first person to ever tell me she loved me. I pondered her in my heart ever since.

"I always wanted to tell her to forgive me. It wasn't that I was totally hard-hearted. I was insecure, lacked self confidence and had a troubled mind. I was worried about my future, somewhat depressed about my grades and I was just nineteen and inexperienced in love. Having mature relationships with the opposite sex was foreign to me. I'm not sure I could have maintained a relationship under those conditions anyway. I had my whole life before me and I did not want to settle down yet. If I could just have told her, called her back, explained things, but no, I just walked out of her life slamming the door of fate. If I could have only asked her to forgive me. I now realize that a *lack of communication is our greatest enemy!*"

Angelica listening attentively, now spoke, "Iben, look behind you—"

I turned and there was Rachael with an aurora of iridescence adorned as a beautiful saint. She seemed not a day older than that fortuitous moment we had met.

What extreme joy raced through my mind and heart as great tears welled up in my eyes! Her golden hair shimmering in the sunlight, her countenance radiating beauty untouched by time. The aural glow of her eyes capturing me—my soul. She was thinking *my* thoughts, waltzing through my mind as fresh as ever I remembered her!

"Iben," she whispered to me, "I have forgiven you. But I must tell you something. I didn't die later that year. Their

Registrar's Office was wrong. It was a case of mistaken identity. I lived another 16 years, marrying and having two lovely children. Then I contracted acute leukemia and died within six months of the diagnosis. My sons were only 8 and 10 years old. I got married after college and divorced two years later. I got custody of the children and he left me for another woman.

"But, I have always wondered about *you*, Iben. You hurt me deeply, left me quietly and killed my heart softly. I never forgot you. I wanted to call you the next day but my roommate talked me out of doing so. It wasn't proper to call boys in those days. I had too much pride to try to amend things between us."

"I pondered your death in my heart for 16 long years, Rachael, thinking you were killed in that car crash which never happened! Such are the foibles of life!"

Angelica revealed an alternative life where Rachael and I were married less than a year after we had met in college. Traveling on our honeymoon, a flatbed trailer loaded with tires came loose, one of which bounced into the path of our car, killing both of us instantly.

"Iben," Rachael continued, "don't be too hard on yourself. God has ordained our destiny to further His goals in our lives. And that was then and *this* is now. I have forgiven you completely. You were young and innocent, sweet and charming. How were we to know that life was to deal us the fate of star-crossed lovers? And now we have ETERNITY! Let us forget the past and rejoice in the present! Remember, Iben, earth has no sorrow that heaven cannot heal!"

The sights and wonders Rachael and I experienced in the next few days were beyond belief!

Somehow we suddenly appeared in a fishing village near Peru, South America. Here a mother had lost her small child, Mary, who had wandered off during the night. We now had another Divine Mission from God to influence the dream of this worried mother. Being a devout Christian hysterical with grief and worry she passionately prayed and petitioned God for a miracle. Angelica produced a vivid dream in her mind telling her the whereabouts of her four-year-old little girl.

So this terrified mother was guided in a vision from her house to where Mary was lost. In a nearby forest her little daughter had spent the cool night and was still asleep when she was discovered. We guided this mother to the exact spot where her daughter woke up the next morning. Mary was quickly found—cold and hungry, her eyes swollen, her cheeks streaked with tears. But she was alive and well! Such are the miracles of the faithful! The mother *knew* that the angels of her Lord were at work here, and her faith, along with the faith of the whole fishing village increased tremendously by this miracle!

In the same community we encountered a man broke into a house and stole a gun. Twenty-five years later the robber's little six-year-old boy picked the gun up and shot his baby sister, two years old, killing her.

Angelica spoke, "So you see, Iben, how the sins of one person many years later can affect the lives of others!"

Like Adam and Eve. I thought.

Nasca Plains/Machu Picchu/Aztecs/Incas/Maya

We continue our adventures, our strange After-Death Odyssey, touring all the wonders of South America.

Arriving at the plains of Nasca, we crossed the Peruvian desert in the southern Andean foothills. Here we discovered ancient weird geometric drawings of giant spiders, birds and other creatures along with enigmatic spirals etched into the ground. We learned the secrets of what these symbols meant, why they were drawn and who created them!

What caused these pre-Incan peoples to make such art? Even a stone calendar was found that could calculate the equinoxes, the growing seasons, the positions of the moon and even the rotation of the Earth! This proved that the Incas had developed the knowledge of advanced mathematics!

We even found a twenty-ton solid block of red sandstone known as the Great Idol, carved with hundreds of astronomical symbols thousands of years old. Some of these strange markings we deciphered proving the Earth to be a sphere, thousands of years before the time of the Vikings or Columbus.

Bingham/Fawcett/Prescott/Stephens

Traveling over the majestic Andes mountains we soared through the lost valleys of the Inca Empire. Whizzing past in a flash of light we waved to Hiram Bingham the late archaeologist, who in 1912, discovered the Lost City of the Incas. He was still studying the Incas' Lost Citadel of Machu Picchu and her "Hanging Gardens" after he had long since died. Here is his reward in the afterlife!

We also learned of the disappearance of the explorer Percy Harrison Fawcett searching for the legendary city of El Dorado and the City of Z. He was lost in these thick jungles of South America and was never heard from again. Fawcett captured the imagination of the entire world and notably, the adventure writer Arthur Conan Doyle who was so inspired over this explorer that he wrote his great novel, *The Lost World*. Interesting enough we discovered what he had been searching for, a great lost civilization even surpassing those of ancient Babylon and Egypt.

We now encountered the strange living civilizations, the "lost tribes" of South America, the Yanomami, the only survivors of ancient Atlantis near the Venezuela border. I learned it grew to about 6 million strong in the 1500s but was decimated down to a mere 300,000 survivors after contact with the European explorers who introduced exotic diseases to them.

We studied the Kranhacarore tribe where 90% of them have been decimated also by the modern explorer's diseases. These, along with many other "lost" tribes we visited, learning all about their ancient customs.

We soared over the snow-clad volcanoes of Popocatepetl. From here we studied the legends of the mighty Aztecs, saw how they build their great cities of Teotihuacan and solved all their fabulous mysteries.

We conversed with the Supernalite, William H. Prescott, who wrote *The History of the Conquest of Mexico* and *The History of the Conquest of Peru* and with him explored the wonder of the Inca empire.

Then, we met the late archaeologist, John Lloyd Stephens,

who revealed the mysteries of the jungle-choked ruins of the Maya empire.

We then solved the riddle of Uxmal's huge "Pyramid of the Magician!" What we learned was beyond belief! Some of these monolithic structures contained sandstone weighing 100 tons, topped with other 60 ton blocks for walls! We found the "Gate of the Sun" in the mysterious city of Tiahuanaco. The average person does not believe such things exist and yet archaeologists have been studying them for hundreds of years!

Then we continued the exploration of the rest of the magnificent ruins of the mighty Aztecs, Maya and Inca civilizations!

Perched upon Machu Picchu's highest peak we then dived 2,000 feet and plunged into the Urubamba River! What an exhilarating dive! Time seemed to slow and yet the canyon walls slowly and forever moved upward—then we splashed into her angry waters!

The *apapaima* and the *piranhas*

Rachael and I, along with Angelica, drifted down the turbulent Urubamba River into Brazil southwest of Peru. Here we entered a tributary much more quiet and peaceful. We approached a small party of white men in their flat bottom boats. We scanned their minds realizing that they were studying the environment to earn their master's degrees and were here to catch a few living specimens of exotic fish to ship back home. They were from one of the universities located in the United States.

Rachael spoke, "Iben, let's listen to their conversation."

"Shall we try to catch one of these big fish?" Their guide questioned.

"Sure, we want to get one for the Adler Aquarium in Chicago," the scientist answered. "Their aquarium should pay handsomely for a fish like this. Transportation for a few fish this size will be expensive but I've already made arrangements."

Rachael and I noticed that they were talking about a huge fish that was swimming beneath them.

"Iben," Rachael spoke, "these fish are the *apapaima*, a strange abnormality because they can breathe in surface air through a pair of lungs, not gills as other fish do."

Something else stirred in the water. Young hatchlings of the *apapaima*.

The graduate students earning extra credit for their summer courses unwary of any danger now jumped from the boats into shallow water to net some of these smaller fry.

"These men," Angelica stated, "do not understand that they have stumbled upon the lost river, the Rio das Mortes—the River of Death which runs through central Brazil."

All was quiet. There was only a slight rustling of the leaves along the shore with the lazy buzzing of insects and a few bird calls. The still water cast reflections of the surrounding tranquil jungle.

All of a sudden one of the students slipped and fell under the water. The water boiled and then turned red as the man screamed for his life. Then I could see under the water hundreds of small fish with razor-sharp serrated teeth literally ripping this man apart! Then Angelica introduced one of the most terrible words in the English language—*PIRANHAS*! The most ravenous fish in the world. Then out of sheer panic and fear the others made haste for the bank. Another student slipped ... the water frothed as the little beasties went for him. Both men were dead in minutes as their bloody bones rose to the surface almost totally stripped of flesh. What a ghastly scene as the survivors watched from the shore in shock and sheer terror! This expedition had had their fill of death upon the tributary so well named, the Rio das Mortes!

The gentle reader should be informed that others in their party were successful in finally acquiring some species of these *apapaimas* and yes, they captured some piranhas also, some of which they termed "genuine man eaters!"

Iguassu

We continued our journey through South America leaving the piranhas far behind. We encountered the Harakbut natives discussing the destruction of their rain forest, along with the pollution of the Amazon.

We found ourselves crossing the Andes. We glided through dense jungles fording steep rocky crevasses observing thousands of butterflies, brightly colored orchids growing in treetops along with various begonias and other interesting wildlife.

A faint rumble of sound, strange and wondrous, now penetrated our ears in this otherwise quiet verdant jungle. Following this roar to the edge of a rocky precipice, we stopped short—

Before us spread the expansive panorama of the *Garganta del Diablo*, the "Throat of the Devil," a terrific mile wide abyss and once again beheld the majesty and power of God! Here the river changed into a boiling frothing mist as it fell into the vast depths below!

We stood in awe of the *Cataratas del Iguassu*! This fantastic palisade formed a semicircular arch over two miles wide. Iguassu is longer and even *higher* than Niagara Falls. That great breathtaking vista which spread before us created magnificent rainbows in the moist humid air.

What a beautiful dreamscape we encountered! The thundering of the Falls was something to behold—another magnificent creation of God, a lost almost forgotten wonder laying deep in the dense verdant jungle of South America!

I must regress here a moment. The Spirit Angelica, Rachael and I, realized that this moment is all that counts, *this existence,* not that old earthly mortal realm which is now but a *shadow*, a dream of some other dimension, as if some other person lived an alien existence in some other life. The caterpillar metamorphosing into the beautiful butterfly. Can the butterfly even remember its earlier existence as a mere worm? What counts, that long ago existence, or the *here and now* of Eternity! Forever loving, forever knowing the wonders and beauty of God, His majesty, His love, His creation, His Divine Purpose for us. His magnificent divine essence and divine mind manifested in His wondrous and miraculous creation and His guidance in all that exists!

"Iben," Rachael spoke, "I have yet to complete my rendezvous with destiny. I have been called upon a Divine Mission to comfort and protect all the police, nurses, physicians, paramedics and firemen throughout the United State and the rest of the world."

Russia, I learned, has infuriated the Japanese by brazenly dumping more than 900 tons of low-level radwastes into a prime squid fishing area in the Sea of Japan.

Angelica stated that one of Maryland's large poultry producers are dumping brownish-green chicken sludge from slaughtered birds outside Berlin, eight miles west of Ocean City. This chicken waste has helped cause the outbreak of the toxic microbe *Pfiesteria piscicida* in the bay area.

"I will monitor the ecological disasters of massive forest fires in California and in the Sequoia National Park where drought is killing millions of trees. Also, the rain forests of South America need protection. Remember, that I have the divine power of *theomorphic ubiquity* to monitor these things all at once, doing a hundred tasks in but a moment of time! We must now go immediately to prepare many of these people to meet their destiny!"

So I bade farewell to Angelica, along with Rachael, knowing full well we could see each other again just by wishing it. What a wonderful thing to visit Rachael after 16 long years of absence. To be able to communicate the desires of our hearts to one another after so many enduring seasons. God bless her!

Chapter Nine

History of the World

*N*ow, another Divine Spirit appeared. Brandishing a sparkling purple robe symbolizing all those killed in war, Historia, stated she was to reveal all the tragedy upon the earth, the fearful slaughter of humanity, teaching me the lessons of recorded history.

So we left South America and traveled back in time—

Shards of dazzling polychromatic luminance twisted and centrifuged us through time. The ground left my feet and I rippled through exotic subharmonic cascades—into the unknown tracts of forgotten history.

THE BIRTH OF CIVILIZATION

Adam and Eve

I actually witnessed the creation of the first humans, Adam and Eve, right before my eyes—by the very hand of God!

Mankind has a reasoning nature to seek out God, separating the human race from the rest of God's creation, as we have already seen. The awe and majesty of the human consciousness! To be one with God in the Garden of Eden! Such communion with God, such a paradise on earth. All seemed so good and pure. All was well.

Interestingly, Eve was created from Adam's rib just as the Bible stated! *Though both man and woman have the same number of ribs, I now understood that God created Eve from the DNA of Adam.* Only a tiny bit of this genetic material— not the complete rib was need to exemplify that she was now a part of the complete gene pool of humanity. This forever proved that the man and woman are "equals" in the eyes of God. He has placed the man over her to protect and nurture her and to keep her safe.

Therefore, the human species has that *reasoning nature* to seek out God making us *different, unique* and *special.* Thus, *Homo sapiens* (wise man) was separated forever from the rest of God's creation—the animal kingdom.

Then I watched the angel of light, Lucifer, come and tempt Eve first with the forbidden fruit. Then Adam, after listening to Eve—sinned by eating the forbidden fruit—also fell under the influence of doubt and shame.

"So you thought the story of Adam and Eve was just a *myth?*" Historia questioned.

What did the Serpent look like? I cannot reveal this esoteric secret of the ages. I was told NOT to write it down so the saints of God can observe this mystery someday for themselves. It must be remembered though that Lucificer didn't "crawl upon his belly" until God cursed him to become a serpent. Another mystery *not* to be revealed until each mortal person meets his destiny... and faces dissolution—as they all will.

Then came the great fall of Adam and Eve from Paradise into the tortures of a cursed earth.

CURSE OF THE EARTH:

1. Lack of communication with God. Humankind lost its ability to commune with the Almighty. Only *through Jesus Christ* can the born-again believer reunite in Godly conversation commonly known as prayer. At the "Fall" humanity lost its *spiritual language,* then after Noah's flood, God further "confused the language" at the Tower of Babel.

2. We cannot commune through mediums such as soothsayers, astrologers, fortune tellers, necromancy, etc. because they cannot break through the barrier between God and Mankind. Their message is lost and distorted through a barrier designated by God in the "Curse of Humankind." Therefore, their petitions with the "Other Side" are lost in distortions, falsehoods and lies. Communion with the fallen angels, demons and lesser "gods of perdition"—are forbidden."

3. Only the *glorified* and *immortal saints* after death can communicate with other humans *if ordained by God*. All of humanity is lost and can *only* reach God through our Mediator, Jesus Christ. Any other means to communicate to God is foolishness and

vanity which opens up the other world of guile, fear, error of truth and deceitfulness.

4. The Curse of Strife and World Wars—including Terrorism, asserted upon humanity. Nations, religions and races fighting against each other have been established through the wiles of Satan.

5. Lost the "Greenhouse Effect," and the human life span was considerably shortened. The canopy above the earth altered—clouds now formed where once a "mist came up and watered the ground." (Gen. 2:6)

6. The tilt of the Earth upon its axis was altered, along with its magnetic fields, doing untold damage to the seasons and crops, and destroying many life forms.

7. Copious amounts of harmful ultraviolet radiation (UV) now enters through our earth's atmosphere. The ozone layer, our buffer against these deadly rays, has been altered. Destruction of this ozone is one of our greatest perils. This mutates the genetic makeup of the skin causing skin cancer and cataracts in the eyes. Noteworthy is that skin cancer is on the rise and will increase 300% in the next 30 years. There is also a *five-times* greater chance of getting melanoma after a severe, blistering sunburn. *Be forewarned that sun lamps and suntan booths are dangerous and can cause skin cancer.* Wear UV protective sun glasses, a wide-brimmed hat, and a SPF sun-screen of at least 30+ when outside. Also, skin cancer accounts for over 700,000 new cases each year and basal cell carcinoma and squamous cell carcinoma represent one-third of all cancers occurring in the United States each year.

8. Astral projection: Lost is the divine ability to travel to different places without actually physically going there. The mind or soul travels to a distant location or to another dimension, then reenters the body. (Dreaming while one is asleep is the closest we can get to this phenomenon).

9. The human body has lost its ability to produce Vitamin C. The special enzyme that converts glucose (sugar) to ascorbic acid was lost to humanity. Many animals today still carry this enzyme—but not humans.

10. (A) Death: The natural breakdown of the DNA in the living cell, implemented as the greatest plague and scourge of humankind … part of the "Curse of God," (Gen. 3:19).

    (B) Longevity (Old Age): The life span of animals and humans has been shortened. Chromosomes which facilitates cell division are now damaged. Free radicals are also produced from cellular energy, all of which enhance the culpability of old age.

11. Woman cursed with painful childbirth (Gen. 3:16). Until recently before the 1900s almost half of all women who gave childbirth died from complications resulting from infections.

12. The mass extinction of many species of animals and plants. Ninety-nine percent of all species of life that have ever lived are now extinct. All the great dinosaurs of ages past died off. Many animals and plants are still dying off at tremendous rates even today.

13. Human intelligence and memory have been altered and shortened. Brain capacity suffered making memorizing extremely difficult ... and cognitive reasoning deteriorated.

14. The feeling of superiority and hubris some people have to control others, whether it is your boss at work, or a spouse, a family member or a friend.

15. All nations are cursed with taxes and the burden of armaments (weapons of mass destruction) costing billions of dollars annually (which could be spent on schools, education, hospitals, health care, cancer research and helping the homeless, etc.). (Think what Hitler could have done with Germany's billions of tax dollars instead of increasing their military might to conquer the world. Or Japan, or Russia, or China? Or what the United States spends each year to defend itself against foreign terrorism or defend itself against the military aggression of rogue nations?)

16. Plate tectonics shifted and split apart all the continents. This separated the human race via oceans, color and religion.

17. Fly and mosquito started sucking the blood of mammals. (Other parasites as ticks, lice and chiggers also cursed to use blood for food and rearing their young).

18. The Earth was cursed to be infertile where before many food bearing plants needed little or no care. Weeds became prolific and multiplied over man's production of eatable foods. Not only did the soil become poorer, the genetics of the vegetables and

grains themselves were altered, yielding less produce. Weather patterns changed along with many climates upon the earth. These weather patterns are also very unpredictable causing drought and famine in some regions and floods and blizzards in others. (Scientists are trying to genetically produce many grains and vegetables to flourish once again to withstand drought, the cold or even flooding). Also, fertilizers, such as Roundup (Glyphosate), are endangering many people and beneficial insects who eat the crops they are used on.

19. The curse of deadly bacteria introduced, such as anthrax (*bacillus anthracis*) and bubonic plague (*Yersinia pestis*). And deadly viruses such as variola (smallpox). So deadly as to control the total population of the human species.

20. STD: Sexually Transmitted Diseases permitted to scourge the Human Race.

21. Humans began to kill animals and eat meat for their food. Wild animals began doing this also. Humankind began to kill animals to clothe themselves. The example was set by God (Gen. 3:21).

22. Wild birds and forest creatures such as squirrels and deer began to fear humankind.

23. The lack of the ability of the human skin to reproduce itself therefore causing the scaring of tissue.

24. Tissue and organ rejection. This is when one donor organ is rejected by the body.

25. Blood transfusions are handicapped with agglutinogens in the red blood cells causing clotting and clumping causing death to recipients. This is known as the curse of the A-B factors and the Rh factor.

26. The acute ability of multi-tasking was lost. We are now cursed to think only one thought at a time or do only one task at a time.

27. The ability of instant travel from one place to another by "thought," known also as translocation, was lost to humankind.

28. The lack of remembering names. We have been cursed by not being able to remember the names of our friends that we went to school with, or those we met while in the service or our many family relatives and their kids. Remembering names is divine, forgetting them, only human.

29. The curse of not having enough balance of energy (i.e. oil and gas) to run our societies causing strife in the world. The United States uses more than 20 million barrels of oil a *day*, about one-fourth of the world's total consumption despite having less than 5% of the world's population. The world needs about 2 million barrels a day in spare capacity to keep the world market stable.

30. The curse of the pubes. Pubescence of the mature species. That hair located on the lower abdominal region of the body including the underarm in the adult.

31. The curse of having to cook our meat, poultry, fish ... and steam our vegetables. Why is this? (1) They

contain complex proteins that are difficult to digest. (2) They can contain many harmful bacteria, such as *campylobacter*, jejuni, E-coli, listeria, salmonella and trichinella that must be killed by cooking.

32. The curse of dementia, neurodegenerative disorders and Alzheimer's disease all springing up in old age.

33. The curse of cancer (leukemia, brain, breast, lung, prostate and uterine, etc.). One in 4 people in the world will someday die of some type of cancer. How does cancer relate to stress, our emotional trauma and the genetics of cell-division?

34. Gullibility and Guile: The problem that the human race is easily deceived and has a hard time determining truth from fallacy. No matter how smart we are, we many times are deceived into believing strange things, conspiracy theories, and things that just aren't true, but believe them anyway. And no matter now illogical, they are still hard to abandon even after the truth is revealed. Examples are the deception of alcoholism, drug addiction, religious cults and many tenacious superstitions.

35. The curse of reckless driving which kills thousands each year upon our highways. This is a type of extreme carelessness (*negilgent homicide*) of your fellow human beings, full well knowing that *even though you have passed a driver's test and know better,* you still do not respect your fellow humans, drink and drive, and text your friends, and can still kill them indescrmately without a thought.

36. Not being able to forgive others that have trasspassed again us. This unforgiveness has cursed

society, family, and friends. Forgiving has the divine potential to change your enemies into friends more than anything else, and the lack of it is pulling civilization down into terrorism, murders, revenge and hate. This unforgiveness even changes our brain chemistry, causing dementia, schizophrenia, and insanity. All sin springs from it. (Mt. 6:12-15). "To err is human, to forgive, divine." —Pope, *Essay on Criticism*

Yes, we are definitely a doomed species ... with no way out ... except through death.

Ancient Civilizations

The Bible states, *And Eve bore Cain, and then bore Abel.* I learned that Cain was a farmer raising grain and fruits, while Able was a shepherd having many flocks of sheep. These first-born sons were required by God's law to give offerings as a sacrifice to Him. Cain's offering was not accepted by the LORD God for it was not a blood sacrifice and Abel's was. (Blood had to be shed for the atonement for the sins of humanity the forerunner of the Messiah, Jesus Christ). Then Cain became jealous rose up and slew Abel, his brother. For this he was cursed by God and taken from his parents to become a fugitive and a vagabond in the earth. And the Lord God set a mark upon Cain lest any finding him should kill him. What was this "mark"? Another mystery to be revealed at the demise of each human life into the mysteries of death.

Cain came to a place called Nod on the east of Eden.

He bore a son, and named the place after him. In time it was built into a great city bearing his son's name, Enoch.

This city was full of evil, wickedness and murderers. It expanded outward and corrupted all the other cities like a malignant cancer until the whole earth was a cesspool of sin.

"Iben," Historia spoke, "can you see any just and righteous people moving upon this ol' earth?"

Noah's Ark

I searched and searched and found only one family … that of Noah. You know the rest of the story! "Was the ark real? Let me tell you about it!"

Then God spoke to Noah and told him to build an ark of gopher wood because it was soon to rain. The people laughed at him. A mist rose up from the earth thus watering the ground at this time. They strangely understood not the concept of rain. They lived in a world what we would call the "Greenhouse Effect." So Noah hired numerous people to build the greatest ship mankind had known. It was 450 X 75 X 45 feet containing one and a half million cubic feet. The ark could have carried almost 600 railroad freight cars, each rail car containing over 2,500 cubic feet where many thousands of animals and birds could stay, along with Noah's entire family of eight.

Granaries were also built to store food for Noah's family and all the animals.

Interesting enough, I learned, the ark had a Grand Purpose and a Divine Mission to fulfill. With His blessings and his anathema upon a generation of humanity gone awry, God helped Noah to gather all the animals. Then a single drop of water hit my head. Then another. I realized the terrible rain to wipe out the human race had begun. The ark's massive doors were shut sealing those evil reprobates all outside in the rain. Those condemned now realized their peril. Their shrieks and screams could be heard as the waters steadily rose and finally and mercifully a long and deathly silence prevailed.

The survivors of the Great Deluge exited from the ark to observed a rainbow in the sky, the symbol of hope and faith that God will never destroy humanity in this way again. Since the whole earth had been cursed, rain now fell from the sky instead of coming up from the ground as a mist.

"Reminds me of the Passover of Exodus 12:12-13, where God's wrath is poured against humanity. *I will smite all the first-born in the land of Egypt, both man and beast; and against all the gods of Egypt I will execute judgment: I am the LORD.*"

My Guardian Spirit was strangely silent.

Historia now revealed how the mighty Egyptians built great pyramids and those massive temples erected around Babylon. We discovered the city of Akkad who produced the first written works. *Gilgamesh*, the great Sumerian legend and epic tale was the first to relate the story of creation and of the flood first mentioned outside the Bible.

Biblical History, Con't.

We journeyed into the "Land of Shinar," and stood before the mighty Tower of Babel! Until now, all the world was of one language and in their pride wanted to build a tower to the heavens! They broke two laws of God here.

First, "let us make us a name," meaning pride in thinking that their nation was the best and its citizens better than other nations. Second, "let us build us a city and a tower whose top will reach unto heaven" was a statement full of arrogance and hubris that their *faith in science* was all that was needed for a meaningful life. But it must be stated that you cannot reach God only through science or technology nor only through mundane ways without Godly faith.

So another "curse" was placed upon humanity. God confounded their language and produced many different dialects! They would now have to come to God for their salvation. They learned that they could not just rely upon the minds of their scientists and philosophers. Nor could they totally rely upon their architects and masons to search out the purpose of life, morality and divine truth. Or even rely upon mathematics, astrology, or science to solve the problems of the universe. They learned that the path of philosophy and secular humanism were *not* the ways to happiness, contentment and total fulfillment.

In other words, we will never be able to solve our many difficult problems. Just like the human race could not solve the problem of sin without Jesus Christ, it cannot solve its dilemma of wars and hate without the intervention of the Second Advent, the Second Coming of Jesus in his glory and power.

Time sped onward. We came upon Lot entering the land of Zoar, leaving behind the cities of the plains. We stumbled upon those lost evil cities, known in the Bible as Sodom and Gomorrah, lying in ruins beneath the Dead Sea!

Historia and I watched in abject horror as the anathema of God's wrath rained upon these wicked and infamous cities and their complete obliteration from the face of the earth! Never before had any city been so utterly destroyed before Hiroshima and Nagasaki, Japan of World War II!

Yes, the story of the Bible came to life before our very eyes! IT WAS ALL TRUE... EVERY GLORIOUS WORD! Some think the Bible is only a myth. And yet, therein is contained more truth in one sentence than in some large tome written by many philosophers or scientists combined!

Now we saw the Pharaoh, Ramses II, and the plagues which befell Egypt ordained by God to release the Hebrew people. We actually saw Moses and the awesome parting of the Red Sea!

"Behold the power of God!" Historia proclaimed.

Moses, under divine influence, waved his arm and the great sea obeyed him.

"This passing through the Red Sea not only was a physical reality, but is also the symbol of humanity passing through death (the wilderness) to the Promised Land or Paradise! The Pharaoh's army pursuing the Israelites was also destroyed, thus symbolizing that someday all the evil of the earth will be erased and that good will prevail."

We saw the legend of Joseph in the Bible unfold before us and how his brothers sold him into slavery and that God through dire circumstances guided him through it all to bless his life.

We observed the burning bush and how God talked to Moses. We watched as Moses descended from Mt. Sinai carrying the Ten Commandments in his hands; and with his wrath kindled threw them into the midst of the blasphemous Hebrews!

"Watch your step, there, Iben!"

He responded grabbing my arm. He swung me

backward just as the ground quaked opened beneath me and the screams of the unbelievers disappear into the abyss!

Moses, their leader, then took the golden calf and ground it to powder throwing it upon the water making the children of Israel drink it (Ex. 32:20). He stood by the gate of the camp and gave the people a choice whether to believe in Jehovah God or reject him. Moses had his men draw their swords against the remaining 3,000 that rejected the LORD.

Next, we witnessed Elisha actually parting the Jordan River so the Israelites could pass through on dry land, proceeding to the Promised Land of milk and honey!

"I had read that long ago, but since had forgotten it," I stammered.

Historia asserted, "Remember Joshua 3:17? The Lord commanded Joshua to attack the Amorites to protect Gibeon. Joshua did, and God cast down great hailstones from heaven on them. God commanded the sun and moon to stand still until the Amorites were conquered!"

"This is tremendous!" I proclaimed. "To actually see the hand of God move outward into the orbit of the Earth … and holding it in the palm of his great hand just enough to actually STOP it!

"Where in the Bible is this found?"

"Joshua 10:12-14, Iben. This miracle was performed by God to enable Joshua to overcome his enemies before darkness befell them!

Green Belt, MD

"Incidentally, several years ago at Green Belt, MD. scientists used a modern computer to calculate the movements of the stars. They examined past events and suddenly their computer halted at a certain time in the past as if jammed. There was a day missing in elapsed time on a certain date, exactly 23 hours and 20 minutes. Then they remembered a Biblical quote, 'not to go down about a whole day.' But where was the 40 minutes missing from the rest of the day?

"Well, in 2 Kings 20:10-11, the Bible recounts a passage that the sun went backward 10 degrees. Hezekiah, on his death bed was visited by the prophet Isaiah. Isaiah informed him that he wasn't going to die and he had requested the above miracle of the sun to move back 10 degrees as a sign of proof. Ten degrees is exactly 40 minutes, plus the 23 hours and 20 minutes in Joshua equals the whole 24 hours the scientists had searched for as being the missing day upon the earth!"

Next we observed the brave little boy David face Goliath and the adult King David sin with Bathsheba. We witnessed the building of King Solomon's Temple and his wondrous kingdom. We saw King David come to power and the split of the kingdom at his death.

Historia guided us to the island of Crete where great palaces were being built. Knossos was one of the most fantastic structures ever erected by civilization. It lasted for 500 years but alas, the eruption of the volcano Santorini destroyed it 3,500 years ago.

We now studied the artistic Greeks and the rise of their culture, and then we studied the Romans.

CHAPTER TEN

The Romans

*H*istoria and I now continued our trek through history.

The Romans came to power in Europe. I witnessed the assassination of Julius Caesar on March 15, 44 B.C., and the Battle of Actium where Octavius won over Antony, where 500 warships battled it out. To witness such real Roman conflicts as these was beyond belief!

We witnessed Hadrian usher in Rome's *Pax Romana*— her peak of opulence when Rome was at her pinnacle of prosperity. A new capital, Constantinople, in Byzantium, Turkey was now created. Constantine was the new monarch of Rome. He was a new Christian proselyte and halted the persecution of the Christians. Thus Christianity was pronounced the new major religion.

Finally, we witnessed the fall of Rome. It was destroyed by the Barbarians and Goths in A.D. 410. These hordes of infidels attacked the Roman army that had been weakened by complacency, divorce, homosexuality, the decline of religion, high taxes, the brutality of her sports, the building of gigantic armaments and dishonesty in business. So, the Roman Empire disintegrated thus ending forever the 1,229 years of Roman power, might and influence upon the world!

Earth's history continued as we expounded upon other events unknown to the recorded pages of history. They are all worth telling but our time and resources could not be allowed to print all we saw and did, nor what the Greeks and Romans as a whole accomplished and built. But as saints of God we saw it *all*, everything that took place, the wonders and ingenuity of the human mind, vast city states and nations ... now "but dust in the wind."

We witnessed the ruins of the Seven Wonders of the Ancient World. As I touched their ruins they appeared once again in their pristine and magnificent splendor proclaiming the technology of their time. We visited the Egyptian Pyramids, the Hanging Gardens of Babylon, the Temple of Diana at Ephesus, the Statue of Zeus by Phidias at Olympia, the Mausoleum of King Mausolos at Halicarnassus, the Colossus of Rhodes and the Pharos, or Lighthouse of Alexandria.

From here, we traveled through massive dust storms in Arabia and discovered the lost city of Haram Bilqis, or the fabled Arabian Kingdom of Sheba.

Solomon's temple

Israel now entered the scene. This country, chosen by God to set an example for the world, had gone for 400 years with only a "tent" as God's dwelling place. Then the Hebrews decided they wanted a permanent temple to worship their God. So God gave instructions to King David to erect it. This Temple was to be "exceeding magnificent of fame and glory in all the earth."

King David wanted to build the Temple but was forbidden because he was a "man of war."

So the honor of building the temple went to his son, Solomon. In today's inflation it would be worth over $5,000,000,000! It was to be the most expensive, most spectacular and most resplendent building ever imagined or erected upon the face of the earth!

The holy design of the Temple was patterned after the Tabernacle. Here resided the ark of the covenant protected by two cherubim, the Golden Altar of Incense and five Golden Candlesticks on the north and south sides containing five tables of show bread therein.

This wondrous Temple of Solomon is thought to have stood on the very rock where Abraham offered Isaac. This is where an eight-sided Muslim mosque is now located, known as the "Dome of the Rock," in Jerusalem.

But why this Dome of the Rock matters so much to the Christians, the Jews or to the Muslim world remains a mystery. Shouldn't people do as their Bible, Torah and Koran teach to love, forgivness, and to help one another and give to the poor? Why must they travel to the very spot where they allegedly think Mohammed left the earth to be in heaven—the very same spot where Abraham was told by God to offer Isaac as a sacrifice? *There is really no real proof that either of them actually stood here—*

This barren rock is called "sacred" by these religions. The folly then lies in tribute to the vanity of the thousands of Jews, Christians and Muslims that pilgrimage to this consecrated spot each year and those killed in "Holy Wars" to acquire this otherwise worthless piece of "sacred" historical property!

Also, the Muslims (Moslems) must make their pilgrimage to Mecca in their ritual known as "stoning the devil," where pilgrims hurl stones at three pillars symbolizing the temptations of Satan. The *hajj* is required of all Muslims at least once in their lifetime and some 2 to 4 million people arrive in Mecca, the Muslim Holy City, every year where thousands are trampled to death or die from heat exhaustion attending these rituals. One year at least 2,177 Muslims were stampeded to death while waiting to stone the devil.

And this is no isolated case. If they so die on this holy journey they immediately attain paradise, they believe.

All that wasted energy! Couldn't all that effort of these pilgrims be used to alleviate the human condition? All that money spent on this journey used to a better purpose given to charity proclaiming their love toward one another? Why couldn't we teach each other to respect all religions and all people? Then I wondered why Christians want to travel so much to the Holy Land to walk where Jesus once walked? What good does this do? Is there such a thing as "Holy Land" anyway? Jesus Christ is alive and well and the Holy Spirit should dwell in one's heart—not in some far away archaic country.

This grand Temple to the LORD was plundered within five years after Solomon's death. Then it was destroyed by the Babylonians in 586 B.C.

We stood in silent wonder at the magnificence of the Temple and were saddened by its final dissolution and fire.

The mighty Empire of King David was split into two

halves, the northern kingdom to be known as "Israel" (in 922 B.C) and the southern part known as Judah.

We now witnessed Nebuchadnezzar, King of Babylon, besieged Jerusalem pillaging Solomon's Temple, looting its vast treasures and taking 10,000 captives back to Babylon. The Hebrews were now a conquered nation and were sent to Babylon in exile as slaves in 606 B.C. Thus the "Babylonian Captivity" commenced upon them for the next 70 years. Then the new ruler of Babylon, Cyrus the Great, released them to return home to Jerusalem once again (536 B.C.).

Interestingly, God wanted the Hebrews (the Israelites) to worship Him only. The Hebrews once again brought the customs of pagan gods back from Babylon on their return. The Babylonians had a goddess named Ishtar (Astarte, or Ashtareth) the goddess of fertility. This is where the Hebrews brought back the *symbols of fertility of the rabbit and the egg* with them and these customs were carried all the way into the Twenty-first Century! Now we know why there is the "Easter Bunny" and the dyed colored "Easter Eggs" come from. Ancient Babylon is the reason. It also should be noted that the word "Easter" comes from this goddess *Ishtar* and is used only one time in the KJV of the Bible in Acts 12:4. New translations have correctly changed the word Easter to *Passover*. The Greek word, "*Pascha,*" is used to commemorate the Hebrews release from slavery in Egypt when the Lord passed over the first-born of the Hebrews and smote those of the Egyptians.

Oddly, I always knew since I was a little kid that rabbits didn't lay eggs. Finally, I now have the answer to the riddle.

CHAPTER ELEVEN

The Ark of the Covenant

(Ref. Josh. 3:13; 6:13-20; 1 Sam. 6:19;
2 Sam. 6:6-7, 12; Ex. 34:1)

"Historia, I have a question. What ever happened to the ark of the covenant?"

"Well, Iben, the ark first of all presented another unsolved Mystery of the Ages! The Israelites traveled with it. It was built of Acacia (shittim) wood and it was gold-plated inside and out having a gold border around the lid. It was hammered from pure gold. There were two golden cherubim, their wings widespread as if to protect the mercy seat. It caused the Jordan River to stop flowing, it caused Jericho's walls to collapse, and it caused the Israelites to prosper. The ark also contained such might from God that 50,000 men were destroyed for only looking into it. Uzzah was also killed for nothing more than attempting to steady the ark as the cart shifted."

It was finally captured, I learned, and the heathen

nations were crushed by its mighty power. The mice overran the country carrying the scourge of plague. Iben, if we can find the lost ark of the covenant we shall also find the Ten Commandments for they were placed inside it!

We entered the old city of the ruins of Jerusalem in a part that had *never* been excavated by archaeologists because it ran about thirty feet under the old city streets. My excitement grew more intense as Historia disclosed the old burial catacombs containing skeletons of those murdered during the fall of Jerusalem in 606 B.C. We passed through these labyrinthine tunnels and weaved our way to an old dry cistern never used again since the siege of Babylon. Here deep within one of these arid dusty caves we discovered a hidden doorway still having the unbroken seal of Nebuchadnezzar's cameo upon it. My skin actually tingled with anticipation!

Here Historia uncovered a crate wrapped in a ragged weathered tarpaulin. Under this, guarded by golden cherubim … *was the actual ancient … lost ark of the covenant!*

"Can I divulge what we found?"

"Yes, Iben, tell the gentle reader what you have seen!"

Here still sealed inside the ark were the actual Ten Commandments before my very eyes! I thoroughly scrutinized the two smooth granite plaques carved from a single block of stone containing PreCanaanite lettering, and could not find a chip or broken spot on any of them! I thought they would be broken because Moses in anger threw them at the Golden Calf when he came down from Mount Sinai.

"Iben, this is the *second* set of the Ten Commandments!" The first were destroyed when Moses threw them but he was commanded to carve out two more tablets on which God then *rewrote* the Ten Commandments."

Also, in the ark we located an *omer* of manna, long since turned to dust. It was found in opaque amphora, its lid still sealed by very hand of Aaron himself! Aaron's rod was observed next. Its colors had long since faded but still had some of the Israelite genealogy etched upon it! It had a gold-plated hilt still intact and was found in very good condition still after all these years. The manna symbolized God's provision in the wilderness. The rod symbolized the authority of Aaron when God commanded the stick to blossom forth buds and almonds.

"It is amazing that it has never been discovered!"

"It will be found in God's due time," concluded Historia. "But Christianity, Iben, is based on *faith*, not artifacts!"

Historia and I witnessed hundreds of unrecorded battles and wars, civilizations utterly destroyed leaving no trace in the sands of time. Whole armies who perished in vain trying to conquer other nations and whole nations who were conquered by marauding barbarians. What a waste of humanity slaughtered by their pride and vanity that marched before our eyes completely lost to the pages of history!

CHAPTER TWELVE

The Christmas Star/The Birth of Christ

*T*wondered if there were any substantial evidence that Jesus Christ really existed?

Jesus' life, I learned from Historia, was one of the best-documented historical facts of antiquity. Many secular writers even outside the Bible mention him. Cornelius Tacitus, who recorded history during the Roman Empire, mentions a deadly fire that destroyed Rome in 64 B.C. Tacitus stated that the Emperor Nero set it but blamed a new sect known as "Christians" for starting it. Tacitus writes that a man named *Christus* was executed by the procurator Pontius Pilate during the reign of Tiberius. All this was inscribed in the *Annals of Tacitus*, XV, 44.

Also, the Jewish historian, Flavius Josephus, mentions Jesus between the death of the Roman governor of Judea about 62 B.C. and the arrival of his successor the High Priest Ananus (Annas) who spoke before the Sanhedrin and brought before them a man named James, the brother of

Jesus, who was called the Christ. This was recorded in the Jewish Antiquities, XX, 200.

Other ancient non-Christian writers such as Lucian of Samosata, Suetonius, Pliny the Younger, etc. including numerous non-Christian Jewish sources and the historically and reliable New Testament, all cannot be explained if Jesus never really existed because they are *eyewitness accounts* of Jesus Christ's life.

Now some Christmas Luminaria appeared before Historia and I. There was Ave Maria, Cantique de Noel, Adeste Fideles, Shengdan Laoren, Panis Angelicus, Melchior, Balthasar and Gaspar!

"Iben, look!" Ave Maria shouted, "The Holy Star of Bethlehem!"

"Yes, Iben, you are observing the very Christmas Star the *Magi* or 'wise men' from Persia had actually observed over 2,000 years ago! They were a priestly caste that specialized in astrology. I can assure you it is *not* Jupiter, Mars and Venus aligned together. This star is *not* the conjunction of Jupiter/Regulus in 2 or 3 B.C., nor is it a supernova explosion, nor is it any other known phenomenon known to mere mortals!"

"I heard someone say that it could be a comet?"

"Oh? In 1871 the astronomer John Williams recorded a list of comets produced from Chinese ancient astrological records. This list stated that two comets, one in March and April 5 B.C. comet #52 appeared near the constellation Capricorn and the other was comet #53 in the constellation Aquila. Could these two comets be those the wise men observed in the night sky so long ago? Number 53 could have been mistaken as a tailless comet but in reality it was just the remnant of a supernova explosion millions of eons ago with its light only became visible to the inhabitants of the Earth in the last 2,000 years, during March and April, 4 B.C. But was Christ really born in 4 B.C? Or 2 B.C.? Or 6 B.C.? So the quest for the 'Christmas Star' continues."

Noel stated that this star was prophesied in the Bible around 800 years before it happened! Numbers 24:17, states, "There shall come a star out of Jacob…" and again in Isa. 47:13, "Let now the astrologers (Magi)… stand up and save you from what will come upon you."

Thus, astrology was now rendered impotent, null and void with its power utterly destroyed. That even the astrologers (the *Magi*) were enlightened by the birth of the Messiah and rightly followed God's glorious light to where the Christ child was born! If the "star" was a comet or just a conjunction of stars, then how could it have led the Magi to the Christ child?

I realized at that moment Ave Maria was the very Mother of Jesus Christ standing before me in all her divine glory, clothed in an iridescent satin gown of liquid silver radiating divine light from her angelic countenance!

In mortal life I would have swooned and fell as dead before her beauty!

In this enhanced state I have now acquired the *divine permission* to divulge from the angels just what this *STAR* was.

"This *star*," Ave Maria continued, "was the *Portal of Paradise* beaming down its light from the astral realm to keep and protect the Christ Child from all evil! The night sky actually split open and a great beam of Holy Light known as the Shekinah Glory radiated its radiance and fire down from the Kingdom of God, slicing through the space-time continuum to the Christ Child! No person, thing or entity could come close to harming the Child of God, Jesus Christ, God's only begotten Son! A Supernatural Light, for a Supernatural Announcement of a Supernatural Birth! And Iben, you will even learn *more* about this *Wondrous Light* later on—and be totally amazed!

"Sorry to tell you, but our calendar is off a few years! Dionysis Exeguus, 'Dionysis-the-Little,' known also as 'Dennis-the-Short,' the sixth-century monk miscalculated Jesus' birth by 4 to 7 years. A more accurate date would actually be 4 B.C. because the Julian calendar is inaccurate!"

"Four B.C.?" I stammered. "I figured Christ to be born on—"

"And Christ wasn't born on December 25 and it wasn't even winter time! You see, Iben, no mortal knows the *exact* date for Christ's birth and the angels have censored it from human knowledge. It could have been around October or May, or even in March. But we must remember that the shepherds were 'watching their flock' during these times when the angels came and announced the birth of Jesus to them.

"In A.D. 354, Bishop Liberius of Rome ordered the celebration of Jesus' birth on December 25. Rome was already celebrating the pagan holiday, the Feast of Saturn (the *Saturnalia*) the birthday of the sun on this day. Now Christians could honor Christ as the 'Light of the World!' Now the western world celebrates the birth of the 'Son,' the Son of God, that is. This is how December 25 became the Christmas holiday!"

Jesus Christ:

The fulcrum on the scale of Humanity,
balancing the weight of good over evil,
justice over corruption, joy over despair—
splitting the fabric of time asunder, dividing the history
of humankind from B.C. to A.D.,
balancing the past with the future,
the Alpha and the Omega,
the Beginning and the End—Past, Present and Future.
A hundred million books and sermons
have been written about the Life of Jesus,
who He is and what He has accomplished.
Yet no mortal has ever completely fathomed,
exhausted, nor comprehended all
that He did for humanity!
It takes DEATH to fulfill all His promises,
to reveal all the love, truth and life
He has to give to his believers.
—The Author

Historia, the Christmas Spirits, and I followed the shepherds as they traveled to witness the Christ child, listening to their stories of how the angels spoke to them and that they should follow this strange "star" to the place where Jesus was born.

While upon our journey I questioned the Christmas Spirits about how the legend of Santa Claus was born and if such a person actually ever existed.

Shengdan Laoren spoke, "Iben, the real Santa—was

known as *St. Nicholas* or *Sinterklaas*, the bishop of Myra. He was born in 270 A.D. in Patara, Turkey. He was an orphan whose wealthy parents were killed in a plague. He used his inheritance to feed the poor, especially widows and children. Today some of his 1,600-year old remains are buried in Bari, Italy and other bones have been located near Antalya, Turkey. Even fragments of his skeleton have even been sent to the Greek Orthodox Church of St. Nicholas in Flushing, New York.

"Being a compassionate man, he helped a nobleman unable to provide dowries for his three daughters to be married by throwing a bag of gold through their window. Word spread of St. Nicholas' good deed and at his death he was made the patron saint of virgins and young girls searching for good husbands. Then Europeans adopted him as their patron saint of the seas. Sailors and merchants adapted him as their symbol of good luck.

"St. Nicholas died December 6th and was celebrated in Europe by a person wearing a red costume. If the children were good they were rewarded with gifts. This gift-giving was celebrated along with Christ's birthday. Some countries still celebrate 'Father Christmas' on December 6th, exchanging gifts in St. Nicholas' honor. St. Nicholas in Dutch translates into Sinterklaas, into English as 'Santa Claus,' and in China … to Shengdan Laoren!"

So the Supernalite before me was actually St. Nicholas, whose legend caught afire the generosity of the world at Christmas time!

We watched as Jesus grew up, attended the Jewish synagogue and waxed strong in spirit and wisdom. I learned the meaning of "**Jesus Christ**." *Jeshus* is the Hebrew form for the Greek word **Joshua** *or "Jesus"* which means "God saves," or "God is Savior." "**Messiah**" or "**Christ**" means, "**the Anointed One**." Jesus was reverently referred to as "**Jesus, the Christ**."

Jesus was also called **Emmanuel**, which means "**God with us.**" He would also be called Wonderful, Counselor, The Mighty God, The Everlasting Father, the Prince of Peace.

Melchior, Balthasar and Gaspar (Caspar) related how the *Magi* or Wise Men from the Orient visited Herod. They represented all those wise astrologers who visited Bethlehem seeking out the babe Jesus. It is only recorded in St. Matthew's Gospel and nothing exists outside this biblical narrative but legends and myths. All that is known about these sojourners were that they were Persians from Babylon and usually roamed the desert in caravans for protection from thugs and marauders. All else remains a mystery. In the eighth century the Wise Men were traditionally given these above names. They arrived in Bethlehem and gave the Christ child their three gifts: gold, frankincense and myrrh. The gold symbolized the tribute for a king and used it throughout their travels as payment for room and board; frankincense was burned with its smoke symbolizing the prayers of the saints; and the myrrh will be used in the embalming of his mortal body after His crucifixion.

With uncanny accuracy and verity, the truth of the Holy Scriptures unfolded before us. We saw the hatred and cunning of Herod plotting to liquidate the baby Jesus—rival heir to *his* throne, so he thought.

We learned how Herod's soldiers went from door to door battering them from their hinges seeking out all the tender and precious babies, chopping them to pieces with their pikes and broad swords. What a horrific sight to see as hard iron pierced through their little twitching screaming bodies, their once shinny blades now dripping with the blood of the innocent! Soldiers slinging down the wounded babies onto the floors of their homes breaking their necks, crushing them to death under foot. One moment alive and kicking, the next—blood and death. Mother's and infant's screams pierced through the black night in unison, their tears mingled together in great sorrow and then the silence of an unquenchable pain.

The horrible and ungodly screams of their mothers wailing over their dead children. Only a mad man could think up such atrocities.

Jesus began to realize that he was the chosen Messiah. Jesus at a young age began to attend daily classes at the synagogue memorizing the Torah and finally proclaiming his Divine Mission and Divine Destiny.

I was now taught all about the esoteric or lost years of Jesus' childhood on which the Bible is strangely silent. What he did and how he acted as a young child was very interesting to us, but was not pertinent to Jesus' Divine Mission. And then he grew up into a man having *no form or comeliness having no beauty that we should desire him*, and a young man of *low esteem* and *poor*, with his hair cropped just below the ears, *unlike* those Renaissance paintings and inaccurate movies portraying him in long stringy dirty hair that we have become accustom to.

We witnessed the Sermon on the Mount and was

totally enthralled as Jesus taught the truths of God! How wonderful to see the crowds, their faces alight with divine wisdom, Godly character and beauty… surely this is truly the Son of God!

The Origin of the Bible

The sermons and parables in the Bible were recorded and the world is still awed and inspired by them over two thousand years later! Such Promises! Such miracles! Such comfort! Yet, Americans take it so for granted that they even have access to it! Alas! Other countries have had Bibles banned and have only a few pages of Holy Writ and blessed even to have these!

I noticed that the Sermon on the Mount and other sayings of Jesus were almost identical with the very texts found in the Bible! I thought Jesus' words were but a paraphrase and yet the gospels contained THE VERY WORDS THAT JESUS SPOKE!

How can this be?

Adeste Fideles replied, "Iben Jair, as we have stated, the scriptures of the New Testament are from *eyewitness accounts* of Jesus' ministry. And those from the Old Testament have been inspired by God's very presence. You wondered how we came to preserve so many of them? For example, we have only a very few copies of Caesar's *Gallic War* complied between 58 and 50 B.C. Of the 142 books of the Roman history of Livy (59 B.C.-A.D. 17) only 35 survived. The *Histories of Tacitus* (c. A.D. 100) only four and one half survived, of the sixteen books of his *Annals, only* ten have survived. There are only eight manuscripts left of *The History of Thucydides*

(c. 470-400 B.C.). The *History of Herodotus* (c. 488-428 B.C.) have all been handed down through generations, the earliest manuscripts are over 1,300 years later than any of the originals.

"Compare these to the Bible, of which there exists thousands of fragmented manuscripts. The Christian Greek Scriptures exceed to within a hundred years of their originals!"

"Most of the above Greek manuscripts," Noel spoke, "have been destroyed though many were written *after* the Hebrew Scriptures. Oddly, even in the face of persecution and penalty of death, we still have more Greek Scriptures (Bible Texts) than those original manuscripts existing from Greece or Rome!

"Iben, the Bible is composed of 66 books written by about 40 different prophets over a period of 1,600 years. Three different languages were used, Hebrew, Greek and Latin. All these writers were imbued with various talents and inspiration. Then after all these years the books they wrote were combined into what is now know as the Holy Bible. It is God's wonderful gift to humanity, an instruction book for the human race, revealing the Son of God, Jesus Christ, as the *only means to salvation*, as seen in Acts 4:12; Jn. 14:6; 1 Jn. 3:23."

Jesus' miracles and parables came alive before us unraveling the wonder, splendor and mystery of God's message toward all mankind. All the multitudes listened and pondered these teachings in their hearts, souls and minds.

Such divine wisdom, and yet almost every Christian in the United States has a Bible in their home and yet only few read it at all and only one in 100,000 has ever read it through from cover to cover, from Genesis to Revelation! *Yet it can determine the destiny of your soul for all Eternity!*

I learned that the Bible was uncannily more accurate than I had ever previously imagined! Jesus and his miracles unfolded before us revealing the total veracity of the Holy Scriptures! There is an old acronym going around that states that the B-I-B-L-E stands for, "Basic Instructions Before Leaving Earth."

How true, I thought.

Toward the end of Jesus' ministry, we watched as he led his twelve disciples in the Lord's Supper. We watched as Judas Iscariot betrayed Jesus for 30 pieces of silver.

> "We see Jesus, who was made a little lower
> than the angels for the suffering of death,
> crowned with glory and honor, that
> he, by the grace of God,
> should taste death for every man."
> —Hebrews 2:9

We stood in total enthrallment and reverence as Jesus observed the Passover— took the bread, symbolic of his body ... broke it into pieces and passed it to his disciples to eat. Then he drank the wine, symbolic of his blood shed for many ... and also passed it around. They then sang hymns and went out into the Mount of Olives. Now the end unfolded upon Jesus' life.

The Crucifixion of Jesus

The peace was broken by the tumult of Judas Iscariot leading an angry crowd to Jesus, betraying him. He was then carried off to the Jewish court where Caiaphas, the high priest, along with the scribes and elders were assembled accusing him of blasphemy—all false charges.

Jesus was taken before the governor to procure the decision for crucifixion. Now Pilate gave the people a choice at a certain feast day to choose Jesus or a prisoner called Barabbas. They chose Barabbas which sealed the fate of Jesus. And then Pilate washed his hands symbolizing his innocence in his decision.

We witnessed Jesus in the common hall, and we wept as they stripped him and put on him a scarlet robe and plaited a crown of thorns upon his head. Then they mocked him, spat upon him and smote him on the head.

As they came out, Simon of Cyrene helped Jesus carry his cross. They stripped Jesus of his garments and tied him naked upon the cross which was resting on the ground. He carried Jesus' cross to *Golgotha* which means in Aramaic, *place of the skull*; or Latin meaning, *Calvary*—both words referencing the place Christ was crucified.

Now a plaque was placed above Jesus' head in Greek, Latin and Hebrew:

"THIS IS JESUS, THE KING OF THE JEWS."
—Matthew 27:37; Heb. 4:14-16

Interestingly I noticed that there was nothing special about this particular cross that Jesus was to be executed upon. It had already been scared with previous nail holes and dark blood stains from other executions. And I suspected it will be continually used after this infamous day. The Romans did not use a fresh cross each time they executed someone. Also, each cross was used many times with many different criminals. And this was no isolated case for there were numerous crosses with criminals hanging upon them almost every day of the week all across Rome. It was their reminder not to cause foment or disagree with the Roman government or face its dire consequences and swift judgment.

Then a group of Roman soldiers held Jesus down and tethered his legs so the pain wouldn't make him kick them. Then two others, one on each side of him, stretched out his arms as they hammered a long sharp nail into Jesus' wrists pinning both of them to the cross-beam almost simultaneously. The right wrist cut through an artery— blood splattering the soldier—fully in the face. Wiping his face, he drew out another long nail, reached down to Jesus' feet—hammering one of them to the cross. He did the same to his other foot, nailing them separately, one just above the other. Oddly each nail that pierced Jesus, I witnessed a bright flash of light that no one else could see except me!

Then the soldiers shoved the crown of thorns down over his head, blood running across his face. More soldiers using a set of ropes stood the cross upright and with a thud, it landed in its hole, jerking Jesus upright making him again wince with pain.

I noticed Mary, the mother of Jesus, now turn her head as in deep unbearable pain as tears welled up in her dark serene eyes.

Blood now slowly trickled from Jesus' face down onto his chest. Also, from his back, still bleeding from his flogging, the cross turned a bright scarlet. I could see his tranquil eyes move across to his mother and some of his friends. He seemed to be in *another world* as his pain became unbearable. I felt something wet on my foot and realized that I was standing in Jesus' blood! Jesus, turning his head, looked directly into my eyes! *He could actually see me!* Such a peace filled my heart! Oh my soul! Such tears I shed unashamedly. Jesus could *see directly* into that dimension which I and all the angels dwell.

Panis Angelicus spoke, "If the people of the Twentieth Century could witness this! How much TV sets would be turned off and the Holy Writ once again become king in the household! To know this is the Way, the Truth and the Life! God help us all! No wonder we have such problems in our great modern and technological age!"

Surely this is the Son of God!

The two thieves were nailed and tied to their crosses. They were then placed on each side of Jesus.

I noticed the sky, once sunny, now turning strangely black and the strong wind whipped between their crosses, stirring up some trash the soldiers and others had thrown down. Then, as the specter of doom, strange pink spider lightning flashed, its thunder even rattling our teeth from the intensity of it… fortelling the evil humanity had done.

Then, six hours later, at the age of thirty-three, Jesus died.

At Christ's death the veil of King Solomon's temple in Jerusalem was torn apart signifying that Christ's believers can once again commune with God *without* a *mortal priest.* We confirm that Jesus is our high priest. I witnessed a deep rumbling under my feet as great boulders split asunder.

What otherworldly powers were released at Christ's death? We were stunned as many of the dead now rose from their graves. Some even went into Jerusalem proclaiming Jesus' sovereignty over life and death!

I saw many legions of angels ready to do battle for Jesus, just waiting for God to give the signal. The whole world held its breath! We were on the brink of the most terrifying battle of all—Armageddon—that of Good versus Evil. There were twelve legions of divine angels ready to annihilate the Roman army and the demons of Satan and from my perspective, only one of these mighty angels could have done the job easily with one capricious sweep of the hand!

His Name is Jesus

In Genesis—our Omnipotent Creator
and our Divine Image;
Exodus—our Passover Lamb and our Shekinah Glory;
Leviticus—our Day of Atonement;
Numbers—our Revelator and Divine Healer;
Deuteronomy—our Rock of Faith;
Joshua—our Divine Path to Prosperity;
Judges—our Deliverer from Apostasy;
Ruth—our Kinsman-Redeemer and Blessed Life;
Samuel—our Anointing and Trusted Prophet;
Kings and Chronicles—our Guiding Master;
Nehemiah—our Restorer;
Ester—our Advocate;
Job—our Pathos and our Restitution;
Psalms—our Peace and Protector;
Proverbs and Ecclesiastes—our Divine Wisdom;
Song of Solomon—our Bridegroom;
Isaiah—our Immanuel and our Prince of Peace;

Jeremiah—our Everlasting Love;

Lamentations—our Redemption from Apostasy;

Ezekiel—our Divine Visitor;

Daniel—our Source of Divine Knowledge;

The Minor Prophets—our Ransom from Hell and Death;

The Gospels—our Shepherd, our

Comforter and our Miracle-worker;

Acts—our Risen Savior and our Holy Spirit Power;

Romans—our Righteousness and

our Free Gift of Salvation;

Epistles—our Divine Light, our

Compassion and our Victory;

Hebrews—our Anchor, our High Priest, our Helper and

the Author and Finisher of our Faith; and

Revelation—our Alpha and Omega,

our King of kings and Lord of lords,

and Designer of our Divine Destiny.

—The Author

So it is with this panorama unfolding before us, those present at Jesus' resurrection could see only the tip of the iceberg! Now we, the saints of God, can see into the *Great Beyond* into an alternate dimension—no one even dreamed of or dared to vision in the afterlife! *There is so much more to reality than the mere five senses can comprehend! So much more!*

Did time stop? Humankind was cut asunder by Jesus' death. The very fabric of time was cleaved in half!

The soldiers thought: *Surely, this is the Son of God!*

All the great Evil Entities of the universe were also

present—ready to war against God's angels! Their leaders were Lucifer, Apollyon, Beelzebub, Belial and Satan. The indignity and blasphemy of it, mocking our Lord and the mighty power of his holy angels!

We were at the brink of the fulfillment of God's divine prophesy. For in one twinkling of the eye from Jesus, with all untimate power, he could have annihilated these demons from the very universe itself!

Also, present were the all-powerful angels of Jehovah guarding and protecting Jesus' precious soul with their shinning 'swords' of flame! With these massive weapons of destruction sweeping to and fro these magnificent Angels were ready to strike at a moment's notice.

Leading the archangels were Michael and Gabriel. They were waiting for the signal from God to strike and destroy all the evil upon the earth. Was it God's Divine Plan to extinguish evil now? We held our breath and waited. Morning came and the earth once again breathe a sigh of relief. The time for the great battle, Armageddon, had passed. The earth was still intact. Evil still dominated the earth but its power, along with Satan's, had been irreparably shattered!

Then early the next morning of the third day, while Mary Magdalene along with many other women were vigil over the sepulcher, there was a great earthquake and an angel of the Lord descended from heaven rolling back the gravestone! His countenance was like lightning and his raiment was white as snow!

Then the angel stated, "He is not here: for he is risen, as he said. Come, see the place where the Lord lay."

And they departed quickly from the sepulcher and did run to bring:

"GOOD TIDINGS OF GREAT JOY! THAT JESUS CHRIST HAS RISEN! HE HAS ACTUALLY RESURRECTED FROM THE DEAD!"

And then the disciples met Jesus along the way! What ecstasy and mirth!

Shroud of Turin

All the Christmas Angels, along with Historia and I, were now running with the women! *To actually be there to witness the resurrection of Jesus Christ!* After Jesus abandoned the sepulcher, his burial cloth was left behind. It stilled glowed from the flash of divine radiant energy as Christ rose to immortality from the grave! It was stained with the very blood of Jesus with the imprint of Jesus' majestic countenance etched upon it! This cloth has been preserved by the Catholic Church and has become known as the—

"So the Holy Shroud of Turin, Italy, is real!" I proclaimed.

"Yes, Iben it is—which confirms what many scientists and the Roman Catholic Church has stated all along … that it is the *actual* linen cloth wrapped around Jesus' body at his burial!"

I realized now that mortal mind cannot understand the complete euphoria and peace the immortal being can have!

Historia and I now continue our journey...

CHAPTER THIRTEEN

Christian martyrs

*H*istoria continued with all the misfortune, foibles, calamity, suffering and pathos of the human predicament through the pages of history.

Christ's resurrection I could now see was the pivot for humankind, splitting time into B.C. and A.D. We all watched the sowing and spread of the Gospel, the "Good News" across the Mediterranean Sea.

In 8 A.D. the apostle Stephen, I learned, was accused by the Sanhedrin for "blaspheming against God," a false charge. This was the *same* Jewish court that had condemned Jesus of blasphemy. Paul was a member of this Jewish court who condemned Stephen to death by stoning. Stephen thus became the first *Christian martyr* and in his death agony he could see into the eternal realm of which we stood. Stephen, like Jesus, looked directly into my eyes at the moment of death! Then many angels guided him into the Kingdom of God!

Ananias and Sapphira lied to the Holy Spirit and the

anathema of God struck them down instantly to their deaths! Andrew, the brother of Peter, went to Asia Minor to minister the Gospel. Here he was caught, tried and we watched in horror as he was crucified on an "X," two crossbeams of wood fixed into the ground.

Peter was caught next witnessing the "Good News." He stated he was not worthy to die as his Savior, and so was crucified upside down on a cross, thus dying a slow and agonizing death! We saw John, the writer of the book of John and Revelation, get condemned to the island of Patmos, where he crossed into an alternate universe— actually witnessing the end of the world ... and the New Jerusalem coming out of heaven! We next witnessed the demise of Bartholomew who traditionally took the Gospel to India. He was eventually caught and flayed alive in Armenia (eastern Asia Minor).

We saw the execution of John-the-Baptist. He was beheaded ... and the list of Christian martyrs goes on and on. We bid farewell to Christ's disciples as they returned into the Bosom of Abraham.

We now traveled with the apostle Paul on his great missionary journeys and witnessed his divine miracles. We visited the newly founded Christian churches all across Asia. We followed him to Rome where he was blamed for the burning of Rome. Here in A.D. 63 we witnessed his rendezvous with the executioner's ax.

Our odyssey of history continued to unfold before us—
Then in A.D. 455 we witnessed the Vandals pillage and burn Rome, a sad day indeed, for the world was plunged into ignorance and darkness for the next thousand years!

Rome was looted and burned without remorse. Gone were the many books and writings of some of the best literature the world had ever produced ... and once again civilization spiraled downward.

We continued to witness the panorama of the past unfold.

We witnessed Martin Luther change the course of Christianity as he nailed his 95 Theses upon All Saints Church in Wittenberg, Germany in A.D. 1517.

King Louis XVI

Now the time was January 20, 1793 in Paris on a cold rainy morning. We could hear the drums of proclamation sounding in the air as King Louis XVI of France, upon a heavily guarded carriage, took his final ride into destiny. Trumpets announced the king's arrival at the *Place de la Revolution* and the carriage stopped at the tall stately instrument of infamy. Thousands of people observed as he climbed to the stage of the sturdy wooden tower, composed of two upright parallels, with a sharp heavy angled piece of gleaming iron at the top.

As the macabre panorama unfolded, Thanatopia suddenly appeared—

As the thunder of the drums roared in our ears, Louis XVI was forced down upon the plank and his neck fitted into the stock. Then as the crowd stood in reverence and silence, the blade suspended above for a brief moment, then split through the air forever changing the fate of history. The king's head toppled. The executioner now held up the bloody truncated head so that the crowd could see it. The guillotine, now splattered with blood, was dashed with buckets of water to purge the machine of death.

Some wept while others fainted at this ghastly sight. Most were stunned that the people could do such a reckless thing. Shouts of… "Long live the Republic!" resonated throughout the mob. The crowd now began to sing the song of revolution, the *Marseillaise*.

So, many times good does come from something bad. I thought.

We witnessed the effluvium from the dead king's body rising and those shadowy dark demons fluttering away from his soul leaving him in peace. The angel Thanatopia was guiding him toward that strange radiating "star" that only we could see.

Chapter Fourteen

The slaughter of humanity continued ... the brutality, the cruelty, the barbarism of it all. History to us seemed an insane blood bath and yet through all this pathos and futility… there were hope and dreams of a better future—the expediency of a better world to come. I wondered if humanity has learned anything from 5,000 years of civilization!

Historia and I continue upon our trek of history. We now witnessed the American Revolution!

The waste and slaughter of humanity continued—

Then on July 4, 1776, we watched the signing of the Declaration of Independence by Thomas Jefferson, John Adams, Benjamin Franklin, *et al*. What a day this was, not only for America, for this day the angels smiled upon the earth and the whole of humanity! All the redeemed in the Kingdom of Heaven were rejoicing over this!

The American Civil War

The American Civil War now commenced. The time…1861.

General Grant, of the Northern, Federal (Union) forces and General Lee, of the Southern (Confederate) forces appeared, all dressed in their Civil War uniforms. They revealed the great American Civil War first hand!

"When war is declared, Truth is the first casualty."
—Arthur Ponsonby: *Falsehood in Wartime*

We witnessed all the major American Civil War battles, Antietam, Bull Run, Chancellorsville, Chickamauga, Cold Harbor, Fredericksburg, Gettysburg, Kennesaw Mountain, Murfreesboro, Petersburg, Shiloh, Vicksburg and many more. They unraveled before us in all their raw fury of blood, gore and death.

Then on Sunday, April 9, 1865, General Lee surrenders to General Grant at a little farm house near Appomattox Court House, Virginia.

One million people had died! This death toll includes troops that had been killed from diseases: about 618,000. The North lost 360,000 men and the South 258,000. Diseases killed far more troops than cannons, bullets, swords or bayonets. Only 110,000 Union soldiers and 94,000 Confederate troops actually died on the battlefields.

We bade farewell to General Grant and General Lee as they evanesced back into Abraham's bosom.

"All it takes for evil to prevail, is for
good men to do nothing."
—Edmond Burke

As human events unfolded before our eyes I learned that God, Jesus Christ and the Holy Spirit, along with the mighty angels were *directing* and *controlling* human destinies unfolding before me, that history was *not* just randomness brought on by evil and cruel empires producing chaos, death, world destruction, hopeless circumstances and vain existences of billions of people. Nor was it just for God's entertainment to toy with the circumstances of desperate people to place pain and misery upon the sinners of earth.

The important lesson I now must proclaim is that God does have a Divine Mission for humanity ... that life does have a meaningful purpose—redemption and salvation embued with divine love and truth.

Then I knew my Divine Mission. That is why I have been chosen to write this book.

WORLD WAR I:

"There is not such thing as an inevitable war.
If war comes it will be from failure of human wisdom."
Bonar Law–Speech before World War I

We found ourselves in Sarajevo, the capital of Bosnia. We noticed a parade moving slowly down the street. Then two shots rang out mortally wounding Archduke Francis

369

Ferdinand and his wife, the Countess Sophie. The date: June 28, 1914.

Now Austria-Hungary declared war upon the Yugoslav freedom movement and Serbia. Now Germany invaded Belgium, and Britain declared war on Germany. World War I had begun. The Central Powers composed of Germany, Austria-Hungary, Turkey and Bulgaria fought against the French and Russian troops.

All sides now faced fierce fighting known as "trench warfare." As the armies dug in, the area turned into *no-man's land*, a quagmire of death and destruction. This lasted for four horrible years, each side using hand grenades, machine guns and the most feared of all—poison gas. The total of masses killed was mind boggling. Nations of the world had never seen destruction of this magnitude in the history of warfare!

We witnessed the horrors of the Battle of Verdun, and the Battle of the Somme where, in a killing frenzy of untold magnitude, tens of thousands of troops were killed in only *days* of fighting—instead of years.

Next we encountered Russia, her thousands of civilians totally unprepared for war—took on the terrors of the machine guns of the advancing German armies. Russia lost over 2,000,000 men fighting along the Baltic and Black Seas.

The sinking of the Lusitania as we have already seen by a German submarine, May 1, 1915, brought the United States slowly into the War. Then about 2 years later on April 2, 1917, the U.S. finally declared war on Germany.

We watched as massive British army tanks, the first ever used in warfare, attack the Germans. The Germans had never seen such steel monsters in their lives! Some of the soldiers panicked, turned and ran, terrified at the sight. Up and down in the trenches they went and those Germans not killed from the machine gun fire were crushed to death under the tracks of these great massive mobile war machines.

An Armistice was finally reached and on November 11, 1918, all the firing ceased along the western front. Germany at last surrendered, and the first war in Europe was finally over.

EIGHTEEN MILLION people had been killed. Ten million soldiers and eight million civilians including women and children had been blasted to bits by bombs and gunfire.

We walked across *no-man's land* in silence. The dead emasculated bodies of soldiers were tangled in the barbed wire dotting the land for miles with their bloody rotting carcasses. The land had become a parched, bomb cratered worthless shell-shocked desolation with nothing for miles but dead splintered trees and fields riddled and blown to bits by cannon, grenade and machine gun fire, smoking and barren of any life whatsoever. The stillness was not even broken by squirrels, rabbits or birds chirping or singing. Nothing but deadly silence... as the wind blew across this bleak and barren waste all created by the handiwork of humanity gone insane!

We glided over the farms of France which were turned into swamps from bomb craters. Total ruin and silent desolation. The stench of putrescent bodies, both soldiers and innocent victims, were everywhere. Great historical monuments and the cathedrals of Belgium were reduced to nothing but smoking rubble. The living envied the dead ... hunger and starvation were rampant.

Again the poignant lesson of history blew across our faces as the Jolly Roger catches wind upon a pirate's ship!

"When the innocent let evil progress by doing nothing," Historia spoke, "all end up suffering. The innocent suffer with the guilty!"

The League of Nations, hope of a forlorn world, was created. It tragically failed in its mission. The Versailles Treaty was signed prohibiting Germany from forming an army over 100,000 men and forbade them to have heavy artillery, airplanes or submarines.

In the Hall of mirrors built originally for King Louis XIV we watched in silent respect as Germany finally signed the treaty to end the most terrible war the world had ever known—up until this time, that is.

Why is it that the lessons of history are so hard to learn? Why must the innocent always suffer at the folly of the greedy and powerful.

Historia—was strangely silent.

Chapter Fifteen

WORLD WAR II:

"If war no longer occupied men's thoughts and energies,
we would, within a generation,
put an end to all serious poverty throughout the world."
—Bertrand Russell: *The Future of Mankind*.

The Spirit Historia and I now continued observing the panorama of world history ... as total war unfolded before our eyes!

The peace generated from The Treaty of Versailles at the end of World War I was but a travesty. Germany began secretly rebuilding her military. Then on Sept. 1, 1938, Germany attacked Poland. Now both Britain and France declared war on Germany. The deadliest war the world had ever known had just been consummated. World War II had begun!

Hitler declared war on France. He threatened to bomb Paris to oblivion unless France surrendered immediately.

France surrendered to save her beautiful cities and her gentle people from slaughter.

Now Hitler made his *first great mistake*! He invaded Russia. The Nazi army marched and fought through their cities like crazed men. But, the Nazis were ill prepared for the fierce cold and these dire conditions of fighting.

Russia had lost uncountable millions of soldiers and civilians in this onslaught of humanity from the Nazi invading forces. Twelve million Russians allegedly died in these battles!

Japan now attacked Pearl Harbor, Hawaii on December 7, 1941, plunging the United States into war. This was the Axis power's *second big mistake*! This brought the United States into the war, whom, to quote Yamamoto of Japan, "We have just awakened the sleeping giant!"

At Pearl Harbor, Hawaii, 21 ships were sunk or seriously damaged and 188 planes destroyed killing 2,403 people.

The next day President Roosevelt asked Congress to declare war on Japan.

We watched in horror as hundreds of death camps sprang up around Germany ... Treblinka, Sobibor, Auschwitz, Bergen-Belsen, *et al.* Here starvation, their fumatoriums of poison gas and firing squads were used to destroy those unwanted by the Nazi regime. Millions of Jews, along with war criminals and communists including Gypsies, Slavs and Jehovah's Witnesses were killed unmercifully—their bodies cremated to ashes.

Warsaw was next. Hitler wanted Warsaw totally destroyed. The Germans invaded the city with tanks and flame throwers burning everything in sight—all buildings, factories and homes. The survivors were finally forced to take to the sewers to flee their wrath. There were few survivors. Those that did survive among the ruins lived like wild animals, hunted down like dogs by German patrols and shot on sight. The Germans now sent in bulldozers and actually obliterated Warsaw into nothing but miles and miles of smoking rubble!

Surrounded by the Russians starving and stunned by the cold, the Germans finally surrendered on February 2, 1943. Ninety-one thousand troops were all that remained of their 285,000 elite fighting division. After the war only 5,000 survived the Russian labor and death camps and their harsh cold winters to return home to Germany.

We discovered Hitler's hideout in the Chancellery in Berlin. We watched as he ordered his wife, Eva Braum, poisoned. He had just married her the day before. Then we witnessed Hitler as he was sitting on his davenport poison his German shepherd with a cyanide capsule. Then he took one himself at the same time he took a German luger, bravely stuck it into his mouth and blew his brains and blood across the wall behind him. Gasoline was poured over their bodies and ignited. Goebbels on hearing the gunfire poisoned his six children. He and his wife were also shot and burned.

Then on May 7, 1945, Germany surrendered. The Nazi rule which Hitler stated would rule for one thousand years ... only lasted nine. But look at what terrible cost these long infamous nine years brought to the world!

The horrors of war continued as the Japanese continued the war in the Pacific. We witnessed the bloody battle on Iwo Jima and the horrors of Okinawa. Here at least a thousand Kamikaze planes were shot down! The Americans invaded the island with thousands of causalities ... and the

Japanese, ordered by their Emperor to fight to their death—
lost uncountable tens of thousands.

The Atom Bomb

Next, the total invasion of Japan by the Allies was about
to take place. The top secret Manhattan Project created a
new experimental device, which was tested at Los Alamos
and Alamogordo, New Mexico. There was now a "gadget"
upon the scene with the code name "Trinity."

Then suddenly Thanatopia appeared—

We now witnessed the end of World War II, August 6,
1945.

Flying high above the island of Japan we encountered a
B-29 bomber. As we neared the plane we could see plainly
written on the fuselage the words *"Enola Gay."* She was
31,000 feet over the Japanese city of Hiroshima, a modern
city of 350,000 people. The bombardier now aimed at the
Aioi Bridge. The *Enola Gay* had just released the world's first
atomic bomb at precisely 8:14 A.M.

We watched in rapt fascination as the ten-thousand-
pound bomb plunged toward Hiroshima. We were only
a mile from ground zero. Then forty-three seconds later it
detonated as a pinprick of purplish-red light 1,890 feet above
the city ... expanding to a mile-wide vermilion fireball of
over 50 million degrees C., as hot as the surface of the sun.

The concussion from the blast spread out from "ground
zero." Buildings and people just vaporized into nothingness.
The awe and incredulity of it. One moment the city, alive
and normal—a nanosecond later—a bubbling cauldron, a
seething raging incandescent inferno!

People looked up and were vaporized into shadows on the walls, steps and sidewalks. Others were blown across the ground, twisting and turning into bloody masses of flesh and bone. Other bodies were blasted and shredded by flying glass and debris before being set afire and burned into red-hot cinders. Still other residence only saw an intense bright light before total oblivion.

From our perspective we could see the angry ever expanding red-black mushroom cloud now forming above the remains of the city. In this boiling seething cloud of superheated air I could make out the souls of nearly 90,000 inhabitants of the men, women and children who were suddenly atomized into nothingness.

Sixty-two thousand buildings were destroyed in one full second. Never had the world seen such destruction. But the lesson of Hiroshima was that there had never been so many killed in an instant of time by only one bomb—dropped from a single plane.

Three days later, August 9, Nagasaki was destroyed by the second atomic bomb killing 60,000 of it inhabitants in an instant.

These two atomic bombs it has been estimated saved over 1,000,000 American troops that soon would be ready to invade the mainland of Japan. The United States and Japan finally signed the peace negotiations aboard the battle ship *Missouri* in Tokyo harbor.

Thus the turmoil of World War II was finally over. The "insanity against humanity" finally ceased. The world was now for a little while … strangely at peace.

Now, Historia revealed that the total men, women, children and soldiers killed in World War II: SIXTY

MILLION. Combining World War I victims of EIGHTEEN MILLION with World War II … makes a staggering SEVENTY-EIGHT MILLION lives snuffed out! But the Angels explained there was another plan for them … *a Divine Plan*!

"Again are there lessons to learn from all this?" I questioned.

"Our lives," Historia stated, "begin to end the day we become silent about things that matter. In the end, we will remember not the words of our enemies, but the silence of our friends."

> "I know not with what weapons
> World War III will be fought,
> World War IV will be fought with sticks and stones."
> —Albert Einstein

If Hitler had Won

Historia now directed me to write this prophecy that might have been.

A strange vision appeared—an alternate universe … a melancholic dark world—where Hitler and his Axis powers divided up the Americas and Eurasia. The atom bomb had yet to be developed. Pearl Harbor had not only been attacked, but Hawaii had been totally invaded and conquered! It was then used as a Japanese base for attacking the United States. So, caught off guard, the United States was in a panic for it was now easy for the Japanese to send their aircraft carriers to the Pacific coastline.

At the same time military ships of the Germans were sent into the Atlantic surrounding the New England states, including Washington, D.C. They now had within their ability to bomb her major cities and factories into submission. New York was the first to be destroyed and many years later we could still see the remains of many of her famous skyscrapers as burned out shells still crumbling to dust. They were never rebuilt. The Statue of Liberty was gone and in her place upon her massive pedestal stood an austere Adolph Hitler, a 150-foot copper statue in his likeness, holding not an eternal flame of freedom—but the insignia of the Nazi regime, the swastika or twisted cross in one hand while the other was extended into the Nazi salute!

Japanese militia was now set up to govern both the federal and state governments. They were controlled with armed guards carrying machine guns at the entrances of shopping malls and all administrative and revenue buildings, including the state and city parks and all the post offices. The Germans, on invading the New England states, now controlled the newspapers, libraries, churches, museums and factories. They were now using America's resources to further their war effort to conquer the world.

The Washington Monument, destroyed by explosives, looked like a broken tooth sticking up from the ground. The top four hundred feet rested silently upon the ground, shattered beyond repair as it collapsed into rubble. The White House was gone, bombed and burned to the ground. It was never rebuilt. The Lincoln Memorial was preserved and an ascetic Adolph Hitler, carved in white marble, was sitting within its massive columns! The statue of Lincoln was loaded upon a barge and sank into the Potomac River. The Jefferson Memorial—vandalized by the Germans, had been used as a target for their artillery fire. Its beautiful columns shattered and scarred by mortar fire ... the Jefferson statue inside ... pockmarked and headless. Future plans were to replace Jefferson with the *El Duce*—Mussolini, leader of Italy, within her majestic columns

New York, humbled by the slaughter of the German army, was only the beginning. Charleston SC, Philadelphia, PA, Atlanta, GA, were also humbled by the onslaught. Then the Japanese in the West invaded San Francisco and Los Angeles—conquering all of California's military bases.

The people of America fought on as a proud nation— but were outmatched by the Axis military might—finally surrendered. Then, as the great Beacon of Freedom fell, the whole world lost hope. Then Great Britain and Australia— succumbed to the realm of evil.

Now the systematic extermination began of those that fought against the Japanese, Germans and Italians. They were herded as cattle into Prisoner of War camps that were set up outside most major U.S. cities and throughout the world. And as in Europe those that rebelled against their authority were forced into these slave labor camps where they were gassed and cremated. Thus included the Blacks, the Hispanics, the Puerto Ricans, the Jews, the Muslims and those political activists unlucky enough to get caught.

By now the masses of people had abandoned the larger cities, for many had been bombed into submission. They moved upon small farms and established agricultural communities. Those who finally surrendered were told to plant fields of corn, cotton and rice. Also, various vegetables and produce were grown for the German Reighstag and the Japanese and Italian coalitions.

We visited the schools and saw all the students, from grade school up, wearing brown khakis with black ties. They were all highly disciplined and motivated individuals, for if reprimanded, their parents were fined and punished and could even be sent to jail for the disciplinary actions of their children!

Then some years later, Hitler declared war upon the Japanese. He wanted them exterminated as well as the Jews, the Afro-Americans and the Chinese. Knowing that they were next, the Japanese and Chinese both declared war upon the Nazis and the German Empire! By now Hitler had attained the atomic bomb and—

And the world was humbled by this. God and his angels wept at the sight … and a surrogate Hell was established upon the earth for the next thousand years … just as Hitler had predicted!

Historia extricated me from this abyss of horror. I again wept unashamedly at the infamy and demise of the United States … as if I had just been awakened from some terrible nightmare.

CHAPTER SIXTEEN

*H*istoria, along with the Spirits of Tragedy and I now toured other murderous wars being fought upon the earth. Next, the Korean Conflict consummated before us ... then Viet Nam—

The things I learned about the human condition as it was pulled, shaped and molded by circumstances *beyond* the control of human intervention. I could understand how lives are changed, altered and wrought by Divine Providence as nation warred against nation as conquered societies intermingled and influenced each other.

Historia stated it was time to bid farewell. She has heard the prayers of the faithful. In Eschede, Germany a high-speed train will soon derail killing over 100 people. Also in Gaisal, India over 400 people will be killed when two commuter trains from New Delhi carrying over 2,500 passengers will collide head-on—

"Also, Iben," he concluded, "an explosion at the U.S. embassies in Kenya and Tanzania will kill over 258 people. Also Swissair Flight 111 at Peggy's Cove, Nova Scotia, will explode killing all 229 passengers. And an Air France Concorde will soon crash near Paris—

"I have heard the prayers of the desperate people of Papua New Guinea and Indonesia, where tidal waves have washed whole villages away. In America, Joplin, MO and Moore, OK, along with many southern states, will be hit with deadly tornadoes—

"In Quebec a runaway train carrying oil tankers will derail and explode—destroying the city of Lac-Megantic killing dozens of her citizens. Also, avalanches in Austria, earthquakes in Taiwan and Mexico—

9/11/01 - Terrorist Attack on America

"So, Iben, with great consternation I must inform you that another horrendous calamity will occur in the near future which will undermine the faith and security of the civilized world! There will be a major terrorist attack against the United Stated of America. Great loss of life will occur and thousands of innocent lives will be lost with hundreds injured in the world's greatest terrorists attack upon American soil. It will be so bad that it will shock America into a new war. There will be more killed here than were killed at Pearl Harbor."

I was stunned.

Could such things really happen?

"Where in American will this occur?"

"My dear Iben, it cannot be revealed as yet—"

"When will this take place?"

After a long moment, she finally spoke, "It will be revealed unto you… "Sept. 11, 2001." It will be a beautiful sunny day … as was that fateful clear day in Oklahoma City … when *your* world changed for all eternity. It will be many times worse than the Oklahoma City bombing."

"How many will die?"

"Thousands, Iben. Thousands. As I have stated—it will literally shock the world."

"What kind of attack will it be? Nuclear? Biological? Chemical? Who would do such a despicable thing?"

Historia was silent—

After some duration, she finally spoke, "Iben, it will be revealed to you in God's due time. I must therefore go and prepare all these soon-to-be victims to face their destiny to meet the Lord … and console the dying and injured strengthening them in the face of this monstrous calamity. I must guide the survivors on their long arduous road to recovery. I must console the families and friends of the victims to understand why such tragedies happen to the innocent and to the unaware. Yet none of those now living upon the earth have the guarantee of tomorrow."

So, she must soon comfort all these people, both the victims and the survivors, for they will be needed to escort these souls into Abraham's bosom.

Historia stated that she was to continue upon her Divine Mission to bring peace to our world—to stop North Korea from contining to test its nuclear weapons and refrain from testing its bio-warheads containing weaponized anthrax, smallpox and plague. And to try to stop Iran from creating nuclear missiles to destroy Israel. And to prevent China from developing more submarines that contain a dozen missiles, each of which carry a payload of 10 nuclear warheads. And to prevent Russia from developing the Avangard, a new hypersonic glide vehicle capable of delivering a nuclear payload to any city in America, 5 times faster than any previous launching system. Now instead of having 12 minutes for the United States to prepare against a nuclear attack, the Avangard will reduced the time to—

With this, Historia evanesced back into the yet untraceable annals of history… and slowly faded away into the vast unknown—

"Whereas ye know not what shall be on the morrow.
For what is your life? It is even a vapor that appeareth
for a little time, and then vanisheth away."
—James 4:14 (Ref. Prov. 27:1)

(THE END OF BOOK II)

Thus concludes Book II of the After-Death Trilogy,
Eternity.
Continue the last and final exciting
adventures of Iben Thayer in
Book III:
The Secrets of Life and Death
and enter God's Kingdom for even more amazing
and miraculous adventures proclaiming
God's Divine Plan and His Divine Destiny for your life.

Now continue Eternity:
of the After-Death Trilogy,
Book III: The Secrets of Life and Death.

Encounter the *Paradisia,* God's
magnificent Celestial City
and witness the Great Tribulation
and the wrath of Armageddon,
the last great battle against Good and Evil.
Solve the ultimate quest for life on other worlds and
unravel the mystery of the *Divinus
Spiritus Primordium.*
Encounter the esoteric Second Death
and the enigma of Time and Space.
Are you, as a Christian ... now ready to meet
your Final and Ultimate Destiny—
beyond the infinite stars?

Eternity

BOOK THREE

The Secrets of
Life and Death

Now continue Eternity:
of the After-Death Trilogy,
Book III: The Secrets of Life and Death.

Encounter the *Paradisia,* God's
magnificent Celestial City
and witness the Great Tribulation
and the wrath of Armageddon,
the last great battle against Good and Evil.
Solve the ultimate quest for life on other worlds and
unravel the mystery of the *Divinus
Spiritus Primordium.*
Encounter the esoteric Second Death
and the enigma of Time and Space.
Are you, as a Christian…now ready to meet
your Final and Ultimate Destiny—
beyond the infinite stars?

CHAPTER ONE

We now continue the unique adventures of Iben Thayer and his After-Death Odyssey. We leave the wonders of the miracle of the creation of the universe, the microscopic world, our journey into earth's core and the lost world of Pellucidar, the ministry of Jesus Christ, and the insanity of war.

Our voyage commences into the Land Unknown. We will learn what wonders the future holds for the faithful believers in Christ and their final destiny into *terra incognita*.

At this instant, Mysterium, the Angelic Divine Counselor, materialized from the Great Beyond—

"I shall now reveal the mysteries of your life."

"This takes us back to the present then?" I inquired.

"Well, not really, Iben, in the sense that you remember it. You see, your trip through the earth and through history has taken you many years to complete."

"Mysterium, could I … I mean is there any way that I could visit my grave since I have died?"

An instant later I appeared back in Stillwater, OK. New

Horizons Cemetery, which was so active on the day of my funeral, now lay before us.

We passed through a recently erected white arch marking the cemetery's new entrance. Just inside this gate I noticed a recently placed upright white granite monolith, standing on a pedestal with the following words etched thereon:

THE DASH

Forever etched upon your tombstone
will be the Date of your Birth
along with the Date of your Death.
Between these two dates—
You will find the Dash.

The Dash represents all you have accomplished
Throughout your dynamic life—
Your dreams, hopes, aims, ambitions, desires,
Thoughts, successes—and failures.

Did you help others?
Or were you a burden?
Did you love people enough?
Or were you filled with hate?
Did you compliment or inspire them?

When you reflect upon your Dash—
Did you utilize all your God-given talents?
Did you live your life to your full capacity?
Was your life full of joy and happiness,

Sympathy and compassion—
Or was it full of sorrow, regret,
Criticism and bitterness?

So, think about your Divine Purpose—
And your limited existence;
Are you the person you want to be?
Have you made a positive difference in someone's life?

Will you improve the life of others?
Now is the time—
For you have no guarantee of tomorrow.
For you never know when the angels weep,
Or if the demons sleep.

Each Hour is a true miracle of existence,
Each Day a bright diamond sparkling
In the infinity of time.

So… remember when you reflect upon your Dash—
Can you still change your life for the better?
For the Dash is short—
As is your lifetime.

Therefore, when your life is over—
Ask yourself the ultimate questions:
With what priceless gift will I embrace humanity?
And how will humanity… remember my Dash?
—The Author

Beyond this monolith scattered among the quiet meadow were many white crosses and tombstones of marble, granite and copper in their neat rows. The cemetery had grown larger than I remembered it. Six years more of countless graves peppered the green valleys and hillocks. I could hear the birds chirping and feel the cool wind. Before me were a number of new graves that had also become victims resulting from that ignominious day in April.

My eyes wandered across the still, serene panorama and then I saw it—my own tombstone! As I read upon its carved granite facade, tears welled up in my eyes. The front of my tombstone was etched with:

Iben Thayer
Born: May 20, 1963—
Died: April 19, 1995
Honored victim of the
Oklahoma City Bombing Holocaust,
April 19, 1995

The back of my tombstone bore the following message also carved in stone:

Metamorphoses

"I have always wanted to travel beyond
the stars into the Great Unknown—
and the Angel of Light will lead
me to my sublime new home!
As a flower blossoms upon
an unmarked grave,

I will bloom in verdant pastures
forgotten as a memory dissolved by time.
As the metamorphoses of the lowly caterpillar
transforms into a beautiful butterfly,
I will soar through strange skies
of mysterious worlds.
I will abandon this Earth forever—
yet will I rejoice in magnificent
treasures of an unknown destiny.
—The Author

Faith's Epiphany

"Iben, I want you to meet someone," interjected Mysterium, waking me from my reverie.

With this I once again found myself just outside the city limits of Stillwater, Oklahoma. Before me was an old house that needed some painting, some shrubs that needed trimming, and some leaves that needed raking—

"Don't be nostalgic, Iben, this is Eternity! Watch and see the immanence of God consummated. In the next few minutes all this will have a tremendous effect upon you."

With this, we entered a bedroom. Lying upon the bed was the silhouette of a human being, the curves of a female.

She just had taken her bath and was resting in her nightclothes from a hard day of work at the office. I could see the heaving of her body as she breathed.

I watched as the sleeping figure shuffled a little, turned and her countenance came face to face with mine. A gentle face it was. With her eyes closed she was resting in tranquil sleep. Recognition slowly came. A feeling of religious rapport overwhelmed me. I was thunderstruck! It was Faith! Time had altered her face some but she was still that beautiful lady that I exchanged vows with on that very special day long, so long ago. It seemed frozen in time, that day did, in which I had the world before me ... the potential happiness of love which all people want ... and yet so few attain.

"Iben, Faith, married again, a fine man named Ambrose, as you are already aware. Sabrina, Ambrose's sister has gone with him to see Faith's mother, Candace, in Bethany, just northwest of Oklahoma City. Candace has been diagnosed with liver cancer. Ambrose, on Saturday, took little three-year old Cassandra with him. (Cassandra, whom I observed in Faith's womb, was already three! My ... how fast children grow up!) So he left Faith alone in the house, for she had to go to work on Monday, for a business meeting and she couldn't take off. She was to travel to Bethany on Tuesday, taking a day of vacation to visit her mother."

Faith was silent, laying upon the twin bed under the comfortable covers exposing her soft brown hair shimmering slightly in the shadows of the twilight haze.

Then I saw Thanatopia—

She shivered and experienced only a stab of pain, then a touch of paroxysm and a slight touch of convulsion.

"Look into her heart, Iben."

I looked—discovering that she just had a massive heart attack! She was dying before me and I was powerless to help her! Her lips and cheek had a touch of blue about them, but she was at total bliss and peace. I fully became aware of her spirit undulating up from her body, hovering above it, seemingly perplexed and confused as she saw us. She raised her hand to block our brightness!

"This is how you looked and felt when you died in the Federal Building, Iben. I am Faith's guardian angel, ready to guide her into the Eternal Realm, the Kingdom of God. You are here to comfort her also."

She saw us as three blinding ignescent beacons of light and at first thought she was only dreaming.

My precious wife who had departed from her worldly body, now gazed our way with fear and uncertainty upon her countenance.

"Go toward the Light!" I proclaimed to her.

"My children," she screamed, "my precious Prudence and Cassandra. I can't possible leave them now! Ambrose, how will he—"

I embraced Faith with all my heart and all my soul. We intertwined as two perfect octaves of harmony, blended together into an oscillating vibration of perfection!

She stated that a day had not passed by without her thinking about me. She told me all about her life after I had died, how she had met this other man, Ambrose, who had become her husband and how wonderful he has been to her. She asked about our children, Hope and Charity, who had died in the explosion that infamous day and about Beth, who had died from Sudden Infant Death Syndrome (SIDS) and what I had been doing for the last few years!

Now Mysterium and I witnessed yet another strange kaleidoscopic dimension, a wondrous hypnotic and swirling portal between two worlds.

Along our way we encountered other prodigious

Luminaria of the Heavenly Hosts including many angels of the Illuminati.

Just behind us presided the Alleluia Chorale, rejoicing and singing praises. We then entered into a swirling tunnel of dazzling divine light.

To be with my wife, Faith—my first true love once again! How wonderful Heaven can be! We now came to an event that entranced us in our new immortal state of being.

THE PARADISIA

A wonderful multidimensional indefinable phenomenon now revealed itself. Let me describe it to you:

> "And I looked, and, behold, a whirlwind
> came out of the north,
> a great cloud, and a fire enfolding itself,
> and a brightness was about it,
> and out of the midst thereof as the color of amber,
> out of the midst of the fire. ... As for the
> likeness of the living creatures,
> their appearance was like burning coals of
> fire, and like the appearance of lamps;
> it went up and down among the living
> creatures; and the fire was bright,
> and out of the fire went forth lightning."
> —Ezek. 1:4, 13

We were now pulled into this this strange aberration of unknown origin. We could see powerful angelic beings, many wonderful Luminaria, seraphim and cherubim, with psychedelic colors swirling all about … spiraling us ever upward toward that great beacon of "Holy Light" in all its supreme majesty!

> "I thought I was dreaming and saw a strange
> staircase leading up from the earth,
> and the top of it reaching to infinity: and
> there were great angels of God
> ascending and descending upon it. I thought
> how beautifully awesome is this place!
> This is none other than the house of God,
> and this is the very gate of heaven."

"Behold, Iben," stated Mysterium, "here resides that *Great Star*, the glorious Celestial City of God!"

It took me a while to understand just what I was experiencing—

A thought came to mind…

> "How can the finite mind of man
> comprehend an infinite God,
> Or a limited existence—an illimitable universe?"
> —The Author

We now entered the wondrous and cabalistic Celestial City of God! Again, I am stuck with the wit of mortal language. This is total obscurity, beyond the human experience, beyond the senses, beyond the imagination, beyond the dimension of reality! As Faith and I entered we met powerful cherubim set as guards along its perimeter.

Do souls, spirits and angels occupy space? I hadn't thought of that before!

This magnificent city was composed of a symmetry of perfectly formed arcs of both positive and negative energy fields spinning in complete equilibrium. I realized, as I neared this structure—it was a grand geodesic globe composed of oscillating rays of pure divine kinetic energy portraying infrangible transparent bubbles or crystal domes laying at opposition with each other.

> "For we know that if our earthly house
> of this tabernacle were dissolved,
> we have a building of God, a house not made
> with hands, eternal in the heavens."
> —2 Cor. 5:1

Within its interior were hyperbaric biospheres resembling wheels turning within wheels dotted with uncountable surrealistic gardens and arboreta. These great ornamental enclosures were plethora with beautiful redolent flowers and trees, insects and animals, mostly unknown to mortals. Thus was the divine nature of this glorious Celestial City of God.

This supernatural city was suspended in the heavens as a colossal brilliant chandelier! It reminded me of the Christmas Star, its lights illuminating all things and all people present. Could this have been the very "star" the wise men and shepherds saw? Or the "pillar of fire" that protected Moses through the desert from Pharoah's army? Could this have been the conveyance that took Elijah up into a whirlwind into Heaven or the strange phenomenon that Ezekiel witnessed? Could it have teleported Enoch to Paradise? Could it have been that shiny object the faithful observed in 1917 in Fatima, Portugal?

Now I remembered the night the *Titanic* sank and that great radiant "beam" splitting open the dark heavens for the deceased to enter through—*that strange light that Abraham witnessed. Jacob's ladder!*

Within this imposing sphere radiated a magnificent cube suspended by electrostatic levitation, containing the home for all of God's Redeemed. This prodigious star illuminated Faith's peaceful and angelic countenance as I had never before seen and was even warming our inner *tripartite* nature, penetrating into our very hearts and minds—and soothing our very souls. What a warm, sensual feeling … it was pure unadulterated LOVE! Divine love, peace and tranquility spread over us as I had never known! What life was meant to be … total forgiveness, well being, completeness and acceptance that I had been born for a *Divine Mission*, that I was a unique individual, and that God had accepted me for what I was (a sinner) and for who I am (a forgiven child of God) knowing full well that He has created me for his own very *Special* and *Unique Purpose*.

This proves that it is not just a pipe dream that humanity will someday attain true supernal happiness, that suffering will be totally eliminated and that we as a member of the human race will be a survivor beyond this little narrow paltry world in which we live! Again, it cannot be described, because a thing must be comprehended and then given a name … and this dimension is beyond the *human intellect*. This does not insult man's ability to reason, it just belies the fact that there are a number of things that *cannot* be explained by science, physics or mortal mind in our universe!

I realized the *Paradisia's* holiness—that God resided here. I now understood that he is omnipresent, meaning

God has *theomorphic ubiquity.* As God can be in your church, he can also be within the *Paradisia*, he can also dwell within you ... and be everywhere throughout entire universe at the same instant! God and his power ... are not limited as humans are, bound to a three-dimensional existence!

A portal of this marvelous Celestial City now glowed and opened, welcoming us into its fantastic interior! There were wonderful paths of gold to follow, all leading to the very core of this magnificent city. There was the path of the Anointed, the path of Faith, the path of Repentance, the path of Forgiveness, the path of Atonement, the path of the Good Shepherd, the path of the Prince of Life, the path of Salvation, the path of the Holy Spirit, the path of Peace, the path of the Receptive Heart, the path of Living Water, the path of the Word of God, the path of Prayer, the path of Victory, the path of Righteousness, the path of Godly Love, the path of Obedience, the path of the Shekinah Glory, the path of Light, the path of Divine Truth, the path of Restitution, the path of Miracles, the path of Humility, the path of Sanctification, the path of Redemption, the path of Witnessing, the path of Eternal Inheritance, the path of the New Covenant and the path to the Rewards of the Saints!

Wonderful, powerful angels of the Illuminati now energized. Coming toward us was the brightest Entity I had ever seen.

With this, Mysterium began to fade away—yet another angel now appeared...

"Iben and Faith ... welcome to the *PARADISIA.*"

"I am Ariel, the 'Angel of Glad Tidings.' As the great pyramid of Egypt symbolized that nation's perfection, so the *Paradisia* symbolizes the crowning *ne plus ultra* of scientific achievement of all ages ... the greatest teleological achievement of pure science—unequaled in the universe! So, as the Ten Commandments were carved by God's very hand, so is this ... *built by the omniscience of God himself*! Welcome to the Kingdom of God within the *Paradisia*.

"This is the miracle like the unique third state of the carbon atom, the Fullerine, or Buckyball concept, a geometric design of graphene, an allotropic form of the element carbon, forming a round hollow geodesic globe. It is divided into two halves.

"The upper sections contain all the divine angels along with the Supernalites. Deep within the bowels of the Celestial City are Satan's minions, and the condemned and imprisoned wicked souls of mankind. They are sealed off in Gehenna by an impenetrable barrier, which separates good from evil."

I now understood what Buckminister Fuller and Benjamin Franklin had been describing, and explaining to me about his "Fullerine" geodesic concept of the carbon atom!

Inside this wonderful Celestial City, I realized that ALL the dead are now once again living, both the good and the evil. But through death, the unforgiven and the unrepented Sons of Disobedience and Sons of Perdition are permanently sealed away from the saints of God, never again to influence them or do them harm.

Another note struck me as being true. All the races have merged together into the Holy Spirit of divine love, and divine righteousness. The *resurrected, living* saints have all been purged into God's Divine Family, another "curse" lifted from humanity!

The *Divine Purpose* of our Celestial City, I learned, is to gather all the souls—both the good and evil. The saints can move to and fro around the earth as you have done Iben Jair, as divine Watchers—influencing those by God's will that need divine help and protection.

The dead who have died in Christ can do untold wonders and miracles through the power of prayer (remember when you toured the brain) and have unadulterated Divine Energy.

Inside our splendid Celestial City of God, I began to hear the most beautiful music! The orchestration and harmonization of the Hosanna and Hallelujah Chorale of millions of angels and saints rejoicing and singing in unison at my rebirth and also that of Faith's ... along with the thousands of others that had died this day upon the earth—welcoming us all into the MAJESTIC REALM OF GOD—FOR ALL ETERNITY!

"Iben and Faith," Ariel continued, "they are all celebrating your CORONATION! Peace is yours! Life inperpetuum is yours! Happiness is yours! Your duties will be *SPECIAL*. They will be what you both have always wished for while upon the earth. Iben, didn't you have an insatiable mind, wanting to learn the secrets of life, matter and the universe? And Faith, didn't you want to utilize *all* your God-given talents? Well, here in our Celestial City both of you can continue exploring these strange new fields of science and strange worlds which now await you. You will encounter many other exotic phenomena you could not understand while mortal—but you will very soon!"

A bright halation of radiant energy, nebulous and incorporeal coalesced and materialized, then split, becoming two separate Entities. I instantaneously recognized them as—

Faith screamed with delight as our two lost twins neared us. Faith held out her arms and hugged Hope and Charity to her breast, weeping and kissing them as great tears of great joy ran down her face! Then little Beth appeared before us, who had died of SIDS at the tender age of one-year old!

At this moment, I realized that God's Divine Purpose had finally been consummated in our lives. Hallelujah! Hallelujah! Hosanna to the LORD! Praise be to God!

What more can I say? We united in the amphimixis of total bliss and completeness. We hugged and kissed each other as only the saints of God can! What tenderness, what congeniality, what amity—what camaraderie and *esprit de corps* we all felt toward one another! My wife and my very own children gone from the earth, but now in Eternity with the LORD, his saints, his Supernalites! We embraced in the Kingdom of God and great tears of joy stained my face!

Hundreds of my friends suddenly appeared that I knew while upon the earth, all of which had died. Friends I had in kindergarten, grade school, high school and college. I learned of their joys and disappointments, all about their friends and and their hardships. And yes, how each of them had died of disease or mishaps, or were killed or murdered or committed suicide. What strange and interesting stories they related to me!

Ariel stated that she must now be leaving. Others must be welcomed into the Kingdom of God.

CHAPTER TWO

$\mathcal{Z}$oe, the profound 'Angel of Eternal Life,' now appeared.

I wondered what denominations would be represented within the *Paradisia*.

"Iben, *none of the great religions nor any denominations whatsoever are represented.* Only those people defined as *"God's children,"* those who are *"Children of Light,"* those that believe that Jesus Christ is the Son of God are redeemed."

> **"Neither is there salvation in any other;**
> **for there is no other name under**
> **heaven given among men,**
> **whereby we must be saved."**
> **—Acts 4:12**

"These Supernalites are all brought together in DIVINE TRUTH, AS ONE CHURCH, IN ONE BODY IN CHRIST, ALL UNITED AS ONE DIVINE FAMILY. Another great miracle of the Divine, witnessed by us, accomplished by God!"

Regretfully many other great religions of the world that did not have Jesus Christ as the center of their worship were strangely absent from this sanctuary. The reason is that none of them believed that Jesus is the true Son of God, died and rose the third day—conquering sin and death ... thus breaking the power of Satan forevermore. Christ died to take upon Him the sins of mankind, who is our High Priest, so that all people, under His blood, would be cleansed from all sin to become righteous in God's eyes. Then and only then could they be adopted into His holy family.

Their false and pagan religions suffered, their lives suffered and their countries suffered from not believing that Jesus Christ is the Messiah, the true Son of the living God.

Here I noticed that many of the mansions God prepared for his people—were vacant.

This was very tragic. Somehow I realized that these were the dwelling places prepared for all the peoples of the earth ... billions that were not forgiven and did not make it to claim God's perfect blessings. So these grand mansions of pristine beauty were now overgrown with weeds and underbrush, dilapidated, sad forlorn derelicts of what might have been.

It must be stated that *all* those upon the earth will be guided into the *Paradisia*. Thus the good and evil start upon this journey called death—and *all* will enter herein. For Jesus took our sins upon himself, cleasing us, so we could become righteous in the eyes of God. But the evil ones—

I now realized that our divine mission is to retrieve all those souls that have died, traveling to all the countries and nations of the world.

Those that knew not Christ as their savior, those of

pagan religions, and all that have *not* accepted Jesus Christ as their personal savior, and those *wicked souls* here deep within our Celestial City must wait for God's *Judgment.* They are kept safely sealed in the Prison of Gehenna in the depths of the *Paradisia.*

Faith, still by my side, had a glorious surprise. Her mother, Candace, suddenly appeared!

"But you, Mom, are in Bethany, OK. What—?"

"I DIED Wednesday, Faith—from liver cancer, two days *after* you did with your heart attack!"

Then Faith wanted to visit with her mother and so we departed. I had my own rendezvous with destiny!

Again, all aboard the *Paradisia,* the rejuvenated souls of the Supernalites, have glowing countenances and the rosy healthful look of youth. Most seemed to be not over the age of twenty, all in their peak of opulence!

THE GRAND REUNION

Zoe now welcomed me into the magnificent sanctuary of the Redeemed. He introduced those whose lives had been snuffed out in the Oklahoma City Bombing. It had now been many years since the carnage had taken place. The look of ecstasy on their glowing countenances of those reunited in jubilation with their loved ones that died will be etched on my mind for all eternity!

Time is distorted when you concentrate upon some pertinent interest—it seems to move faster. In the Afterlife, it seems to travel even *faster*! Many of my other friends on the earth finally made their peace with the Lord and passed on into Eternity as I had done.

The following people are those I knew while upon the Earth, who lived on after I died.

First of all, my secretary Mary Ann's son, Jason, now appeared. Remember, he choked to death while eating hot dogs. Our *Divine Mission* to his family seemed futile in that we didn't help prevent his death. But, in that visit they learned to accept his fate, they stopped having those proscribed séances ... and their faith was strengthened, his parents joined a church, were baptized, and even starting teaching Sunday school!

The Holy Roster of Saints

Those affected by the Oklahoma City Bombing now stepped forward. One mother's lovely eyes once again lit up as she was reunited with her two small children! I will never forget the vestal joy which filled her face. It went beyond words—beyond ecstasy, beyond all mundane and corporeal things!

All 168 people that died were reunited with their loved ones, families, friends and babies. What a day of all days to remember ... such happiness ... such effervescent ecstasy! I loved every one of them as my own family! And, I realized that they were my family in the Kingdom of God! The holy communion and amity we felt at this moment I will never forget! This was a day of pure unadulterated rejoicing and singing that the world has never seen—since the days of Adam and Eve before their fall from glory!

This revealed that there was something for all these

people to look forward to, to hope for after their death—that of being reunited with their loved ones!

Praise the Lord! Hallelujah! O Happy Day!

I must state here that the little babies who died in this incident were still as little babies in the afterlife. Once their parents were reunited with them again, these babies will age as normal as if they were still living upon the earth. Then they will grow up in their enhanced state of glory in the care of their parents. This is because there is something innately primordial in life to raise their young, whether it be bear cubs, little ducklings, or the human species. Those that have had their parenting terminated upon the earth by tragedy will once again have the opportunity to rear their young! All these children will age as normal, then reach their peak of opulence and will be preserved forever as perfect mature living individuals, looking perpetually young!

With this, my deceased Mother and I, now as Children of Light, embraced each other in our new empyrean existence! One by one all of my deceased family coalesced before me The mirth I have now was exceedingly wonderful and complete!

Now others paraded forward. I had a little trouble recognizing my great grandparents from all those black and white, faded and torn photographs in dusty and worn out family albums, whose names have long ago been forgotten. Here they were in their pristine glory! I was in total ecstasy! Those that had died older than twenty have become young again! They were a paragon of perfection, having no acne scars, no excrescence, nor any blemishes upon their countenances. They beamed from the glory reflecting pure ecstasy and perfect bliss direct from the energy and radiance of God.

They were totally purged from their earthly worries and sins under the mercy and blessings of total forgiveness. Those living were all reunited with those that were killed— what mirth, what wonderful solidarity, such companionship! Such happiness—such pure eternal divine ecstasy!

I noticed a long line of people and a person who I could vaguely remember in my former life came forward from this line and gave me a firm handshake and then hugged me with great compassion.

"Iben Jair," Zoe continued, "all these present now welcome you into the Kingdom of God! Each person here was saved by your teaching the Bible in Sunday School classes and your fine example of Christ in the latter life. You were an influence to them all, and now they want to tell you how much you have meant to them, to honor your former life, and warmly welcome you into eternal glory."

So each of these people came forward and hugged me as the pure unadulterated love of God flowed between us, the mirth and joy of being a part of the sanctified Family of God! Nothing I ever dreamed or thought of prepared me for this! *Total fulfillment! The perfect abundant life the Lord proclaimed!*

Notably, I also saw many victims of suicide, saved by the grace of God. I was taught that this was an abomination that would be judged harshly, but I saw a merciful God and that there were many victims of this malady here! I wondered why and it was revealed that suicide many times ran in families, thus becoming a *genetic abnormality* in the brain, along with the *lack of dopamine* and other psychotic chemicals that determine personality. Since the human doesn't understand just how the brain works and does not comprehend the psychosis, schizophrenia and paranoia that determine suicidal behavior, the taking of one's life is better to be left to the realm of the Eternal.

Reunion Victims of Disasters

Next, I saw those precious victims that were gunned down at their schools in the United States and other countries. I watched as those from the massacre at Columbine High School, Littleton, CO (1999) were reunited with their friends, their faces full of tears of joy as they met their parents and loved ones after all these years! Reunited in holy exaltation they all joined in singing in the Hallelujah Chorale, praising God for his miracles and great wonders, their eyes full of divine love.

Also present was a student at Columbine High, a sweet blond teenager, Cassie Bernall, who was asked by her killers if she "believed in God," and then was unmercifully killed. We know her answer, which shook the civilized and religious world. She went to glory, a martyr for the cause of Christ! Singing with her were many of her friends and teachers who also died on that infamous day in one of the worse school massacres the world has ever seen.

These were singing with school students killed in the shooting in Springfield, OR (1997), and the Jonesboro, AR shooting (1998). Also present were those young boys killed in the Pearl, MS High School shooting (1997), the victims from the Ft. Worth Baptist Church along with those at

Virginia Tech University, Blacksburg, VA (2007) and those students killed in the massacres of Heath High School in Paducah, KY (1997), those of Benton, KY (2018), and the Parkland, FL Marjory Stoneman Douglas High School (2018), where a lone gunman massacred 17 students on Feb. 14, Valentine's Day.

These victims were reunited with those from Jokela High School, Finland (2007) where a teen killed five boys, two girls and their female principal along with the victims from the Westroads Mall, Omaha NE, (2007), when a 19-year old gunman open fired with a SKS assault rifle killing 8 and then himself.

They met the 6 victims who were stabbed and shot in Isla Vista, CA (2014). They were all UC Santa Barbara students, killed by a deranged, depressed and suicidal student angry because the sorority girls on campus didn't like him and wouldn't date him.

Then those murdered victims were all reunited with these from Tuscon, AZ, where at a shopping mall (2011), a lone gunman who wanted to assassinate Congress woman Gabrielle Giffords shot and killed 6 people and injured 13 others.

These were reunited with the students from Oslo, Norway on the island of Utoya at a Summer Youth Camp (2012) where a gunman killed 69 of them along with the detonation of a car bomb in central Oslo which killed 8 more.

These victims were reunited with the Aurora, Colo. Massacre (2012), where a lone gunman killed 12 watching *The Dark Knight Rises* at the suburban Denver theater.

These victims were all reunited with those 20 elementary school students killed from the Newtown, CT, Massacre at Sandy Hook Elementary School (2012), along with their 6 teachers. These were reunited with those 13 soldiers waiting to be deployed overseas who were killed by a Muslim Army psychiatrist at the Fort Hood, Texas (2009). These were then reunited with those 12 murdered at the Washington Navy Yard (2013) by another deranged gunman about 2 miles from the U.S. Capitol, Washington, D.C.

We welcomed into Paradise all those on the Las Vegas Strip, who were massacred at the outdoor country music festival (2017) starring singer Jason Aldean, when a lone gunman from his room window on the 32nd floor of the Mandalay Bay Resort and Casino, shot into a crowd of 22,000 people, killing 58 of the concert attendees, while wounding over 500 others. The assassin, an accountant and heavy gambler, then committed suicide in his room at the resort.

All these victims were united in glory, singing and praising the Lord with those of many other church and school massacres, mall and restaurant shootings too numerous to mention.

Then I saw all those that died upon the earth from AIDS, cystic fibrosis, cerebral palsy, polio, malaria … and the deaf and the blind, all healed of their maladies in the Kingdom of God. All these were rejoicing and singing and playing their melodeons, guitars, flutes, virginals and the glorious Divine Glockenspiel Clavichord!

In this rejoicing Chorale I spotted my family members,

along with Faith, my wife in the old world, all singing praises in the Hosanna Chorale to the Lord. All being caught up in the divine music of the vox angelica.

Also in the Holy Hosanna Chorale was the famous Rock and Roll ensemble of the 1950s. Buddy Holly, the Big Bopper (J.P. Richardson) and Ritchie Valens who were traveling by air to their next concert in 1959 to be held in Mason City, IA, when their plane crashed in foul weather, killing all aboard. Interestingly, Ritchie Valens tossed a coin with Tommy Allsup to determine who would fly to Mason City. Ritchie Valens won the toss—and the rest is history. They had no idea it was really to see who would live or die. Those on the plane who died were all here reunited in Paradise rejoicing in the heavenly realm of glory! They were singing their praises and adoration to their Lord for their salvation!

All quieted as Boxcar Willie, America's singing hobo, now sang his hit song, *I'll Ride That Last Train to Heaven on Rails of Solid Gold.*

All were reunited in ecstasy as they accepted and welcomed me to join them in their happiness! O Happy Day as all were reunited with each other once again!

We watched the grand reunion of the "King of Rock and Roll," reunited with his mother, father, his wife and his dear daughter. Elvis' *twin brother*, who died at birth, was here also. Oddly, his brother, now in Heaven, could sing better than he could!

Here was one small girl who wrote about the Jewish Holocaust in a very famous diary. She was captured in Holland by the Nazis during World War II. Her family was incarcerated in the concentration camp of Bergen-Belsen in

1945, where her whole family perished. She died of typhus in this camp at 15 years old.

> "It's a wonder I haven't abandoned all my ideals,
>   they seem so absurd and impractical.
>   Yet I cling to them because I still believe,
> in spite of everything, that people are truly good at heart."
> —Anne Frank (*The Diary of a Young Girl*)

Not far from where this young lady lived, the first licensed woman watchmaker in Holland, Corrie ten Boom, now appeared. She wrote, *The Hiding Place*, about the horrors of the Nazi death camps. She, along with her family, were taken to the Death Camp—Ravensbruck. She was the only survivor. Her older sister, along with her youngest sister—including her Grandfather all died there. Now they were all here in glory—reunited together!

The victims of all the Nazi Death camps now came forward! We saw all their happy faces reunited with their families once again! I will never forget the ecstasy upon their countenances! Such are the happenings in the Celestial City of God!

I met those who died in World War I and World War II. I also met the honored dead, whose bodies lie in the Tomb of the Unknown Soldiers, Arlington, VA.

The victims of all the battles of the French Revolution, the American Revolution, the American Civil War, the Korean War, the Viet Nam War, and the Gulf War now appeared.

I saw the Wright brothers who are credited with the world's first flying machine. They were visiting with the astronauts who died in the Apollo I fire in 1967 at Kennedy Space Center, Florida. They had all been celebrating their reunion with those who died in the launching of the space shuttle, *Challenger* (1986), and those of the space shuttle *Columbia* (2003).

I met all those innocent children killed at the McDonald's restaurant (1984), in San Ysidro, Calif—where 21 people were shot and killed by a lone gunman.

Reunion Victims of Disasters, Con't.

We met Ms. O'Leary, whose cow overturned a lantern setting her barn ablaze, which started the Great Chicago fire, where in 1871, produced one of the greatest conflagrations the world had ever witnessed! I met Mrs. O' Leary, atoned from her guilt of starting this accidental fire, and met the hundreds of victims that died in it!

I met the victims of the Iroquois Theater fire, Chicago, IL, of 1903 … where 602 people were burned alive in the worst theater fire in American history. These were reunited with those victims of the Coconut Grove night club, (1942) at Boston, MA. A fire broke out—killing 491 people. These were then united with those of other fires, namely The Station nightclub, West Warwick, RI (2003) where 96 fans of the rock group Great White lost their lives to the ensuing conflagration!

These above victims were rejoicing with the victims from the KISS nightclub in Santa Maria, Rio Grande do Sul state, Brazil (2013) which killed over 233 university students when a fire broke out from a pyrotechnics display.

These were rejoicing in heaven with those victims from

the Lame Horse nightclub of Perm, Russia (2009), killing 152 people. These were reunited with those of the nightclub fire in Buenos Aires, Argentina (2004), where 194 people died. These were reunited with those victims of a disco fire in Luoyang, China (2000), where 309 people were killed; and these were reunited with those of the Ozone Disco Pub fire in Quezon City, Philippines (1996), where 162 people died. These were reunited with the Beverly Hills Supper Club victims in Southgate, KY (1977), where a fire killed 165 people … and these were reunited with those that died in a fire in the Rhythm Night Club, Natchez, MS (1940), killing 209 people.

We met the victims of the Ringling Brothers-Barnum & Bailey Circus fire (1944), where the tent caught fire killing 168 people.

These victims now met those from the Sao Paulo, Brazil conflagration in a 25-floor skyscraper which caught fire (1974), where many office workers jumped to their deaths, killing 179 people.

Those victims of New London, TX explosion (1937), now marched forward. Their gymnasium accidently exploded, killing 413 people, including the whole senior class of 92 members, save one, from a natural gas (methane) leak. We now watched that one survivor be reunited with his classmates after all these years! (Today the compound ethyl mercaptan is added to methane to give it a pungent odor so a leak can be smelled to warn people of its presence—for it is extremely deadly).

Now we visited the victims of the Triangle Shirtwaist Factory, New York City (1911), where some 850 girls were sewing clothes in a sweat shop. The fabric caught fire creating a raging inferno which whipped through the 8th story building. Not being able to escape, 145 of these girls leaped from the building—killing all who jumped. A witness said that the fire was so intense he saw a bright entity, the "Angel of Death," hovering over the burning building guiding the girls to their infamous doom!

These now met the victims from the Kansas City Hyatt Regency Hotel (1981), where two massive 36-ton 120 foot-long "skybridges" fell at a "Big Band" dance, injuring 300 people—crushing 114 of them to death.

Now those that succumbed aboard the fateful *Titanic* appeared. There was the filthy rich now reunited in death, living modestly, no better or worse than those poor immigrants of the lower decks they died with! They had lost all their money—but attained the wealth of eternal life!

Now the ship's 8 band ensemble played once again those songs from that fateful and forlorn night so long ago. For a moment all the souls aboard our Celestial City of God respectfully quieted as those special church hymns, giving courage and bravado to those victims as the great ship dipped further and further into her watery grave. *Nearer, My God, to Thee* and *O God, Our Help in Ages Past* echoed through the great halls of another time, another place … in the grand Kingdom of God! Those of the *Titanic* were now introduced to those victims of the *Andrea Doria* that collided with the *Stockholm* head-on July 25, 1956. Forty-six passengers aboard the *Andrea Doria* were killed including 5 crewmen aboard the *Stockholm*.

These victims were reunited with the 32 victims of the *Costa Concordia* who were killed when the cruise ship hit a barrier reef off the coast of the tiny Tuscan island of Isola del Giglio, Italy in 2012.

And in Fuxin, China (2005), an explosion deep down in a coal mine that killed over 200 workers were now reunited with those of the 1942 China disaster where 1,549 workers died. These were then reunited with those of West Virgina where an American coal mine killed 11 workers in 2006.

We met the 35 victims of the Alpine tunnel under Mont Blanc connecting Italy and France (1999). Twenty tractor-trailer trucks and 11 cars exploded which burned for days.

All these innocent victims were here wonderfully rejoicing in their hearts now living the abundant life promised by Christ to all His believers. They were in total peace—free from fear and pain, residing in unadulterated ecstasy and comfort within the heavenly kingdom knowing that nothing can ever harm them again!

Lady Liberty

A very interesting lady now arrived. Her name is unknown to the world, and yet will be forever more. Yet millions of people view her each year! She will never be known to the mortals! Yet she lies in the heart of all those who have fought for the cause of freedom. Yet, I, alas, have also been told not to reveal her name—yet you know her. In 1851 the Second Empire in France was in turmoil, being founded by Napoleon III. On a cold December after Napoleon had seized power, Bartholdi, walking down a dark Paris street, saw a young woman, a torch held high in her hand, leading the way through some barricades. Suddenly, a bullet struck her. As she died, her torch ignited those barricades set up to hinder the enemies of Napoleon. Bartholdi never forgot this tragic scene, and the unknown woman's ultimate devotion, a martyr to the cause of liberty. He was so inspired from this incident at the age of 17, he was compelled to create a shrine in her honor, which has now been immortalized in hammered copper and resurrected in New York Harbor—that ultimately became known the Statue of Liberty!

World Trade Center Reunion

The victims of "The Day of Innocents," now paraded forward. This was when four skyjacked airliners crashed into the New York World Trade Center's two skyscrapers, the Pentagon and a field rural Pennsylvania, where 2,977 people died, including 343 firemen and 76 police officers. (This was 574 more than died at Pearl Harbor). It was the worst terrorist attack upon American soil and the worst terrorist attack upon the face of the earth! Again the tears of pathos trickled down their glowing faces, all welcoming me into God's wonderful Kingdom!

Now those innocent children, the victims of the silent holocaust stepped forward. Those millions and millions killed from abortions. Those precious children who were conceived from rape victims and murdered by the unwilling mothers who refused to give them birth. Sweet precious innocent children never having the chance to be a viable human being, now had their chance at life for all eternity! They all radiated divine countenances for they have received the love of the angels and divine beings.

One Tiny Miracle

Week One: One tiny sperm penetrates the ovum—DNA choreographed into an amphimixis of ecstasy—the miracle of life has begun.

Week Two: I have become the grand potential of the human race, designed by God, imbued with a divine soul—made in His Image, transforming one tiny living cell into an enigma of a trillion cells.

Week Three: My little heart is fully formed and has already started beating—though another 10 weeks will pass before my heartbeat is detected by my mom's doctor.

Week Four: My mind is growing—as are my little bones. I can now feel pleasure and pain.

Week Five: Mom, will I have curly flaxen hair like my dad and deep blue eyes like you? In the sanctity of the womb I'm drifting along weightlessly pondering the wonder of the world to come.

Week Six: I think someday I will play tennis. My parents don't know it yet, but I'm going to be a little boy! I'll tell you more later, but now I have the hiccups.

Week Seven: My little hands and feet are growing stronger. Woops—was that a little kick? Did you feel that mama?

Week Eight: My eyes and ears are developing nicely. Mama, are you listening to Beethoven? I'd like to play the piano someday. I am in an ethereal and tranquil dream pondering the mystery of existence.

Week Nine: Wow! I think I'll become a scientist and probe the secrets of life—maybe find a cure for cancer. I am determined to change the world for good.

Week Ten: I'll suck my thumb while I ponder the beauty of a sunset—and the glory of a rainbow and the wonder of a twinkling star. I seem to be in a surreal primordial dream—but will soon encounter a beautiful reality.

Week Eleven: I will grow up—fall in love—get married, have children. I am now only a stranger to my mom, but will someday look into her deep saturnine eyes with a profound love. What will my name be, mom?

Week Twelve: Today, my mom killed me.

—The Author

Note: *One Tiny Miracle* is dedicated to all the millions of babies worldwide that have died from abortions.

Zoe stated that he must be leaving—then evaporated as smoke from a snuffed out candle.

CHAPTER THREE

Hell

(Ref. Mt. 8:12; Mk. 9:48; Rev. 16:10)

*A*nother angel now appeared—
"Call me Mystagogue. I am here to initiate you into the enigmas of Hell. It is time for you, Iben, to visit the Other Side, 'The Prison of Gehenna,' a place of shadow and sinister beings, located in the bowels beneath the City of God."

With this, I began descending down a steep and narrow twisting bright vermilion staircase. As I descended, I very cautiously broke through a membrane that separates good from evil. A strange barrier, where Good could enter, but Evil could not exit. I realize that I was now alone in a strange deep abode of darkness and gloom. On reaching the bottom of the stairs I entered a huge dimly lit cavern with ebony arches stretching high above. Here I discovered a number of haunting propylons expanding over my head leading to different paths with these words etched on them:

"BEWARE! THE VALLEY OF THE TERATOGENY AND THE CONDEMNED SOULS OF HELL"

With much trepidation I entered and literally walked through the gates of Hell. I learned that it was constructed in concentric dark Mephistophelian labyrinths in which to trap the soul. Many of these disconcerting paths led into other more despicable paths which eventually led to ultimate and total confusion—all spiraling downward toward ultimate insanity.

Within moments I was totally bewildered. There was the path of the Antichrist; the path of Sorcery; the path of Abomination; the path of Immorality; the path of Blasphemy; the path of Idolatry; the path of the Reprobate Mind; the path of Hubris; the path of Pornography; the path of Addiction; the path of Revelry; the path of Hatred; the path of Wrath; the path of Murderers; the path of Variance; the path of Foment; the path of Revenge; the path of Sedition; the path of Heresy; the path of Hypocrisy, the path of the Hardened Heart; the path of Insipience; the path of Mammon; the path of Avarice; the path of Gluttony; the path of Satanism; the path of Deception; the path of Necromancy; the path of Apostasy; the path of Despair; the path of Desolation; the path of Variance; the path of Contention; the path of Terrorism, the path of Anarchism; the path of Atheism; the path of Nihilism; the path of Secularism; the path of Deism; the path of Humanism; the path of Syndicalism, and the path of Communism.

In trepidation I chose the path of the Reprobate Mind. As I descended, I began creeping down into a void of utter darkness; a smoking pit of choking brimstone burning with the fires of iniquity. I wondered why I decided to visit Hell, and realized it was to enlighten the gentle reader that such dimensions actually exist. I wanted to forewarn the unbeliever against the iniquity of evil, lest YOU might be more than just a mere visitor to the place of eternal damnation and eternal sorrow in the agony beyond death.

"But the children of the kingdom shall be cast out into outer darkness; there shall be weeping and gnashing of teeth;" and "where the worn dieth not and the fire is not quenched." —Mt. 8:12; Mk. 9:46, 48

Here were the condemned that had gone to church all their lives—but had never heard the "Plan of Salvation" preached. Others that were here used their church for only a "country club" and for business contacts.

The path of the Reprobate Mind now grew more frightening … an abomination of desolation. A forbidden place destined to see the anathema of Jehovah, and the curse of Judgment upon all that are incarcerated therein.

Peering through dark formations of twisted, mangled debris, I could see deformed ghouls, termagants, jinns, and seducing bat-like demons all observing me with their cold hollow eyes, glowing red in the dark. Here resided creatures with vicious talons that not only tear and bleed the skin and disembowel the unwary, but brandish razor-sharp claws that actually rip and shred the very *souls* of mankind.

I stepped cautiously around the most horrible serpentine creatures of the eternal night whose prehensile tails were like that of scorpions, with terrible stings to render excruciating pain to the condemned of God. Still other wicked demons too evil to gaze upon, snapped at my ankles. One less quick and agile as myself could easily be snatched by the foot and dragged into the black pit of profound obscurity.

These Rulers of Darkness slithering in the shadows were the very minions of the Antichrist. I even spotted some fallen angels and unclean spirits who were at Jesus Christ's crucifixion. Their unholy stares pierced my very soul, condemning me for trespassing in their cursed domain.

I had lost Mystagogue for a moment and realized I couldn't find him. Dare I continue into this horrid place of eternal damnation? If I become hopelessly lost in this forbidden place, could I ever find my way out? In these haunting shadows I stumbled across the Teratogeny. What made them, I wondered, follow the paths of wickedness, evil and ultimate destruction.

Diabolus now appeared, along with little imps, goblins, orcs, gnomes and demons. They skittered all about my feet like nasty rats.

I could feel the chill of the eternal night and sensed the horrible chimeras creeping ever closer. The rustling of web-like structures hanging from the canopy were not from the wind—but the subtle movement of evil spider-like specters lurking everywhere. Could they snare me in their grip and hold me against my will? The Cerastes hanged in festoons from these glistening webs just above my head, hissing everywhere waiting to trap the unwary. Their poison was to destroy the souls of those condemned to these infernal regions.

Psalms I was now quoting—hoping this will ward off the evil pressing so close. I now came to a towering archway surrounded by barbed wire, with a strange succinct epigram etched across it—

427

Solfatara

I could now see something digging itself out of a smoking pit, entangled and bleeding. It was a ghastly apparition … some dead forgotten disheveled, ragged impuissant zombie, oozing purulence. It dragged itself forward bound by a heavy chain of "crimes against humanity."

It spoke, "Iben, fear not … for I cannot harm you … you are a saint of the Divine and those that dwell here have no power over you. I am the concierge of Hades known to the mundane world as Adolph Hitler, the infamous Fuhrer of Germany, the mass murderer of millions."

Hitler's head, at that moment, toppled from his shoulder hitting the ground with an audible thud. Unperturbed, he stooped down, groped for it, rose once again, placed it upon his neck not noticing one of his eyes hanging on his cheek.

"Welcome," he continued, "to this province of Hell know as Solfatara. Let me introduce you to many others who dwell here."

With this, the cortège of the wickedest souls who ever lived marched forward. Hitler's Elite Gestapo told their ruthless tales of all the horror they etched on the history of humanity.

Next Josef Stalin, insanity in his eyes of stark terror of some innominate evil stalking him through the corridors of Hell, related how he killed 4.2 million of his own people in the 1920s. During his unholy reign of forced collectivization, he had millions shot or sent to labor camps.

Pol Pot, the Khmer Rouge leader, one of the century's most infamous mass murderers now appeared. He killed untold millions in Cambodia between 1975 to 1979. He died in 1998, thus ending the Khmer Rouge insurgency of Cambodia for 19 years. What stories he related made my skin crawl—even in my enhanced state of being!

Here we met Chang Hsien-Chung, who in 1640 A.D. murdered millions of people in only a few short years on Szechuan Province in China! Miles upon miles of this entire province was transformed into a mountain range of body parts—hands, feet, heads and torsos.

Next I conversed with Nero, Rasputin, Ivan the Terrible, and Dracula (Vlad the Impaler), the latter being much more terrible than the myth which Bram Stoker conjured up in his book, *Dracula*. Vlad was impaled here as he had impaled thousands of his hapless victims. As the spit turned roasting him alive over the fires of Hell, he told me of his macabre tales of murder and pillage.

We now entered new cross-roads and chose the path of Murderers.

The entourage of reprobates continued—

The deadliest serial killers of them all now appeared. Their ears still ringed with the curse of the screams of their victims as they reaped the judgment and anathema of God!

A mass murderer from Russia crawled forth. He killed 100 people and fed them to his supper guests!

Here we found many cult leaders who brainwashed their followers into killing themselves. I recognized the leader of Heaven's Gate Cult, where in 1997, in San Diego, he commanded all 39 of his followers to commit suicide to leave the earth to rendezvous with a UFO trailing behind Hale-Bopp comet.

We discovered members of the Jim Jones Religious Cult

of mass suicide in Jonestown, Guyana, South America, in 1978, where 913 people, almost a third being young children, took cyanide-laced Kool-Aid killing all in their newly established primitive community.

Many of the gangsters from Chicago and Las Vegas arrive to tell their tales of vice, graft, carnage and revenge.

The assassins of world leaders along with numerous infamous serial killers now came forward, dragging their chains of woe and sin: Jack-the-Ripper; the Zodiac Killer; the Night Stalker and the Hillside Strangler. And still the depraved continued along Hell's smoky pathways including the Skid Row Stabber, the Trailside Slayer and the Sunset Slayer, all among the mass of humanity en route to the fires of Gehenna, "where the worm dies not and the fire is never quenched."

Another mass murderer in Arkansas related how and why he murdered all 16 members of his family Christmas Eve as they all arrive to visit his home to celebrate Christmas.

Yet another reprobate told how he killed and fed many of his friends and their children to his pet alligators.

Infamous rogues, malefactors, hoodlums, bank robbers and thieves told their horrid tales of pillage and murder.

Another mass killer now appeared. He was the murderer of over a dozen people, to whom he fed to his award-winning pigs at the state fairs!

The "Boston Strangler" related how he killed 13 women between 1962 and 1964. Sentenced to life in prison, he was stabbed to death in his cell in 1973.

One person related how he killed and ate over 15 children.

A homosexual man told how he enticed young males

to his house. The police dug up over 30 bodies of young adults in his yard.

One man who worked in a packing house told how he married over 55 women and killed 15 of them.

Next I saw a medical doctor who tried to play God. The once-beloved English family doctor killed over 260 patients—all by lethal injection. Psychologists learned that Dr. Harold Shipman was actually *addicted* to killing, as others are to drugs or alcohol.

Again we intersected other paths ... that of Deception—

I located thousands twisted in a massive human knot, those condemned that had taken advantage of the aged people that were abused and duped into having their fortunes eliminated by con men. Also embedded here were condemned reprobates, those that tricked others along with those who forged hot checks on their accounts, or took advantage of paying victims in advance to do construction work which was never done, or never finished, or not in compliance with set laws or criteria. Those telemarketers that deceived others over the phone we also found here intertwined and tangled within this massive human knot, all dangling from a tether—roasting alive above the unholy fires of Hell.

Freedom of Religion

Now we entered the path of Terrorism—

Before me, as I entered these most noxious depths, there appeared horrible demoniacs stinging and torturing *all* the terrorists who have murdered the innocent. Within these smoldering pits of perdition, were those who died inflicting wounds and havoc on others, destroying many innocent lives. This included *all* those involved in the terrorist organizations, along with their twisted networks of radical Islam.

God condemned their crimes against humanity … justice and punishment served to all the suicide bombers and assassins of the world.

Then we finally discovered the Islamic terrorist responsible for flying the planes into the World Trade Center and the Pentagon. We felt the heat miles away and witnessed a frightening flaming arc of fulminating plasma intense enough to cauterize the very souls of these repugnant beings… their fate sealed in a supernatural fire.

The Koran doesn't advocate murder and sedition for the cause and spread of Islam. Does it not state that any form of violence against innocent civilians or even the persecution of minorities contradicts the *basic principles* of their religion? *Doesn't one of Islam's major fundamental teachings proclaim that the killing of one person is equal to the slaughter of all humanity? And the saving of one person is equal to preserving the whole of humanity?*

Yes, we have the tenet "Freedom of Religion" in America. We welcome religious freedom in our great country of the United States, but as someone succinctly stated, "freedom ends where evil begins."

Crossing over a boiling river we now came to the path of Murderers—

Here I met a vast number of deceased world leaders of communistic, tyrannical and terrorist nations. Yet many of these dictators were so buried in the depths of Hell, I dared not visit them. They were isolated from any visitors, and kept chained to the weary souls they deceived, partners in crime, sent into perdition, and this chained line of victims turned and twisted for miles through these smoldering depths of eternal gloom.

Many infamous racists and anti-Semites appeared next. Here were all those who think that their race is superior. It's their way, or the highway. Here were all those racial radicals, doomed to promote darkness and prejudice throughout the world.

Next we entered the path of the Atheist—

Here were those who pushed to eradicate public prayer and Bible reading from our schools. Here were all those fools (Psalms 14:1; 53:1) who were also trying to ban *under God* in the "Pledge of Allegiance to our Flag," "In God We Trust" from our coins and "The Ten Commandments" from our court houses and capitol buildings. Here we found them all.

And the reprobates marched on and on, telling their stories of wickedness, horror and death.

Wicked Biblical Kings and Rulers

We entered the path of the Hardened Hearts—

The infamous Rich Man mentioned in the Bible now appeared. After all these long millennia he still calls Lazarus in vain to cool his tongue in this pit of fire.

The Evil Kings of the Bible now sauntered forth:

There was King Saul who rejected God, and tried to kill David.

Ahab, king of Israel, next stepped forward. He was the wickedest of all their kings. He married Jezebel, a Sidonian princess, an imperious, unscrupulous devilish woman, a demon-incarnate.

Ahaziah, wicked king of Judah, told of his brutality.

Athaliah, queen of Judah, impudent, wicked daughter of the infamous Jezebel related her foibles...

Sennacherib, king of Assyria, son of Sargon II, who invaded Judea...

Jehoiakim, king of Judah, a hard-hearted and wicked king related how he tried to kill Jeremiah several times, but failed.

Then Jezebel stepped forward, wife of Ahab, who killed the prophets and caused Naboth to be put to death. She told about her violent death, how she was thrown to the horses. "And when they went to bury her; but they found no more than her skull, her feet, and the palms of her hands."

Herod the Great told how he murdered his wife, along with his sons, to keep the throne of Judah. He was responsible for the "slaughter of the innocents" when all the little babies in Bethlehem were killed trying to liquidate the Christ Child.

Herod Antipas, 33 years after Herod-the-Great's rule over Judah told how he killed John-the Baptist and mocked Christ.

Next Nadab, king of Israel, appeared. He killed all the house of Jeroboam.

Later on, we spotted Ananias and Sapphira present, who both lied to the Holy Spirit and were struck down dead. Sapphira, his wife, was incessantly enticing me deeper into Hell's smoking realms, showing me all sorts of bizarre ghouls and anarchist. Judas Iscariot (the disciple who betrayed Christ for 30 pieces of silver) was also here.

"Iben," Hitler spoke, "all that you see is much worst than that revealed in Dante's *Divine Comedy*. If you go back to Earth, write and tell of that which you have seen here today. Make no mistake, there is a Hell, and it is waiting for all those lost and evil souls that have altered the status of peace and tranquility breeding foment throughout the world. Cursed are those malicious and dastardly persons which have sowed the works of the flesh, namely adultery, fornication, uncleanness. lasciviousness, idolatry, witchcraft, hatred, variance, emulations, wrath, strife, seditions, heresies, envyings, murders, drunkenness, revelings, and such like… shall NOT inherit the kingdom of God. BE YE WARNED!"

Hitler's Judgment

Hitler now seemed to be in a catatonic trance with an insane gloss in his eyes mumbling some redundant phrase over and over to himself. We now found ourselves once again near the pit where Hitler emerged. Slowly he wandered off a short distance toward an arched gateway, emblazoned with an epigram above it. I realized it to be an entrance to another section of Hades surrounded by barbed wire and an electrified fence. Hitler kept mumbling *Arbeit Macht Frei,* over and over, echoing in my ears, *ad nauseam*. Then I realized just what this phrase meant! "Work Will Make You Free." It was the same infamous lie he had placed over the archways of numerous Nazi death camps scattered across Poland and Germany! Now he himself was condemned to one of these many prison camps—reserved for insane rulers and demented kings!

"I have reaped my reward, "Hitler continued, "and now for my punishment—sent to Satan's concentration camp of untold misery, though its final details have yet to be revealed even to me."

With this, the chain binding Hitler tightened and unmercifully dragged him screaming and kicking through this arch into that smoking pit of brimstone from which he came. His screams could be heard until the awesome stench of vomit and the black muck of tainted sin once again oozed over him, stifling what was left of his lungs, and for a long while I could still hear those gurgling bloody screams echoing in my mind as I journeyed beyond the duration of my welcome.

Retracing my steps through the horrid miasma of Solfatara, I realized I had been traveling in chaotic circles, that even the frightening path that I was now on ... was fading away—disappearing totally in front and behind me. I was hopelessly lost in these despondent labyrinthine tunnels wandering endlessly and insanely through blind smoldering corridors and fiery blistering cul-de-sacs.

Black smoke choked me—total darkness cloaked me. Panic and fear. The demons were closing in. Was I hopelessly lost in the depths of Solfatara? My worst nightmare was beginning. I began to pray to Heaven. The words of Hitler once again echoed in my ear ... "fear not Iben, for no harm will come to you," and yet—

Then I could hear the demon's scream for me and their

rustling approaching even closer and closer. Great fountains of tears came and I began to pray out loud. Dizziness and vertigo ... thick smoke ... a frenzied choking ... then my consciousness was fading ... blackness—

I then heard a divine voice, "Thy sins be forgiven thee, arise and walk."

Then as I opened my eyes, miraculously the thick heavy smoke somewhat cleared. A brilliant glowing pearlescent propylon arching above my head, read, "STRAIT" ... and I realized it to be that "narrow gate" Jesus proclaimed as the only way to salvation!

Immediately I entered through this gate and raced up a great magnificent bright and glistening staircase spiraling heavenward toward redemption as fast as I could. As I neared the top I sensed a fresh rapport of divine love enveloping me.

Mystagogue, as the wind of divinity, now appeared brandishing a flaming sword of protection, mercifully plucked me from these deranged paths of chaos. At the top of these stairs, I now prostrated my body before this mighty angel, being thankful and in ecstasy of being purged from the fires of Hell. He raised me up stating that God and Jesus Christ only are worthy to be worshiped.

So I survived the perils of Hades, this noxious dwelling of death, Satanism, and horror.

Oh, to be redeemed from Solfatara, that pit of perdition. To be mercifully plucked from these indigent reprobates, the sons of perdition. It was good to be back into the warm divine grace of God and the fresh sweet air of atonement!

"Thy word is a lamp unto my feet;

and a light unto my path."
—Ps. 119:105

I pondered all that I have seen in my heart, mind and spirit.

The Celestial City's Interior

We now explored the alternate planes of our Celestial City of God, and saw the great splendid wonders the Almighty had prepared for his redeemed.

Mystagogue now invited me to the grandest of rejoicing and frolicking I had ever seen! I recognized my parents and all my acquaintances, old girlfriends and grade school friends of youth. I traced their life stories from kindergarten through high school, college, on to their occupations and their marriages.

I learned about the children they bore, and how the Angel of Divine Providence molded each individual life. I came early to the conclusion that we are all brothers and sisters on this earth, and we are all interrelated to each other. I learned how one person far removed from our lives can indirectly affect us. Just incredible!

The Elysium Gardens

Mystagugue and I penetrated still deeper into our Celestial City. There were conservatories of ecological, biological and geological natural wonders. There were enchanting zoological, botanical, aeroponic, hydroponic and aquaponic gardens of surreal beauty within sensuous cascading waterfalls. Also present were variegated and exotic wildlife, which are both endangered and extinct upon the earth. Vast exotic Triassic and Jurassic parks where living dinosaurs roamed free coexisted with fantastic Archeozoic, Proterozoic, Paleozoic, Mesozoic and Cenozoic reserves of bizarre animals long thought dead were now living peacefully before us, our view extending as far as the eye could see—and *far beyond* the imaginings and beliefs of mortals!

Do plants have souls? Mystagogue proclaimed that God's most peaceful creations, the flowers, bushes, shrubs and trees also flourished after death in God's magnificent *Paradisia*. We could easily commune with these plants and they actually responded to our thoughts! We penetrated still further into God's spectacular Kingdom. Yet other surprises prevailed that will only be revealed after death!

I was now feeling the pure divine kinetic energy of my new immortal body—extraordinary divine powers, propelling me onward to completion. No malice toward anyone. No hate toward anybody. All that was gone in the instant I died. Only total peace ensues me onward to perfection.

Mystagogue stated that he must be leaving—that he must now bestow spiritual blessings and favor upon those that are pure in heart, for they shall see God.

CHAPTER FOUR

The Grande Musique Suonare:

I realized that here in Eternity I am destined to do great things! All *thinking* and all *actions* are totally pure and wholesome.

The Divine Spirit, Harmonia, now appeared. She revealed a vast spacious chamber known as the *Grande Musique Suonare.*

I came upon a new concept—thought produced music. I knew in my old life I could not play a note nor read music.

"Remember, Iben, how difficult playing the piano was while upon the earth?"

All of a sudden I had this great desire to think "classical," and a cavalcade of great composers came to mind. With an excited vibration of my total being, I entered the Grande Celestial Auditorium and began to play a wonderful modulated ultrasonic divine *Glokenspiel-Clavichord voix Celeste.* It is an electronic rhythmic light-to-music modulator, covering *all* the instruments of the orchestra, with many other unworldly gismos not yet invented upon the earth.

They produced wondrous ultrasonics and supersonics never heard nor conceived by the ears of humankind. Embued with this spiritual gift, I thought of a song and waved my hands over the top of its glass-like incandescent baubles and polychromatic crystals. As the music flowed, wonderful kaleidoscopic colors glowed, casting a thousand rainbows over the walls and ceiling.

Now as my soul played forth from this grand melodeon the great music from Handel's Messiah, the angels of heaven themselves wept great tears of joy and mirth!

I played the great masters of Bach, Beethoven, Chopin, Debussy, Mozart, Schumann, Schubert, Strauss, Rachmaninoff, *et al.* Beautiful, divine music flowed from this magical melodious "glockenspiel!"

Then I played the music of Brahms, Gershwin, Liszt, Tchaikovsky, Stravinsky and Wagner. I played them all *perfect* the *first* time! It would have required a lifetime to play these composers correctly as they had intended for them to be played, and a penchant for doing it. I had neither in the old mundane life. Yet *this* music was very different in that I could perceive different dimensions of frequencies never before experienced by man.

I was in complete ecstasy! What magnificent music flowed abundantly from my mind and soul into the cosmic vibrations of this celestial sphere!

As I played, these eximious composers now appeared. I communed with them all! The late-great contemporary musicians paraded before me, and *still* the cortège continued!

We composed totally new divine music together into the exotic realm of "polytonality." How I did this was a new supernatural gift, written upon a "new song" created upon our hearts now embued with divinity!

Wonderful also is that these composers have *still* been creating *original* divine symphonies. Beethoven, who turned deaf at the age of 28, could now *hear* his wonderful symphonies once again—along with the hundreds of other masterpieces he has since created! Eternity overflowed with thousands of *new* celestial songs expressing realms of total delight found only within the kingdom of God!

> "As we acquire knowledge, things do not become
> more comprehensible, but more mysterious."
> —Will Durant

Harmonia stated that she must be going ... but yet another Spirit will soon reveal—

The Grandisio Celestial Arte Museo

The Divine Spirit, Artistica, now appeared. Instantly we arrived at the *Grandisio Celestial Arte Museo.* It was at this moment empty of any Supernalites.

I spied a blank canvas. Lying on the table were hundreds of variegated acrylics in small vials coruscating their brilliant colors in thousands of beautiful hues covering the *total* spectrum.

The empty canvas was resting upon an easel, ready for the imagination of the infinity of thought. On my palette I mixed cerulean and cobalt blues with titanium white and created a sky as I remembered in a different life. Then I created, using van dyke brown, yellow ocher and cadmium yellow some majestic mountain ranges. It was all my unique style and I must say, it turned out superb! In my old life I couldn't even paint the barn!

Trees would be nice. I picked up a fan brush and touched it in sap-green and with thousands of tiny strokes, created trees and marsh grasses. Now appeared a beautiful azure sky with billowy white clouds, and with dark rich indigo I formed a lake shimmering in the sunlight!

Then I decided to paint what I had seen within the *Paradisia*. New prismatic *multidimensional* paints presented themselves a great challenge. To capture on canvas those new exotic creatures, supernatural landscapes, and strange kaleidoscopic skies! I had never tried to master the concept of a fifth and sixth dimensional world, art in a surreal super-reality of existence—wondrous enchantments of which I have just now become aware. In a few minutes of divine inspiration, the magical dreamscape I now created even surprised me! What a wonderland of incomprehensible beauty, a finished masterpiece of extreme ecstasy!

The Great Artists

The canvass was filled, and the challenge completed just as a Supernalite, a very young man dressed in an old renaissance style appeared. His name—Antonello de Messian. He was from the classical antiquity of the Italian Age of Art (c. 1500 A.D.) with his painting, *The Death of St. Sebstian*. This is the famous saint with arrows piercing through his body, one of the most famous paintings in the world!

"My dear Iben Jair," Antonello spoke, "welcome to Eternity! You are going to have the best time ever! As you might not know, St. Sebstian was caught and tried for his religious beliefs and tied to the execution stake and shot through with arrows. Most people think this killed him, but he lived through this, and after his recovery, was actually stoned to death!"

Here in this Art Museum of our Celestial City thousands of paintings of antiquity resided, all that looked as fresh as if they had been painted only a few days before! Then I discovered that some of them *actually* were only hours old!

The cortège of artists continued ... Sandro Botticelli, who painted, *The Virgin Adoring Her Child* and *The Adoration of the Magi* and the *Last Communion of St. Jerome*; Giovanni Cimabue, who painted *Madonna and Child with Angels*; Leonardo Da Vinci, of the Italian Renaissance, who painted, *The Last Supper* and *The Mona Lisa*; Michelangelo, another artist of the Italian Renaissance, who painted the walls and ceiling of the Sistine Chapel with *The Creation of Adam* and the *Last Judgment*; and Giotto di Bondone, also an Italian Renaissance painter, who painted his famous works of *The Descent from the Cross* and *The Madonna Enthroned*.

Then appeared a man, small in stature, uncommonly disheveled in appearance ... and yet had a wonderful original glow in his eyes and a vitality in his being.

"May I enter?" he humbly requested.

"Of course, sir," I returned, offering him my smile.

He offered his hand to me and I shook it in the American tradition.

"Dear Iben Jair, I am respectfully at your service. My name is Francesco le Broussart."

Who is le Broussart? I had never heard of him!

"Le Broussart," he continued, "that unknown painter who was *never* given the chance to succeed while upon the earth. You see, my parents laughed at me when I informed them that I wanted to be a great painter! Then mitigating circumstances forced me to take one menial job after another. Then I got married and the children came along making it impossible to develop my penchant in painting. I studied all the great artists at the library in Italy and tried to get ahead, but alas, all my efforts fell to the wayside. At twenty-two I got sick and gradually got worse, contracted 'painter's colic' from lead paint poisoning that finally resulted in severe dementia. With this my dream died—and four years later so did I. With this death, the world missed the development of the WORLD'S GREATEST PAINTER, THE WORLD'S GREATEST ARTIST!"

The other artists made way for him and I immediately learned that le Broussart was the center of immediate attention of all the other artists of our Celestial City. He was the master they all stated, and he was the unknown artist which painted *St. George and the Dragon*, an early 15-Century Italian tempera painting, (the only extant painting by him) from the Byzantine School of Art! If given the chance, he would have become the *greatest* painter ever born of woman!

Since the last shall be first and the first last, the FIRST PRINCIPLE aboard the *Paradisia*, the Celestial City of

God, Francesco is FIRST, the greatest of all living artists and painters known—and unknown!

We discussed the artist's different styles, their lives, their paintings and their creativity. The history of art came alive before our eyes. They stated that they also continued painting here in our Celestial City of God, producing thousands of neo-classicial paintings that had never been seen by mortal man.

I communed with Jan van Eyck and Hieronymous Bosch discussing paintings many of which were lost, stolen or ruined through the ages, and how our colors and paints compared with the originals.

Others who entertained us in the Art Museum were Vincent van Gogh who allegedly killed himself. He had an argument with Paul Gouguin, who he threatened with a knife. For this, in deep remorse, he sliced off his own ear as punishment for having this altercation with him! (His ear was now healed and he has been forgiven and purged of his insanity!)

Raphael, El Greco, Peter Paul Rubens, Pablo Picasso and Salvador Dali now appeared. Many of these were multi-tasked artists who were not only painters, but also experts in sculpture, not only molding the graceful human body, but grand masters of architecture—designers of cathedrals, castles, museums and administrative buildings.

How exciting! What solidarity to be able to actually converse with these great artists of genius. It was just unbelievable. God is so good! Eternity is such a paradise!

These artists and I communed for what seemed like months. How long these events lasted was hard to tell, since a "thousand years is as one day, and one day is as a thousand years."

Artistica told me it was time to leave. Many people need to learn about the beautiful world which surrounds them ... for many have only been surrounded by an ugly environment and abject poverty with no time to enjoy the beauty of life. But in Eternity they will all soon understand—

As Artistica dematerialized, she introduced yet another Spirit—

CHAPTER FIVE

The Grandisio Bibilothecaire Humaniores:

Thesaurus, the "Angel of Divine Wisdom," now appeared. He guided me to a great beautifully framed oracular mirror possessing strange metaphysical properties. Its surface, a strange vitreous membrane, undulated as a ripple in a pond. As I touched it, my hand penetrated through and then my whole body was pulled into it. I realized it to be a *vast intellectual dimension.*

> "Reading is to the Mind,
> what God is to the Soul."
> —The Author

I found myself surrounded by millions of divine scintillating diamonds—all shapes, sizes and colors. I learned that these 'diamonds' were actually books, not bound with leather, nor their pages composed of cellulose, but composed of—extraterrestrial sempiternal substances.

Thesaurus introduced his companions Incunabula and Scriptoria, or to you Iben Jair, the custodians of the *Grandisio Bibilothecaire Humaniores*, or the Grand Library of our Celestial City!"

"Iben," Thesaurus spoke, "these books are composed of imperishable substances, containing the divine wisdom of the ages. These books are, indeed, totally indestructible, and will last for all eternity!"

Scriptoria informed me that the average person spends two hours a day watching TV and only 19 minutes actually reading. I also realized that these crystals would totally *absorb* my mind and come alive as a movie, but a movie played in my imagination, totally unique and personal!

Incunabula revealed wonderful books and scrolls written by the prophets of the Old Testament, the Law of Moses (the Torah). Also there were the traditional New Testament manuscripts, including *all* the *lost letters* (epistles) of Paul, many of which did not make it to the New Testament.

"Iben," Thesaurus continued, "this library also contains *all* the wholesome, spiritual and constructive books every written, as they looked before antiquity overtook them— copied in the ink of their time, totally preserved in *pristine condition*. Here resided the original texts of the languages of hieroglyphic, hieratic and coptic papyri, Hebrew, Greek, Semitic, *et al*. Included also were the *whole* texts lost and destroyed in the old world and *all* the lost texts that were written in the libraries of Babylonia and Assyria."

"Iben," Incunabula spoke, "we even have all these very ancient scrolls as fresh as the day they were written! Also, the Hebrew Torah is complete, its "D" (Deuteronimic code), "P" (Priest), "J" (Jehovah) and "E" (Elohim) documents of the Holy Scripture, not mere fragments, but the *complete lost texts*! The Nash Paytrus, found in Egypt in mere torn and tattered fragments, is here in its complete and pristine condition!"

Scriptoria explained how these books were preserved as they were sealed in an immortal elixir making them durable as diamonds, which they are, diamonds of literature, and much more precious. These before me contained the *living* divine wisdom of God.

He questioned me, "Can a stone or diamond talk to you a thousand years, nay *many* thousands of years ago? We now have our answer! All these immortalized books can reach you, telling of days long ago, and carry their wisdom to you over the ageless past!"

I spotted the eminent scientist, Joseph Priestley, here within this grand library, in ecstasy, studying all his personal priceless manuscripts on science he wrote which were lost to humanity, destroyed by fire during the French Revolution.

Thesaurus revealed the actual lost works of Philo, Thucydides, Aristides, Duranzo (the Greek historian), Heraclius, Trajan, and those of the Talmuds.

He now disclosed those ancient manuscripts: the envy of the Vatican library at Rome! The Dead Sea Scrolls were here—not in old torn fragments, but the *whole complete parchments*, the preserved scrolls in mint condition penned by the Essenes! Yes, the "Gospel of Thomas" and the "Angel Scroll" were here also! ALL the lost texts of the Bible were present, along with thousands of ancient k*oine* or common Greek manuscripts in parchment and papyrus in *mint condition* from which the Holy Bible was composed. Here were wonderful manuscripts from the *Alexandrian Codices;*

the *Vaticanus Codices*; the *Origen* texts along with hundreds of others, including the actual Jewish and Jerusalem *Talmuds*! Again, these were the *original complete pristine manuscripts*, not mere worn, torn and partial fragments worldly libraries now contain!

The Apocrypha

Here Incunabula unveiled many ancient scrolls, known as the "apocrypha," or concealed, hidden books of the Bible. These were the "lost" documents that were *not* canonized by the Council of Jamnia in A.D. 90. They were disapproved as authentic" (inspired and written by the Jewish prophets themselves) by the early Church of which mere fragments now exist upon the earth. Then at the Council of Trent (1546 A.D.) the Roman Catholic Church confirmed most of the works as canonical (the Prayer of Manasseh and 1-2 Esdras were still *not* accepted). These latter volumes were then known as the "deuterocanonical" ("second canon").

Here in pristine condition of our Celestial Library resided *all* these apocryphal books, including *The Assumption of Moses;* the codices of *Jubilees*; *The Song of the Three Holy Children*; *The Prayer of Manasseh; The History of Susanna; The Sibylline Oracles*; *Bel and the Dragon; I and II Maccabees*; along with thousands of other manuscripts lost to humanity. Most of these documents have been *rejected* as being "inspired by God," and caution should be a factor in accepting them because, it should be noted, that Mohammed used some of them extensively in writing the Koran, establishing his religion of Islam, c. 600 A.D.

Notably, Jesus Christ did not write any of the New

Testament. The disciples Matthew, Mark, Luke and John *recorded* what Jesus proclaimed *as eye witnesses*. Luke wrote Acts, about Paul's missionary journeys, and Revelation was written by John of Patmos.

Then Thesaurus revealed a beautiful flawless diamond, perfect and complete, composed of uncountable carats illuminated and filled the whole library with beautiful divine radiance, the nimbus of Holy Light … and I realized that this was the HOLY BIBLE IN ITS PERFECT TRANSLATION!

And there before me—illuminating a beam of light as a radiant stained glass window, embedded in the library wall, were —with Moses' fingerprints still upon them … the *actual* TEN COMMANDMENTS, carved by the very *finger of God*, brought from Mt. Sinai, handed to Moses— which he threw in anger.

These two tablets were the only broken and chipped documents in the whole library, and were not in the diamond format, but exactly preserved as God had carved them and handed them to Moses, still coruscating the Divinity of the great "I Am," the Almighty God!

We now met thousands of authors who were *still* writing their books *even after their death*s! Before me lay rows and rows of every divine spiritual book written by the hand of humankind and the millions that the Cognoscente had continued to write. Paradise is such a busy place.

Also, among these lost books was the book of *Jasher*, a compilation of songs celebrating the glory of Israel, mentioned in the Bible in Josh. 10:13 and 2 Sam. 1:18.

God had bestowed another miracle upon his eternal saints, the Supernalites, the "GIFT OF LANGUAGES," the polyglot. Therefore, the new-born saint could read them all in their original languages. The *CURSE OF BABEL* had been abolished!

Incunabula now unveiled the ancient books from the Library of Alexander, Egypt, that burned in 300 B.C. This destroyed much of the esoteric knowledge of the ancient world. Also, we discovered the encoded and *decoded* books by Nostradamus!

The Book of Life

Scriptoria now revealed the mysterious book of immortality ... radiating its divine light across the library. My heart stopped when I realized it was *not* the Holy Bible ... but the very *Book of Life*. It was turned to the "T's." With the greatest trepidation I desperately searched for my name: "Thayer, Iben," and I did *not* see it. My heart stuck in my throat and sweat beaded upon my forehead. Then the book mercifully turned its pages as if by magic to the "J's." Then a wonderful divine glow highlighted a new name. My name that was *changed* to "Jair." "Iben Jair." It was there! I was saved! Hallelujah! Glory to God in the highest! Great tears of joy burned down my face as I fell upon my knees thanking and praising God for his great miracles and blessings for my eternal life!

All these Spirits now bade me farewell.

"Iben," Thesaurus concluded, "we must continue to help the 26 million Americans in the United States who cannot read—to learn this divine miracle of the printed word, unique only to *Homo sapiens*. For knowing how to read, not only separates us from the lower animals, it is truly a Divine Gift from God!"

"A good book is the precious life-blood of a master spirit,
embalmed and treasured up on
purpose to a life beyond life."
—John Milton

"The very language in which they were conceived may die,
but the thoughts themselves triumph
over bronze and marble.
An author becomes a book. And what better
metamorphosis could he desire?
—*I Love Books* by John D. Snider

"Without the love for books the richest man is poor."
—Author Unknown

"Language is more important to the mind,
Than light is to the eye."
—Anne Sullivan (Helen Keller's teacher)

Thesaurus, now leaving, introduced yet another exotic Spirit—

CHAPTER SIX

The Plasmaphysiks Laboratory:

"*I*ben, I am the Divine Spirit, Transurania. Welcome to the Plasmaphysiks Laboratory."

Now appearing was one of the great physicists of recent times—Albert Einstein!

"Welcome, Iben. I have been expecting you! Micronia, a while back told you that I have been a very busy man lately. So, let me announce a unique experiment in quantum chromodynamics that I have been working on."

The Newtonian Anti-Gravity Oscillator
The Synchrophasotron

Einstein then guided us into a very mysterious place. At its center resided a Newtonian anti-gravity oscillator embedded within a quantum-particle catalytic fusion breeder. In other words, a time reverter enabling us to travel back into the past or forward into the future. I realized that I was already utilizing these effects, traveling into the past—but didn't realize until now its source.

Encircling this was a massive synchrophasotron generating strange subatomic particles, such as the quarks, the hyperons, the baryons, the Higgs bosons, the mesons, the muons, the gluons, the gravitons, the pions, the kaons, the antiproton, the tachyons, *et al.*

Einstein also revealed all these exotic particles that have an ethereal existence of only a few nanoseconds upon the earth—thrive here in plasmas held between magnetic fields … for *years*! Such are the paradoxes in our Celestial City. We also learned that without God creating the Higgs boson, the universe of stars and galaxies, along their solar systems of planets and all their innumerable life forms would not exist, because no atoms could have ever formed!

I noticed some Supernalites engrossed in intense study delving into the secrets of matter, atoms, subatomic particles, antimatter and all of their electro-magnetic forces. They were of different time periods, but continuing their learning in total humility—*now taught by Jesus Christ and his angels.* With the "gift of recognition" I realized some of them to be none other than Alessandro Volta, Nikola Tesla, Georg Simon Ohm, Ernest Rutherford, Joseph John (J.J.) Tomson, Robert Millikan, James Clerk Maxwell, James Chadwick, Glenn Seaborg, Niles Bohr, Max Plank, and numerous others—

Once again Jesus came over and welcomed me into this enticing realm of divine knowledge. And with complete humility as a young inquiring baby gazes upon a page of print, knowing somehow he will decipher the knowledge contained within, so will I, with my new-born existence, learn the mysteries of these dynamics flashing and blinking before me—and will, with an anxious curiosity, master their many intriguing secrets revealing the mysteries of astral travel and the phenomenon of time-warp—penetrating deep into strange multiple dimensions and anti-matter universes.

Transurania then revealed fantastic new sub-atomic particles of matter completely filling out the rest of the periodic table, ranging from elements that do not exist upon the earth at all, and which worldly physicists are just now beginning to unravel! Other eccentric elements we studied totally completed the series of lanthanides (rare-earth elements), the actinides (radioactive elements), and the superactinides (radioactive elements above the atomic number 103 in the Periodic Table)!

Totally awesome! I pondered.

We thanked Einstein for his grand experiments and insight—

Then Transurania was called to another mission … and so introduce yet another Spirit—

The Biologia Vita Misterioso

The Divine Spirit, Genetica, and I now entered a large chamber where thousands of Supernalites experimented in still other glorious biogenesis laboratories, resolved to solving all the riddles of the creation of terraformation of organic life on foreign planets. Here in the *Biologia Vita Misterioso,* resided grand pathophysiologic, embryologic, genomic, oncologic, biochemical, electrochemical, bioenergetic, cytogenetic, epigenetic and cryogenic laboratories — unraveling the secrets of all life, from the miracle of chlorophyll and genetics in plant replication, to the secrets of animal meiosis and mitosis.

They were solving the age-old riddle of why Nature (God) created the molecular building blocks of life, the amino acids, in a *left handed* configuration, known as *chirality.* Geneticists of today's advanced technology can only create *right handed* amino acids, and are therefore baffled at creating life in the laboratory.

Yet others were studying and analyzing the secrets of protein synthesis, genetic cloning and sequencing techniques, hybridization, electrophoresis, even cloning blood factors to cure hemophilia, genetically engineering antibodies and vaccines for treatments against all types of viruses and cancers.

Genetica revealed new techniques in synthetic biology, metagenomic sequencing, and cryosurgery ... discovering thousands of various pharmaceutical medicines to help in the cure of hundreds of deadly diseases which now plague humankind.

With our great minds hungry for knowledge, we delved even further into the secrets of protoplasm, its mitochondria, ribosomes, chromosomes and genes, and into the very mysteries of the nucleic acids of DNA. We further studied the retroviruses, breast cancer; sickle-cell anemia; cystic fibrosis; Alzheimer's disease; achondroplasia (dwarfism, caused by the mutation of an ovum or a sperm); progeria (abnormally fast aging); Down syndrome, muscular dystrophy, along with hundreds of other genetic diseases, including HIV

(Human Immunodeficiency Virus); and AIDS (Acquired Immune Deficiency Syndrome)!

I was totally enraptured as I was given a lab apron, goggles and gloves, and was initiated to partake in the unraveling of nature's very mysteries and secrets kept hidden from mortal man from the beginning of time—*until now.*

Genetica stated that she must be leaving. Another divine Spirit will now continue guiding me—

CHAPTER SEVEN

I was introduced to the Divine Spirit, Victoria. She revealed in the upper "sphere" of our Celestial City two massive canopies or twin domes, consisting of clear impregnable crystal spanning high over the very center of the *Paradisia*. The first one was the *Grande Observatorium* where resided a wonderful mechanical orrery revealing all the galaxies—where the secrets of astronomy were taught. There were also all sorts of telescopes, refracting and reflecting, X-ray and radio telescopes, solar, infrared, ultraviolet and gamma ray ... and exotics such as the anti-matter and multi-dimensional scopes ... along with numerous others yet to be invented upon the earth.

The other dome, the *Grande Consistorium*, consisted of an integration of the *Acta Santorium* and the *Sactum Santorium*.

Victoria now revealed the utmost divine sanctuary of the Elohim. This ineffable wonder consisted of an interlocking antechamber having expanding concentric rings leading to the predominant Sactum Santorium. This Sactum revolved around a divine inimitable nucleus—the Holy of Holies.

Within the *Grande Consistorium* resided the most eminent Honorarium and the Cognoscente of all time.

THE SACRARIUM del a ROTUNDA

The Honorarium and the Cognoscente
(Rev. 4:11; 21:4)

Victoria and I moved to the very exact center of this Rotunda. Here dwelled the *Sactum Santorum*, or the Holy of Holies. Here grew the Tree of Life. It kindled a scintillating flame as the burning bush of Moses, the *Veni Sancte Spiritus* sounding as a rushing mighty wind. The Great White Throne was surrounded by twenty-four elders in white garments having golden crowns upon their heads, each holding a golden harp and golden bowls full of the prayers of the saints. Then I saw four living creatures, too strange indeed for mortal eyes—and too eccentric to describe, shouting "Holy, Holy, Holy, Lord God Almighty, who was, and is, and is to come."

Here resided the very Son of Man, the Sacrificial Lamb. Upon Jesus, a golden crown represented his complete authority. Now holding the *Book of Life* he was interpreting the prayers of the faithful to all present. He was teaching "the Honorable Saints" the *Divine Wisdom* and *Divine Power* of the universe, along with the *new language* of the Divine. A language I will soon learn spoken by the very angels!

There were people present from every continent standing before the throne and before the Lamb. They all wore white robes and had palm branches in their hands. They all cried with a loud voice, saying, "Salvation to our God which sitteth upon the throne, and unto the Lamb." And all the angels stood round about the throne and about the elders and the four creatures who fell before the throne on their faces worshiping God, saying, "Thou art worthy, O Lord to receive glory and honor and power; for thou hast created all things, and for thy pleasure they are and were created."

Victoria revealed that the white robes were presented to those redeemed that remained faithful and had come out of the Great Tribulation and washed their robes in the blood of the Lamb. These faithful are now before the throne of God, serving him day and night. These were the Illuminati and Cognoscente, those *chosen* to be the honored messengers and emissaries of God.

These great cherubim lowered their fiery swords beckoning me toward the Tree of Life. As I neared it, searching for its precious once forbidden fruit, I saw one like the Son of man, clothed with a white garment down to his foot, girded about with a golden girdle. His head and his hair were white like wool, as white as snow; and his eyes were like a flame of fire, his feet like fine brass as if they burned in a furnace; and his voice like the sound of many waters, and out of his mouth went a sharp two-edged sword … and his countenance did shine as the sun. Glory!

From out of the flashes of lightning and peals of thunder I witnessed the presence of the very Lamb of God, the Messiah, the Alpha and the Omega, Emmanuel, the very Prince of Peace and the Prince of Life. He had a book sealed with seven seals and was holding the keys to Hell and of Death.

CHAPTER EIGHT

The Grande Consistorium
around the Throne of God

*V*ictoria was given the honor of revealing all those great saints, blessed for all eternity, that promugulated the Word of God to better humanity.

I witnessed many concentric circles of the Illuminati all of which revolved around the Grand Throne of God.

The circle nearest the Throne was composed of the twenty-four Elders. Also resided here were the Angelic Divine Counselors. These all wore orphreys interwoven with liturgical symbols representing their fields of endeavor and interests.

The next circles were composed of the magnanimous souls of the *Santi Belli*. They were the sanctified women,

Tom Knight

those elite honored saints. Here presided the spiritually enlightened women, all radiating the nimbus of the Divine.

They were dressed in radiant apparel representing their spiritual rewards and the work in which they were involved, symbolizing their esoteric knowledge.

Notably the women were FIRST in the Kingdom of God! After being once considered as slaves, controlled by men, persecuted by society as being inferior, and told to keep silent in the church, I now realized that we are *all* considered by God to *be on equal standing,* "... there is neither male or female; for ye are all one in Christ Jesus."

From my viewpoint I spotted Rachel and Leah, Rebekah, Esther; Jesus' Mother, Mary; Martha, and Mary Magdalene… Joan of Arc (heroine of France); Lottie Moon (missionary to China); Mary Slessor (missionary to Africa); Amy Carmichael (missionary to India); and Edith Cavell (English nurse, martyred during WW I by a German firing squad for the cause of liberty); Florence Nightingale; Sarah Pierrepoint (Jonathan Edward's wife); Madame Guyon ... and Princess Diana of England, conversing with Mother Teresa of Calcutta, India—as they did in their worldly life!

Mother Teresa, if you remember was that Catholic nun of the *Missionaries of Charity,* who worked untiringly with the "poorest of the poor" in the slums of Kolkata (Calcutta), India. She won the Nobel Peace Prize in 1979 against "crimes of poverty." In her depressed worldly state, she candidly confessed, "There is so much contradiction in my soul. Such deep longing for God, so deep that it is painful, a suffering continual, and yet not wanted by God, repulsed, empty, no faith, no love, no zeal ... Souls hold no attraction. Heaven means nothing, to me it looks like an

464

empty place. The thought of it means nothing to me and yet this torturing longing for God. Pray for me please that I keep smiling at him in spite of everything."

Here she was ... in Heaven, forfeiting her blue-trimmed white saris for an honored gown of liquid silver and gold ... forgiven for her lack of faith, her "dark night of the soul," an unsettling and contentious period of spiritual doubt, despair and loneliness that many of the great disparaged mystics experience.

We saw millions of other unsung women heroines, those who kept the faith and taught their children the great precepts of the Bible. Many here were the Christian women who were battered and abused wives upon the earth, and now exalted and honored for all eternity.

The middle circles embodied many of the the patriarchs, devout men who kept the faith when all odds were against them. From my vantage point I could see Abraham, Moses, Lot, Israel, Joshua, Benjamin, Shadrach, Meshack and Abednego, David, along with some of God's chosen prophets.

We located all of Jesus' beloved disciples: Andrew (the fisherman), Bartholomew (Nathanael), James (son of Alphaeus), James (son of Zebedee), John (the Apostle), Matthew (the Tax Collector), Philip (the Healer), Simon Peter (the Evangelist), Simon (the Canaanite), Thaddaeus, and Thomas (the Doubter). I also realized that Judas Iscariot (Christ's betrayer) was *not* present.

Also here was Christ's apostle, Paul of Tarsus, founder of the first Christian churches across Asia and writer of most of the New Testament! Here also were all the martyrs for the cause of Christ. I recognized John Baptist de La Salle (father of modern education), John Wycliffe; Miles Coverdale; James Moffatt; and thousands of others too numerous to mention.

The outer circles contained many Christian ministers such as St. Augustine (*Confessions*); St. Thomas Aquinas (*Summa Theologica*); Thomas A. Kempis (*The Imitation of Christ*); Quintus Tertullian (*Apologeticus*); John Calvin (*Institutes of the Christian Religion*); Martin Luther (*On Christian Liberty*); William Tyndale (translator of the Kings James Version of the Bible); John Knox (*Book of Discipline*); John Bunyan (*Pilgrim's Progress*); Jonathan Edwards (*Sinners in the Hands of an Angry God*); Charles Haddon Spurgeon (*Sword and Trowel*); Matthew Henry (*Matthew Henry's Commentary*); with hundreds of others—such as Hudson Taylor (Christian missionary to China); William Carey (the father of modern missions); William Booth (founder of the Salvation Army); Oswald Chambers (*My Utmost for His Highest*); A.W. Tozer (*The Pursuit of God*); John Tauler of Strassburg; Jacob Behmen; Samuel Rutherford; Brother Lawrence (Nicholas Herman); James Fraser of Brea; David Brainerd; John Fletcher of Madeley; William Wilberforce; Robert M. McCheyne; John Laycock; John Dickie of Irvine; William Ashley (Billy) Sunday; Dwight Lyman Moody; John Wesley; Henry Martyn; John Huss; Jim Elliot; George Whitefield; Charles Finney; David Livingstone; Cyrus Ingersoll (C.I.) Scofield; and Billy Graham, the great modern evangelist ... naming only a very few among thousands of other anointed ministers.

The outermost circles, as for as the eye can see, were composed of the greatest ancient and modern thinkers of renown. Now for the first time different scientists from different time periods could actually communicate with each other and discuss their discoveries! Here were many of the great geniuses of science and gifted inventors.

I met honorables such as Euclid, Paracelsus, Archimedes, Claudius Ptolemy, Nicolas Copernicus, Robert Hooke, Isaac Newton, Antoine Lavoisier, Thomas Edison, Joseph Priestley, Sir Humphry Davy, Michael Faraday—

In the last and largest circle resided the great statesmen and legislators, from honest judges to great presidents representing every period of time throughout history. Here were the honorable Christians—just and honest rulers, viceroys and knights, which ruled the world in the past, along with many royal sovereigns, honest kings and fair queens representing many countries and nations. Here also resided many great physicians, poets, philosophers and writers. In this row I visited Albert Schweitzer, author of *The Philosophy of Civilization* and *The Quest of Historical Jesus*.

All these aforementioned people were all communicating and understanding each other perfectly in that angelic language which God had perfected in the Garden of Eden before the fall from grace by Adam and Eve. I noticed one fine gentleman in this circle and I could have sworn it was that famous learned man of the letters, William Shakespeare of Avon!

In all these outer circles were the many unsung heroes, the unknown and dishonored, those selfless martyrs lost to posterity, but nevertheless *chosen of God*. Those forgotten people who "kept the faith," those who were good parents, and those who diligently went about their jobs, tasks and duties, doing what was right, suffered and were persecuted because of it.

My Honored Grandmother

I noticed an honored Supernalite who rose up and took on the countenance of my Grandmother! Goodness, with little formal schooling, what was she doing here in the midst of these sages and great thinkers. As I listened, I realized they were in a deep dissertation, and *she* was leading the conversation, waxed in deep divine wisdom and knowledge so profound, that many of *them* were stunned to silence!

She solved how China's bird flu jumps from chickens to humans and how swine flu jumps from pigs to humans. She also solved the enigma of how HIV traveled from monkeys to humans! She has recently developed a vaccine against Shingles, a painful nerve and skin infection caused by the herpes virus and is developing vaccine against many dangerous flu viruses.

Grandmother also was experimenting with the banana genome and genetically sequencing chocolate (cocoa) to withstand diseases and cooler weather. She is also developing the new process of lab-grown in vitro meat. This "clean meat" will be processed *without* the need of slaughterhouses. Chicken and duck meat can be grown in vitro, *without* the need of actually killing cattle or poultry.

She is also developing synthetic shrimp—which are shell free! And there is no need to peal them or disembowel them either! They are actually being created containing no animal protein, but made only from algae!

Victoria now presented her Divine Reward and she received a standing ovation in her honor.

Now my Dad, Hugo L. Thayer, was honored next. He had solved the problems of the electric, hydrogen and solar cars. He also perfected the thermionic sodium heat engine which has no moving parts and converts heat directly into electricity!

Then, little Beth, my daughter who died of SIDS, now mature and grown, was now honored. She stood and proclaimed that she had found the cure of Sudden Infant Death Syndrome (SIDS)! She also discovered a new cure for primary amebic meningoencephalitis (PAM) which is caused by a microscopic single-celled amoeba known as *Naegleria fowleri*. This insidious microscopic "blob," that eats the brain—is, with few exceptions, 100% fatal.

Beth was presented her Divine Reward and was honored as an honored Illuminati. She now rejoiced in the grace and humbleness of her accomplishments.

My Apotheosis

After much duration studying in the biogenesis laboratories, *my* apotheosis or coronation commenced. Victoria led me once again into the Grande Consistorium.

I had just finished the Human Microbiome Project involved in sequencing the DNA of all the beneficial and pathogenic microbes found inside the human body.

I was now ready to bestow this knowledge to the

scientists of the earth! This genome project led me directly to solving the enigma of mental retardation, schizophrenia ... and Alzheimer's disease! Then I solved the riddle of the intelligence quotient (IQ) making cognitive perception and intelligence more predominant in one mind than another.

Then Jesus Christ, in all his radiant glory, honor and majesty, left the very throne of God, came over and congratulated me! Jesus wrapped his great holy arm around my shoulder as tears of wonder filled my eyes with mirth and joy. Then as I gazed upward into Jesus' face, he wiped those great tears away! Completely incomprehensible to mortal mind! Then I thought of that Bible verse ... "And God shall wipe away all tears from their eyes..."

As I trembled to my knees, then prostrated myself to the floor in remission and total humility, he reached out with his right hand, that very nail-scarred hand, and placed his hand in mine! Ah, the joy of that moment—equal to nothing I had ever experienced! The Spirit of the Messiah, united with my own spirit triggering a surge of Divine Kinetic Energy more powerful than a lightning bolt. An epiphany that cannot be related to mortal man!

At this moment I felt the effulgence of his holy kinetic energy—the Holy Spirit revitalizing my mind. It permeated through me, stimulating, enlightening, enhancing and purging my intellect! My mind increased as a nuclear fireball and expanded into numerous dimensions—of which the human race can only imagine!

Divine knowledge became cogent, appealing to my mind as the eyes have an affinity toward light.

Then ... at that instant ... I opened my new-born eyes and for the first time saw "his face like the appearance of lightning, his eyes like lamps of fire," the very ... FACE OF GOD. The grandeur of it all! The scintillating conflagrance of the most-high God, possessor of heaven and earth, and his glorious powerful-all-consuming thermoluminescence permeated my total consciousness. I was catapulted at light-speed through endless kaleidoscopic shards of space-time continuum.

(I realized that no mortal could have gazed upon this pure and Holy Divine Kinetic Energy, the Primum Mobile, the Vini Creator Spiritus, those pure vital forces of the universe—and live!)

For these accomplishments Victoria now honored me as one of the Elite Chosen to be henceforth blessed for all eternity! As a savant of the heavenly, *I had acquired that Divine Spark of ne plus ultra of perfect enlightenment.* I had for an instant become totally infused with cognitive powers beyond imagination, and divine genius beyond my wildest dreams. *I HAD NOW BECOME ONE OF THE FAITHFUL ILLUMINATI.*

Other Supernalites Honored

Faith, now taking the floor, related how she had just discovered a cure for breast and colon cancers. She also discovered a vaccine against the human papillomaviruses (HPV), a sexually transmitted disease, the most common sexually transmitted disease (STD) in the U.S. This virus causes genital warts and increases cervical cancer risk. (Faith was my precious wife in the corporeal existence I once knew).

Next to Beth sat Rachael, my old college sweetheart, who had just perfected better influenza, malaria, AIDS and Zika vaccines. She also discovered artificial (synthetic) blood (developed from perfluorocarbons) to be used in humans. I learned that artificial blood has been used in keeping experimental mice, rats and dogs alive for years!

Yet many others were studying the mysteries of "de-extinction," using genetic transcription, gene splicing and gene sequencing to actually bring back extinct creatures. Exotic birds, such as the passenger pigeon, the dodo, the moa, the great auk could be brought back to life, along with some of the even larger creatures such as the zebra-like quagga, and eventually the giant woolly mammoth.

Will this esoteric biogenetic engineering technology eventually lead to the resurrection of the now extinct dinosaurs?

It was now revealed what discoveries *all* these thousands of honored Supernalites had made to further humankind! Absolutely awesome! *Soon many of these miraculous inventions and discoveries will be presented to the minds of the scientists and physicians of the world, many of them thinking that they alone solved the problems they were analyzing!*

This divine knowledge and answers to prayers of the faithful will all be sent down to the Earth. The faithful mortals upon the Earth will now receive this *divine intuitive knowledge.* They will believe that these ideas coming to them are only their own original ideas, or their unique insight, or from their intuition, or solely from their subconscious mind. *They will believe that their great ideas just popped into their consciousness—not realizing that these ideas literally came from the heavens! That it is these Watchers of God who actually helped them.*

This also reminded me of the prophets in the Holy Bible that had attained divine insight, but those around them did not believe them either.

Now Victoria revealed another phenomenon. She explained that we can't see all those calamities that did *NOT* occur while we were upon the earth—those dire circumstances that run into the trillions *that never happened.* We only knew of those that *actually happened,* not those *prevented* by the Guardian Angels and the Angelic Divine Counselors. Those calamities that *did* actually come to pass—their pain and severity were lessened by these divine and holy Eudemon.

Victoria stated that another Divine Spirit will reveal yet more wonders. With this Victoria just disappeared—

CHAPTER NINE

The Conundrum of Sports in Heaven

The Spirit, Angelena, stated that we were to solve another paradox in the Heavenly realm. I wondered if there will be sporting events in Heaven?

"Playing sports in Heaven," Angelena spoke, "is a *physical impossibility*. Why is this? Well, there are no losers in Heaven. Everyone is a winner. Everyone is victorious. Therefore, if two teams or people are pitied against each other, how could both win?

"So if both teams will *win*, how can they play each other? Sports are combative, or a struggle. In Heaven, the saints (all born-again believers) have a divine spirit and are by divine nature, non-combative and *united in divine love and are one in Christ*. In the physical universe, each team or participant's carnal nature trys to prove that they are better than each other, a gross type of arrogance and vanity. Since we as saved believers are all perfect, all are possessed with *perfect spiritual talents*, so competition is therefore of no consequence in Eternity. (One person thinking they are better than another person is the reason for strife and rivalry ... and, many times, why wars are fought).

"For instance, if a person plays pool. The first person that starts the game will be the winner for they will sink all the balls and thus win the game. Football, soccer, tennis, baseball, golf, etc. if each team is *perfect*, there will not be any errors. Each offensive football scrimmage will be a winning play. Or each defense team would totally protect their goal against aggression. The same for tennis. There would be no wild balls, all would be hit over the net, all would be returned correctly. In soccer, how could you hit the ball into the goal and have the other team perfectly defend the goal? In bowling, everyone will get a strike the first time a*nd every time* you threw the ball. In golf, everybody will get a hole-in-one. In baseball, everyone will hit a home run, or the outfielder would always catch the fly ball, the ground ball would always be caught in time and thrown to first base for the out! The simple game of Tic Tac Toe will always result in a draw. In the game of chess, all playing will result in a stale mate.

"Think of all the disappointments and low esteem sports has caused the masses of humanity throughout all the years of 'agony and defeat.' Again, there are no losers in Heaven!

"Iben, don't you think enough time and energy and money has been wasted trying to augment the athlete's pride and arrogance? Neither do we need sports to promote scholarships, for in Eternity we have no colleges or universities as mortals conceive them.

"Nor do we have any stadiums or gyms costing millions of dollars, no wasted time practicing in meaningless competition against each other trying to prove someone is better than another person, whether for fame, honor, or egoism. Sports breed bullying and pugnacity. And look at all the performance-enhancing drugs athletes are now using. It's plain 'ol drug abuse. Some athletes use steroids and excessive amounts of testosterone, even Strychnine—rat poison to enhance their muscles! Yes, athletes will sell their souls for fame and fortune.

"At death, the born-again believer (as already seen) is imbued with divine wisdom and divine knowledge way beyond all the colleges and universities our physical world can offer."

"How about horse racing or dog racing?"

"The horses or dogs," Angelena answered, "are all *equal in abilities*. They will not have to be trained to satisfy the whims of humanity.

"Hunting and fishing sports are also a physical impossibility in Eternity. These sports harm and kill animals and fish. *In Heaven there is no death, so how could these things be?*

"Those that love the sport of shooting the bow and arrow and their pistols and rifles for target practice upon the earth, would have found it boring in Eternity, for they would hit their targets dead center—every time. They will be happy to forfeit yet another fruitless act of competiion for other more important *spiritual activities*. In Eternity we will have no arms or weapons—only the special weapons of God will be used against the evils of Satan.

"Gambling and playing card games as contract or duplicate bridge will also be impossible. For how can all the players be dealt the perfect hand? *The fact is that we will have all we need, and all our wants will be doing the will of God.*

Material things will not be needed or required and there will be no pride to be a winner—*for we will be in a new spiritual realm of love and peace.* Our new empyrean existence will be *beyond* desiring fame and money—and the *glory of the win* will be nothing more than a faint memory.

"The lottery will also be an impossibility. Winners in this game win all the loser's money. Since there will not be any *losers* in Heaven, this also cannot be."

"What about the violence of football?" I asked.

"Football can cause damage and injury to the athlete. Football is exceptionally brutal because it can cause *Chronic Traumatic Encephalopathy* in the brain."

"What about boxing or karate?"

"They can also cause brain damage, and cause physical harm, though they are mostly used for defense, which is, of course, totally obsolete here.

"The same goes for bull-fighting and rodeos. Both the athletes, matador and the animals can be hurt or killed. So why should such sports exist in Paradise?"

"Yes, I understand that many people's lives are caught up in either playing or watching these sporting events. *Being mesmerized by your favorite players is known as hero worship, a type of idolatry, and is forbidden by God. People's minds will have to be reprogrammed to set aside mundane and worldly things and learn to see the grander plan God has for each of us in Eternity. Worldly ways and worldly thinking will be forfeited and replaced by spiritual and divine worthwhile purposes with awesome divine spiritual gifts.*"

"How about the Olympics? Don't they promote *unity in spirit?*"

"The problem with the Olympic games, Iben, is that they

promote themselves, their self-interests and *the country they are from.* Pride of Country is usually not a problem—but this "patriotism" makes one country think that they are better than the others, even if it's only in sport competition. All these countries are of different races, nationalities, religions, ideologies, and of many various languages (no unity here). This positive attitude for country does lead, many times, to war. (Look at Germany and Japan in World War II, and the *cultural wars* we are now having between foreign countries ... and their influence (and terrorism) against the United States. Also, all Christians and all people need to be promoting *world unity and peace*, not trying to just win the "gold" or "silver" or "bronze" metals for their *own* particular country. *This is somewhat beyond the secular thinking of most people, but we need to get hold of this principle or our world will be lost.*

"This is why it is so hard for the average person to comprehend the divine or spiritual existence because they are so caught up in this mundane world with secular thoughts."

More Disasters

"I must now comfort those victims of two commuter trains which will collide in Mozambique, killing 196; in Savar, Bangladesh, in a high rise building, the world's worst garment-industry fire will kill 1,127 people; in Yingxiu, China, an earthquake will kill over 80,000 people; and an earthquake will decimate L'Aquila, Italy, killing more than 150 people, and California will soon be hit by massive forest fires, mud slides, and another major earthquake.

"In Madrid, bombings by al-Qaida will blow apart four

commuter trains, killing 192 people (the worst terrorist attack in Spanish history); a deadly terrorist attack on India's commuter trains will kill over 200 people and wound more than 600.

"There soon will be another horrific event in Belsan, Russia, located in the Caucasus Mountains. Terrorists will blow up School Number One, killing 344, including 170 children.

"And in Southerland Springs, Texas, a church massacre will kill 26 people. It will be the deadliest shooting in Texas history."

As Angelena faded away, she introduced another Spirit—

"Heaven goes by favor. If it went by merit,
you would stay out and your dog would go in."
—Mark Twain

Pets in Heaven

(Isa. 11:7-8; Rev. 21:4)

Felicity, was now to be my divine guide to other uncharted dimensions of the Celestial City. I was introduced to all my pets I enjoyed in my childhood. How they survived death, I understood not, for I was taught that only human beings contained "souls." I learned that all life, even fauna and flora contained that vital bioplasmic energy, which survives death. Logically, after all, *animals and plants have no sin and cannot sin, so why should they perish at death?* And wouldn't Heaven be a drab place if it were as bare as the deserts or lifeless as the moon?

Now my little female domestic white pet duck my Uncle Iben had won at the County Fair, Wibble Wobble strutted forth … quacking, perky as ever, happy to see me as I was to see her, gently nibbling my cheek as I grabbed her up in my arms in sheer ecstasy! Then her mate with a little brood of ducklings rushed up to greet me!

Smokey, my little black dog, jumped upon me next … what a feisty little creature he was, licking my face and wagging his tail in happiness! Then my childhood rabbits, Liberace and Fuzzy, both hopped forth. Then my little pet parakeet "Sparkie" flew toward me. I held out my hand and she lit on my finger chirping her happiness at our re-acquaintance! Even my little pet hamsters ran up to me, encircling my feet and my pet turtles in the old life now ambled toward me and let me rub their heads! *They all survived death.* What a reunion those sweet little pets and I had!

"As boys shoot sparrows for sport,
the sparrows do not die in sport, but in earnest."
—Unknown

Even the little innocent birds I had killed with a BB gun flew down to greet me, forgiving me of taking a life—that of a sparrow, who, with many other creatures, are all ordained to be blessed, to enjoy life and be happy.

Mosquitoes, ticks, mites and chiggers, I learned, also survived death (for they sinned not, but were cursed by God in the fall of Adam and Eve to suck blood). They were *changed* by God into *new creatures* which didn't need the blood of animals to survive. The exceptions, which were uncreated by God, were the *viruses*. The viruses and all forms of cancer, all of which cannibalized cells for survival, perished into complete oblivion. The bees, wasps, ants, spiders, scorpions and snakes and all other harmful creatures that prey on others were changed into benign creatures that didn't have stings nor fangs to harm other creatures.

There is no death in the Celestial City, so this presents another mystery of how all these creatures (including humans) no longer need to kill to feed themselves, for all born-again creatures got their total sustenance from Divine Kinetic Bioplasmic Energy. Such are the mysteries in the Afterlife!

With this, Felicity, stating that she must be leaving, vaporized as the morning dew—

CHAPTER TEN

The Celestial Voyage Commences

*W*e are now preparing for our embarkation into the Great Unknown. Our great Celestial City was resting in a wheat field when it levitated silently and steadily up into the heavens creating mysterious energy vortices, known as crop circles. These wondrous concentric rings of all sizes and shapes will charm, beguile, and confuse scientists and ufologists for years trying to discover their origin! Did we place hidden meanings and messages in them? And if they are even deciphered, will prophecy be fulfilled—

We are now departing Earth because it is wearing out. We have been upon it for many years exploring all its wonders and seeing how pollution has played havoc upon her ecology.

Another wonderful and magnificent Celestial City Ship now appeared. The *Shekinah Glory*—will stay behind gathering all the souls upon the earth destined to die after we leave. Our Celestial City was plethora with billions of glorified saints sealed within the Kingdom of God full of divine love, pure in mercy and grace, atoned by Jesus Christ. Also those that have rejected Christ's salvation such as the unrepented and the unforgiven—were here also, but now sealed within her Prison of Gehenna.

Another Angelic Divine Counselor appeared—

"Iben, my name is Aurora. I will now be your guide to further explore the vast wonders that await us. *Our great Divine Destiny has arrived!*"

In an instant we split through the clouds entering the edge of space looking back at a magnificent blue oval—our Earth. We encountered the solar wind, an ionized electrical plasma known as the Van Allen Belt.

Pollution of the Earth

Mt. 24:3, 7; Mk. 13:8; and Lk. 21:11

"This plasma," Aurora continued, "actually protects our Earth from the sun's intense radiation. This is the reason a comet's tail always points *away* from the sun. The solar wind deflects it! The Van Allen Belt acts as a buffer, trailing behind the Earth for forty thousand miles!"

We explored the ozone layer, which protects the earth from deadly ultraviolet radiation. We learned that chlorofluorocarbons (CFCs), hydrofluorocarbons (HFCs), nitrogen oxides and methane are major sources of this pollution. But down closer to the Earth ozone can be harmful acting as a noxious pollutant found in smog, damaging the lungs and destroying plants. This thinning of the ozone layer can cause skin cancer in humans and cataracts in the eyes! Alarmingly it can also damage the chlorophyll in the leaves of plants.

"Why could this be serious, Iben?"

"Let me think a moment. … Humans depend on plants for their nourishment. For without plants, the animal population and humans would all die! And if our oceans warmed up, the polar ice caps would melt, causing the rising of the sea."

"Your perception has served you well, Iben."

"Also," Aurora continued, "the beautiful Monarch butterfly maybe on its way to extinction. This tenacious insect actually flies from Canada clear across the United States into Mexico upon a journey of 3,000 miles. But deforestation, drought, climate change, and avocado orchards are crowding out the Monarch roosting areas. The weed killer *glyphosate* (trade name "Roundup") along with 2, 4 D herbicide are also destroying the milkweed. These plants are the *only* food source for the Monarch larvae. To further harm the Monarch, some species of milkweed contain a mysterious protozoan known as *ophryocystis elektroscirrha*. This parasite retards the development of the pupa thus weakening the mature butterfly to fly south."

"So pollution is rampant throughout the world, huh, Aurora?"

The Greenhouse Effect

"This takes us to the so-called *Greenhouse Effect,* where global warming is produced by an excessive amount of carbon dioxide from burning fossil fuels such as coal and oil. The greenhouse effect will destroy the world as we know it—*and it is happening NOW!*

"These gases are causing the Great Lakes to warm up leading to massive die-offs of the baby bottlenose dolphins and extinction of the polar bears."

Antarctica, I learned, is warming up causing the acidification of the oceans and the melting of her ice caps. Cold water absorbs more carbon dioxide which, in turn, melts the ice. This melting places the plankton (protozoa) in peril, along with animals that feed on it, as do the many penguins and Arctic sea birds. This plankton is even the basic food for the huge whales and seals.

All around the world, I learned, that mountains are losing their glaciers. Glacier National Park in Montana, Mt. Kilimanjaro, Africa's highest peak, Cotopaxi, Ecuador, Greenland, including those in Switzerland, are all losing their snow. In a few decades global warming will raise the level of our oceans, submerging New York City, the Netherlands and even the coastline of California.

"If global warming continues," Aurora confirmed, "by the end of this century—we will see the quickest shift in climate change since the last ice age some 10,000 years ago!"

As Venice has succumbed to the rising ocean, now Bangkok, Thailand, is one of 13 major cities worldwide in peril of rising water! Also, it should be noted that as the oceans of the world grow warmer, their water expands, needing more volume. This phenomenon of *thermal expansion* creates even more flooding and endangerment to our coastal cities.

This greenhouse effect, I learned, also makes it possible

for beetles, such as the Asian longhorned beetle, the elm bark beetle, and the emerald ash borer, all foreign species, to kill trees otherwise immune to them. The winters are not cold enough to kill off these insects, so they destroy millions of trees each year across the United States. These dead trees become the fuel which leads to great conflagrations as happens every year in the western United States.

Even one gasoline driven car can spew close to 20 pounds of carbon dioxide into our atmosphere *each year*, polluting our atmosphere.

China, the United States, and the European Union have all increased their carbon dioxide emissions. The cause? The use of coal is the biggest carbon emitter—and it is rising because of cars and airplanes using carbon-based fuels.

Methane, soot, and refrigerants also absorb much of the heat in our atmosphere increasing this greenhouse effect. We must also remember, Iben, that a person can live five weeks without food, five days without water, and only *five minutes* without air.

I now realized that we are at the very brink of doomsday—the end of human civilization. It should be noted, that at least one of every eight plant species in the world—and nearly one out of three in the United States is under threat of extinction! It has been predicted that there are more than 16,000 animal and plant species in peril, including the hippopotamus, the polar bear, and the desert gazelle. A quarter of the world's mammals, one in eight bird species, and a fifth of the sharks and rays are in trouble of extinction.

I also remembered that Christ foretold a period of increasing famines, pestilence, drought, floods, and other natural disasters. He revealed a grim specter indeed, from world famine, to great conflagrations and war of which the Earth has never seen.

I now realized that the LORD gave us stewardship over his creation and we, as the human race, have abjectly failed at this responsibility.

Yes, mankind has implemented the greenhouse effect, deforestation, global warming, over fishing and the extinction of countless species. *We are still in grave danger from deadly radioactivity from nuclear testing and human activity has grown so intense and evil… that it may soon lead to total annihilation and ultimate extinction.*

"I will show wonders in heaven above,
and signs in the earth beneath: blood,
and fire, and vapor of smoke.
The sun shall be turned into darkness,
and the moon into blood,
before that great and notable day of the Lord come; …"
—Acts 2:19-20 (Mt. 3:12)

"This is known, Iben, as the Great Tribulation," Aurora continued. "Pollution, plagues and earthquakes are all fearful signs linked to the 'Second Coming,' and other great wonders in store for the inhabitants of Earth."

Now we were far above the Earth observing it from our *Grande Observatorium*. We saw a lonely tiny blue and white marble, our dear Earth, already thousands of miles away, swimming in the sparking black ocean of space. I now realized that I was looking back at the only home I had ever known. My origin, my old friend, planet Earth! I sensed a realization that this might be the last time I would ever see her, my beloved planet. All I am and all I have known has originated from this tiny speck of cosmic dust drifting around a modest star in the unfathomable void of an endless and incommensurable universe!

Earth's civilization has increased in violence, selfishness and greed, spanning ethnic hatreds and wars as we have already seen. Could there be devised a better system, or better yet, some *universal tenet* to replace the antiquated, out-dated thinking mortals have placed upon their society?

Aurora taught me—

The Creed of Humanity

**THE INHABITANTS OF THE EARTH
NEED ONE DIVINE GOAL:
TO DEVELOPE THEIR TALENT AND PASSION,
TO LIVE LIFE TO THEIR FULL POTENTIAL,
AND TO KNOW THAT EACH PERSON
IS TOTALLY UNIQUE, CREATED
IN THE IMAGE OF GOD
TO BE REUNITED SOMEDAY INTO
GOD'S HOLY FAMILY—
OR BE CONDEMNED TO PERDITION
FOR ALL ETERNITY.**

**THE DIVINE MISSION OF HUMANITY:
TO ENCOURAGE SELF WORTH,
TO PROMOTE RESPECT, TO BE
ACCEPTED BY OTHERS,**

**AND TO BE CHERISHED AS
FELLOW HUMAN BEINGS.
NO PERSON SHOULD BE
RIDICULED OR HARASSED,
BUT SHOULD BE TRULY LOVED.
EACH PERSON SHOULD LIVE WITH DIGNITY —
AND DIE WITH HONOR.**

I learned that this *Divine Principle* is what is needed upon the Earth! Only by Jesus Christ's return will all this be fulfilled and accomplished!

I wish I could enlighten the Earth's people about what I have just witnessed! Would they believe me? They would probably say that this destruction of the oceans was still very far into the future, so let us eat, drink and be merry. Let posterity and our great grand-kids worry about the ol' Spaceship Earth. It should be acknowledged that pollution causes many types of cancer and over population already causes the death of hundreds of thousands of people throughout the world *each year.* Is this a precursor of the beginning of the end for humanity?

"Iben Jair," Aurora continued, "the Earth contains a *finite ecosystem* of limited resources. And yet almost a million children in Madagascar and Africa will die *each year* before they reach 3 years old of starvation and famine.

"Remember Pellucidar in the earth's interior? Here also was a limited ecosystem. Animals and plants had learned to limit their supply of food, making sure future generations all had enough resources to survive. But if they failed—remember the mass suicide of the theropod dinosaurs, and the Lemmings of Norway?"

"How about the uniqueness of our Earth?"

"Good question, Iben. The Earth is just at the right limit from the sun so that it does not boil all the oceans dry. So, is this uniqueness a fortuitous accident? Is our organic carbon life a mere freak oddity or remote gamble spawned by mindless matter?"

"We have cheated the question, Aurora, and have already seen the answer of how the Divine Being and Great Architect of the universe, God, created the heavens and the earth."

"By being made in the image of God," Aurora concluded, "at death we are no longer limited as mere physical and mortal beings. We are now ready to fulfill our ultimate destiny: to explore and to learn, to become *Masters of the Universe!*"

"But ye are a chosen generation, a royal
priesthood, an holy nation,
a peculiar people, that ye should show
forth the praises of him
who hath called you out of darkness
into his marvelous light;"
—1 Pet. 2:9

"When I consider thy heavens, the work of thy fingers,
the moon and the stars, which thou hast ordained,
What is man, that thou art mindful of him?"
—Ps. 8:3-4

We finally bid farewell to our Earth. We now were traveling toward our new destination—

Aurora slowly faded away as a thin whisp of smoke from a burned out candle. She now introduced yet another Angelic Divine Counselor—

CHAPTER ELEVEN

The Moon

"*I*ben, I am Celeste, and will be your guide throughout the solar system.

"Behold, the MOON! Another of God's great Wonders! God placed it around the Earth to stir her oceans. Without the moon, Iben, life on our planet would be a total impossibility, reducing it to a barren wasteland. Also, few people have thought of this … that the cycles of the moon regulate our calendar, and also the rhythm of the menstrual cycles of fertility, of conception and of birth of the human species, and that of millions of other creatures living upon and under Planet Earth."

The moon has not only inspired poets and dreamers, it has also kindled the imagination of many great writers and scientists. With her beautiful beguiling smile, always lighting up the Earth's darkest nights with her soft entrancing glow.

Now we were getting wonderfully close to the moon. We could see the goddess Luna in all her glory. Her face pockmarked from thousands of meteor strikes.

It would take, I learned, about 81 moons to equal the mass of the Earth. Its gravity is approximately one-sixth that of our home planet and it is about 250,000 miles from the Earth, creating the cycle of months and the measurement of time. The very word 'month' is derived from the name of the moon!

We hovered less than 10 miles above her surface. What a wonderful lost world God has created for us to explore!

Celeste confirmed that the moon is slowing down the Earth's days and it acts as a gravitational gyroscope to stabilize the 23-degree tilt of her axis. Without the moon, the Earth would tilt as much as 85 degrees off vertical. (Vertical is defined as perpendicular to the plane of Earth's orbit around the sun).

"A few degrees wouldn't matter anyway would it, Celeste?"

"Well Iben, a mere 1.3 degrees shift in the Earth's tilt—resulted in the ice ages!"

So God in his infinite wisdom placed the moon in orbit around our planet, because without it, life could not exist!

We orbited across numerous deep crevasses, vast plains and hovered silently over Mare Imbrium and the Oceanus Procellarum.

The crater Posidonius came into view, along with the impact craters Aristarchus and Copernicus, all created by fierce meteoroid explosions.

You should have heard these late astronauts, Cyrano de Bergerac, H.G. Wells, and Jules Verne, who created their exciting adventure stories about traveling to the moon, all conversing with each other!

How wonderfully strange to be able to understand all their science jargon and technical words and advanced mathematics!

"Look, Iben, we are nearing the South Pole-Aitken Basin, which is seven times deeper than the Grand Canyon, the deepest impact crater in the whole solar system!"

Celeste asked whether any of us wanted to explore the moon's surface. As my childhood playmates and I explored the creeks around our neighborhood, we were now translated to her beguiling craters!

Here we explored the terrain and some of the original landing marks of the pioneer Luna explorers of Apollo 11, 14, 15 and 16 missions.

We located an American flag still parading its glory upon her surface, along with some footprints of the Apollo 14 and Apollo 15 Missions. One astronaut, in total awe and reverence, as tears of incredulity overcame him, had stopped and touched one of his own footprints on Fra Mauro, pushed into the soft lunar dust back in 1971. He even found a couple of the golf balls he hit while upon the Apollo mission!

We then journeyed to the meandering, mile-wide gorge of Hadley Rille. We explored these massive mountain ranges and discovered what lies beneath the feet for future moon explorers? My excitement grew—

We left Hadley Base and moved south of the equator and studied Jules Verne Crater and the impact crater of Tycho. Then we continued on until we reached the Sea of Dreams.

Then, I learned, we were to explore a little known cave which originates from an extinct volcano. We will travel through its lava tube into the very center of the moon!

We traveled through this dried lava tunnel, and were overwhelmed with the wonder of it all! We encountered the moon's original crust of volcanic rocks discovering tiny crystals of feldspar, zircon and pyroxene. We also found tektites (formed from meteor impacts) scattered throughout various Luna caves.

I thought I should *not* tell you a little secret ... but Celeste stated that I could release this bit of information! It could stun the world! I hope it will kindle further study and voyages to the moon to prove its validity!

Still deep within one of those subterranean lava chambers we discovered nitrogen, ammonia and oxygen. Deep in these caves—did we locate some microscopic living extremophiles? Or some strange bacteria, known to exobiologists as *cryptoendoliths*? They can be found on the Earth in the most extreme places, like the deserts and mountain ranges of our world.

Then I experienced a strange vibration or trembling throughout this cavern. This *moonquake*, or seismic waves filtered their way through these subterranean tunnels causing a single long rumble through its rocks then faded into the dark distance beyond. After a short duration we located the moon's core and discovered small bits of glass, tiny glass balls called "spherules." A few were shaped like pears, dumbbells and even teardrops—very similar to those tektites we had mentioned earlier.

From the moon's strange depths, we traced our path back to her surface and made a very interesting discovery! Frozen water was found in both her northern and southern poles!

We were then teleported back to the *Paradisia*. Instantly,

we arrived once again in our Celestial City proclaiming the splendid wonders of the Almighty!

Celeste informed us that it was time to leave the moon, for even greater wonders now await us!"

With this, the *Paradisia* rose from the moon's orbit and headed for our next neighbor in space—

CHAPTER TWELVE

Venus

I must state something here. We traveled to Venus in how much time I cannot tell. This is because Earthlings are use to the days and nights caused by the Earth turning upon its axis. Without the Earth and moon spinning around each other how can we tell time? Why do we need time? For we were now in Eternity! We traveled to Venus almost instantly! Ah, Venus! What wonders await us! The Romans named her—Venus, the Light Bearer, after the goddess of love.

We entered massive thick, yellow clouds of carbon dioxide and sulfuric acid swirling in incandescent whirlwinds of a million miles per hour! The surface temperature of Venus is 900 degrees F. making it hot enough to melt lead! Her circumference is 23,600 miles. Venus turns from west to east, instead of east to west as the Earth!

Venus is 67 million miles away from our sun and orbits it every 225 Earth days.

Our hypervision penetrated through her dense clouds.

We entered strange, massive and bizarre volcanos and craters. "The Tick," a volcano, had a summit plateau 35 kilometers across with dark vicous lava flowing from its giant gaping caldera and lava overflowing her rim! As we neared we could see many other great ridges of massive craters, cracking and folding over each other!

We orbited over Sif Mons, Gula Mons and Maxwell Montes, her great volcanoes. We next passed Aurelia, a meteor impact crater, named to honor the mother of Julius Caesar, and the double-ringed impact crater of Cleopatra.

We explored the "Seven Pancakes of Alpha Regio," having volcanic domes some 18 miles in diameter and two miles high.

A cyclone was brewing and huge lightning bolts struck these massive domes, expelling nerve racking concussions exploding in our ears! Static lightning permeated through the angry clouds producing an eerie glow. The stench of sulfur was everywhere!

We noticed that Venus has "beauty marks" consisting of lakes filled with hot boiling red and white lava. The solar wind from our sun helped erode her oceans. The lack of water further contributed to a runaway greenhouse effect, resulting in an extremely hot volcanic planet that rains sulfuric acid.

I continued exploring a volcanic tunnel deep into the interior of Venus. I then noticed that I alone had ventured into this pit of hell and had trepidation that the others were already back on the *Paradisia*. I shouldn't have worried because many angels and watchers were following me, though I was not aware of them. As soon as I reached the surface of Venus once again, I found the rest of the exploration party, and all of us were once again teleported up. So guardian angels were everywhere, whether you or I can see them or not—protecting and directing our path without our even knowing it. *Even after death!* I still have much to learn!

All were accounted for and Celeste stated that we were now on our way to—

Mercury

We now traveled to the planet closest to our sun. We again arrived, it seemed, in only moments, though Venus and Mercury are millions of miles apart.

Mercury rotates on its axis one and half times, while it travels around the sun on its yearly orbit. She is only a little larger than Earth's moon and has a diameter of a little over three thousand miles. Her surface, as we can see from our orbit, is also scarred with great craters.

We passed over "Caloris Basin," 810 miles across!

We explored her thin atmosphere of helium and arrived at the ridge of the Caloris Basin. Mercury and all her mysterious craters were studied, and yes, we entered her caves and learned things that mere mortals only dream of.

Then we were teleported once again aboard our *Paradisia* and headed directly into the—

Our Sun

(Dan. 3:8-28; Jn. 10:10)

I thought that there was something wrong with our wonderful navigation system aboard our Celestial City!

How could we survive getting any closer to our Sun than a few million miles. Could our wonderful interdimensional *Paradisia* withstand the fires of— The heat alone was—

Yes, we, without a doubt, were heading straight for it! I learned that our Sun was a huge undulating, blazing sphere of fulminating gases, radiating light, heat and energy. Bubbling as a hot cauldron, tremendous heat and pressures deep within the Sun, fuse 654 million tons of hydrogen into helium *each second*—releasing 4 million tons of energy! Oddly, helium was discovered in the Sun before it was found upon the Earth! The Earth utilized only *one billionth* of the Sun's total radiant energy and gets enough sunlight in a few days to equal that of burning all the earth's forests, including her entire oil and coal reserves combined!

Thermonuclear fusion, the processes of the hydrogen bomb, is what powers the Sun. Its diameter is 864,000 miles, and could hold 3,300,000 Earths inside her! It contains no solid material, it being too hot, remaining a gaseous state of hot ionized plasma. The Sun rotates from east to west, and parts of it spin at different speeds, causing swirls and undulations throughout her surface—all the way to her core.

Great tongues of fire and prominences now explode thousands of miles from her surface—licking at our Celestial City causing it to vibrate under this heat and pressure. Frightening sounds of static electricity crackled all about as great electrical sparks danced upon our *Paradisia's* outer surfaces.

Then to my horror, I realized that we entered the photosphere, encountering a darker "sunspot," somewhat cooler than the surrounding surface. Huge convoluted plasmatic swirls engulfed us as we spiraled down through them. Here it seemed the Sun's bubbling and frothing super hot gases were determined to destroy us. This sunspot, I realized, was a twisting tornado which sucked us *down* into such pressures the human mind cannot comprehend, reaching a 100 billion atmospheres at 16,000,000 degrees C!

We actually penetrated into her chromosphere, then entered her corona, then dived down into her photosphere—thousands of miles deep. Here was the Sun's nuclear fusion zone—her very core! Here resided a strange world of hyperactive nuclear particles being torn apart by the great heat and intense pressures, distorting and splitting matter into forms never before imagined!

From such extreme pressure strange fire bubbled all around us. The apprehension I felt plunging deep into this fiery cauldron overwhelmed me. Plasma outbursts were everywhere.

I began to fear the worst—

Can such things be happening?

"Iben," Celeste spoke, "as you are aware, we are still in our state of *Interdimensional Transposition.* In this way we are traveling through the Sun without getting burned up in its scathing heat.

"Ye of little faith! You remind me of when Shadrach, Meshack, and Abednego were thrown into the fiery furnace and discovered a fourth person within this fire? The fourth person being like unto the Son of God? And the fires had no power over them, nor was a hair of their head singed, neither were their coats burned, nor even the smell of fire had passed over them!"

Our Sun, I learned, is a very ordinary star, actually a

yellow dwarf, between the hottest blue stars and the coolest red stars. Rigel, another star, which we will someday study, is 15,000 *times* more luminous, and 36 million of our Suns could fit into Antares, a red super-giant!

Imagine the pressure and heat given off from those suns!

Our Sun has been burning like this for over 5 billion years and has burned off about two thirds of its hydrogen, but still has about 2 billion years left before it will expand in a supernova, vaporizing all its little family of planets. Then it will become a burned-out cinder, shrinking down into a white dwarf or neutron star, about as big as Earth. It will then be very dense and will weigh several tons per cubic inch!

Our craft went to hyper-speed through the interior in a long horseshoe loop, which we rode through the superheated energized plasma. Spiraling through its spicules once again, we convoluted beyond the Sun's surface, exploding in a solar flare catapulting our Celestial City millions of miles into deep space. What a roller-coaster ride through the interior of the Sun! And yet, our Celestial City, our *Paradisia* survived … and the souls of God continued to live that abundant life the Lord has promised his believers!

Our great *Paradisia* was not even smoking when we were flung outward from her surface riding the crest of a solar prominence!

We were flung from the solar flare finding ourselves in the midst of a great geomagnetic storm that increased our velocity to the speed of a comet! Our *Paradisia* was boomeranged once again toward our home—our beloved Earth.

Celeste stated that she must be leaving—

CHAPTER THIRTEEN

The Great Tribulation, The Apocalypse & The Rapture

(1 Th. 4:13; Rev. 16)

*N*ow a great trumpet sounded in the Celestial City of God—an "alarm" of such magnitude God's angels, Empyrealites and Supernalites had never known!

Powerful and intense Eudemons came forward from the unexplored dimensions of the *Paradisia*.

The powerful Archangel Michael, Supreme Commander of the Heavenly Hosts, spoke:

"Saints of God, be *not* alarmed. We are *returning* to Planet Earth. We will now partake in the Grand Finale of Earth's turbulent end. The Great Tribulation is upon us!"

We orbited the Earth at a few thousand miles above its surface. Poor Earth … how I longed for her once again! I now observed the place of my birth—my only home I have ever known, that unique and lonely world in the black diamond studded sky. At this moment I strangely wondered how many days or months had I been away? Or had it actually been years?

Then, understanding these things as they unfolded, I saw thousands of saints from the House of Israel as they manned their awesome and powerful wands of destruction. Powerful Empyrealites, the great warriors of God's army appeared, along with the great and powerful Archangels of the end times. They were ready to war against the evil angels of Satan!

I stood in awe of what unraveled next. Those upon the Earth gazed upward to see the heavens glow as with the Star of Bethlehem—then splitting open as a great bolt of lightning—

Jesus Christ and his legions of mighty angels now descending over all the inhabitants of the Earth!

The miracle of the Rapture now commenced.

And the dead in Christ will rise first. Then we who are alive and remain shall be caught up together with them in the clouds to meet the Lord in the air. And thus we shall always be with the Lord.

The great scenario now unfolded. From the Throne of God … The Lion of the Tribe of Judah, the Root of David, The Lamb, Jesus Christ, upon the golden altar, now breaks open the seven-sealed scrolls … and releases the Seven Vials containing the Seven Plagues—

We witnessed those unfaithful now remaining upon the earth. They were cursed with hail mingled with blood and fire. Great earthquakes shook the earth. The sun became black as sackcloth, the moon became like blood, locusts with stings of scorpions cursed humanity. Beast escaped from the bottomless pit as the great red dragon, Satan, was released to war against the divine angels of God. Diseases came upon those that had the mark of the Beast (pagan tattoos?) and those that worshiped his image. The oceans and rivers went sour with their dying fish. Darkness cloaked the earth with rattling thunders and fantastic spider lightnings as its inhabitants gnawed their tongues with fear and pain. Rivers dried up and no fresh water was found. Those still alive cursed the living God for their plight as apostasy prevailed—and humanity's faith perished.

ARMAGEDDON!

(Rev. 19:19)

It was then I realized we were at the very end of modern civilization. We were to fight for the cause of God and Christ against the forces of evil—to purge the earth and cleanse her from all iniquity!

The wrath from the *Paradisia*, our Celestial Kingdom of God cannot be fathomed nor described.

The scenario unfolding was awesome. Thousands of other mighty Entities of God, having power beyond all comprehension, stood ready. Jesus Christ now drew battle plans to war against the evil nations of the earth and Satan's armada. The mighty Archangel Michael, now leads his mighty fortress in the final attack upon all the wiles of the devil!

THE PAROUSIA or *THE SECOND ADVENT*

The earth was under the Great Tribulation. All the nations upon the earth could no longer recognize the forces of good over evil. As the Messiah, Jesus Christ returned, he was wearing a golden crown and in his hand he carried a sharp sickle to gather his faithful flock, "the wine of the earth," destroying many of the nonbelievers, "in the winepress." *All the nations of the world were corrupted and warred against Christ.* Evil and apostasy ran rampant. Those *without* the Mark of the Beast were saved in the first moments of Second Advent, the Ascension of the Saints, known as "the Rapture." Those evil citizens that dared to battle against Christ were dealt the Final Judgment—*without mercy.* Jesus came to crush and burn to oblivion the reprobate nations in a mighty earthquake and plague of hail, "And every island fled away, and the mountains were not found!"

Now Armageddon continued into outer space. The Dragon, the Great Harlot, along with Beelzebub and the Antichrist, warred against El Shaddai, the Lord of Hosts.

Satan and his minions got blood at Calvary when Jesus was put to death. Now they were prepared to go the *full measure* against God. Great Evil Ships of Damnation, containing the plethora of profanity, appeared before God's armada. These Great city-ships commenced for the final storm.

Armed and ignescent, ready to fight the Ultimate War, the great divine celestial city ships of God, the *Paradisia* and the *Shekinah Glory,* aimed their awesome "ignescent swords of annihilation," those austere and deadly weapons of strange fire, unknown to science, directly at the evil Armada of Perdition, Satan's army. Satan's armada of city-ships had their awesome weapons of might aimed and ready to battle against God!

At the cross where Jesus was crucified, the great powers of God were ready then as they are now for the final showdown.

The great Archangel, Michael, opened his mouth to make known the mystery of the Gospel:

"Be not afraid nor dismayed by reason of this great multitude; for the battle is not yours, but God's. Be strong in the Lord and in the power of his might. Now put on the armor of God for that evil day has commenced upon the earth. Have your legs girded with truth and have your torso protected by the breastplate of righteousness. Don the gospel of peace, and the shield of faith, and the helmet of salvation ... and unsheathe your sword of the Spirit which is the word of God ... BECAUSE WE ARE GOING TO WAR!"

Archangel Gabriel now spoke,

**"GOD IS STANDING BY TO GIVE THE SIGNAL
TO RID THE WORLD OF EVIL.
STAND BACK AND WATCH THE
ANATHEMA OF GOD
HIS WRATH AND MIGHTY POWER
TO BE POURED UPON SATAN
AND THE EVIL OF THE WORLD!"**

"ARMAGEDDON!

THE FINAL CONFLICT OF GOOD VERSUS EVIL HAS COMMENCED!"

All of a sudden Almighty God gives the signal to attack! Satan's armada now tensely waited above the plain of Mt. Megiddo. The evil city-ship, *Wormwood* leaves her armada, becoming the first to attack God's Empyrealites. This ship of Satan fires her awesome and terrible weapon of destruction. A hot spidery dendrite of plasma slices toward the *Shekinah Glory*. It completely misses and streaks across the sky as a lightning bolt, striking the earth thousands of miles below! This fearful bolt of plasma, hot as the sun's interior, struck the earth cutting a swath of terror as nothing ever seen or imagined!

For many miles along earth's surface, this bolt twisted through the capital of Arkansas creating an awesome path of destruction. Little Rock's skyscrapers detonated like firecrackers while other buildings simply melted like an ice sculpture from a blow torch. This blinding bolt continued along the interstate, vaporizing cars and tractor-trailers, turning the interstate into a black goo that ignited instantly. Whole neighborhoods and forests kindled into flame. Continuing toward downtown, Little Rock's capitol was obliterated, then the bolt melted all buildings across the center of the city ... all structures disintegrating before our eyes, turning into a massive conflagration! This deadly bolt swept across the Arkansas River instantly vaporizing the water, turning the dry riverbed into a molten river of lava!

This firey bolt, more fearful than a lightning strike,

swept across Clinton National Airport (Adams Field). Airliners instantly exploded like scorched popcorn. The airfield vaporized into a vast molten lake of fire. Across North Little Rock its shock-wave continued across Jacksonville, hitting Little Rock Air Force Base, setting its fighter jets ablaze, and reducing their runways, buildings and C-130 cargo planes into fire and bedlam. The cities of Jacksonville and Cabot were reduced to puddles of molten lava. Then it swept through Searcy obliterating it from the face of the earth.

Now these evil craft of Satan blasted their great fiery dendrites directly at Mt. Megiddo, in the Plain of Jezreel obliterating it as nothing ever seen upon the humbled earth. Proud cities and verdant forests of the world were reduced to massive firestorms. Great deserts of the world were turned to molten glass. Total mountain ranges were erased as whole continents returned to the deep. Vast amounts of ocean water boiled and vaporized—separating the water into its elements of hydrogen and oxygen—igniting instantaneously. Whole flotillas and squadrons of warships upon the oceans and seas of the world were totally obliterated. Thus the scourge of the Earth had begun.

Then God's awesome army struck back with a terrible blow—

The Shekinah Glory fired striking the *Wormwood* dead center, cutting this great vessel of evil almost in half. Shuddering it began to disintegrate, falling in her *coup de grace* spiraling slowly downward toward the Earth, fire consuming her fuselage as a sparkler burns itself into oblivion.

Those evil angels aboard these vessels of iniquity were

now teleported and sealed within the Gehenna of the *Shekinah Glory*. Armageddon ruptured into the War of the Worlds! The great battle of Good vs. Evil continued … as Satan's army attacked the earth. Huge flaming streaks of strange fire crisscrossed our vulnerable planet, destroying everything in their path. Many great cities simply disappeared under the wrath of these awesome weapons and were totally burned into obliteration. The curse against the Earth had begun.

The *Mephistopheles* attacked next. She fired at the *Shekinah Glory,* hitting her full force. She shuddered and spun out of range, then fired back hitting the *Mephistopheles* at point-blank range. This mighty dendrite of sizzling plasma hit Satan's ship dead center as the energy of the divine seared apart her bow in one fatal blow.

We of the *Paradisia* now fired a deadly bolt directly into Satan's armada. The *Beelzebub* vaporized into a vermilion ball of fire. The Antichrist along with other conquered evil angels and vermin which she contained were teleported aboard our ship and incarcerated within her great Gehenna with mighty angels guarding them all with their swords of fire.

These heinous malefactors and hobgoblins, along with the criminals of the world, will never again be free to influence the souls or minds of humankind.

The *Paradisia* took direct hits from those massive puissant bolts of plasma, but sustained no damage whatsoever! We traveled through the interior of the sun—how could we really fear the weapons that Satan and his minions could throw against us!

Then, God turned upon the apostate Earth with final Judgment, finishing the destruction with flaming fire. Those of evil, that had rejected God, his sacred principles and commandments, now met His wrath with everlasting destruction!

CHAPTER FOURTEEN

THE MILLENNIUM AND THE
SECOND ADVENT:
(Rev. 20:1-3)

THE VICTORY OF THE LORD
HAS COMMENCED UPON THE EARTH!

*J*esus Christ now returns to Earth setting up his fair and just rule for a thousand years. Thus the MILLENNIUM is at hand. We, aboard the *Paradisia,* returned to heal Earth's great battle scars and to collect the souls of the dead which succumbed in Armageddon.

The carnage was awful, whole cities upon the Earth obliterated, billions of people dead. Vast destruction, pollution and diseases were rampant everywhere!

Those great bolts of energy seared our Earth with terrible crisscrosses of disaster and calamity. The Earth was actually altered upon her axis, with *all* her major cities completely obliterated—rivers and streams changed courses, her terrain changed forever. Deserts resulted where once fertile soils and farmlands presided. Vast ice sheets vaporized causing the oceans to overflow their shores, inundating verdant islands and swamping vast continents. A thick shroud of lethal smog, a poisonous pall of death, had choked the lands of the world. A dreadful nuclear winter now engulfed the poor devastated Earth.

The Mystery of Earth's Restoration

A great miracle now took place: THE MYSTERY OF THE RESTORATION commenced. Jesus, now having the power of complete sovereignty, guided the revitalization and bioremediation of our eviscerated Earth.

He appointed the mighty Archangels as overseers, teaching the divine precepts of God, "the author and finisher of our faith." Therefore, they now directed the great task to replenish the Earth back to the original Garden of Eden as before the Fall of Humanity!

We learned from the angels how to use various plants to break down many of the most dangerous cancer causing chemicals known to mankind. Many plants can absorb such toxins as carbon monoxide, nitrogen dioxide, formaldehyde, benzene, ammonia, etc. There were also lethal levels of pollution in our atmosphere such as arsenic and chlorine and the land ran rampant with dangerous radioactive isotopes such as tritium, cadmium, polonium, thorium, plutonium, selenium—

We were taught how to use sunflowers, for example, to remove deadly radio isotopes from the ground and atmosphere. These were also used at Chernobyl. Oysters we used to purify contaminated water, along with those zeolites, those tiny hollow rounded atomic structures which absorb dangerous radioactive wastes.

And one of the smallest of all God's creatures now played a great part in cleaning up our oceans and seas. The brine shrimp have a novel protein that can purify water. Their skin, or outer membrane, can actually filter out the dangerous heavy metals such as lead, mercury and arsenic.

The Great Mentor and Son of God, Jesus, taught us that "GOD IS LOVE," and all people upon the Earth can learn to live with one another in peace and happiness.

Some of the Divine Principles taught upon the refurbished Earth were:

Short Courses in Christian Living

1. Each person is a unique individual, designed and created in the Image of God, to live a fulfilled and abundant life, that Image being reason, rationalization, and the promise of immortality beyond time.

2. Each Christian has a *Divine Mission,* anointed with a specific *Divine Goal.* You just have to ask God for the wisdom and guidance to seek it, and the faith and courage to live it.

3. Each "born-again Christian" has a Penchant, Talent or Spiritual Gift ordained by God to discover and develop. There are *No Exceptions.*

4. When one door of opportunity is closed or slammed shut, God will ALWAYS open another one for you. "Do not let the cloudy skies of yesterday, stain the blue skies of today."

5. Prayer is the Key to the abundant and successful life. Pray to God his for blessings, comfort and peace. Ask Him to bless your friends and enemies. This will prove of great value, though you may never realize it.

6. Count you Divine Given Blessings and Godly Favor—having a good marriage, good health, enough food, shelter, warm clothes, etc.

7. The Christian has the awesome potential of divine insight and inspiration. To always see things through faith and hope, that good always conquers evil, that Jesus destroys the darkness of the soul and is the true Light of the world. We have the *Divine Power* to create a better world in which to live.

8. Remember, God directs your life and no matter what happens—He sends his angels to guide and protect you. (Psa. 91:11)

9. God will never place you in a situation you cannot get out of—or better yourself from "because the foolishness of God is wiser than men; and the weakness of God is stronger than men." (1 Cor. 1:25)

10. No matter how bad it seems—God always has a *Divine Purpose* for you and has all things under control. *No Exceptions.* We, many times do not know what the future holds, but we know who holds the future.

Chapter Fifteen

After the thousand-year Millennium, we once again boarded our *Paradisia* that had patiently waited beyond the clouds with the *Shekinah Glory*. We realized that Satan, his evil minions and the miscreants of the world were all sealed and imprisoned. God's Ultimate and Final Plan, along with his saints (the Sons of Light) anticipate their great fulfillment, Divine Mission, and Ultimate Destiny after the Lord's millennial reign upon the Earth was complete.

We now continue our strange odyssey—full of their esoteric, strange, dark and forbidding secrets. Within that impeccable perfection of our great Celestial City, the *Paradisia,* JESUS CHRIST, OUR MESSIAH as SUPREME RULER AND DIVINE KING, PERFECT, JUST AND FAIR, reigned in all his glory. His forgiven and purged saints, now sealed by God's Holy Spirit, were catechized in the precepts of the LORD. Satan, now impotent, was bound these thousand years. The redeemed in Christ were ready to abandon and forsake our earth, to continue upon their Divine Mission and journey into *terra incognita*, the Great Unknown.

United into one great family—the *Divine Family of God*, all the Supernalites were conversing and communing with one another. The angels were enlightening us to the etiquette of family relationships, the esoteric nature of the universe and the aesthetic qualities of the enhanced abundant life. Though we were not bound in marriage, Faith and I had a solidarity that could not be equaled upon the Earth. We were beyond the physical aspects of our secular beings, and *loved everyone in the Spirit of God* as we never could have attained in the pure physical realm. We were much more fulfilled in our divine relationships, for we realized that God is love. The problems associated with worldly marriage was a thing of the past. *The old life of which I was born—was beginning to fade away slowly but surely.*

With great divine wisdom we proceed into the vastness of the universe. Our friendship, amity, solidarity, and *esprit de corps* were now equal with the holy angels—

> "Neither can they die any more; for
> they are equal unto the angels,
> and are the children of God, being the
> children of the resurrection."
> —Lk. 20:36

Our journey to the stars continues, as we of the *Paradisia* gather under the cupola of the *Grande Observatorium*. We saw the great and intriguing armillary sphere, featuring all the wonderful ecliptic and concentric rings and celestial circles representing the millions of planets and stars. There was also a manificient Laser Interferometer Gravitational-Wave Observatory locating massive black-holes clandestinely hiding throughout our vast intriguing universe.

The Angelic Divine Counselor, Celeste, once again appeared to introduce all the wonders of —

Celeste interrupted my thought, "Iben, look out through the crystal cupola!"

I did and saw a strange sight—

"Iben," Celeste spoke, "you are looking at the moons of Mars."

We passed Phobos (Fear) and her other moon, Deimos (Terror) and on the latter—viewed a huge impact basin.

We then searched for life upon these moons. Then continued on to—

Mars

The intriguing red planet, Mars, loomed nearer and nearer. Enveloped in mystery, it was like an old friend. As a child I looked up into the vastness of space, exploring this red planet with my imagination and a small telescope and the wonder of a child, and pondered if life would ever be found upon this enigmatic world, so far from our own. A famous quote came to me:

"Imagination is more important than knowledge."
—Albert Einstein

We dived beneath the wispy thin clouds of the Martian atmosphere of carbon dioxide observing hundreds of impact craters. Now we explored the vast Vallis Marineris Canyon complex.

Our party of Supernalites, guided by Celeste, were teleported to her surface. What a wonder to actually stand upon the alien red sands of this strange and mysterious planet!

We felt a strange vibration below our feet a few minutes after appearing upon Mars. I realized it to be a *marsquake*! Yes, even Mars has similar tectonic quakes as our earth and moon. In ages past it had a global magnetic field, powered by a revolving mantle and a metallic core producing a dynamo effect. This electric field is now long gone, but its rocks still contain reminisces of magnetization left over from this phenomenon millions of years ago.

Also, we observed long extinct lake beds and mysterious river canyons, carved by water eons ago. We learned that Mars even once had a nice thick atmosphere, but over time the solar winds have stripped much of it away.

Did its soil beneath contain any micro-organisms such as *chemolithoautotrophs*—strange mineral-eating life forms as has been recently discovered in hydrothermal vents deep within our oceans of earth? Did we locate any liquid salt water under the plains or deserts of Mars? Did we discover the exotic *Methanococcus jannaschii,* that one-celled archaean non-classifiable species having strange alien DNA, that we had studied earlier upon the earth? Could it have been carried from Mars to earth in meteorites long ago, and then somehow adapted to our world?

We crossed the strange valley of Candor Chasm and the Valles Marineris canyon complex. Not far from these we decided to explore Olympus Mons, the largest volcano on Mars (three times as high as Mt. Everest)! Here we encountered fierce dust storms as we studied many wonderful gigantic buttes and boulders.

We crossed the Cydonia region above the Tropic of Capricorn, photographed long ago by the 1976 Viking Orbiter that captured some enigmatic apparitions, the specters of wishful scientists who wanted to believe that organic intelligencia once stood upon this dusty red planet. The Orbiter spacecraft sent back to the earth some controversial images of strange humanoid faces and mysterious pyramids. Found scattered along the Ares Vallis region, among the buttes, mesas and escarpments was a "lost city," known as The Fortress, The Tholus, and The D&M Pyramid. We explored the interior of these enigmatic pyramids, many times the mass of those in Egypt!

Were these huge structures natural formations, man-made, or Martian made? Were they just the strange phenomenon known as *pareidolia*, where we see patterns as faces or creatures in clouds, or that a round yellow circle with two dots and a curved line could form a smiley face? Or could they really be the ruins of some lost city constructed thousands or even millions of years ago? Did some ancient civilization erect these clandestine structures and then vanish below the red sands of the Martian surface? Or did we sometime, in the very ancient past, have advanced technology that could have placed *us* upon Mars thousands of years *before* our own pyramids were built? An enigmatic advanced civilization that at one time thrived in it's glory, and then once again crumbled to dust, lost to humanity? I was told *not* to reveal this esoteric knowledge. It will be revealed in God's due time. And in the answer to this unsolved baffling mystery lies one of the strangest conundrums that mere Earthlings will ever face!

The wonders that were revealed as we stayed upon Mars was beyond our wildest dreams.

Asteroids

Leaving Mars, Celeste continued teaching me the wonders of the universe. We now found ourselves in the midst of a great asteroid belt between Mars and Jupiter. Could they have once belonged to a planet between Mars and Jupiter, that encountered an unfortunate fate that was, maybe, hit by a comet? All these asteroids combined still would not make up a world as big as our earth. But if long ago there was a planet that encountered such destruction, much of it could have been reduced to dust in a massive explosion—vaporizing most of it, leaving only larger chunks to orbit the sun.

Strange Meteorites and The Blob

(Hoyle and Wickramasinghe Theory)
(*Methanococcus jannaschii*)

Did we in fact discover even a greater mystery—the remnants of some once-living fossils embedded deep within these asteroids?

Sometimes these asteroids break from their orbits, and over millions of years come crashing down upon the earth as meteorites. Many of these are embedded with strange crystals of amino acids and cholesterol—all tale-tail signs of ancient organic life!

Here we discovered the dwarf planet, Ceres (also known as the largest asteroid). The deeper we penetrated into her warmer rocky core we found a black tar-like substance, actually primitive amino acids, the building blocks for the carbon unit of life! Could there be strange life forms such as dormant parasitic blobs of protoplasm hidden within her deep fissures? Could it be possible for one of these small asteroids, to someday actually be captured by our gravity and fall to the Earth containing—?

"Some of these asteroids we discovered," Celeste spoke, "did indeed contained strange prebiotic compounds! Ever hear of the Allen Hills Meteorite?

"Anyway, the Allen Hills #84001 Mars' Rock was found in the Antarctic in 1984. Hydrocarbons, the building blocks of life, were determined to be much older than scientists believed that life had originated upon the Earth. Yet, other hydrocarbons such as carbonaceous chondrites have been located in meteors 4.6 billion years old—the same age as the solar system, including our Earth!

"Iben, have you ever heard of the Hoyle and Wickramasinghe Theory? They have formulated a trilogy, *Diseases from Space*, dismissing Darwinism and asserting that all infectious diseases, such as the bubonic plague, Ebola and Marburg, came to Earth by *cosmic genes* found in comets."

In fact, we again thought about those strange one-celled organisms, *Methanococcus jannaschii*, that live on our earth that can survive in boiling oil. Remember, we discovered them around the subterranean ocean vents that we studied earlier and learned that their DNA is *very different* than most all other living things. But could they have actually *first* come from asteroids that had fallen to earth as meteorites thousands of years ago?

"Wouldn't the heat generated from the blast of a meteorite destroy any chance for life to form?" I asked.

"It should be noted, Iben, that even in intense forest fires the dormant seeds of the Lodgepole and Knobcone pines survive. These seeds stay dormant for up to 25 to 50 years, then the intense heat melts the resins that seal the cone scales and releases the seeds to germinate in the burned out desolation. In fact, a conflagration is actually *needed* for them to germinate!"

This was a somewhat unsettling thought. For when a child I remembered seeing the horror movies, *The Andromeda Strain* and *The Blob*. *The Andromeda Strain* was about a deadly virus from outer space infecting and killing out a small town in the United States. *The Blob* was about a meteorite that fell to earth containing a pulsating indefinable amorphous parasitic gelatinous protoplasmic living alien biomass which could absorb human flesh on contact. *These movies might not be as far fetched as I had once imagined!*

"Yes, Iben, you are right!"

"Scientists must be cautious of bringing in any alien life forms, such as the above, or spores, or viruses from visiting other worlds. Hyperbaric space laboratories such as the Bio-4 labs we have already visited are now being built by NASA to study and control such ALF's (Alien Life Forms) if any are ever found! When foreign worlds are ever again visited, such as the Moon or Mars, these astronauts, their space rocks, and their alien artifacts, will be quarantined in these special labs for a period of weeks. All the inhabitants of earth just might be thankful someday that they have them! Scientists are still debating life's origin, if it is only an anomaly or not, and whether they have found the remains of life or any prebiotic compounds traveling through space for the last billion years or so!

Panspermia or Cosmozoic Theory

"Iben," Celeste continued, "have you ever heard of the *Panspermia* or the *Cosmozoic Theory?*"

"Not really?"

"Well, the Panspermia Theory and the Cosmozoic Theory are both really much the same. You see, they both state that the original spores of life came upon the Earth from some other planet or alien galaxy. The only question is that at some point, life still had to originate from some *original source* for it to be traveling through space. So the enigma still is unsolvable. How did life originate in the first place to be traveling through space for all these eons of time?"

"By the divine hand of God." I answered.

"Iben, you are getting so smart!

"But the major concern is that many huge asteroids orbiting our sun, will someday approach earth with deadly aim. Earth be forewarned!"

Celeste pointed out many dangerous "earth-grazers," known as Near Earth Asteroids (NEAs). These were laying directly in earth's path and could hit anywhere on earth with an impact of a hydrogen bomb.

Some asteroids from five to ten miles in diameter have in our past actually hit with the earth. One massive asteroid allegedly caused the extinction of dinosaurs some 65 million years ago.

"Iben, on June 30, 1908, an object about 150 feet across exploded over Siberia, known as the Tunguska event, unleashing a 20 megaton blast that leveled hundreds of square miles of forest! The one that wiped out the dinosaurs, as we were enlightened earlier, exploded about 65 million years ago in Central America, forming the Chicxulub Crater along the Yucatan peninsula. This meteor was about 10 miles across! When it exploded, it took half the plant and animal species with it!"

"Wow, the impact was that strong?"

"Not the impact, Iben," continued Celeste, "but the resulting nuclear winter causing dust clouds that held the planet in a dark, cold grip by blotting out the sun's light for the next few hundred years!

"Then in 2013, a 13,000-ton meteoroid 62 feet across plowed through the skies over Chelyabinsk, Russia, a city of a million people. This sky visitor, glowing 30 times brighter than the sun, was traveling at 42,000 miles per hour when it exploded high in the atmosphere. With the power of a 500 kiloton blast, it blew out windows and injured hundreds of people causing a path of destruction over 50 miles long. For a moment Russia had thought it had been attacked by a nuclear bomb, but it finally proved to be a small meteor on its final approach to earth. Luckily, no one was killed."

I then learned that our earth had a number of major extinctions around every 26 million years—known as the Extinction of Species Theory. Could these devastating events be caused by massive asteroids colliding with the earth? This finally congealed into the Alvarez Theory, where scientists found a strange radioactive iridium layer throughout our planet, produced from a large meteorite, probably the one that annihilated the dinosaurs.

So there are *two* layers of iridium. One from this impact that annihilated the dinosaurs—and the one caused from radioactive fallout from thermonuclear testing during the 1950s.

Chapter Sixteen

Jupiter's Moons

"*T*ben," Celeste continued, "we are now passing Europa, one of Jupiter's four biggest moons."

Here we discovered a bizarre world barren as our Antarctica. What wonders await the first astronauts to set foot on lonely Europa! What resided under this thick ice? Here we actually found a brine ocean many miles deep. What Alien Life Forms (ALFs) if any, did we encounter?

There was something odd about the surface of Europa. It consisted of a huge plain of magnesium sulfate, and around this huge desert of Epsom salt, were—

Were there strange undefinable extremophiles swimming in this brine ocean? Were there SLIMEs (Subsurface Lithoautotrophic Microbial Ecosystems) actually surviving here? Were there strange alien bacteria and fungi, known as *bibliocryptozoans* inhabiting these eccentric waters?

Known to biologists as *meiofauna*, could there be organic alien life, fantastic undulating mycoplasmas swimming here, millions of miles from our Earth?

"These meiofauna," Celeste explained, "that live upon the earth consists of flat, segmented worms, known as *gastrotrichs*. They have bristling spines like the tiny blood worms of fresh water streams. Some strange microscopic tardigrades, or water bears, can even survive in a vacuum, can be cooled down to a minus 456 degrees F., and even survive, heated to 304 degrees F. They can also withstand more than 1,000 times the radiation of a human, and the extreme pressures of 6,000 atmospheres, equivalent to 88,200 pounds per square inch! That is six times the pressure at an ocean depth of 32,800 feet! If harsh conditions persist, they can dehydrate themselves, and roll up into a ball as a sow bug does. In this state they can exist for more than a century!"

Could organic life really exist on this alien moon? Did we find microbes or strange bacteria that have replaced phosphorus in their DNA, with its look-alike, but toxic cousin, arsenic? Could we discover here a very different form of bacteria that could change the way astrobiologists view life in our universe? Were there *tholins*, an organic soup of exotic molecules that could produce primitive life forms? What mysteries did the oceans of Europa conceal? But does the formation of life take more than just the right atmosphere, heat, gravity, water, the formation of macromolecules and the "chance" to germinate? *Is there some "Unknown Factor" that needs to be present?*

Will mortals ever explore this alien landscape of this Terra-X, and discover weird creatures on this strange and alien moon of Jupiter?

The closer we came to Jupiter's surface, the more moons we discovered! There was one little moon, now known as

Valetudo, traveling in a circular path the same as Jupiter, but directly in the path of other moons that are traveling in the *opposite direction*, as a person going down the wrong way on a one-way street. Someday this strange moon's luck will run out and collide—

We visited *all* her many moons searching for life forms. We bid these moons farewell, for we were soon entering the swirling mysterious clouds of Jupiter herself!

Jupiter

We encountered the biggest planet in our solar system, Jupiter. We witnessed beautiful but radioactive auroras, very deadly to humans, extending far into space—produced from her magnetic core. Then we descended into her gossamer rings, and entered through this exotic halo and plunged into her thick atmosphere.

Jupiter has now swelled around our vision. Her rings were of utmost beauty. We plunged through these tiny pieces of debris as though they weren't even there! As we drew closer, these rings of brilliant colors faded, becoming mostly chunks of colorless debris, as large as buildings. It was an alien world of frozen ammonium hydrosulfide and large chunks of ammonia ice crystals. But when Jupiter's surface and the stars shined directly through them—they refracted into a kaleidoscopic wonderland of magic!

Nearer and nearer we plunged into her atmosphere. Her Giant Red Spot was a massive Jovian anticyclonic storm, with fierce winds circling a calm central eye. As we descended, we could see that her gaseous layered atmosphere consisted of terrible great ribbons or bands of hydrogen and helium gases, blowing fiercely in all directions.

As we plunged further into Jupiter's hydrogen and sodium atmosphere, we finally encountered its surface of water ice. Penetrating deep beneath this, we discovered a solid core of metallic hydrogen!

All the building blocks of life were present—but under all this pressure—did we, in fact, find life?

Jupiter's atmosphere is extremely cold at minus 140 degrees C. Her gravity is so intense, that she retains all her gases—even hydrogen can't escape her gravitational pull!

Saturn's Moons

As we left Jupiter, we continued our journey across our vast solar system, continuing our quest for divine knowledge and wisdom, proclaiming *all* of God's mighty handiwork!

Next we explored Saturn's many moons. Enceladus was the most intriguing. She lay before us in all her mysterious splendor! Deep beneath her craters and puzzling land formations were wonderful geysers spewing icy jets of frozen sleet and liquid water.

Did we find alien life upon Enceladus? That mystery will be left to the astronomers and their space probes from planet Earth to someday discover for themselves.

We studied and explored all her many moons, many of which veiled the secrets of the genesis of life. Some had dense atmospheres composed mostly of nitrogen. Others contained significant amounts of cyanide. Oddly, cyanide, extremely deadly to Earth animals, may be a necessary precursor to the formation of life on other worlds! Did we in fact find any exotic life forms aboard these remote moons of Saturn?

Saturn

Through the *Grande Observatorium* we now witnessed the majestic gossamer rings of Saturn. She is the second largest planet in our solar system.

I learned that Saturn is actually less dense than water. If placed in a tub of water, she would actually float! (Though it would have to be a mighty huge tub!)

I have been intrigued with the wonder of Saturn ever since I had first looked into an astronomy book about this beautiful heavenly body.

Her rings were like a huge record or disc with prismatic colors of every variegated hue. Boldly into these majestic rings we now flung our *Paradisia*. Again, we were unaffected by all this debris, and had no fear of collision as we passed right through them.

Her rings were composed of varicolored conglomerates of rock and obsidian glass covered with methane and ammonia ice crystals. Saturn's beautiful surface clouds of assorted stripes, reflected their soft entrancing hues of orange, pink and the pastel blue of her wonderful countenance. Now enchanting and graceful Saturn proudly paraded her bewitching rings swirling as precious jewels, dancing upon the neck of some beautiful princess, dressed in her finest apparel upon her wedding night!

Translucent silicas of various colors of her rings now sparkled in my eyes. At that moment I realized that I was hopelessly in love with her, and such a sight has never been dreamed of or comprehended by the mind of all humanity! The moons of Saturn even glowed through these rings like diamond chips through the varicolored aurora of a Divine Being.

Again, only a Creator could design such a spectacle! And, those that had only recently regained their sight, I wondered if God had created these wonderful rings for these nascent eyes, or were these spiritual eyes especially created to view such immense wonders! Those saints aboard the *Paradisia* that were blind upon the earth as Helen Keller, were now in such ecstasy and rapture at viewing this Great Wonder of the Lord's creation. Maybe to be just one of the most beautiful phenomenon the universe has ever produced!

Here millions of miles from Earth in the rapport of total divine love, we watched this spectacular resplendent show of these hypnotic rings of such surreal beauty—known but to the angels and to the "Sons of Light," the Supernalites, the glorious Saints of the Eternal.

This had to be one of my greatest highs upon this fantastic voyage through space! We stayed I know not how long transecting these wonderful rings suspended 100,000 miles above Saturn!

> "The heavens declare the glory of God,
> and the firmament showeth his handiwork."
> (Ps. 19:1; 115:15-16; 121:2)

Did Saturn contain any life forms?

Leaving Saturn was a sad time. I fully realized that I

could never find another paragon of beauty as wonderful as her to visit and explore!

But again, to my great surprise, other fantastic worlds and alternate dimensions were beckoning us onward, enticing me with their insatiable wonders.

Uranus

Uranus came next into view. Uranus loomed above us as a great mysterious entity eclipsing the black sky—beckoning us into her clandestine domain. What will she teach us? She also had a series of rings, and we traveled through them all. They were jagged rocks of all sizes, dull and opaque, of a different structure than those of Jupiter or even Saturn, and not nearly as surreal.

Uranus had an atmosphere of methane. Was her mantle and core composed of many different crystals of *superionic* water? That is water, under tremendous pressure, behaving both as a plasma, and as a metal acting simultaneously as a solid and liquid at the same time! Could life exist in such a world?

Neptune

Neptune now grew in our sight.

We entered through Neptune's narrow rings and penetrated her thick blue clouds, discovering she also had a methane atmosphere. Then we landed upon her icy shell surrounding a metallic rocky core. There was also a strange white spot as massive as the one on Saturn. It also had a weak magnetic field less than that of the Earth. Alas, once again I could not reveal if Neptune contained life.

Leaving Neptune, we also explored all of her moons—unraveling their many hidden secrets.

Pluto

Pluto, we discovered, was much more than just a low density snowball of frozen gases. Her atmosphere was complosed mostly of methane. We even saw an awesome pattern in the shape of a valentine heart, and realized it to be a solid glacier, miles long, of dense methane ice. Crossing mile-high mountain ranges of thick solid water ice, we explored her many jagged peaks, even discovering some active volcanoes. Then we entered her dark forbidden crevasses, where any mortal explorer could slip—and fall for miles. Then we continued deep within Pluto, discovering her rocky radioactive core. Did we find a liquid ocean? Was the interior of Pluto warm enough to harbor life?

We now visited Pluto's largest moon, Charon. It was also very interesting holding strange secrets of her own! Now we explored *all* of Pluto's many moons, including Nix and Hydra and her smallest just-discovered moon, Kerbros. What did we discover upon these distant moons? The angels told me *not* to divulge their many clandestine secrets.

Comets and Planetoids

Beyond Pluto, we traveled to other wonders way beyond the Kuiper Belt, on into the Oort Cloud, composed of comets and old debris left from the creation of our solar system.

Next we explored the 2.5-mile wide comet 67P/Churyumov-Gerasimenko, some 311 million miles away from Earth, hurtling through space at 41,000 mph.

We also discovered and explored 2014 MU69, or Ultima Thule, meaning, "beyond the known world." It was really one tiny planetoid composed of two small spheres which collided and fused together millennium ago. The larger object was to be known as "Ultima," was 12 miles across, while, "Thule," the smaller one, was about 9 miles across. It is around 1 billion miles *beyond* Pluto.

Another planetoid was, Quaoar. It was named from the mythology of the Tongva people of Southern California. Did we in fact find some tiny microscopic spores upon it?

On the very fringes of our solar system, we passed the NASA spacecraft, *New Horizons*, coming to yet another small world... 2003 UB313. This planetoid was named "Xena," after the former TV show, Xena, Warrior Princess, and her little orbiting moon, "Gabrielle," after Xena's faithful companion. Xena, we discovered, has a diameter of 1,800 miles.

We encountered another strange icy world known as 215 TG387. Could this someday become Planet Nine of our solar system? Also, known as Goblin, we discovered it was just a little larger than Earth taking 40,000 years to travel around our sun … much farther away than Pluto—around 200 billion miles.

Also, traveling through the Kuiper Belt, we discovered, Sedna. It was named after the Inuit goddess of the ocean. What wonders lay in wait on Sedna? Did she have a companion, a strange rocky moon orbiting her, keeping her company in the vastness of sidereal space? Again we were cautioned not to reveal too much of her intrinsic secrets and wonders.

We concluded that Sedna was about the same size as Pluto, but was she really a planet? I then realized that she is as much a planet as Pluto was! Could Pluto now be considered a "dwarf planet," or just another planetoid, orbiting our sun? We'll leave those question to worldly astronomers and their mundane classification system while we continue to enjoy all the miracles and mysteries that God has created in his grand and wonderful universe.

We also found a large cometary planetesimal we coined the Immanuel Velikovsky. We named it after the scientist who formulated the theory in two of his quasi-scientific books, *Worlds in Collision* and *Earth in Upheaval,* that proclaimed God sent a comet into earth's orbit in the time of the Exodus in the Old Testament causing the Red Sea to part thus saving the Israelites from the Pharaoh's army!

We now explored Comet Wild-2. A probe launched way back in 1999, known as the *Stardust* was to meet up with Wild-2 and bring back samples for Earthlings to study. We were close enough to observe its head, or coma. We explored Wild-2, traveling at 175,000 miles per hour. In the comet's center did we discover some amino acids, the organic precursors to life? As Wild-2 neared our sun it began melting and disintegrating, spreading her beautiful display of ionized gases into a wondrous diaphanous veil extending millions of miles into space.

Our sun was now only a tiny flicker of light sparkling in the heavens, a common star twinkling among billions of others in the vastness of space. Soon enough, the comets, one by one, will disclose their many secrets as more probes will be sent into the heavens to unravel their exotic mysteries.

Our Celestial City has now transversed past the termination and bow shocks at the edge of our solar system, leaving it far behind. Plunging through the heliosphere, a bubble caused by the solar wind, we now moved on. Beyond this—lay the interstellar vacuum of space.

> "In all chaos there is a cosmos,
> In all disorder a secret order."
> —Carl Jung

NEMESIS

Then another huge comet lost in space and totally unknown to the astronomers of the earth, now sailed into view—

We watched as she sped by on her way to meet her destiny. In a little while the Angelic Divine Counselors migrated toward the center of the canopy under the rotunda. All the saints of God quieted, and an uneasiness permeated throughout the Celestial City. All the saints grew anxious, but attentive.

Celeste spoke, "Fellow Lords of the universe, the Sons and Daughters of Almighty God, we have some very profound news. The earth of your origins is at its closure. Behold … *Nemesis* … that comet whose path is on a collision course—"

I watched in rapt fascination as this comet crept closer to our earth more dangerous than a speeding bullet. It was protected by our moon which took the full brunt of the impact. The comet blasted a huge angry crater into the moon all the way to her core—almost shattering her in twain. Then to my horror I realized that our moon wobbled and shuttered and slowly and methodically began a deadly spiral downward toward the earth. As the moon altered the earth's spin, it began slowing down, the days grew longer as did the nights, and time as we once knew ceased to exist. Now those upon the earth saw an incredible sight of ever enlarging blood moon with a fulminating impact crater spewing out toxic gases enveloping our planet. Great massive tidal waves and intense conflagrations sprang up obliterating everything. All her great civilizations were methodically erased. Then the moon, as a prophesied specter of doom, closed upon the hapless earth, vaporizing her atmosphere and her great oceans. Then after a short duration—mercilessly collided. There was a bright flash of light signaling the earth's *coup de grace*. Our earth, along with our moon, were instantly atomized—expanding into a glowing ball of intense incandescence, a brightness which lit up the dark sky as a supernova, then just as quickly faded into the vast coldness of extinction. Planet Earth's demise had just been witnessed. That little "Garden of Eden," that little "Oasis in Space," that little "Home in the Heavens," was vaporized in an instant, and was no more. An unsettling silence swept over all those aboard the *Paradisia*, a profound reverent quietness permeated all those that witnessed this pathos.

Sic transit gloria mundi
"So passes away the glory of the world."

"But the day of the Lord will come as a thief in the night,
in which the heavens shall pass away with a great noise,
and the elements shall melt with fervent heat;
the earth also, and the works that are
in it, shall be burned up."
—2 Pet. 3:10

"To see a world in a grain of sand,
And a heaven in a wild flower,
Holding infinity in the palm of your hand
and eternity in an hour."
—William Blake

CHAPTER SEVENTEEN

$\mathcal{W}$e had now traveled beyond our Earth … over 9 quintillion miles.

Thus ended our tour of the Solar System. What vast divine knowledge had we learned so far from journeying beyond the edge of our Milky Way galaxy? We now bade it farewell, like small children for the first time leaving their house in which they were born. That little boy or girl now venturing outside to explore their backyard, then onward they go exploring the forests and streams. Compare this to our *Paradisia,* leaving our solar system to see other strange and beautiful island universes scattered across the heavens. What wonders in God's vast creation now awaited us?

The *Paradisia* accelerated through our Milky Way galaxy—*far beyond the speed of light.* Then I remembered once again this strange phenomena of *theomorphic ubiquity.* As we once traveled through the oceans of our world, we can now travel *anywhere in the universe faster than the blink of an eye by just thinking about it, transcending beyond one galaxy directly into the heart of another, exploring them all (almost it seemed, simultaneously).* The human mind cannot comprehend such things as *thought travel or living within the extradimensional realm of the angels. So,* in writing this narrative, I must keep such phenomena within the range of a *three-dimensional reality.*

Spiraling galaxies—island universes were now scattered before us. Each contain billions of stars of swirling suns 100,000 light years across and about one hundred million light years apart. Huge spiral arms composed of uncountable stars, stilled by the vastness of space, spread before us ... enticing our imagination and curiosity.

Massive swirling galaxies beckoned us forward—great pinwheels of spinning light and energy, island universes, vast, incomprehensible. Were there orbiting these suns numerous solar systems containing intelligent beings more advanced than we? Wondrous beings who live in the great unknown vastness of illimitable space? Strange human-like companions on a similar journey of enlightenment and knowledge; alien beings totally unaware of our existence as we are unaware of theirs?

I looked totally enraptured and mesmerized into these uncountable stars—and knew that my Divine Destiny was soon to be found within their midst—

Celeste now addressed those in the *Grande Observatorium:*

"Lords of the Universe, spread before us as billions of white diamonds upon ebony velvet, the stars and galaxies beckon us forward to explore the mysteries of the vast unknown—God's fathomless creation.

Mortal man, *Homo technologicus,* in his paltry little

mundane body could never explore the mysteries of the *Eternal*, the most-high God, and conceive what now awaits us. The human body, bound by time and its circadian rhythm, hinders humankind from experiencing all the things we have *already* experienced beyond death and their narrow limited perception will prevent them from having the necessary *vision* needed to understand such wonders and the vast potential of the human mind—and *why* it was really created!"

"THE MASTERS OF THE UNIVERSE, THE SONS OF GOD... *PARTAKERS OF THE HOLY PRIESTHOOD... WELCOME TO THE FIRST DAY OF SCHOOL!*"

Away at School

"I love to think of my little children
whom God has called to himself
as away at school—
at the best school in the universe,
under the best teachers, learning the best things,
in the best possible manner.
O death! We thank thee for the light
that thou wilt shed upon our ignorance."
—Bossuet

We, of the *Paradisia* observed the vastness and sanctity of the nebulae, stars and galaxies of island universes. Uncountable stars, sharp and crystal clear as on a warm summer's night, now sprinkled the ebony sky as bright diamonds. I had never seen such a sight!

Divine Wisdom

"Come to us, ye who seek Divine Wisdom,
and have insatiable curiosity of the universe.
Come, drink the Sweet Wine of Divine Knowledge,
and eat the Holy Manna of Divine Truth—
for herein lies the Secrets of Life and Death."
—The Author

Miles became a foreign unit of measurement, as our *Paradisia* sped into the unknown. Our sun was but a twinkling star among billions, soon to disappear in the sparkling vast infinity—

We now reached the termination shock, or the beginning of the heliopause, where the sun's gravitational pull begins to ebb, and cold interstellar space begins.

I noticed a strange object gliding silently through space having parabolic and telemetry antennas. It looked man made! What could be so far out in the universe as this? Upon it a golden plaque contained a symbol of the hydrogen atom, which produces the characteristic 21-cm radiation and 14 stars as seen from our sun, including their binary codes. From this they could extrapolate where the probe originated. At the bottom of the plaque was a facsimile of our solar system including a symbol of the craft journeying beyond the planets. There was a male and a female image of some anthropoid beings also etched into it.

I suddenly realized it to be *Voyager I.* This spacecraft was designed to travel for eons until some unknown civilization might encounter it. It is still moving through space at the speed of a comet!

We were all a little disappointed that the residents of the *Paradisia* were the first and only "civilization" to discover it, now centuries after it was launched! It will regretfully be the last remaining object, created by Earthlings, we will ever encounter.

On board *Voyager*, we found something very interesting. I was allowed to analyze this probe and spotted some nanobacteria, microscopic life forms, strange stowaways upon this man-made craft. These microbial extremophiles, to my surprise, were *not* alien in origin but actually came from the earth! All space probes from our planet were suppose to be sterile, but alas, this was not the case. Microbes such as these were also found on the Apollo spacecraft and surprisingly *survived* traveling to the moon and back in the early 1970s! They can withstand 3,000 times the lethal dosage of ultraviolet radiation of humans and the intense cold, heat and vacuum of space! Yet, could these spores live for millennia without dying—to be revived someday in a far distant alien solar system?

Leaving it, I wondered if any alien civilization would ever discover *Voyager's* existence. This antiquated vehicle of *Homo technologicus* was now as primitive as a vagabond upon an island, throwing out a message sealed in a bottle to drift across a vast ocean of space for all eternity. Will this "bottle" ever be retrieved by exotic beings along a strange seashore on another alien world? And the world from whence it originated has already vanished eons ago! What are the odds of this message ever being disclosed? Yet some of these bottled calls for help have actually been found many years later drifting upon some foreign beach! What are the chances that this probe will ever be discovered? This forlorn message in a bottle, *one of the earth's last surviving relics*?

Again, will any alien civilization ever pluck this probe from the vast ocean of interstellar space, decipher its message, play its golden plated copper phonograph record with the recordings of Shakespeare, and other great literary giants and classical music composers, listen to "Hello" in our 60 different languages, and the call of the baleen whale—and wonder …

Will some cosmic alien from some unknown galaxy of some unknown world, decipher *Voyager's* message, and travel to a place between Mars and Venus—and ponder what all those little asteroids mean, being the remnants of the Earth and her moon which was struck by the comet, *Nemesis*. Will they try to reconstruct the pieces of the puzzle, to learn how this space debris was created, and if there was some mistake made in interpreting *Voyager's* message?

Will some alien species ever explore pieces of these asteroids, and find a spore of life? Will any remains ever be discovered of a civilization that once inhabited a little blue planet? A planet of great diversity that contained vast salt oceans and mountains, fresh lakes and streams, great cities and monuments to its dead heroes—a world full of laughter and pathos, encompassing the realities and the dreams of the universe?

Then would they also find within our solar system, the asteroids between Mars and Jupiter … and ponder if yet two other unfortunate planets long ago collided or were attacked and obliterated by some advanced alien civilization?

Then *Voyager*, reflecting a gamma ray, winked a sparkle of light at us, bidding its final farewell ... and in a moment was gone, disappearing forever into the vast uncountable stars.

We have now explored our solar system in billions of miles. As our sun disappears from view—this concept of *miles* becomes totally meaningless to describe our next destination through the universe—

We visited the wonders of variegated galaxies, all lying quintillions of miles from our sun. It must be stated that we of our wonderful hyperspeed and interdimensional Celestial City, have now voided the spacetime continuum. Being beyond a three-dimensional reality, we need little sleep, and being away from the Earth as it rotates, giving us our days and nights, time as we once conceived it, became also meaningless. Eternity took its place as we sliced through great fathoms of space, becoming exobiologists. Were we to solve the Anthropic Argument where *Homo sapiens* is the divine masterpiece of creation? Were we especially designed by destiny, to search for intelligent life much like ourselves inhabiting other planets in alien galaxies?

Why are we as a species, so innately curious about intelligent life on foreign worlds? Were we to partake in God's divine plan of terraformation, that grand cultivation of exotic planets in foreign solar systems orbiting alien suns in distant galaxies?

Were we destined to encounter the souls of other deceased intelligent beings that had died upon alien worlds? Was this yet another Divine Mission from God? To sweep through the uncountable stars, gathering the souls of his flock into the *Paradisia*, bringing them into the Kingdom of God?

Did these foreign worlds we explored have exotic, unique and bizarre life forms? I now realized another reason we die and acquire a new glorified body and become a new spiritual creature is because we could never survive the foibles of unnatural worlds or their pressures (remember the cores of the Earth, Jupiter and our Sun), heat and coldness of sidereal space, the effects of gravity and the forces centrifugal and momentum—and actually travel into huge planets and stars of cold and fire, and feel not the uneasiness of any of it!

So our *new* measurement of distance will be the light-year. One light-year is equivalent to 6 trillion miles, and there are 10,000 stellar systems within 100 light years of our solar system.

We must remember that the distance of our own Milky Way galaxy is 120,000 light years across, and 30,000 to its center!

While aboard our Celestial City we partook in such wonderful *esprit de corps* between the angels and many other Supernalites. Such rapport and angelic harmony ensued between us that *time became an illusion—it had been virtually terminated.* We were exceedingly happy and joyful, full of the promise of the abundant life! There was such an expression of total divine love and amity between each other, all in unison and tranquility, existing in God's holy family.

Another problem about mortal flesh in three-dimensional space and time is that it can never transverse the quadrillions of miles it would take to travel to the stars.

Therefore, *only in the resurrected state, in the realm of the Supernalites*, could we ever hope to accomplish it!

So this is yet another reason for death? To free the supernatural body and its soul to transverse beyond the speed of light, and journey to the stars unhindered!

"This can be accepted as fact, Iben." Celeste confirmed.

But, we also realized that *not* belonging to the mundane world, meant that we were beyond the laws of science and physics, and could go to the stars in only an instant, instead of millennia.

I was stunned. Was this possible? What did it matter? Aboard the Celestial City we could now explore God's vast domain for all eternity without worrying about old age and other limiting factors of the mortal body!

CHAPTER EIGHTEEN

Are We Alone?

*W*e now realized there could be thousands of exoplanets (planets outside our solar system) teeming with exotic life forms. How many of these planets containing intelligent life will we ever discover? Could there be civilizations much more advanced than ours? Could they teach us how to live peaceably without nuclear weapons, bring us cures for cancer, solve our energy crisis, or even teach us now to produce more nutritious foods?

What will these aliens look like? Intelligent, anthropomorphous beings made in God's image? Could they be considered *human* only because they *look* like us? Our concept of humanity may have to be redefined. This image might be in the traditional form of the human body or could be in the *intellectual* or *reasoning power* of an individual (no matter how strange the physical creature may be). They could be repulsive insect or spider-like creatures, or maybe just huge, grotesque brains or mere parasitic blobs of protoplasm, or even strange microscopic animals or plants—all having vast intelligence. What will we ask these exotic creatures? Do they have souls? How will these eccentric creatures fit into God's divine design?

These above thoughts can be unsettling and beyond the average person. It definitely will upset the way we perceive our universe—our God, and our own status in the vast ocean of unfathomable, uncountable stars. Could we stand being in God's kingdom in the company of such enigmatic creatures and have God value them as much as he now does us? Welcome to the brave new world of alien extraterrestrial intelligence we may soon encounter. We had better get ready to face these questions, for the answers may be forthcoming all to soon.

Celeste stated that it was time for her to bid good bye. Other angels will now continue being my guide throughout the vast universe. They stated they were needed to maintain the stabilization of planetary orbits and protect planets from deadly cosmic and gamma radiation resulting from supernovae explosions. With this, they just vanished as whiffs of smoke, back into the vast unknown.

Extraterrestrial Life?

Another Angelic Divine Counselor, Cosmo, now appeared, ready to reveal the uncountable galaxies—to seek out strange new worlds...

What did we discover in the solar systems of the mighty galaxies? I was told *not* to keep the reader in suspense, but to illuminate all the majesty and wonder of space.

We studied a small rocky planet, Kepler 186f about 500 light-years distant from our sun. It was orbiting a cool dwarf star. It was about the same size as Earth, having a solid land mass. But did it contain oceans of water? Did we, in fact, find any life forms upon it—or even intelligent life?

Later we encountered another very special planet about 4,000 light years away from our solar system. We found it to be composed of compressed crystalline carbon—or, in other words … *solid diamond*. This strange diamond planet was orbiting a neutron star known as a pulsar. It had a mass 20 times the density of Jupiter and circled the pulsar in a very tight orbit about the size of our sun, every 2 hours.

"Iben," Cosmo spoke, "our Milky Way galaxy contains billions of Earth-sized planets which exist in the circumstellar habitable region, also known as the Goldilocks zone. These special planets are neither too hot nor too cold for organic life."

We found billions of modest stars much like our own sun, containing these unique and diverse planets, but still only a very few of them resulted in intelligent anthropomorphic life. I didn't realize the Earth was so rare and exotic with her vast salt oceans, unique carbon cycle, benevolent gravity, thick atmosphere, elliptical orbit around the sun, spin and tilt for her growing seasons, and exceptional moon to stir her oceans. We discovered that most galaxy centers were barren of life because of intense X-rays, gamma rays and ionizing radiation. Their outer edges were also barren of life because of the lack of iron, silicon and magnesium—the heavy elements needed to form terrestrial type planets on which life can flourish. Of the 200 billion stars in our Milky Way galaxy, we found about 50 billion suns similar to ours which might support around 11 billion Earth-sized planets that could harbor intelligent life.

What did we, in fact, discover?

Cosmo and I now explored the galaxies discovering—

Journey through the Galaxies

Did life, or intelligent humanoids, live on any planets within our own galaxy, the Milky Way?

We visited the planet Proxima b, about 4.2 light years distant. It was a little larger than Earth and orbits Proxima Centauri, our sun's closest neighbor, a red dwarf. It is in the "habitable zone" meaning that life *could* be possible. But in reality, did Proxima b contained life?

Yet, on a small terrestrial planet, orbiting the red dwarf sun, Gliese 581, we discovered wonderful and fascinating dinosaur-like creatures. We named this planet "Maple White Land," in honor of the unexplored land in Arthur Conan Doyle's, *The Lost World*.

Andromeda, our sister galaxy, also contained billions of Earth-sized planets—but only a *very few* of them were seeded with *intelligent* life in any form. One pitiful little planet we did discover contained mutants, with DNA altered beings. These bizarre humanoids survived a most terrible war of hydrogen bombs in an unthinkable nuclear holocaust of unprecedented horror that destroyed their civilization. They had the advanced technology to produce these dreadful weapons, but not the wisdom to control them. The pollution from these doomsday devices produced radioactive fallout, rendering horrible mutations which altered and disfigured every living thing on their planet in a pathetic devolution gone mad! We termed this sad world, *"Moreau,"* a desperate and pathetic planet of pathos, after a novel by H. G. Wells, *The Island of Dr. Moreau.*

Within the Trifid Nebula we discovered a rogue planet we named *Verboten Syncytium* ("forbidden protoplasm") containing living parasitic gelatinous viscous protean bio-masses or "blobs." Lord forbid any human to land upon this strange and dangerous planet. I thought this was just a nightmare from some science fiction movie, until I saw those horrible plasmodiums devouring organic animal life with an insatiable appetite!

In Orion's Belt we encountered numerous solar systems, with one planet containing a wonderful advanced civilization, having the means for space travel, but only reached their nearest moon. They realized it was too expensive and gave it up for more practical things, like feeding their poor, and developing backward nations to sustain a good quality of life. We named this planet, *Cipango,* a marvelous world of beauty and wealth (a mythical land that Columbus never found).

Within the Virgo cluster we discovered a small group of planets dotted with the "Floating Cities of Felicity." These crystal domed cities were erected upon terrafirma. These vast metropolises were miles across—canopied over with an expanse of huge impenetrable bubbles of transparent glass. These cities, in turn, rested on transparent tempered glass pedestals harder than steel, rising hundreds of feet into the air, looking like huge mushrooms. Here exotic humanoids resided as their beautiful translucent cities revolved slowly upon these great towering columnar posts. Each city had it own unique and special design, and for some unknow reason, each city could fly off its pedestal, leaving their upright column to be inhabited by yet another floating city taking its place!

The planet itself had little or no atmosphere, but the inhabitants inside these "city ships" were very comfortable, *creating special jobs to fit each person's talents and interests.* We named this planet, *Utopia*, from Sir Thomas Moore's book by the same name.

The Tarantula Nebula contained many solar systems. On one we discovered a planet full of cryptobiotic life, worm-like intelligent nematodes. We named this planet, *Erewhon*, an imaginary land from a book by Samuel Butler.

On a planet contained in Tau Ceti, we discovered a planet of Cyborgs which existed along with Androids in a peaceful relationship. Though both were very different, they learned to live in peace, creating a wonderful society where crime was nonexistent. The only strange thing about them was their inability to have emotion or feel the lost of a love one when they died. We named this planet, *Medamothi*, meaning "nowhere island."

Omega Centauri contained a small planet on which thrived the Symbiotes, an intelligence anthropoid species mutually dependent on each another, a coexistence of two diverse life-forms, as some ants and aphids upon the Earth have commensalism. The ants protect and care for the aphids, and they, in turn, exude a sweet juice which the ants eat, thus both kinds of insect life benefit helping each other to survive. We named this planet, *Symbiosis*.

The Pleiades cluster contained a planet in a modest solar system, where the Simulacrums or cybernetic organisms were created by humanoids of flesh and blood. This planet we named, *Frankenstein*, after a book by Mary Shelley, where the humanoids instigated all the wars against them. The Simulacrums, more intelligent, stronger and more durable than their creators, won the wars—killing thousands of the humanoids. Yet the cybernetic Simulacrums honored peaceful relationships and were actually more benevolent, caring and loving than their flesh creators.

The Hercules cluster contained a solar system of two planets about the size of Earth and they all traveled in the same orbit around the same sun. They were only a few million miles apart, looking to each other as a great blue softball painted with clouds and sharing a common moon which orbited them both in a figure eight! Each civilization knew nothing of the other's existence! They all had intelligent life upon them, but they were not interested in astronomy and only observed the stars and their sun for their planting and harvesting seasons and pagan astrology, nothing more. They lacked the curiosity to seek out what the stars actually were, leaving that to the poets, philosophers and dreamers.

Stephan's Quartet of galaxies contained a rather large solar system, where there were three planets of the same size with intelligent life, with each in concentric orbits of only a million miles apart. The inhabitants of each planet visited the others via flying saucers! They all got along with each other, though their skin was different shades (I mean bright red, blue, orange, green and yellow!) Oddly, a red and blue person could mate—and have a green baby!

Within the Seyfret's galaxy clusters we discovered a couple of planets with intelligent life. One planet we coined, *Scyphozoa,* on which intelligent giant protozoa lived. Each organism was about the size of a soccer ball and lived in colonies forming one great interconnected community containing "hive intelligence." Each individual creature could break off and become a free living entity at any time, rejoining the colony to become one hyper-intelligent organism! Oddly, we found *aluminum* in their enzymes. It is poisonous to most life forms, yet here, these protozoa utilized aluminum as easily as other organisms use magnesium as a source of cell metabolism.

The mysterious Whirlpool Galaxy contained a giant sun consisting of a vast solar system of over a hundred planets and upon one we discovered intelligent Metazoans. These strange beings could live without the fear of famine, for they could grow their own body parts as food. (This sounds very strange indeed until one realize that the female of our own species produces "mother's milk" which comes from modified sweat glands to nourish their young).

Within the Centaurus A galaxy there existed a strange solar system having a planet a little smaller than Earth, thus having less gravity with a mimetic life form of strange spores that replicate their genetic code of any organism they come in contact with. True to the Panspermia Theory, to survive harsh conditions upon their planet, these pods blast their tiny spores into sidereal space. Through eons of time whenever these spores reached another planet containing life, they copy their alien DNA and learn to survive in a copy-cat world to perpetuate their species. We named it, *Micromegas*, from Voltaire's, *A Trip to the Moon*.

Located deep within the Magellanic Cloud, we found one planet having tiny inhabitants. We named it, *Lilliput*, in honor of the novelist Johathan Swift, who wrote, *Gulliver's Travels*. It was a world of four-inch high intelligent little people, who coexisted among a race of benign five-foot tall giants. These giants were benevolent and good, and helped the Lulliputians to build their own homes. The giants had fun building rows of little "doll houses" for them to live in, designing complex neighborhoods, constructing their road systems and administrative buildings—instead of trying to conquer and make slaves of them. The little people, to help the giants, cleaned out their rain gutters and sewer systems, worked on their car engines and tight plumbing jobs, installed wiring, conduit systems, and air conditioning and heating ducts in their attics and crawl spaces of their homes!

The Cartwheel galaxy contained a nice little Earth-size planet, where everybody was compatible with each other, loved one another, and were interested in helping one another. (This was the only planet in the several star systems which we explored that had intelligent beings that could actually get along with each other without war)! We named it, *Shangri-la*, after the fabled imaginary perfect utopian society in James Hilton's novel, *Lost Horizon*.

This galaxy also contained an average sized planet with exotic life, *not* created with the carbon-based hydrocarbon molecular structure as we know it, but composed of *silicon*. These "silicates" were organisms which utilized mostly silicon and molecular phosphates to regulate their cell metabolism!

Our Quest for Intelligent Life, continues...

I still questioned Cosmo why there seemed to be so little *intelligent life* among the star systems we visited. I now understood the *uniqueness* of the Earth, but something else troubled my mind. There were numberous reasons why intelligent life was so very rare.

Cosmo explained that asteroids, along with neighboring planets, and their moons in unstable orbits, can collide into each other—erasing many, if not all life forms. Another scenario is that a planet may tilt on its axis too much or revolve too slowly or too quickly—where their growing seasons are destroyed or impossible to form. Their sun could also expand into a supernova burning up any planet orbiting it. A supernova or coronal mass ejection (sun burst) could also emit cosmic or gamma rays of such intensity they could fry their planet.

Yet, another explanation is that a planet's plate tectonics could crumble, submerging whole civilizations under oceans and seas. Also, these miraculous "plates" may *not* even form on many planets, creating a world of water only, where land creatures could never exist to develop complex societies. Also, a planet may never create any water whatsoever during its formation. It could also be too small to sustain a breathable atmosphere, or just have a tiny solid core enveloped in poisonous gases.

A planet could also produce robots with artificial intelligence (AI), species more durable than their flesh creators. These metallic beings could easily destroy their flesh creators and dominate their species. (The wonder of space and seeking out creatures containing organic life forms, may be only a *human* trait).

Also, upon terra firma, pestilence could suddenly break out becoming epidemic, or some new disease could arrive from a meteor, totally destroying their species (as the insidious Smallpox virus could potentially do if its vaccine fails, as could other exotics such as Marburg or Anthrax) altering or killing all intelligent life upon their planet.

Even an ice age could undermine their civilization, or a runaway greenhouse effect, as happened to Venus, could destabilize them. Sometimes in numerous civilizations, technology exceeds intellect—the civilization actually annihilates itself through war with the misuse of weapons of mass destruction such as thermonuclear, antimatter, or particle-beam obliteration.

Yet, another unique, special, and *most important reason,* I learned, is that the *Divinus Spiritus Primordium* (*DSP*) has not yet reached these foreign and exotic planets to create any forms of life, primitive or intelligent, upon them.

Then we discovered within Eta Carinae Nebula, a perfect little planet, almost the exact size of Earth, with just the right distance from their sun, containing mountains and streams, clouds with rain ... with warm salt oceans and even fresh water. *Yet it was totally devoid of all life*! Strange indeed. I wondered why and—

I realized that this little planet had been perfectly designed by God—yet the *spiritus vitae* or "divine spark" of the *DSP* has not yet been "ignited." This sounds too fantastic and out of the scope of secular knowledge, but were we actually ordained by the *Spiritus Sanctus* to help manifest organic life, or even *design a little moon to stir her oceans* so life *could* begin? I knew not how to accomplish these awesome and mighty things, but with the help of God and his angels—

Cosmo and I visited all the wonders of the heavens, the sanctity of space where no imagination of humankind can comprehend!

Our Magnificient Quest was finally answered! Yes, other alien planets upon strange vast galaxies did contain exotic life forms, both primitive and complex. But, alas, only a very few of them had anthropoid intelligent life! Even so … with intelligence … could we consider them "human?"

We visited *all* the constellations which sprinkled the heavens above us—thousands of nebulae, including the massive Horsehead Nebula. Regretfully, the Horsehead Nebula lost its shape and color as our *Paradisia* approached it, like a newspaper picture loses its pattern the closer you get and the use of a magnifying glass renders the image into a series of indistinguishable dots of black and gray.

We next visited yet other intricate nebulae, some shaped as hourglasses (holding the secrets of time as we now can't comprehend), massive pinwheels suspended in variegated clouds of swirling gases, huge stilled tornadoes of uncountable stars, suspended in vast oceans of prismatic stellar dust.

We studied many galaxies, strange and mysterious, known and yet *unknown* to science. Oddly, I must mention this in passing, that some of the galaxies and suns we encountered were nothing but light in the heavens. As we neared them with our hyper-speed they became nothing but ethereal wisps of dying embers—their galaxies and solar systems long since burned into oblivion. Thousands of these galaxies as we neared them, just disappeared in the Stygian darkness of space, their light extinguished billions of years ago. Yet, other complete galaxies we discovered, were lonely, having no life at all within their midst.

We observed wonderful galaxies of untold beauty as NGC 4650-A with a strange "polar ring" intersecting its center—the results where two dissimilar galaxies are colliding with each other—and we are seeing it *now* for its light is just reaching us—though it has *already* happened over a billion years ago!

Did we sow the seeds of organic life among the stars? Did we set up the precursors of terraforming planets among enigmatic alien solar systems?

Were the lost tribes of Israel destined to seed the stars of infinity? I then realized that these "lost tribes" were really known now as God's new adopted family of born-again believers!

This gave the biblical passages in Genesis
a totally new interpretation:

"And I will make thy seed to multiply as the stars of
heaven, and will give unto thy seed all these countries;
and in thy seed shall all the nations
of the earth be blessed;"
—Gen. 26:4

Now we encountered the grand exotica of the universe, the pulsars, quasars, dark matter, white and brown dwarfs, and strange tiny wrinkles in space that are the seeds of nascent stars.

We discovered what causes the mysterious dark matter. The visible stars, galaxies and nebulae only compose about 4% of the *known* universe! We encountered eccentric *dark matter* which composes over *one fourth* of the universe and exotic *dark energy* which composes about 70% of the entire universe. This dark energy is also an *unknown factor* which surrounds many galaxies, and is actually being *repelled* by the galaxy's gravitational field. This antigravity pressure is causing the expansion of the universe. *I then realized that most of the universe is not composed entirely of three dimensional matter as we normally conceive it.*

I learned all about general relativity and quantum mechanics and the paradoxes of Einstein's cosmological constant. I was enlightened on how they all fit into the Grand Unified Theory (GUT) of fundamental forces (known also as M-Theory), that confirms the existence of many parallel and alternate dimensions of time and space … namely the 5th, 6th, 7th, 8th … on into the Nth dimensions.

We learned all about pulsars—those mysterious lighthouse beacons, flashing their eerie light out across the universe! Were they remnants of collapsed solar systems, or the collapse of massive suns, or were they the remains of super-condensed galaxies?

The least understood phenomenon plaguing astronomy—the source of extremely powerful bursts of gamma rays, now flashed through our universe. Where were these bursts of energy coming from? Were they generated when a neutron star is sucked into a black hole? Or were they coming from exotic cracks between multiple dimensions beyond time on the edge of infinity?

Another mystery we encountered, was that our known universe is just one strange bubble among millions! Cosmic inflation is defined when the Big Bang formed separate universes inside one another as space is warped into hyper-speed. This is how our own universe came to be when God spoke it into existence.

Now we saw an alarming phenomenon indeed. The Milky Way galaxy, and our nearest neighbor, Andromeda, two great island universes, colliding into each other at 300,000 miles per hour!

"Oddly, Iben, many other galaxies have collided in this manner," Cosmo confirmed. "The Antennae galaxy was formed when two spiral galaxies collided with each other! It took these two spiral galaxies a half-billion years to move through one another distorting them into one great elliptical galaxy."

Cosmo stated that he must now be leaving—

CHAPTER NINETEEN

The Judgment of the Lord
(Rev. 20:6;14-15; 21:8)

*T*he *Paradisia* has now traveled over 15,000 million light years and has reached the extreme limit of the known universe. *My mind has totally expanded beyond all the experiences of humankind.* I am on the brink of becoming fully imbued with the Divine, something that *Homo sapiens* can never attain except through death! I am becoming satiated with the power of omniscient divine knowledge!

Distance and time have become meaningless. We are traveling through vast tracts of space exploring whole galaxies as a person sailing across an ocean discovering new unknown islands! Only our ocean is that of deep uncharted space ... and our islands are exotic mysterious universes!

Chaos

The Archangel Michael now appeared. He announced to the Sons of God:

"NEW MASTERS OF THE UNIVERSE, divine citizens of the Holy Priesthood—we have traveled beyond the billion galaxies and are at the very edge of known matter. What lies before us is a vast void of nothingness, containing just one last unknown and mysterious globular cluster. It is known but to the angels as Chaos. Will Einstein's General Theory of Relativity—be confirmed—or discarded?"

This unknown cluster, I observed, had a nefarious dark X or an enigmatic nebulous cross etched across it. Was it a precursor of doom and impending danger, a warning for us to stay away? As we entered into this "cross" we found ourselves orbiting the edge of a blue fuzzy doughnut shaped circle of incandescent gases. It was an accretion disk ... numerous light years across, and even more *massive* than our Milky Way galaxy!

Michael, the Archangel, spoke, "We have arrived at an event horizon orbiting the very edge of Chaos, a black-hole binary containing two crepuscular swirling masses of infinity where time and space are warped beyond the comprehensibility of the human mind ... where huge suns and even whole galaxies have disappeared into its gaping abyss. Where gravity has no limits and has bent, stretched and convoluted the fabric of space into anti-matter, exotic dark energy, and strange plasmas where all corporeal things cease to exist!"

I hugged my children, as I watched a huge island universe

of a billion suns disintegrate as it drifted into this tunnel of terror, and was then condensed into a tight diamond of pink fire, flashed brightly, and then to my horror, literally winked out of existence.

In this dark foreboding maelstrom, I witnessed numerous horrible vultue-like apparitions—the Demons of Damnation—ready to devour the lost souls of humanity. The great angel Apollyon, was guarding the dungeons of the bottomless pit. They were here, waiting for the unrepentant souls, to be judged by God.

Apollyon spoke,

"THE JUDGMENT OF THE LORD IS AT HAND!"
(Mt. 3:12; 13:24-30; Lk. 3:17; Mk. 9:42-50)

"*Those judged guilty will be cast into Gehenna, and those sealed in the righteousness of the Lord will be saved.* So, now the Almighty LORD will separate the wheat from the chaff—and judge the wicked—and the faithful."

Gabriel, the Archangel spoke: "Fear not, the enlightened saints of God, for there is yet to come *A Divinus Novus Ordo Seclorum*, "A Divine New Order of the Ages"—for the exalted and chosen of God. Keep the faith! Death is swallowed up in victory!

"Iben, you will see wonders that no one has ever before witnessed. Terrors like nothing ever comhrehended by the mind of man—

"Iben, you, are nearing the realm of the condemned of God—to totally convinced others that those of perdition will never partake in the blessings of the saint, for they will soon tread through strange darkness into an unknown universe in an unfathomable fire—

Fear struck my very soul. Thanatopia now appeared—

The shock wave from the disintegrated galaxy which entered the black hole finally reached our Celestial City, pulling and sweeping us beyond the event horizon toward the bottomless pit of Chaos. We inexorably were being engulfed down its mighty throat!

The *Paradisia* shuttered and groaned as it swirled beyond the event horizon into this strange double vortex wormhole from which nothing, not even light can escape!

Then I realized what this is all about. It is the SECOND DEATH. This is *terra incognita!* I now realized there is a world beyond the senses. Was I to discover yet another clandestine world— *beyond the dimensions of which I was now existing?*

We were entering THE ULTIMATE UNKNOWABLE.

The Bridge of Dreams/The Second Death

I touched Faith's hand. I realized the terror of my wife's nightmare of a terrifying vortex when I toured her mind. I remembered a long sususpension bridge spanning over a vast virulent maelstrom, an unknown void or abyss ... enshrouded in a dense fog of a strange Stygian darkness. It was an immense cauldron of swirling clouds far below, miles in diameter—a hugh hurricane with this gaping hole at its center ... its final destination unknown. I watched in great trepidation as the bridge began to sway with large numbers of helpless people sliding and falling from it, screaming and enexorably disappearing into this deep strange pit of dark oblivion inexorably disappearing into—

Faith's dream … I remembered, *symbolic of what*—

Buckminister Fuller and Benjamin Franklin's words came hauntingly back to me—about traveling to and actually surviving in an anti-universe of anti-matter.

Of all the awe-inspiring mysteries of our existence, I realized that what lies before us is the *key* to the Kingdom of God. We are born but to die and yet we survived this! Next comes the SECOND DEATH, and yet, I secured the faith that I can survive this also. Was it some precognition that I had? I wanted to keep the faith—but this could also be the ULTIMATE END! An eternal existence is well nigh impossible for mortal humanity to comprehend. The human mind is only finite. Yet, in this enhanced state of the Supernalite, are our minds also finite? I now realize that they have merged in that hypostatic union and have become infinite with the mind of the Eternal.

The first death sowed the seed for a more abundant life. Just what will the *Second Death* sow for us? I had great trepidation upon entering this black hole, I will not lie, but I also realized that I had survived the first death, and that just maybe—

Keep the faith, Iben Jair, keep the faith! I kept telling myself.

The sight and reality of a black hole is a complete terror totally against the human experience, an unfathomable unknown equation, a vast indefinable involution that the human mind cannot comprehend.

The event horizon is known as the Schwarschild radius,

and nothing happening inside can ever be communicated to the outside.

"As death and the grave!" I Confirmed.

Faster still we traveled in a giant parabola, spiraling into a double helix near the adjacent gaping mouth of Gehenna, the bottomless pit, toward the singularity, where the very universe ceases to exist. How *long* it took there was absolutely no way of knowing, for we were melting into a strange conundrum beyond time—where a second could be stretched into a thousand years, or a thousand years into a second. We watched in horror as the universe we once knew blurred, distorted, and then disappeared for all eternity.

Jesus Christ now appeared upon the Great White Throne holding the Word of God and opening the Book of Life. "And the dead were judged out of those things which were written in the books, according to their works."

Our *Paradisia* shutters in terror, the crystal canopy vibrating as to shatter at any moment—then an extraordinary thing happened ... the bowels of our Celestial City disengaged and actually cleavaged in half! The austere amorphous voice of Apollyon, the angel of the bottomless pit trumped, "ALL HOPE ABANDON, YE WHO ENTER." With this echoing in our ears, the KING OF KINGS, AND LORD OF LORDS commenced JUDGMENT, separating the wheat from the chaff.

The Prison of Gehenna, where the Antichrist and Satan's vanquished army of profligate angels resided, along with all the UNREPENTED SOULS—those evil entities, whoremongers, sorcerers, reprobates, sadistic and depraved criminals, the abominable, idolaters, murderers, blasphemers, malefactors, miscreants, atheists, and terrorists, which caused havoc upon the earth from all ages past—spiraled down into the bottomless pit, the SECOND DEATH.

This Prison now convoluted and tumbled into this endless nothingness—and within but a moment of time— disappeared into a strange iniquitous void—the only dwelling God had forfeited. All these evil transgressors and anarchists swirled down into this gaping maelstrom— vanishing into the capital of Hell, Pandemonium, and her lake of fire.

Thanatopia gave me the honor of peering into this vortex ... where all evil souls that have blasphemed against God are destined, and I saw what even God prevented the angels of heaven from knowing—

A swirling vortex engulfing the sons of Belial, Beelzebub and Lucifer, including Satan and all his minions of fallen angels ... the anathema of being completely abandoned from God. Gehenna, an incoherent and ignominious anti-universe—a plasmatic conflagration of searing heat to *burn the souls*—the excruciating pain, that *ultimate scream of damnation* ... echoing through the darkness ... for all eternity.

I released my mind from this inferno of those judged by God—who are, "cast into outer darkness into the furnace of fire, the wailing and gnashing of teeth, where their worm dieth not, and the fire is not quenched."

We followed above the "Prison of Gehenna" until it was but a tiny speck which disappeared into the fiery clouds of brimstone, and then snatched into its firey jaws of total and ultimate vacuity—

I now noticed that the *Shekinah Glory*, trailing behind

us, crossed the event horizon, following us into the abyss, and split and jettisoned her evil cargo incarcerated within her "Prison of Perdition," those UNREPENTED SOULS AND ANGELS CURSED BY GOD, that were gathered *after* we had left the Earth. Now they were also judged by God, condemned, and cast into Gehenna—tumbling and screaming as a yet another blazing blasphemous bomb into the bottomless pit."

Ultima Thule/Destination Unknown

I wondered about the fate of the *Paradisia, w*hether it could survive the *ultima Thule*—that unknown region, the farthest limit and degree of the known universe. I began to pray.

I sensed the Judgment of God upon us—Lord have mercy—

All the redeemed Supernal Beings of God (his redeemed saints sealed in Christ) were now witnessing the spectacle unfolding before us. The reality of our normal universe was strangely warping and disintegrating—

We were entering the singularity, a dark choking abyss, engulfed in an aphotic plasma—

One by one God's chosen faded into a strange state of complete catatonia, then sank into the final dreamless sleep ... into the ultimate unknowable, down further and further into that strange black unconscious void where all things cease to exist—

"Death thou hast seen in his first shape on man;
but many shapes of Death,

and many are the wayes that lead to his grim Cave,
all dismal; yet to sense more terrible
at th' entrance then within."
—Paradise Lost, John Milton, Book XI

I now became conscious of a strange vibration … something very faint … an extremely faint sound a million billion times below the range of the human ear … one note 57 octaves deeper than that of middle C on the music scale.

This haunting sound of super-heated gases steadily increased in crescendo as the dissipation of matter was annihilated into energy—accelerating at extremely high rates of speed, heated by millions of degrees.

As we entered into the ripples of incandescent super-heated matter, this sound was changed in tempo into an excruciatingly loud roar frothing in our ears as we neared the termination point—deafening loud, nauseatingly loud—these extreme vibrations shattering our minds—

Those Supernal Beings who were sealed in Jesus Christ were now shrouded in this vast enigmatic whirlpool—

Blackness—nothingness … the darkness of infinity … then an unconscious starless void—

We found ourselves plunging deeper and deeper in this minacious maelstrom, directly into the *singularity*—

The *Paradisia* pirouetted and spiraled down into a reversed parallel vortex *opposite* Gehenna. For an instant, we became the fastest thing in the universe, where breath, depth and height become meaningless—time stops, dimensional space terminates, and all known phenomena cease. My last conscious thought was a quote I remembered—

"Now I am about to take my last voyage,
a frightful leap in the dark."
—Thomas Hobbes: On his deathbed, Dec. 4, 1679.

The White Hole

We penetrated into the ultimate unknowable—

Then out of this black nothingness, beyond time and space, glowed a single pinpoint of light in this vast whirlpool of eternal night ... Divine Light, the Presence of the Holy ... with such warmth and love—a magnificent spinning polychromatic gateway lay before us. We of the *Paradisia,* in fear and trepidation, now plunged through this spinning psychedelic Iris of Transfiguration, an ingress—

Here we found ourselves swirling through an anti-universe of multiple dimensions and multiverses of pure divine ecstasy. Einstein's Special Theory of relativity $E=mc^2$: mass into energy—energy into mass ... was now a proven reality!

This strange phenomenon we had encountered was known as the "Bifrost bridge" referring to an old Norse legend, a link between two worlds ... or in modern physics— the Einstein-Rosen bridge.

The Black Hole of Chaos had been conquered—the *White Hole*, I discovered, was a reality!

The nimbus of the Holy permeated all about. The atonement of God's saints was reconciled! Within this new realm of existence, I discovered that many members of my family, relatives and friends were still with me.

Through all this, I now realized that I was still holding Faith's hand in mine!

After we had crossed the Schwarchild radius, I realized that our universe was now strangely *without evil*, and that Jesus Christ, The Messiah, our immortal Savior, now reigned for all eternity—the curse of the Garden of Eden had been totally lifted, with all evil finally vanquished! *The saints of God were finally vindicated!*

The New Jerusalem

I saw a new heaven and a new earth; for the first heaven and the first earth were passed away. And I saw as a bright sparkling diamond, the holy city, now coming down from God out of heaven, coruscating the divine Light of the Lamb of God ... the most miraculous ineffable wonder ever dreamed or imagined within the realm of pure ecstasy! So we disembarked from our *Paradisia* and entered our new home, the New Jerusalem. It was now unveiled before us, pristine, empty and waiting—the divine home of *Jehovah-Shammah,* "The Lord is there." The New Jerusalem is ready to be occupied by His saints—as the bride is ready for her husband, to fulfill and complete God's divine prophecy.

After transcending the Black Hole and arriving through the White Hole, I wondered just where we were in our relationship to the three dimensional universe of which we once belonged? Is it beyond the mind of man to comprehend such things as a strange indefinable interlinear dimension that God has promised to His faithful?

What existed beyond this Black Hole? What was the nature of the exotic White Hole we now entered? Could we be living within an enigmatic phenomenon that science may *never* be able to fully explain or living an existence that the mind of mortal man may *never* be able to fully comprehend?

Had we entered into an anti-matter universe or an eccentric reverse universe? Were we existing in an anomalous parallel universe, or were we in an unfamiliar alien cosmic vacuum? Were we floating within a tiny particle of cosmic dust, or were we a glimmer within a tiny snowflake, or even encapsulated in a tiny photon of light? Could we be living within a geometric "point," having no length, height or width? Could we be living in a strange indefinable "cosmic bubble" or in a "positronic plasma," or even existing within a numinous nebula? Could we be in an "atomic interstice?" Or were we entangled between dimensions, living in a warp in time on the edge of infinity ... suspended beyond our known reality within the glorious twinkling eye of God?

I realized that the Black Hole was allegorical of death also. We could not have known what was hidden before us until we entered in ... and once inside, could not communicate to the outside to tell others what we found (as in the grave). Again, I had nothing to fear as we were swept *beyond* the Second Death. I kept the faith that God and Jesus Christ had a UNIQUE REASON for me to exist beyond the sphere of a limited three-dimensional universe.

Jesus Christ, at his death on Calvary, transected the Black Hole eons before to prepared his magnificent divine dominion under the complete Sovereignty of God, for all his faithful and redeemed believers. We now realized all those redeemed saints aboard the *Paradisia* were imbued with a SPECIAL PURPOSE and a DIVINE MISSION God had ordained when humankind was created in His Image.

So we anxiously passed from our *Paradisia* and entered into our "rest," our new glorious heavenly home—that glorious realm of tranquility, comfort and serenity, beautiful beyond description of mortal language.

The Kingdom of God encompassed the very Holy of Holies, where God reigns with complete integrity, fairness and justice—with total divine power and authority. Here were the Supernalites ... all enraptured in total harmony, full of exceeding grace, having an all invigorating, inspiring and rewarding future—

Hallelujah! Salvation and glory, and honor and power unto the LORD, God Almighty!

Complete Metamorphosis

The thoughts beyond that of mortal mind and that of God's new language now brings us to a paradox. Again, I must be leaving you, for I am changing, metamorphosing into a totally new creature. As my "self" now expands beyond mortal capacity or understanding, so are my thoughts becoming divine, and my language is becoming infinite and of the Deity.

"My Divine mind now accumulates vast
tracks of wisdom at a moment—
and can converse with a hundred minds at an instant.
It has increased, knowing no bounds,
as divine knowledge, truth, and wisdom
has become cosmic, knowing no limits."

"I AM IN TOTAL COMMUNICATION
WITH THE LORD,
AND HAVE GONE BEYOND
THE LIMITS OF PURE THOUGHT
INTO OMNISCIENCE."

CHAPTER TWENTY

The Theocentric Universitas of Astrophysics and the Centro de Astrobiologia

Our Divine Mission and Ultimate Destiny

Another magnificent Divine Spirit now appeared. Charisma, 'the power of the Holy Spirit'—

"Iben," Charisma stated, "remember those galaxies we passed that had already disappeared and burned out in the eternal night before time began? Their light being extinguished long before we had a chance to explore them? And still other island universes which had travailed in birth and death, as we passed vast oceans of interstellar dark matter where we thought nothing existed? And still other great spiraling galaxies, that were so distant, that we were never aware of them, whose light never caught up to us in our travels?

"Our *Divine Mission* is to sail upon yet *another odyssey*, to search and find these lost galaxies and antimatter universes … those galaxies that exploded, vaporized, or were burned out long before we encountered them. We will visit the constellation of Quadrans Muralis, and the nova, Aquilae, both of which have disappeared, and no longer exists in star atlases. These, along with thousands of other exotics that have vanished, we will explore—*that now exist beyond the uncharted depths of the universe.*

"Iben," Charisma continued, "we will travel through space and beyond time exploring intriguing passageways of the Einstein-Rosen bridges and enter strange antimatter universes and multiverses, those more enigmatic than the star system from which we once called our home, the wondrous Milky Way galaxy.

"We will also partake in God's grand scheme of galactogenesis, the actual formation of new and extinct galaxies and nebulae throughout our physical and incorporeal universe. We will encounter dark matter and dark energy yet conceived, and alternate universes—*yet to be created.*

"We will be departing very soon, and you Iben, as a Son of Light, have become an honored member of the *Theocentric Universitas of Astrophysics,* and of the *Centro de Astrobiologia.* We are now preparing to search out and explore these missing planets, galaxies and stars—*to fulfill our ultimate destiny.* We have transcended *beyond our known reality* and possess the divine power and knowledge to warp space, and even reverse time, exploring extrinsic galaxies which have crystalized within alternate dimensions.

"We will also monitor the terraformation of many planets God has chosen for cultivation—seeding intelligent organic life into His Special Creation ... for His Special Purpose as He ordained with the Earth *before* the fall of

Adam and Eve. We will also kindle *spiritus vitae*—to imbue this *special anthropomorphic life* with Theocentric Spirit.

"Therefore, we request your noble and honorable presence to travel with us on a great new adventure. Departure is imminent. We will continue exploring unknown regions, the *terra incognita* of vast tracts of bizarre antimatter universes, strange formidable dark matter, and inimitable clandestine dimensions of time and space still yet to be discovered, initiating the power of the *Divinus Spiritus Energia* throughout our grand universe—and of a billion others."

After this speech the Angels disappeared once again into the great cosmic infinity.

Were we to be the *divine architects* of the universe? To actually help design exotic worlds and gestate life upon them? And were we to gather still more souls and spirits, who have died upon these foreign and alien worlds? Should I stay in this renascent existence, or embark upon this new glorious odyssey Jesus Christ has preordained for me?

I shall soon decide upon the fate of my New Destiny, and Divine Mission still yet prepared for me before I was even conceived in my mother's womb.

Meanwhile, I must now leave you to enjoy this wonderful life of bliss, having total peace and tranquility in perfect communion with my Savior and of the Eternal God Almighty.

**I NOW UNDERSTAND THAT GOD
HAS EVERYTHING UNDER CONTROL,
AND DOES NOT FORSAKE US
IN OUR TIME OF NEED.**

**THAT THE HOLY BIBLE IS TOTALLY TRUE,
THAT THERE IS— WITHOUT DOUBT,
A LIFE SO WONDERFUL AND BEAUTIFUL,
A LIFE OF EXTREME HAPPINESS
AND FULFILLMENT,
A LIFE OF COMPLETE ECSTASY
IN THE HEREAFTER
AS TO BE TOTALLY INCOMPREHENSIBLE
AND MYSTIFYING TO MORTAL HUMANKIND!
GOD IS STILL ON HIS THRONE,
AND ALL IS WELL WITH THE UNIVERSE.**

God Bless and farewell …
Until we once again meet beyond that sacred door—
DEATH …
and life's fulfillment beyond time …
to dwell with God in a New Heaven and a New Earth.
So shall it be—
FOR ALL ETERNITY.
Grace be unto you, and peace, from God our Father,
and the Lord Jesus Christ.
AMEN! SHALOM!

ADIEU MES AMIS JE VAIS LA GLOIRE
(Farewell, my Friends! I go to Glory)

HALLELUJAH!

TO THE SANCTIFIED
AND
REDEEMED
OF GOD
THROUGH CHRIST:
WELCOME TO THE
GRAND
AND
ULTIMATE
BEGINNING!

May God bless all the readers of this book.

EPILOGUE

"We are reading the first verse of the first chapter
of a book whose pages are infinite…"
—Unknown

"Life is rather a state of embryo, a preparation for life;
A man is not completely born till he
has passed through death."
—Ben Franklin

Eternal Life is an exciting realm transcending the mundane existence of anxiety, remorse, hate, sorrow, frustration, anger, pride, and greed. It is a life surpassing the senses, a *hyper-reality*, where all is well. It is an exuberant life in total ecstasy and divine fellowship with God, Jesus Christ, the Holy Spirit, the glorious powerful and majestic Angelic Divine Counselors, the Illuminati of the Divine, the Cognoscente of the Enlightened, the Watchers, and fellow

Paranormal Supernal Beings, those Supernalites, "the Sons of Light," God's expurgated Saints! The veil of ignorance and darkness has been lifted by Christ, and is replaced by a spiritual life of *total perfection* and *completeness* in the glory of the Lord!

"Who shall separate us from the love of Christ?
Shall tribulation, or distress, or persecution, or famine,
or nakedness, or peril, or sword?"
—Rom. 8:35

Purpose of Being Born

"I now realize
that the true purpose
and meaning of being born *is* to die!
For only in death
will life's greatest and enigmatic
questions be answered,
and life's greatest rewards be fulfilled."
—The Author

In Conclusion

*I*n *Eternity*, I have wanted to elucidate the reader into a wonderful reality of God's divine love, peace, tranquility, and happiness. *Its pages can translate you into a truth many seek, but only a very few have the will to discover, or the faith to believe, or the enlightenment to understand.*

God's divine revelation is too precious to throw before petty minds. "Give not that which is holy unto the dogs, neither cast your pearls before swine, lest they trample them under their feet, …" (Mt. 7:6).

So think about them, ponder them, keeping an open mind on the subject of death, for there are many novel ideas contained within these pages. Elucidate yourself to other possibilities that you have not thought of before. Read this book as you would any classic of literature.

> "A closed mind is the only prison from
> which you cannot escape."
> —Unknown

I hope that I have shown that science and religion can

coexist side by side. It's the theories which usually get science into trouble. Science is the *accumulation of facts within a three-dimensional reality,* and extrapolations from *incomplete data* lead to erroneous and false assumptions. Hypotheses created without all the facts being presented (as in the creation of the universe, the demise of the dinosaurs, and the process of evolution), can be bogus. The problem is when scientists draw these conclusions, they are taught as facts, but "facts" that they can change and alter as more evidence is gathered or discovered. Many times in the past they have been proven wrong! *When all the facts are in, then the theories will coincide with the truth.* They will then be congruent and in unison with the Bible, and the precepts of God.

So *only* beyond the grave can humanity acquire those enigmatic *facts* that will prove the Bible, and determine the cause and effect of our universe. In Paradise we will also attain that grand reward of eternal life, that total fulfillment and happiness promised by God and Jesus Christ.

So a human being must die in order to be transformed, as a butterfly hatching from its cocoon, a miraculous divine spiritual metamorphosis. Christians should recognize *death as only a gateway* to all the marvelous blessings God has for us. So why should we have that great fear and trepidation, as we see the egression of our departed loved ones? Why should we fear the *shadow of death,* as we *all* will ultimately pass through this portal, into a greater and more wonderful state of existence and enlightenment?

"According to Jesus, life in the future world
is related to "many mansions,"

a term variously understood to mean many
places of sojourn, many homes,
or many planets to visit." —Billy Graham, *World Aflame*

Within death lies a great mystery. In Gen. 3:22-24, the angels guarded the tree of life so that Adam and Eve would not eat of it, and live forever upon a cursed earth of lawlessness, rebellion, hate, and transgression. We also should remember that Jesus holds the keys to death and immortality.

Death can be compared to a tiny seed planted in the soil which germinates and grows to maturity. God's children, those saved through the blood of Jesus Christ (Jn. 12:36; Eph. 5:8), will now bloom into the great magnificent blessings of a new spiritual body (1 Cor. 15:35-57); and the promise of the Great Harvest of Judgment, dividing the wheat from the chaff (Mt. 3:12; Lk. 3:17), proclaiming the wrath of God, separating the wicked from the righteous (Rev.14:15-20).

It must be remembered that flesh and blood *cannot* inherit the kingdom of God. Understanding death's *true purpose,* will give us more peace and tranquility toward the "Grim Reaper."

Most people have heard of "life-as-we-know-it," referring to an existence in the organic carbon based state, as exobiologists have defined it. But how about "life-as-we-do-*not*-know-it?" That life which can NOT be probed with scientific instruments in the laboratory? But is life just a *biological* phenomenon? If not, then there is a distinct possibility that a *nonphysical aspect of human personality* can exist beyond death. So this is what the "other life" after death can be, a life of true beauty—a magnificently awesome existence beyond our imaginations. Quantum physicists have now actually discovered interspacial worlds far beyond ours, vast enigmatic multi-dimensional universes, and Euclidean wormholes where our souls, when separated from our bodies, could *actually survive*. Where we could encounter a hyper-reality, and a cognitive perception—illimitable. This phenomenon, known as "Spirit Athanasia" in the near future, could become a proven reality.

In the immortal words of the Holy Bible let me depart with some last thoughts upon the mystery of the Afterlife:

"The last enemy that shall be destroyed is death."
—1 Cor.15:26

The paradox of death will increase our faith and renew our hope of a better life, energizing us to a new refreshing experience, and into a glorious and wonderful existence.

God will soon enlighten his saints, through death, to all of life's great mysteries. We know that *The Great Unknown* lies in wait for us all. It will someday be revealed that a *Divine Purpose* and *Divine Plan* for a new life beyond death is a solid reality. God's Word, the *Holy Bible*, proclaims these truths to us now in this life … BEFORE we have to experience this translation of the spirit.

"He will swallow up death in victory;
and the Lord GOD will wipe away tears from all faces;
and the rebuke of his people shall he take away
from all the earth; for the LORD hath spoken it."
—Isa. 25:8 (Cp. Rev. 21:4-7)

It should be remembered that death is
already a vanquished enemy!

Are YOU ready to face death? Nothing can separate us from the love of God—not even death. The Christian has the promise that Jesus Christ will greatly bless our lives now—and for all eternity.

Again, remember that YOU will someday die. All natural life dies. May you, after reading this book, have more enlightenment upon the riddle of life, and more peace and solace about the enigma of death—that portal to a new and glorious beginning!

In closing, I will relate the story of the great composer Handel.

For three weeks, George Handel would not leave his house. He ate little, read his Bible and composed a musical masterpiece. After Handel finished the "Hallelujah Chorus," he turned to his servant with tears in his eyes.

"I did think I did see all of heaven before me and the great God himself," Handel stated.

I hope after someone reads this book, that they might state as much. I hope you have been encouraged by this epiphany, and that God will richly bless you, now and for all eternity!

"Death—the last sleep?
No, it is the final awakening."
—Sir Walter Scott

"Life is real, life is earnest,
and the grave is not its goal;
Dust thou art, to dust returnest,
was not spoken of the soul."
—Longfellow

Togetherness

"Death is nothing at all. I have only
slipped away into the next room.
Whatever we were to each other, we still are.
Call me by my old familiar name.
Speak to me in the same easy way you always have.
Laugh as we always laughed at the little
jokes we enjoyed together.
Play, smile, think of me, pray for me.
Life means all that it ever meant. It
is the same as it always was.
There is absolute unbroken continuity.
Why should I be out of your mind
because I am out of your sight?
I am but waiting for you, for an interval,
somewhere very near, just around the corner.
All is will. Nothing is past. Nothing has been lost.
One brief moment and all will be as it was before—

Only better. Infinitely happier.
We will be one, together forever.
—Kevin Healy, who wrote his own obituary
before he died, May 10, 1986.

A DREAM WITHIN A DREAM

Take this kiss upon the brow!
And, in parting from you now,
This much let me avow—
You are not wrong, who deem,
That my days have been a dream;
Yet if hope has flown away
In a night, or in a day,
In a vision, or in none,
Is it therefore the less gone?

All that we see or seem
Is but a dream within a dream.
I stand amid the roar
Of a surf-tormented shore,
And I hold within my hand
Grains of the golden sand—
How few! yet how they creep
Through my fingers to the deep,
While I weep—while I weep!

O God! can I not grasp
Them with a tighter clasp?
O God! can I not save
One from the pitiless wave?
Is all that we see or seem
But a dream within a dream?
—Edgar Allen Poe

I sincerely hope and pray this *Word of Knowledge* before you, has presented a deeper meaning of God's truth and has helped fulfill God's Divine Purpose in your life.

If you think this message has been profitable, please share it with others. Remember,

"A grief shared is half a grief;
A joy shared is twice a joy."
—Anonymous

**"And the peace of God,
which passeth all understanding,
shall keep your hearts and minds
through Christ Jesus."
Phil. 4:7**

**"The LORD bless thee and keep thee;
The LORD make His face shine upon thee
and be gracious to thee;**

The LORD lift up His countenance upon thee—
and give thee peace."
—Num. 6:24-26

Hosanna—
To God be the Glory!

Praise be to God!
Amen!

Printed in Great Britain
by Amazon

16893531R00350